PAT BARKER was born in Thornaby-on-Tees in 1943. She was educated at the local grammar school and at the London School of Economics where she studied economics, politics and history. She taught history and British Constitution at a College of Further Education in the North-east but left in 1970 to have her first child, a boy. Her daughter was born four years later. *Union Street*, her first novel, was published by Virago in 1982 to great critical acclaim. In 1983, Pat Barker was chosen as one of the twenty 'Best of Young British' novelists; she was also joint winner of the Fawcett Prize for Fiction and runner up for the *Guardian* Fiction Prize. Her second novel, *Blow Your House Down*, was published in 1984. She lives in Durham with her husband and children.

The Century's Daughter is Pat Barker's most brilliant achievement yet – the story of a working class community seen through the eyes of Liza Jarrett, born on the last stroke of midnight as the twentieth century begins. Liza grows up in the First World War, marries Frank – mystic, faith healer and unemployed steel worker – and brings up her children through the hardship of the Depression. Surviving the sixties and seventies, she meets Stephen, alienated from his parents and his job as a community worker, who comes to Liza to offer help, but stays to be helped. A remarkable mixture of naturalistic style and poetic sensibility, this outstanding novel captures the taut, hard humour and warmth of people who have had short shrift both in literature and life.

D0388480

Other novels by Pat Barker:

Union Street (1982)
Blow Your House Down (1984)

THE CENTURY'S DAUGHTER

Pat Barker

VIRAGO

For my children
John and Anna

Published by VIRAGO PRESS Limited 1986
41 William IV Street, London WC2N 4DB

British Library Cataloguing in Publication Data
Barker, Pat
The century's daughter.
I. Title
823'.914[F]   PR6052.A648/

ISBN 0-86068-606-X
ISBN 0-86068-611-6 Pbk

Typeset by Goodfellow and Egan, Cambridge
Printed in Great Britain by
Anchor Brendon, Tiptree, Essex.

1

'No point being eighty, is there?' said Liza. 'If you can't be a bit outrageous?'

And certainly she looked it, Stephen thought, with her scarlet headsquare tilted crazily over one eye, giving her the look of a senile pirate.

'I'm sorry I didn't let you in when you come before. Thought you were some bloody do-gooding cow from the social.'

That – give or take an udder – was exactly what he was, but he didn't want to risk rejection now by saying so. Instead he handed her the letter he'd brought with him.

'Oh, I can't manage that,' she said, and tapped the corner of one eye. 'Cataract.'

'I'm sorry,' he said.

'You will be.' She cackled merrily. 'Well, we've all got it to come, haven't we?'

But he couldn't imagine ever coming to this. To be the sole remaining inhabitant of a street scheduled for demolition. Isolated, helpless, threatened with eviction if you didn't agree to conform and get out.

'How long have you lived here?'

'Since 1922.'

That didn't sound like senility. Of course they were hoping she was senile: it would be so much easier to get her out.

'But it must be lonely living here now. No neighbours.'

'I'm never lonely,' she said. 'I've got Nelson. And there's Mrs Jubb.'

Mrs Jubb was the home help, but who the hell was Nelson?

1

Liza pointed to a corner of the room, where Stephen could just see, half-hidden under a grubby nightdress, the bars of a cage.

'That's Nelson?' he asked.

'That's Nelson. Would you like to see him?' Without waiting for an answer, she whipped the nightdress off the cage. In the dark and dingy room, there was a flash of scarlet as Nelson stretched his wings.

The cage looked cramped for such a big bird, but then the bedhead was caked with parrot shit, so evidently he wasn't always caged. Perhaps the old woman *was* confused. She was certainly odd.

He looked around for coal to put on the fire, because the room was cold as well as dark, but remembered that she probably couldn't afford to burn much. All the more reason to get her into sheltered accommodation, quickly.

'Does Mrs Jubb come in every day?'

'Have a heart, they've just cut her hours again. She comes in more often than she's paid for as it is.'

'But not every day?'

'No.'

'What about your family?'

'I've got a married daughter, but she lives down London. Anyway, she's crippled with arthritis, she'd be no good if she was here. I can shin up the stairs faster than she can.'

'Anybody else?'

'Only grandchildren.'

Stephen went back to the parrot, since this might be a real barrier to moving her. Pets were not allowed on the Parkhouse development.

'Have you had him long?' he asked, indicating the parrot's cage.

'Seventeen years.'

'That's a long time.'

'It is. I got him out of a pub – the King Billy. You won't remember it, it was pulled down in . . .' She hesitated, but only for a second. 'Nineteen-sixty-seven. Nelson was well known, he used to drink, sing songs, do all sorts, the men used

2

to vie with each other, you know, who could teach him the worst words. When it got pulled down the old bloke in charge was more or less put out, and the woman he went to lodge with wouldn't have Nelson. And I used to go along and see George now and then, he had no family, you know, never got married, but he was a real nice lad, and when she said he had to get rid of Nelson oh, he very near broke his heart, he says, "Liza, whatever am I gunna do?" So, I says, "Oh, cheer up, give him me, I'll look after him." That way, you see, he could come and see him whenever he wanted. But he didn't live long after. Wicked old cow killed him. I said it then and I say it now.'

'What sort is he?'

'Oh, I couldn't tell you that. George got him off a sailor.'

Stephen got up and walked over to the cage.

'He's a bit nervous with strangers.'

But Nelson didn't seem particularly nervous. He sidled towards Stephen along the perch, ruffling his neck feathers coyly.

'And you can't half tell he's off a sailor, 'n' all,' Liza said. 'He comes out with some funny expressions.'

Stephen bent closer to the cage, but though Nelson peered at him closely – even stretched one feathered thigh towards him, cautiously, like an aging stripper – he did not speak.

'He's shy,' Liza said.

He didn't give that impression. Stephen went back to his chair and sat down. Liza peered at him, rather suspiciously, he thought. She had remarkable eyes: the pupils, starved of light, were so wide that the irises had vanished. No matter how closely you looked at them they seemed to have no colour but darkness. He wondered how much she could see.

'It depends on the angle,' she said.

He dismissed the idea that she had read his thoughts. He began to talk, as persuasively as he knew how, of the advantages of centrally heated maisonettes. On the ground floor, too. No stairs. She'd broken her hip a year ago, the doctor said. Wouldn't it be nice to have no stairs?

'I broke it in the yard,' she said.

Then there'd be other old people for company. When she

wanted company. Nobody was forced to join in, but they usually got together a couple of afternoons a week, to play . . .

'Bingo.'

'Whatever they want to play.'

She pulled a face. 'Why do they always think you want to play bingo? I've never played bingo before. Why should I want to start now? And as for other old people, they think because you're over eighty you've got to be friends. But people my age don't make friends – we're too old. You look at each other and you think, "Oh, she can still see all right," or, "He gets around," but you don't make friends. How can you? To make friends you have to tell people about yourself. If I started telling some poor old bugger about meself now he'd be dead by the time I'd finished. No, young man, you bugger off back where you come from and tell 'em I don't want it.'

'You ought to think a bit more carefully before you say that.'

She lowered her head, like a sulky bird, and turned away from him.

He hesitated, not knowing how blunt he dare be. 'They *can* put you out, you know. They're not bluffing.' He talked about redevelopment areas, planning blight, compulsory purchase orders, bailiffs, eviction. Most of it meant nothing, he thought, though he saw her flinch at the word 'bailiff'. He went on, 'And by that time, you see, the offer of a maisonette mightn't still be open. They're very popular. And then it would have to be . . .'

'I know what you're going to say. The workhouse.'

'I was going to say: St Hilda's.'

'The workhouse.'

'It's not like that now.'

'Do you know, I've heard my father say he'd gas the lot of us before he'd see us end in there?'

It was a chasm, he thought, a chasm that no amount of rational argument could bridge. He tried once more, 'The important thing for you to realize is: they *can* put you out.'

'I won't be here when they come.'

4

'Oh.' He smiled, to humour her. 'Where will you be?'

But she just shook her head.

He looked at his watch – discreetly, he thought – but she caught the movement.

'Aye, go on, you're wasting your time.'

'Could I just check a few facts?' he said. 'Before I go?'

'Yes, go on.'

She watched him get out his notebook and pen.

'Your name's Liza Wright?'

'Yes,' Liza agreed, '*née* Jarrett.'

It was such a perfect imitation of his own official voice that he might have suspected parody, had he believed her capable of it.

'And you're eighty years old.'

'Eighty-four.'

'But you said . . .'

'I meant eighty was the turning point. After that there's no sense bothering what people think.'

'So you're the same age as the century?'

'To the minute,' she said.

He stared.

'Oh, yes. Almost to the second. Me Mam'd got herself reckoned up to the end of January, and she was never far wrong, she was the local midwife, you know. She could put her hands on a woman's stomach and very near tell the hour. When they used to go and fetch the doctor to a woman in labour it was always, "Who's with her?" "Mrs Jarrett." "That's all right, then." But she was never registered 'cause she couldn't read. Anyway, as I say, she wasn't expecting me till the end of January. She hadn't even given up work. In fact she'd just got her hat on to go out to a woman when *whoosh!* – all over the oilcloth. Well, she got herself off to bed and sent for *her* midwife – mucky old bugger she was, you could've planted a row of taties in her neck – and settled down to wait. Then just before midnight, she says, "Hey up, it's coming." "Never in this world," said the old wife. Didn't like me mother. Took too much of her trade. "*You'll* still be here this time tomorrow night." Then the clock started to strike

5

midnight and, my God, did she have to stir her pins, because there I was, very near fighting me way out. Water everywhere, bloody great pool of it in the middle of the bed. And if me Mam hadn't had the presence of mind to pick me up and wallop me I'd've drowned there and then because all the midwife did was gawp. But there was a piece in the paper about it, on the front page, and it said: "The Century's Daughter." Me Dad treasured that bit of paper, and then after he died it come to me.'

Telling the story of her birth had animated her: her cheeks had flushed to the same hectic colour as her shawl; and suddenly, in Stephen's eyes, she ceased to be a case, a social problem, a stubborn, possibly senile old lady, and became instead what she had called herself: the century's daughter.

He saw how time had moulded, almost gouged out, the sockets of her eyes, how two deep lines of force had been cut into the skin between nose and lip, how the hand that came up to grasp the scarlet shawl was brown-speckled, claw-like, but finely made. He saw, too, that her neck was grained with dirt, that there was dirt in the lines of her face, that the scarlet shawl was stained with parrot shit. None of this mattered. Like a rock that wind and sea have worked on since the beginning of time, she needed to apologize for nothing, explain nothing.

Stephen went out into the yard to get some coal. Evidently in wet weather the yard flooded, for the ice, thinly coated with snow, creaked and gave way beneath his feet.

There wasn't much coal left: he had to grope with his bare hands under the sludge to find any. When, finally, he had managed to fill half a bucket, he stood for a while assessing the condition of the house. There was a broad streak of green down one part of the wall, where the guttering had sagged. The bedrooms must be cold and damp: no wonder she'd brought her bed downstairs close to the fire. When there was a fire.

He turned to look at the other houses in the row. All their windows were boarded up, but here and there he could see

6

a board hanging loose, where somebody had succeeded in breaking in. Some of the houses were used by drunks, others by teenage gangs sniffing glue. He wondered whether Liza knew and hoped she didn't. Surely to God they could get her out of here without having to frighten her.

A few specks of snow drifted down on the wind.

When he went back into the living-room, Liza was on her knees by the bed, dragging a heavy box from underneath it.

'Here, let me do that,' he said.

She paused then, leaning on her stick. 'If you could just lift it for me,' she said.

He bent down and lifted it onto the bed. It was an old metal box, not as heavy as her weakness had made it seem, painted on the lid and sides with dancing figures, women holding their clasped hands high, dancing in a ring. Behind the women, almost in the shadow of the trees, were two other figures. One was so shrouded in a long robe that neither age nor sex was visible; the other was a young man. The draped figure held something in its hands, but the box-lid was so filmed with dirt that Stephen couldn't see what it was.

'That's very beautiful,' he said. 'Have you any idea how old it is?'

She climbed slowly onto the bed and waited to get her breath back. 'No idea,' she said, at last. 'It used to be me Mam's. I used to play with it when I was a lass. But how old it is I couldn't tell you. Me Mam got it off her grandmother, so it must be old.' She started to rummage around inside the box. 'I've got that newspaper cutting somewhere. I thought you might like to see it.'

Stephen got down on his knees and started to place tiny nuggets of coal here and there on the almost-dead fire. Each one hissed and spat, and, as the glowing embers disappeared beneath them, his face darkened. Then he began to fan the fire with the cardboard top of a Weetabix packet he'd found propped up by the hearth and, as the flames took hold, his shadow began to grow on the wall behind him and his face re-emerged into the light.

It was a blunt-nosed, high-cheek-boned face, the face of a

7

man who is nearing thirty and therefore no longer thinks of himself as young. A tired, self-disciplined, lonely face, though he would not have described himself as lonely. Rather as if at some time in the past loneliness had bitten in so deeply that he carried the scar long after the wound had healed. He knelt with his hands clasped loosely between his knees until he was sure the fire had caught, then put the piece of cardboard back and wiped the coal-dust off his hands. 'There,' he said. 'I think that should go all right.'

'I've found it,' said Liza.

While he'd been busy with the fire she'd been emptying virtually the entire contents of her box onto the bed. 'Loads of old rubbish,' she said. 'I keep telling meself I should chuck some of it out, but I never seem to get round to it. Anyway, here it is.'

He took the scrap of paper she held out to him. It was a dark gingery-brown, so discoloured by time that it looked burnt; and the creases, from long folding and unfolding, had become cuts. Gently, he disentangled it, and started to read.

'Your mother must've been very proud,' he said, when he'd finished.

'We-ell, she was and she wasn't. She liked the newspaper bit all right – it was me she wasn't keen on. I was the seventh and she'd lost four. Three of them in one week. Took more than a bit of paper to make *her* jump for joy. Especially over a girl.'

'She didn't like girls?'

'No, she was all for the lads. And yet out of fifteen kids, ten were girls, and out of the nine that lived, seven were girls. Poor old Mam, she must've thought she was cursed.'

'What about your father?'

'Oh, he was tickled pink. He used to take that to the pub and show it round. Then when I got a bit older he used to take *me* to the pub and show *me* round. He used to get dressed up, and he had a lovely watch-chain, me father, gold but a very reddish-gold, and he used to hold this gold watch up to me hair, and it was the same colour. Oh, he thought that was marvellous.'

Stephen handed the scrap of newspaper back, and she smoothed it out against the counterpane.

'He was a grand man, me father. Never kept me mother short of money, if he had it she got it. And if he wanted money for a pint, rather than just take it, which a lot of the men did, he used to race for it. He used to say, "Come on, you silly buggers, you'd put the money on a hoss, back yourselves instead." And out they'd all go and put their jackets on the ground for the starting post and he'd race them. Sometimes he'd come straight from work and they used to say, "You're never gunna race like that, are you?" and he used to say, "Hey, don't you worry about me. I can beat you buggers wi' me boots on." And he could'n'all.'

Her face kindled and glowed in the light of the fire. She was not so much recalling the past as reliving it.

'They used to call him Ginger-black, because he had this bright red hair and a black beard, and I think meself that was why he made such a favourite of me, I was the only one that'd got his hair, the others were all dark like me Mam.'

She started to pile papers back into the box. Stephen wondered whether he should offer to help, but guessed that the contents were too private for that. A thought struck him.

'You don't keep money in there, do you?'

'Why, no!' She gave him a scornful look. 'I haven't got any to keep.'

But he wasn't altogether convinced.

'You're almost out of coal, you know.'

'That's all right. He comes tomorrow.' She looked at him. 'It's bound to be a bit low, look at the weather we've been having.'

Even allowing for the weather, the house was cold and damp. It had the feel of a place that has not been adequately heated for years.

'May I come and see you again?'

'So you can soft-soap me into a home? No, thank you.'

'I won't soft-soap you. I won't put any pressure on. I promise.'

She looked at him and evidently liked what she saw. 'All

9

right then,' she said, grudgingly, 'you can come.' A long pause. 'I'll trust you.'

It was early morning when he went to see Liza again. Mrs Jubb, Liza's home help, answered the door, holding it half closed against the wind and peering round it, suspiciously. Even when he said who he was, she was in no hurry to let him in.

'She's not good in the mornings,' Mrs Jubb said. 'It takes her a while to pull herself together. As I dare say it will us at her age.'

The look she turned on Stephen was frankly hostile. There was no way of telling whether she'd taken an instant personal dislike to him, or whether this was her attitude to everybody who represented 'authority'.

'I won't stay long. I just came to see how she was.'

Liza was huddled deep under the bedcovers. The shawl had slipped from her head and, for the first time, he could see her hair, what was left of it. She was very nearly bald: her scalp showed pink through a thin covering of white, like the down on an owlet's back.

She was old, grey, drained of life.

Above her on the bedhead was Nelson, free of his cage at last, stretching out the emerald green and scarlet of his wings.

'Hello,' Stephen said, gently, bending down towards her.

From the bed came the musty smell of old woman and not-quite-clean sheets.

'I've just come to see how you are.'

He waited, but it was clear she couldn't speak.

As he straightened up, aware of Mrs Jubb behind him, watching, willing him to go, he was struck by the contrast between the greyness of the woman and the splendour of the bird, as though her life had somehow gone to feed the brilliance of his plumage.

'The parrot must be a problem when you're cleaning,' he said to Mrs Jubb, as she opened the front door to let him out.

'If it is I'm not complaining.'

10

He looked back, as his car turned out of the street. She was still there, on the doorstep, watching him go.

'I'll never get used to this place,' Jan said. 'Before I came here I didn't know places like this existed.'

The Clagg Lane estate was trapped between two motorways. On his first visit it had taken Stephen an hour to find his way into it: every entrance seemed to be blocked by concrete bollards built to protect small children from the constant stream of lorries on the main roads. This was his fourth visit, but he still wasn't entirely sure of the route and he had to drive slowly, trying to recognize landmarks. It was no use looking at road signs: they'd all been uprooted or turned back to front, as if the inhabitants of Clagg Lane expected an invasion.

'That's the turning there,' Jan said, pointing.

'Are you sure?'

'Yes. I remember the dog.'

The dog, a big, almost black Alsatian, was tied to a stake in the front garden of a house whose every window had been broken. It had run round so many times at the end of its tether there was a circle of bare earth in the grass.

'You're right. I remember him, too.'

A few minutes later they were there. Stephen turned the car slowly into the drive.

'Looks quiet,' he said.

'Don't you believe it,' said Jan.

Just as they got to the bottom of the drive Tony, a boy of about eight, leapt onto the bonnet and hitched a lift, grinning and jabbing two fingers in the air when Stephen rapped on the windscreen and shouted at him to get off.

Stephen got out of the car. Immediately, Tony squared up to fight him, grinned from behind clenched fists, and then jabbed at his shoulders and chest. Stephen reached up and lifted him off the car, swinging him round a couple of times before setting him down on his feet. 'Now go on, scarper! You know you're not supposed to be here.'

'Our Sean'll thump you.'

11

'Last time you were here he thumped *you*.'

Tony shrugged. He pulled himself away from Stephen, aimed a parting kick at his ankle and ran off round the corner of the building.

Stephen and Jan looked at each other and took a deep breath.

Red paint daubed the walls of the building: 'Mac is a wanker', 'Stew is a puff', 'I have a ten-inch prick'. *Congratulations*, Stephen thought sourly, and walked in.

A smell of blocked drains from the girls' toilets: evidently his appeal to the caretaker had gone unheard.

'Do you think you could try this time?' he asked Jan. 'I don't think he likes me.'

'I don't think he likes anybody.'

At this time of the evening the hall was never crowded. Two or three of the older boys had gathered round the video and were watching, or sleeping through, a film. A larger group of fourteen- and fifteen-year-olds were playing pool, watched by one of the girls. And the other girls, four or five of them, had gathered round the kitchen door, and were threatening the trainee worker, Colin, with gang rape.

Jan was trying to interest that lot in the formation of a gymnastics team, God help her. But she had a way with them: she got the doorway unblocked at least.

Colin looked slightly embarrassed. 'I just popped in to make a cup of tea.'

He was very young, and the scattering of freckles on his white skin gave him a perpetually surprised look. Or perhaps that was the girls.

'I think we should get out there,' Stephen said, though the attractions of hiding in the kitchen were apparent to him too. 'You have a go at the pool lot, I'll go and talk to Whitey.'

'You'll be lucky. He hasn't woken up all afternoon.'

'Does he ever wake up?'

Colin nodded, gloomily. 'Yes.'

The two young men by the video were asleep. It still amazed Stephen how much time they spent in sleep, though he knew this turning of day into night was a conscious and deliberate decision, a way of filling in the endless hours when other people were at work.

One of the young men, Whitey, was an albino, and the other kids told a story to explain why. His father had kept ferrets in a council flat where no animals were allowed. One day, seeing a man from the housing department on his doorstep, he'd panicked and pushed the ferret he was holding up his wife's skirt, where it bit deep into her thigh. (Twat, somebody always put in here, in case you'd missed the point.) Nine months later she gave birth to a son with white hair like a ferret's, and pink eyes. In their constant telling and retelling of this story there was something of the magic of fairy tales.

Though there was nothing magical about Whitey. On the screen, a car crashed and burst into flames. He woke up long enough to watch the people inside it burn.

'Bloodthirsty little sod, isn't he?' the other boy said.

His name was Brian Jackson. He stood out, in Stephen's mind, because he was angry and the others weren't. Most of them just accepted the situation and tried to find ways of passing the time pleasantly, until things 'looked up' – something they never seemed to doubt was going to happen. Not one of them, Stephen thought, had begun to suspect that the absence of work might be permanent. But Brian was different – sceptical, intelligent, and bitter. Therefore, to Stephen, more interesting.

'You were awake all the time.'

'Yeah. Just didn't fancy watching that.'

'What *do* you fancy doing?'

Brian looked startled. 'Here, you mean?'

'Yes.'

'I don't know.'

'Nothing much seems to be happening. I wondered if you had any ideas.'

'What do you want to happen?'

'I don't know, that's why I'm asking you. Workshops? Discos?'

'Money?'

13

'That's my problem.'

'It was Maurice's problem, too. Look what it did to him.'

'That's not what I heard.'

No response.

'I heard some of the kids smashed the place up. Deliberately.'

'Yeah. Well, perhaps *that's* what they want to do. Smash things up. Have you thought of that?'

'Yes. But I can't run the place on that basis, can I?'

'That's your problem. Nobody's paying me to worry about it.'

So much for enlisting Brian's help. They watched the film in silence from then on.

Whitey's legs twitched once or twice, he muttered something and tried to swallow. The effort brought him awake and he began watching the screen as if he'd never left it.

'Boring,' he said, when it was over.

Stephen got up to rewind the tape. Whitey wandered off to watch the pool game and Stephen expected Brian to follow, but he hung around instead.

'I'll help you with that,' he said. 'It's too far on your own.'

The video recorder had to be returned to the caretaker's house at the end of every session. Anything left in the building was stolen or smashed.

'There's no need to bother. I've got the car.'

'I'll help you outside with it.'

Silly to go on refusing. 'Thanks.'

'You don't want to pay too much attention to me,' Brian said, as they heaved the video recorder onto the back seat. 'I get pissed off with people helping the unemployed and getting paid for it. It's the only growth industry there is.' He grinned. 'Time we had our cut.'

'Get paid for being helped?'

'Why not? It's bloody hard work sometimes.'

He stood there laughing. For the first time Stephen noticed that there were purple love bites on the side of his neck. 'Are you going back in?' he asked.

'Aye, for a minute. I'm gunna ask Whitey if he fancies a trip down-town.'

Benefit day. The fortnightly piss-up.

'I'll see you around,' Stephen said, as he got into the car.

'Yes.' Brian bent down to the window. 'And don't park your car there, you're asking for trouble.'

When Stephen got back to the club, six or seven of the younger kids had gathered round the front door and were pounding on it with their fists. 'Let us in, you mean bastards!' Tony had shinned up a drainpipe and was screaming defiance from the roof.

Colin appeared at the door. 'Piss off home, will you?' he shouted.

Not a fortunate suggestion. Tony walked to the edge of the roof, pulled out his cock, and aimed a jet of piss straight at Colin. Even as Stephen thought, *You little bastard*, he saw how beautiful Tony was, with his tiny clenched buttocks and the great golden arc of piss glinting in the sun.

'You filthy little sod, I'll murder you,' Colin shouted, as the jet hit him full in the face.

Stephen waited until Tony's bladder was empty. Then he pushed through the crowd and tried to persuade Colin to go back into the hall, but Colin was furious and only interested in getting his hands round Tony's neck. Behind him the door swung open, undefended, and the kids swept in, jumping about and cheering.

There were now about twenty people crammed into the room. The pool game was abandoned. The cues came in handy as spears, as the teenagers chased the younger kids around the room and tried to put them out. Tony appeared from nowhere and climbed onto the table where he jumped up and down, shouting and waving his arms like a miniature Lord of Misrule.

'What do we do?' Jan asked.

'Close. I don't see what else we can do.'

'If they'll go.'

A fight had broken out in the far corner of the room between two girls, Vinnie and Teresa. They rolled over and over on the floor tearing each other's hair and scratching. Gradually, as they attracted more attention, a circle formed,

15

and even the younger kids stopped running about and stayed to watch. Teresa was a big girl. As Stephen reached the front of the circle, he saw a trickle of blood on Vinnie's neck. Immediately, without thinking, he went into the circle and pulled Teresa off her.

They stared at him blankly for a second, then, jointly, screamed. Stephen was too bewildered to know what to say.

'Hitting lasses?' Whitey said. 'I dinnaw.'

'I haven't hit anybody.'

'Yes, you did,' said Vinnie.

'And he grabbed me tits,' said Teresa, with a glance at the boys.

'Now you know that's not true, don't you, Teresa?' Jan said.

'He did, miss,' said Teresa, looking not at Jan but at Stephen – a look of such blatant invitation that he blushed.

'Whatever possessed you?' Jan whispered.

'I didn't do anything!'

'You should've left it to me.'

Stephen took a deep breath and closed his eyes. When he opened them again, Whitey and Scrubber were watching him, shaking their heads.

"*Mucky bugger*,' he heard one of them say, as he walked past.

Stephen went to see Liza again the following day and she was refreshed.

'Sorry about last time,' she said. 'You get like that when you're old. Up one day, down the next.'

'I've brought you some flowers,' he said, putting a bunch of daffodils down on the bed.

'Flowers in a sick room,' said Mrs Jubb, coming in from the kitchen, 'take every bit of oxygen out of the air.'

'I'm not sick,' said Liza. 'I'm old, and no amount of oxygen'll cure that. Put them in a vase for us, will you, pet?'

Mrs Jubb took the flowers and retreated to the kitchen.

'A cup of tea would be nice,' Liza called after her. 'I have to be careful what I say, you know,' she whispered to Stephen. 'She could be very awkward about me bird.'

16

'I've brought Nelson something, as well,' he said. 'Sunflower seeds. That's what they like, isn't it?'

'Oh, yes, he'll eat any amount.'

Stephen pushed one of the small, striped seeds through the bars of the cage. Nelson transferred it from beak to foot before he began, very delicately, to nibble.

'I saw a programme about them on the telly,' said Mrs Jubb, coming in with the tea. '"Nationwide". There was this bloke, he was trying to breed them and it said anybody that had a lonely parrot they had to send it in.'

'Do you think he's lonely?' Stephen asked.

'Why, no!' said Liza.

'You never know,' said Mrs Jubb, 'he might be fancying a bit.'

'Gerraway,' said Liza, 'he's long past.'

'Not according to this bloke. He says they can still be fancying at seventy.'

'My God,' said Liza, 'just like a fella.'

'That's what I said to me husband. He says I hope they get more chance than I get.' She put her cup of tea down on the hearth. 'Have I to let him out?' She looked at Stephen. 'We generally let him have a fly round in the mornings.'

'That's all right by me.'

Nelson needed no urging. With a flash of scarlet he swooped across the room and landed, beak open, on the back of Mrs Jubb's chair.

'Ooh, this is the bit I can't stand,' she said. The bird edged closer to her, stretched out its neck and began to nibble her earrings. 'He loves doing this and it goes right through me.' She hunched her shoulders and threw her head back. 'In any case,' she added, pushing Nelson away, 'I'm not sure about you now. You could be a randy old git.'

After they'd drunk the tea and Mrs Jubb had taken the cups away, Stephen got up to go. Liza waved him to sit down. 'She'll be off in a minute,' she said.

Sure enough, a few minutes later Mrs Jubb came back into the room, knotting her headsquare.

'You know what you could do, don't you?' she said, looking

17

at Stephen. 'Instead of harassing her? You could clear that lot out.' She jerked her thumb at the wall. 'I was coming down the back arch with her pension the other day and I bumped into Whitey and all that lot pushing a wheelbarrow full of floorboards. I says, "What the hell do you think you're doing?" They says, "Aw, we're from the Gas Board." I says, "Don't come that with me, son. *Gas Board*." It was that bloody Peter Taylor, what do they call him – *Zit*. That lot. You want them out of there. They're burning them bloody floorboards and it's not safe. They'll have the whole bloody row on fire before they're through.' She checked the set of her scarf in the mirror. 'He's a right little waster, him. His Mam had him to a lion-tamer.'

'Now you know that's only a rumour,' said Liza.

'Is it heck. She hung round that bloody circus till she looked like a tent pole. Six months later she was out here.'

After Mrs Jubb had gone, Liza said, 'Bring your flowers in, pet. I won't get the pleasure of them out there.'

When Stephen came back into the room with the vase, he said, 'She doesn't like men much, does she?'

'Oh, you'd be surprised! It's social workers she doesn't like. Had too much to do with them.'

'Where do you want me to put these?'

'On the table there where I can see 'em. You shouldn't go wasting your money on flowers for me.'

'I don't think it's wasted.'

Neither did she, he thought. She patted the shawl into place around her head like a young girl. Then, straightening her pillows, she said, 'So what did they say, then?'

'Who?'

'I don't *know* who, do I? Whoever sent you to get me out of here.'

He hesitated, but respected her too much to offer less than the truth. 'They asked me whether I thought you were confused . . .'

'Gaga!'

'. . . and I said you weren't. But there's a doctor been to see you, hasn't there? A specialist?'

'Yes,' she admitted.

'And I'm afraid . . .'

'Nelson shat on him.'

'I'm afraid his report wasn't very favourable.'

'He asked such bloody stupid questions: who was the prime minister. I told him I was trying to forget.'

'Well.'

He watched her huddle down in the bed and face the prospect of losing her home.

'Nothing's going to happen overnight, you know.' The truth was they didn't have the money to knock the houses down. 'And I'll do anything I can to help.'

'Yes, I know you will.' She looked round the room. 'But I've been here such a long time.'

He patted the cover near her feet. 'Would you like another cup of tea?'

'I'll be awash. Aye, go on.'

Stephen looked round the kitchen. It had been dark when he passed through it to get the coal, and he hadn't seen, then, how inadequate it was. One tap. Cold water. And when he turned it on there was such a juddering and shaking of ancient pipes that lumps of plaster fell off the wall and landed in the sink.

'Don't touch the wall!' Liza called.

Her hearing must be fantastic. 'It's in a bad state, isn't it?'

'No point doing anything about it now.'

But there *would* have been a point, earlier. For the first time in many years, Stephen allowed himself to know that he was angry.

When he came back into the room, she'd got out of bed and was sitting in her chair by the fire. So small a space, he thought. A few steps encompassed her entire world.

'It's like being told you're going to die,' she said. 'I mean, you always know you are but, somehow, to be told, to know that's it's weeks and days, not years . . .' She held up her hands with the fingers spread, as if time were streaming through them. 'You have to try and make sense of it, don't you? If it's ever going to make sense, it's got to be now.'

19

She was leading Stephen down a path he'd never expected to walk, with her or anyone. He said, carefully, 'I don't know what sense you want it to make. I've given up trying to make sense of mine.'

'Already?'

'Yes,' he said, and felt frightened because he hadn't known till now that it was true.

2

After Stephen had gone, Liza sat for a while staring into the fire. He'd built it up for her before he left and so it was not in the state she liked best: there was a bank of black coal smoking and smelling of wet dust, rather than the glowing caverns and bleak, shadowy, overhanging cliffs that stimulated her imagination to enter again and explore the long country of the past. She tried to poke life into the fire, but it sputtered, sullenly, releasing trapped gas, and burned, if anything, darker than before.

It would have to be the box. She pulled it out from its hiding-place and knelt beside it, not wanting to open it but simply to touch the lid. She could hardly, now, see the pictured dancers, or the figures in the background exchanging their mysterious gift, and yet they came to life beneath her hands, and their movements flowed through her.

Monday. Wash-day. The fire hidden by a clothes-horse draped with Dad's long johns. Monday was the worst day to be ill, because of the smell of wet wool, and cabbage, and the cold, dank, cheerless room. Mam was in the scullery, heaving buckets of water onto the boiler, grunting with the effort, and whenever she reached or stretched you could see the swelling she kept hidden the rest of the time. She was getting fat again and when that happened you knew to keep out of her way.

'Can I help, Mam?'

'You go and lie down. Best way you can help is keep quiet.'

Liza went back to the sofa, feeling small and weak and useless, but was drawn back to the scullery again. Her Mam's

21

hands were bleached white, the fingertips pleated from their long soaking. When she sensed you standing there she turned and tried to brush her hair back with her elbow.

'Can I get the box down, Mam?'

Louise didn't answer, she was too taken up with wringing the last drop of water from a shirt. But probably she wouldn't have answered anyway. She often ignored Liza, simply pretended she wasn't there.

Liza went back into the living-room and watched the grey drops of water gather on the leg of her Dad's long johns and drip, one by one, onto the floor. When he came in from work, he would lift her up and swing her round and though that made her headache worse she didn't mind. She just wanted to nestle up close to him and feel his prickly black beard and breathe in the heavy smell of iron dust on his clothes. The iron dust was what made the work, but once, when her Mam complained, her Dad said, 'Don't argue with your bread and butter,' and Liza had wanted to laugh, it was so funny, her Mam arguing with a piece of bread and butter.

Perhaps when she didn't say anything it meant Liza *could* go and get the box? The more Liza thought about it the more probable that seemed.

She crept upstairs, past the clock that had chimed midnight at the moment of her birth. She knew if she ever heard this clock chime midnight again something wonderful or terrible would happen, everything would be changed. Night after night she lay in bed, crammed between Harriet and Sarah, and tried to stay awake, but her bedtime was at eight, and by midnight she was always asleep.

The clock, by day, was different, ordinary, though she always stopped at the turn of the stair and had a word with it, since its presiding so dramatically over her birth made it seem like a friend. But at night, as Liza went reluctantly to bed, it changed again. It knew about midnight and magic. It knew Liza was special, not just anybody, like the kids at school or even her own sisters thought, but different. 'The Century's Daughter.'

The century was ten years old now, and so was she.

22

The box was kept inside a much bigger box, underneath the spare blankets and the winter coats. A smell of mothballs, and there they were, in the corner, purple and crumbly, like big sweets. Once, when she was little, she'd tried to suck one and got smacked. Carefully, she pushed the blankets aside and lifted out the box.

She'd seen everything there was in the box, and knew all the stories about them, too, because she'd pestered and pestered until she did, but that only made it more interesting. There were papers, certificates and things, that weren't interesting, but she didn't pay any attention to them. Only to the newspaper cutting that announced her birth. She handled that gently, because it was beginning to yellow with age.

What she liked best were the photographs. One of her grandmother, a tall, straight-backed woman, standing by a chair.

'When did she die?' Liza would ask, though she knew the answer perfectly well.

'Nine months before you was born. I thought, "My God, it's never her coming back, is it?" But as soon as I saw you, I knew it was.'

'Did you love your Mam?' Liza asked, timidly.

'Course I loved her,' Louise said. 'She was me Mam, wasn't she?'

'Am I like her?'

'The spitting image.'

Liza looked at the photograph and could see that yes, she *was* like this fierce, hard woman, so perhaps that was why her Mam didn't like her. Except her grandmother's hair was scraped back into a bun, whereas Liza had hair all over the place, hair you could do nothing with, her Mam said, tugging on the comb.

She picked up a locket and opened it to see the hair, the hair of her great-grandmother, who'd gone off to war with her husband, a drummer, and had once washed the Duke of Wellington's breeches, while he played cards on the drum with his officers. That was a long time ago, almost a century, though the hair in its twist of black ribbon was still bright.

23

Liza got up and carried the locket over to the mirror. She didn't dare put it on because she'd got into trouble once for doing that, but she held it up against her chest, and turned from side to side.

But then she heard the front door creak, and her Mam say, 'Eeh, it's never that time already, is it?' and there was a stamping and trampling of feet as Harriet, Sarah, Winifred, Esther and Beatrice pounded upstairs to take their school pinafores off. Liza put the box away and slipped downstairs again, unobserved.

A minute later Edward came in, whom she loved best of all the family, except her Dad, and he made her laugh, asking if she'd had vinegar and brown paper put on her head.

'Yes, she has,' said Louise. 'You can laugh. You'd be glad enough of it if your head ached.'

'Be goose-grease as well tonight,' Edward said, but Liza didn't think that was funny. When she had goose-grease on her chest Harriet and Sarah complained of the smell and made her sleep at the bottom of the bed where their feet poked into her all night.

Tea was ready in minutes. Louise cut seven doorsteps of bread, fried them in dripping, and gave one to each child. For Edward there was a small piece of bacon because he was a boy and had left school. Liza looked at the dripping, then round the room at the smeary mouths of her sisters, and her stomach heaved. 'Here,' she whispered to Harriet. 'Can you eat mine?'

Harriet jumped at the chance.

'I didn't think you'd manage that,' Louise said. 'Now can you lot make yourselves scarce? I can't be doing with you under me feet.'

Sarah said, 'Howay, Liza, let's play gluepots.'

'You might be playing it,' said Louise. 'But she certainly isn't.'

'Aw, Mam . . .'

'Never mind "*Aw, Mam*". If you're too ill to go to school, you're too ill to play.'

The girls went out. Edward went upstairs to read. Liza knew she'd get into trouble if she disturbed him, and it wasn't fair.

24

Her Dad could read, Edward could read, but as soon as her Mam saw a book in her hand it was 'Liza, run round the shop for me will you, pet?' or 'Liza, if you've got nothing to do, them socks need darning.' The only place *she* could read was the midden, and if she stayed there too long it was syrup of figs, or castor oil if her Mam's leg was giving her gyp. She knew Liza wasn't constipated. It was just because she couldn't read herself.

It would've been nice to have one of the books now, though probably she wouldn't've been able to read it, because her headache was really bad. She lay down on the sofa and closed her eyes.

The room was warm now, full of the smell of hot linen, and the clothes-horse had been pulled back so you could see the fire. Great flame shadows climbed up the walls and fought each other, an endless battle that wove itself into Liza's dreams, so that she cried out and turned restlessly. She heard the *thump, thump* of the iron on the board, the faint clatter as Louise put it back on its stand. Once she opened her eyes and saw her mother take another iron from the fire. Louise held it close to her cheek, then licked her finger and tapped the hot metal. Her spit sizzled as it dried. Satisfied, she ran the iron over a piece of old cloth and carried it back to the table. She looked tired. But she always looked tired, except for sometimes right at the end of the day when she took her hair down and brushed it in the firelight, and the children, watching, knew she'd gone away and left them, and then they would pester and pull at her until she came back and was her old snappy, exhausted self again.

Liza tried to sit up and the attempt brought on a coughing fit. Immediately, the iron went back onto its stand and Louise came across to feel Liza's forehead.

'I thought so,' she said, 'I thought you looked a bit hot.' There was no sympathy in her voice, only impatience. 'Well, you'd better go on up to bed. Go on. I'll be up in a minute.'

Liza trudged upstairs to bed and crawled between the sheets in her underwear. Her thick woollen stockings itched, but it was cold in the bed without Harriet and Sarah, and she had to have warmth from somewhere. For a long time, she lay and shivered. Then, suddenly, she was too hot. She stuck her arms and legs out of the hot tunnel her body had made, but soon there were no cool places in the bed.

From outside came the voices of children playing. She listened hard and thought she could hear Winnie's voice. They were playing skips under the lamp three doors down, and quarrelling over whose turn it was to hold the rope. For a moment Liza thought she would get out of bed and wave to them, but it seemed such a long way across the bare floor to the window.

Instead she closed her eyes and listened. She could hear the rope whistling as it turned, the scrape of boots on the cobbles, a cry as somebody was out. Then voices chanting, steadily.

> Mary Ann Cotton,
> She's dead and she's rotten.
> She lies in the grave with her eyes wide oppen.
> Sing! Sing!
> Oh what shall I sing?
> Mary Ann Cotton is tied up with string.
> Where? Where?
> Up in the air!
> Selling black puddings a penny a pair!

It was terrible about the open eyes in the grave, Liza never liked singing that bit, but it was worse lying alone in the dark listening to it. Mary Ann Cotton had murdered her children, all twelve of them, and her step-children, too, nobody really knew how many, and she did it by making them drink arsenic from a teapot. She pretended it was medicine and made them drink it, but the more they drank the worse they got. They were in awful pain, but she didn't care, she just wanted them out of the way, she didn't love them.

Liza screwed her eyes up tight. She could hear Mary Ann Cotton climbing the stairs, the rustle of her skirt, then the creak of the banisters as she leant on them. She was turning the corner, past the clock, coming up the last few stairs. You could hear her breathing . . .

26

Liza forced herself to open her eyes. A woman's shadow was growing on the wall. She came into the room, holding her hand up to shield the candle. You could see the dark shadows of bones in the red skin. Her face was candle-gold and smooth, but the black eyes stared.

Liza whimpered and tried to wriggle away.

'Why, Liza, what on earth's the matter?'

A hand, grave cold, came down and felt her head.

'Well, there's one sure thing, no school for you tomorrow. I'll just have to send Harriet round and say I can't go to work.'

Louise set to work straightening pillows and sheets. Then got the goose-grease out of her pocket and started to rub it on Liza's chest. Her hands were big and rough and Liza wanted to cry out with pain, but she kept quiet. At last it was over.

'There. That should do it,' she said. 'Now don't push the covers off. I know you're hot but I don't want you getting chilled.'

Liza's Dad came up to see her as soon as he came in from work, bringing with him into the room the smell of iron. The backs of his hands were covered with red scars, like tattoos, where the iron dust had got in through cuts or burns on his skin. But these hands were very gentle as he smoothed back Liza's hair.

'Are you asleep, flower?'

'No. Where's Harriet and Sarah?'

'Oh, never you mind about them. They'll be up in a minute. Do you want anything?'

'No, I'm all right. You won't go away, will you?'

'No, I'll stop here a bit. You go to sleep now.'

A few hours later, in the middle of the night, she threw up. She lay there, half-conscious, crying from the misery of wet on her neck, and then her mother came. She pushed Harriet and Sarah out of bed onto the cold oilcloth and they complained bitterly. Then she started to wipe the sick off the bed. Like raw egg, it slid about and wouldn't be picked up. Louise chased it across the pillow, only to see it slither down onto the sheet.

'You stupid little bugger,' she said to Liza. 'Why couldn't you be sick on the floor?'

Her voice sawed on. She stripped the bed and put a clean sheet on. You could see the swollen belly quite clearly as she bent and stretched.

The younger children, asleep in the other two beds, began to wake up.

'There,' said Louise with a catch in her voice. 'Now look what you've done.'

Liza climbed back into bed. She felt useless, humiliated by her mother's anger, by the contempt that was always directed at *her*, never at any of the others.

Later, just before dawn, when Liza's cough was bad again, bare feet padded into the room.

'Mam?' she said.

'Yes.' A hand rested, briefly, on her forehead. 'You're nice and cool again now. You'll be all right.'

The following Friday, Louise decided she couldn't afford to miss any more work. For the past few months she'd been going to Mrs Wynyard's to do rough cleaning, front door steps, scullery floor. Since Liza wasn't well enough for school, she would have to go too.

That morning Liza's sisters lined up to get ready for school, one behind the other, each brushing the hair of the girl in front. Today, Liza's hair was done by her mother, who pulled at the tatters and cotters as if her life depended on it. 'Ouch!' said Liza, and jerked her head away.

'You be a good girl, Liza. I don't want you showing me up down there.'

Liza didn't say anything. She was wearing her Sunday dress and pinafore, and hardly dared sit down.

Louise took her by the hand and they walked down Newport Road together, quickly at first, then more slowly, as Louise's leg began to hurt. They passed the shops they knew, the tripe shop, the boiled-boot shop, the second-hand-clothes shop, Dennison's, the butcher's, whose bloody aprons sometimes came into the house to be washed.

'You're better going out to work,' Louise said, as she passed this shop. 'It's all very well your Dad saying, Take work in, but

28

it doesn't do you any good, that. It's still the same four walls.'

There'd been a row when her Mam took this job. Dad didn't want his wife going into service.

'It's not *service*,' her Mam said.

'I don't know what else you'd call it.'

'I'd call it cleaning.'

'It's bad enough me slaving for the Wynyards, without you skivvying after them as well.'

Now Louise jerked Liza's arm. 'Mind, Liza, you stay with me in the scullery, or play out the back. They won't mind you playing in the back garden, I shouldn't think. But *don't touch the flowers*.'

Liza walked on, stiff-legged, because her boots pinched. 'Lucky to have boots,' her Dad said. Lena Lowe didn't, she had to stop off school.

The streets they were walking down now got posher at the far end, and in the next street the houses had little gardens and steps leading up to the front doors. Liza jumped up once to catch an overhanging branch, only to be pulled down to earth. 'Liza, what have I just told you?'

But Liza was silenced by her first sight of the Wynyard mansion. It stood well back from the road at the end of a long gravel drive and had a broad double staircase leading up to the front door.

Liza got hold of her Mam's hand and forgot that her boots pinched as they crunched over the gravel towards those steps.

'You don't go up there,' Louise said, as Liza put her foot on the bottom step. 'You go round the back.'

Her voice was hushed, as if she, too, had been frightened by all that crunching. They started to walk round the side of the house. Liza noticed that her mother was wearing Edward's cast-off boots, and that a loose sole flapped and flapped as she walked. Probably she'd been wearing them for a long time, but Liza had only just noticed. She let go of her mother's hand and walked a little apart.

'Now remember, Liza, don't do anything to show us up.'

Two girls were in the kitchen, wearing black dresses and ugly caps pulled low to hide their foreheads.

29

Louise stood just inside the door and waited to be noticed.

One, who was fat and rosy, though a bit sweaty, giggled when she saw Liza. The other, who was yellow – skin, teeth, hair, everything – said, 'I dunno what they'll think about *that*.'

'She won't be any bother. I'll make sure she keeps out of the way.'

An older woman, wearing ordinary clothes, came into the room. 'This your daughter, Mrs Jarrett? Well, I don't know.' She looked down at Liza and pretended to consider. 'She's a bit gristly, isn't she? I shouldn't think I could give them that for their dinner.' She bent closer. Liza could see hairs growing out of the mole on her chin. 'They're big eaters, the Wynyards, you know.'

Liza was indignant. As if she was young enough to believe the Wynyards ate people!

'Oo, what a face!' the cook said. She straightened up. 'It'll be all right the once. Just don't let them see her.'

'And *you*,' she added, turning to the two girls in black, 'oughtn't to be here.'

The girls bustled out. Liza followed her mother to the scullery, a cold, dark room, with one window, very high up. Too high to see out of. Louise filled a bucket of water and began to scrub the stone-flagged floor. Liza scuffed her feet, not knowing what to do. If she picked anything up, Louise told her to put it down. In the end she just watched her mother's hand driving the scrubbing brush across the floor. The skin was so red it looked like raw meat, but the bubbles that grew between her fingers were domes of iridescent blue and green. Fascinated, Liza reached down and burst one.

'For heaven's *sake*!' Louise snapped. 'Find yourself summat to do.'

Liza wandered out into the garden. It was late spring: the heads of the daffodils were brown and papery, roses thrust up red leaves towards the sun. There was a pool at the far end, underneath the high wall, and Liza walked towards it. An old, almost-white goldfish swam slowly across, looking as bored as she was.

She couldn't think of anything to do.

She went back into the scullery and rubbed herself against the door. Most of the floor now was gleaming wet and she'd get wrong if she tried to walk across it. Her Mam rocked from side to side as she scrubbed, trying to ease the pain in her leg. Under the sacking apron, her belly sagged.

Liza went away again, but this time not into the garden. She pushed open the door that divided the servants' quarters from the rest of the house and walked through. She listened for a full minute, but there was no sound. Everything seemed to settle around her. Even the motes of dust sifting about in a shaft of sunlight seemed steady, permanent. She let go of the servants' door and it clicked shut behind her.

She went into the drawing-room, which was pink and blue and overlooked the long garden at the rear. A green light filtered in through branches and leaves. The wooden floor was pale and so highly polished that she stood on a squashed and blurry reflection of herself, which moved as she moved. She began to dance slowly across the floor, one hand holding out her skirt, the other clasped in the hand of an imaginary partner. Turning, turning. She saw herself in a big mirror and danced towards her reflection, but the sight of her pale face and deeply shadowed eyes brought her back to earth again. She looked down at her boots and best dress, and then around at the plump, pink cushions piled up on sofas and chairs.

She moved round the room, stroking the cushions, feeling the silk catch on a flap of skin where a blister had burst. Once, a door opened and closed somewhere else in the house and she froze, until her skin told her it was safe to move again. She thought, *This is where they live, the Wynyards, this is where they eat and sleep and talk and laugh*, and she remembered her father's hands, scarred with iron dust.

Footsteps in the hall, *flap-flap*, and her Mam came in, furious, but also awed by the room she'd never seen before.

'You haven't to be in here,' she said, whispering like she did in church. 'Howay, now, out the back.'

The yellow, not-nice girl followed her in, and her skin got dingier in the green light.

31

'You won't half cop it, you,' she said, but to Liza's surprise, she didn't sound angry. Instead, she plopped herself down on the pink cushions and looked at Louise. 'Supposed to be modern, this. Can't be doing with carpet.' She looked at the floor. 'I know every grain.'

'Have they got children?' Louise asked, looking at the furniture and thinking what nine had done to hers.

'Three boys, away at school. One girl. Miss Elizabeth. Snotty little madam. "Do this." "Fetch that." "Ellen, you haven't done my . . ." You'd think *she* was the Missus.'

Liza listened, and in her imagination she became this girl, who looked out of these tall windows, at the rosebeds and the lily pond and the high walls.

'We'd better be going,' Louise said, but she said it reluctantly. She stood taller in this room, moved more freely, as if some cramping corset had been taken off.

Ellen ignored her. 'You'd think wouldn't you, with all this, they'd have a bit of human kindness, a bit of respect? Don't you believe it. The first month I was here, I was polishing under these rugs and I kept on finding money. Sixpence. Half a crown. Once it was a crown. And, you know, I just put them on the mantelpiece, and that was it. But I went back to the kitchen and I says to Mrs Hayes, "Hey, they aren't half careless with their money." She says, "What do you mean?" I says, "Well, they keep dropping the stuff. Every time I pick the big rug up there's money underneath." Oo, you should've seen her face. She says, "I thought she'd stopped that," and she says, "You show me what you found." Well, I brought her in here and there it was, I'd just popped it down there beside the clock. She says, "I'll show you what we're gunna do", and she went and got a big jar of glue, and she glued the half crown to the floor. Then she put the rug back on top of it and she says, "There, that'll learn her. Time she learned to treat folks with a bit of respect." I was shaking in me shoes because, you know, I thought I'd get into trouble, but anyway nowt was said, and when Boxing Day come round I got a crown in me envelope. I was over the moon, but when Mrs Hayes saw it she says, "Aye. Conscience money." She speaks up to Madam does Mrs Hayes. It's a good job for her she cooks as well as she does, because I think she'd be out on her neck if she didn't.'

Louise was fascinated, but beginning to feel uneasy as the minutes ticked past. Ellen had become flushed, almost reckless.

'Don't let *her* go into service,' she said, pointing at Liza. 'It's a dog's life.'

'What else is there, round here?'

'Marriage. It's got to be better, hasn't it, scrubbing your own floors?'

Louise could have told her a thing or two about that, but was prevented by a footstep in the passage.

'Hey up,' said Ellen. 'Little Miss Snot-nose is back.'

Liza would have liked to see the girl, but in spite of all her brave talk Ellen was anxious to get them back into the kitchen without meeting anybody.

'Give the front steps a do,' said Mrs Hayes. 'If you hurry up, you can just get them finished before Mrs Wynyard comes in.'

Louise filled a bucket and flapped her way round to the front of the house. She looked smaller and dowdier now, as if the drawing-room that had given her temporary height and freedom of movement had also drained her vitality. Liza trailed behind, her head full of the girl who lived in the house. If only she'd asked Ellen more about her. Not that it mattered. Her imagination was already busy weaving a future in which she and this girl were friends. Meanwhile, Louise put a square of hard sacking on the second step, knelt down and began to scrub.

Liza sat a little further down, her hands underneath her bottom so that her dress didn't come into contact with the step. She looked up: the sky had thickened, congealing to a dense white. A carriage drew up at the bottom of the drive and a lady got out, one hand raised as if in acknowledgement of a lift. She walked rapidly towards the steps, taking off her gloves as she came.

This could only be Mrs Wynyard. Liza looked round for her mother, frightened because she sensed they shouldn't be there.

Mrs Wynyard began to climb the steps, then stopped short as she saw Louise.

She frowned. 'What on earth do you think you're doing?'

Louise thought she wanted to get past and, still on her knees, began to shuffle out of the way.

'It's no time to be doing this. This should've been done hours ago.'

'I'm sorry, Madam. Mrs Hayes . . .'

'Mrs Hayes should know better.'

Louise pressed herself back against the wall. Then, as Mrs Wynyard swept past, Louise smiled, a timid, apologetic smile, that seemed to get onto her face without her knowledge or consent. Liza saw it and her face tightened.

'What's up with her?' she asked.

Louise was flushed from the encounter. 'You're not supposed to be seen,' she said. 'You're supposed to skivvy after 'em and get it all done and out of the way while they're flat on their backs, or out enjoying theirselves. She doesn't fool me.' Louise picked up the sacking and started to walk, slowly, down the steps. 'Some so-called *ladies*'d be sat in their own muck like loonies if they didn't have us to run round after them.'

Liza followed her mother back to the scullery.

'Well, anyway,' Louise said, as they walked down the drive an hour later, 'did you enjoy yourself?'

'No,' said Liza, 'I didn't.'

They walked on in silence. 'Why did you smile?' Liza wanted to ask, but you couldn't ask that. There were a lot of things you couldn't ask, either because the words didn't come, or because you knew already, without being told, that there were no answers.

They walked along Newport Road, past the tripe shop, the second-hand-clothes shop, the boiled-boot shop. Liza held tightly to her mother's hand, and every step was punctuated by the *flap-flap* of Louise's torn sole, sounding to Liza like the *b-b-b-b-b* of a blocked tongue.

3

Stephen went home by train.

Habit, really. When he first left home to go to university he'd always come back by train. As the years passed, those three hours on the train came to seem more and more like time-travel, a slipping back through railway cuttings and tunnels not merely into his own past, but into the country's past. You looked down on banks of smoking houses, on steelyards that no longer made steel, up railway lines axed so long ago that rose bay willow herb thronged the track.

That was years ago. This journey was shorter, minutes rather than hours. He hardly had time to sit down before the steep sides of the cutting shut off the sky. The train rocked and swayed, encased in its own roaring. Then, abruptly, rushing towards him, the platform, the barrier, the high glass roof he remembered so well.

When he got to his parents' house he stood outside for a while, staring up the path at the window. Only when it occurred to him that his mother might look out and catch him standing there like that did he walk up the path and try the front door.

Locked. Serve him right for arriving like a stranger.

He went round the back. The back garden had a vegetable patch, neglected since his father's illness. Yellow stumps of cabbages stuck up like decayed teeth. Beyond the fence, the ground shelved steeply to a stream with a few ragged hawthorn bushes. Their lower branches were draped with white rags, as if left there by a river in full spate, though in all the years Stephen had known the stream, there had only ever been a few inches of coppery brown water, hardly enough to cover the occasional tin can or cast-off shoes.

Some children were playing down there now. The wind carried their voices back to him, and the sudden excited barking of a dog.

He lifted the sneck and walked in.

At first he thought the room was empty, but then saw his mother's head over the top of a fireside chair. She'd fallen asleep, head back, mouth open, hands lightly clasped between loosened thighs.

Without waking her, he sat down in the opposite chair and stared into the fire.

Although he had made no sound, an awareness of his presence seeped into her mind, so that her face tightened slightly and her tongue began doing complicated things with saliva and teeth.

In the end, she came awake quite suddenly.

'Oh, Steve,' she said, and gazed rather breathlessly round the room, 'you should've let us know you were coming.'

She didn't give a damn whether he let her know, as long as he came. She was angry because she'd been observed asleep and defenceless. She wiped the lenses of her glasses on the hem of her pinafore and put them on again.

They laughed at each other through glass. Then he came over and bent down to kiss her.

'Hello, Mam,' he said.

He wasn't going to get round her as easily as that. 'If you'd let me know I could've had something ready.'

'It doesn't matter. I'm not hungry.'

'I've got a bit of bacon in for your Dad.'

'I'm not hungry.'

'Oh, you must have something.'

Food was communication. 'All right,' he said. 'But nothing much.'

She went into the kitchen. He looked round the room, which hadn't changed for years. Two photographs on the mantelpiece: one of Christine's wedding, one of himself in degree gown and hood. He remembered having it taken, the

36

bright sunlight, how they'd had to squint into the camera. His father, overawed by the tall buildings and the long lines of figures in gowns, had put on an accent nobody had ever heard before or, mercifully, since. Stephen had expected timidity and deference from his mother. His father's behaviour mortified him.

'How's Dad?' he called through into the kitchen.

'Pretty much the same. He doesn't change much.' A pause. 'He goes to the doctor again on Wednesday.'

'Where is he now?'

'Upstairs, having a lie down. Don't go up.'

'I wasn't going to.'

She came back into the room carrying two cups of tea. 'Look what I've done,' she said, holding out one of the best cups. 'Making a stranger of you.'

His father's cup, British Rail best, was put on the hearth to warm.

'We were ever so pleased when you wrote and said you'd got this job.'

'Yes,' he said.

He got up and stood with his back to the fire, but this position, assumed in his father's house, made him feel uneasy and he soon sat down again.

'Did you come by car?'

'No, train.' As he said this, he wondered why. The car would've been so much more convenient. Only he could not, then, have relived those earlier homecomings, and perhaps he needed to do that. 'I do enough driving,' he said. 'I get tired of it.'

'You never came just like that?'

He looked down at himself and realized he had no coat. The fine hairs on the surface of his sweater were matted with rain.

'Yes.'

She looked at him, flushing with concern. 'You want to be a bit more careful. You should think about your chest.'

He laughed, an angry, barking laugh. 'Oh, my chest's all right,' he said.

37

Almost without realizing it, he looked down into the grate. Not once, but several times a day, his mother got down on her hands and knees and cleaned off every trace of his Dad's phlegm. Once, when she'd been ill, Stephen had tried to do the job for her, only to give up halfway because he was too sick to go on.

He held the cup to his face and his glasses misted over. He felt a slight, pleasant tingle as his pores opened.

'Is the new job all right?'

'Yes,' he said.

She smiled. 'I don't even know what it is you do.'

'I'm not sure I know myself.' He saw from a slight movement of her head that she felt rebuffed. 'I try to get things going for unemployed youngsters.'

'Jobs, you mean?'

'No,' he said, 'ways of passing the time.'

Bleak, perhaps, but accurate.

'And I help run an advice centre, you know, heating bills, benefits, things like that. Debt. I don't find that easy, because in the end you have to sit down and do the sums.' He smiled. 'You know what I'm like at that.'

'Your Dad used to try and learn you.'

'Yes.'

Scraps of paper and a stub of pencil on the green tablecloth. Himself bored, not really listening. Checking you'd got the right change. Working out stoppages on the back of a cigarette packet. What possible relevance could that have to him?

'Anyway, I bought myself a calculator. That does most of it.'

He thought, now, his father might have enjoyed those sessions, with pennies and scraps of paper and bits of chewed pencil, passing on something he knew, before the incomprehensible Latin and algebra shut him out forever.

Upstairs, a floorboard creaked.

'Is he still looking for work?'

She looked away, smoothing an imaginary crease in her skirt. 'Oh, yes.' She looked up at him, quickly, and away again. 'He'll not stop.'

'Time he did.'

'He can't stop, Steve. You know what he's like.'

He stopped speaking as his father came into the room.

'I thought it was your voice I heard,' Walter said. 'Well, how are you?'

'I'm all right. What about you?'

'Not so bad.'

His chest, tightening in response to the slight effort, had begun to wheeze.

'I'm getting too old for that,' he said, with a gesture towards the town where every day he went looking for work.

'You've been told to stop often enough,' Margaret said.

'Aye, well.' He sat down, panting slightly. 'Long as you keep looking, they can't say you're a scrounger.'

Stephen sat on the sofa beside him. 'Has anybody ever said you were a scrounger?'

'It's not what's said, is it?'

'Howay, now, Walter,' Margaret said, 'come and have your dinner.'

'I want to talk to the lad.'

'You can talk to him while you eat. These taties'll be boiled to mush if you don't get a move on.'

'Switch buggers off.' He went to the table, grumbling a bit, but liking to be chivvied. 'Have you had owt, our Steve? You can have half this, you know. I don't eat much.'

'You'd eat more if you smoked less,' said Margaret.

'I don't smoke anywhere near as much as I did. Anyway, it helps the pain.'

She made a little noise in her throat, half-acknowledgement.

'I don't want anything, Dad. I had a big breakfast.'

After a few minutes, Walter pushed the plate away. 'I'm not all that hungry,' he said.

'Well, it's a damn shame letting good food go to wrack and ruin.'

'It'll not go to wrack and ruin. I'll have it for me supper.'

You could see how glad he was to get up from the table and come back to the fire.

They sat, father and son, facing each other across the

hearth, like a pair of electric plugs that wouldn't fit into each other, until Margaret came and sat between them, giving them, by her mere presence, connection and purpose.

'Is your stomach bad?'

Walter pulled a face. 'It's not good.'

'You should get the doctor.'

'Aye, you try telling him,' Margaret flashed. 'I've said all I can.'

He saw the fear on her face.

'I'm off to see him on Wednesday, and why, I don't know, because all he does is give me pills.'

'Well, if they ease the pain . . .'

'Is there a lot of pain, Dad?'

Walter stared stubbornly into the fire. 'I don't know, this stuff's rubbish. You can't get a good blaze.'

He bent down and shovelled coal onto the fire. Each of them felt the sudden, darkening chill.

'He's never liked hospitals,' Margaret said. 'It was all I could do to get him to go and see your Gran when she was dying.'

There was a moment's uneasy silence.

'Anyway,' Walter said, 'tell us about your new job.'

'There's nothing much to tell, really.'

'I could never see why you had to pack the last job in. I bet you're not getting paid as much for this'n, are you?'

'No, I'm not.'

'No.'

'Look, I got worried about some of the decisions I was taking. I just . . . started to question what I was doing.'

'*Started to question what I was doing.*' The mimicry was accurate and vicious. 'Bloody hell, man, where do you think I'd've been if I'd *started to question what I was doing*? Turning the same bloody crank handle forty, fifty, sixty thousand times a day for thirty bloody years. Where do you think I'd've been if I'd questioned that? Aye and where would you've been 'n'all? Up shit creek with your arse hanging out of your britches. That's where you'd've been.'

Stephen had had enough. 'I'll tell you why I left the last job. There was a little boy, a baby, about six weeks old, and his Mam spilt boiling fat all over him. By accident. *She said.* And I had to decide whether he should go back to her. You don't *sleep* after a decision like that. And whatever you might like to think, Dad, that is *work.* I don't care if I never get a spot of bloody grease on me hands,' he said, holding them out towards his father. 'I *work.*'

'I don't know about work,' his Mam said, the pair of you can swear.'

She turned the conversation to Christine and the eldest of her three children, who had just started school.

'Bright as a button, the teacher says. I says, he'll take after our Steve.'

'My God, I hope not.'

Margaret chattered on about Christine's children. Walter nodded off, his head hanging a little to one side.

Stephen looked at him and whispered, 'He really is bad, isn't he?'

'Yes,' she said. 'He worries the life out of me, but what can you do? He won't listen.'

'Can't our Christine have a go at him?'

'Oh, she does. But she can't get round all that often, you know. Not with three.' She stood up. 'Are you stopping? It's just that if you were I could mebbe give her a ring.'

'No, Mam, I'd better be getting back.'

She looked from him to his father, but said nothing. She knew the score too well to waste time announcing it.

In the kitchen he said, 'If he gets any worse you will give us a ring, won't you?'

She clung to him, suddenly, and started to cry.

'I'm only a few minutes away.'

She let go of him then and smiled. 'Yes, you are, aren't you?' she said.

Light years, he thought, closing the door behind him. And they both knew it.

4

Everywhere the wind whipped up little whirlpools of dust, picking up scraps of paper and carrying them along until it tired of them and let them drop. And yet this wind brought no relief from the burning heat. In the back alleys between the houses, flies crawled on the slicks of night soil from the middens that had been emptied the day before. If you went too close, they rose up in a swarm, black and buzzing, heat made palpable. Then settled again, immediately, as soon as you'd walked past.

The women sat on their front doorsteps and fanned themselves. Toddlers played in the street, bare-bottomed and streaked with dirt, poking the dry earth between the cobbles with bits of stick.

One of the toddlers fell over and screamed, 'Liza!' at the top of his voice.

Instantly, a young girl got up from the doorstep of one of the houses and came running across.

'Come on now, you're not hurt.'

But he continued to scream. She set him astride her skinny hip and carried him into the house, where a woman sat by the empty grate, rocking herself. A crutch was propped up against the wall behind her.

'Not again,' she said.

She took out her old, slack, blue-veined breast and pushed the nipple into the child's mouth. He struggled on her lap and she slapped his bare bottom so hard that he started to cry, and fought against the breast.

'There's no point going on like that,' the girl said. 'Here, give him me.'

42

The woman didn't reply, except to point her breast at the girl and squeeze. A jet of milk shot out and hit her in the face. She leapt back.

'Oh, Mam!'

This was her mother's unvarying response to anything that resembled disobedience in her daughters, especially this daughter. But more even than disobedience, she punished hope, daydreaming, any sign of a belief that their lives could be different from hers. *Squirt*, went the milk, and said, more clearly than words, *There is only this. Don't think you can escape.*

But Liza was strong.

Louise's leg, which had been getting worse for years, swelled up and ulcerated after the birth of the twins, so that now she could hardly walk at all. One twin had died at three months. The other lived to be nearly a year old, but then had to go for an operation at Leeds Infirmary. The older children saw their parents off on the train, and a week later watched them come back, straggling apart, their father carrying a small coffin in his arms.

After that, Louise lost all patience with children. This final baby was too much. At night when he bit her breast she shouted and slapped his little bottom till Liza got up and took him into her bed, sometimes plugging his mouth with her own scrag-end of tit. No milk there, but still he sucked and hiccuped himself to sleep.

'I think it's time Dad was a bit more bloody careful,' Edward said, when Jimmy was born.

'Why?' asked Liza. 'What has it got to do with him?'

Edward stared at her. *'Don't you know?'*

No, she didn't know, Liza thought, watching Jimmy's plump little hand pump her mother's breast. Didn't know a bloody thing, though guessed, from scuffles and whispers after dark, and the remarks boys called after her in the street.

'Edward and me are going out,' she said.

'Oh, aye? There's plenty to be done here, you know.'

'Yes, I know there is. I do most of it.'

Louise set Jimmy down on the floor. His face, flushed with milk and heat, immediately crumpled and began to cry again.

Louise got hold of his arm and dragged him round to face her. 'You go on like this,' she said, 'and I'll give you summat to cry about that you'll remember all your bloody life.'

Jimmy, understanding the threat, if not the words, stopped grizzling.

'He cries all the time because you shout all the time,' said Liza.

'Oh, I shout all the time, do I? I wonder why.'

Edward came downstairs, fastening the top button of his shirt. He was tall, dark, well dressed, and his mother's face lit up as she looked at him.

'We're off to the river,' he said.

Louise was torn between her need to keep Liza in and her inability to deny Edward anything.

'I just want Liza to do one little job for me. It'll not take her a minute.'

Edward nodded and went outside to wait on the step.

'What is it?' said Liza, suspiciously.

'I'll show you.' Louise was struggling to stand up. She got one hand on the crutch, but it slithered away from her and clattered on the floor.

'Just pick that up for us, will you, pet?'

Liza knelt to pick up the crutch. But Louise reached it first. She lifted it, high, and brought it crashing down on Liza's back.

'There!' she said. 'That'll give you summat to think about while you're sat by the river.'

Liza gritted her teeth and waited for the pain to pass.

'Don't you ever ask me to pick that up again,' she said, 'because I won't. As far as I'm concerned you can stick in that bloody chair till you rot.'

'Job done all right?' Edward asked, as she joined him on the step.

'Oh, yes. It wasn't much.'

They walked quickly and in less than an hour had left the town behind. Out here in the country the heat was different: it didn't frazzle you the way it did in town. It just made you thing of shade and water and wanting to lie down. Liza scuffed her feet in the dust, raising a separate cloud with every step. The hedges on either side were dusty green, and there was a smell of hot tar. Her mouth was dry.

'How much further to the river?' she asked.

'Not far. You can see it from the top of the hill.'

You could see it, though almost hidden by trees. Better still, there was a warm breeze now, just enough to ruffle the sticky hair at the nape of her neck. Edward talked excitedly all the way down the hill. At home he sat on the front step and read the newspaper and talked politics to anybody who'd listen. He and Dad had rows about it, because Dad was a Tory. He grumbled about the Wynyards and the wages they paid, but in the end he thought they were all right. Now, though, it was all the Kaiser. Dad was all for having a go at him and so was Edward, so they didn't have rows any more.

The woods were green and still. A thick mulch of last year's leaves covered the ground, and their feet sank into it. Within a few minutes they had reached the river. The water was shallow and clear enough to see shoals of tiny, dark fish, and their shadows beneath them on the sand. Liza slid her hand into the water and her fingers looked bent.

'It gets deeper further on,' said Edward. 'Let's go up there.'

They walked along the river path, their feet crushing wild garlic until the air was heavy with its smell.

Edward went behind a bush and stripped down to his long johns, while Liza sat on the bank and took off her stockings.

She heard a scuffling of leaves and a white figure ran past her. It launched itself in a white arc through the air, the water burst in showers of spray and foam all round it, and then there was a dark, sleek head moving out into the centre of the stream. Liza got up and stood on the edge of the bank to watch.

'God, it's cold!'

'What did you expect?'

'Warmth! The sun's been on it all day.'

He swam further out into the river and floated, his white, almost transparent skin dappled with the shadows of leaves.

Liza sat on the bank, envious and sticky.

'Why don't you come in?' he said.

'I can't!'

'You could paddle.'

Liza tucked her skirt into her drawers, and waded out into the water. She wanted to feel angry, because this was yet another restriction imposed by her sex, but the heat was against it. When she stood still, the minnows, which had scattered when she moved, returned and tickled her feet. She looked up and laughed.

And froze. There was a man watching them from the opposite bank.

He came down to the river's edge and waved.

'Look,' said Edward. 'It's Peter Graham.'

He was the son of the vicar of St Chad's, the church the Jarrett children attended every Sunday morning, scrubbed and starched, for an hour of boredom and misery. He and Edward had sung in the choir together and been firm friends for a while until, at the age of thirteen, Peter went away to school, and Edward left school altogether to work at Wynyard's. Their friendship had been one of those passionate, pre-adolescent attachments, that can't lapse into indifference as adult friendships do. Whenever they'd met since, there'd always been the crackle of hostility in the air.

Edward flipped over onto his back and called out, 'Why don't you come in?'

Peter raised the costume he was carrying, 'I'm going to.'

In spite of the heat, he came out in goose-pimples as he took off his clothes. The air felt strange, exploring the hidden surfaces of his skin. When he came out from behind the bushes, Edward was standing in the shallows waiting for him. They looked quickly at each other's changed bodies and then, rather self-consciously, at the river.

'Is it deep enough to dive?'

'Not here. There it is.'

Peter ran across the bank and dived into the water. He began to swim quickly away from the bank, light flashing off his arms as they rose and fell.

'It's cold!'

Edward laughed. 'You get used to it.'

'Do you remember when we used to come here to swim?'

'Aye. And your Mam always thought you'd catch your death.'

'I nearly did once.'

'That was you diving in before you'd tested the depth.'

'You said it was all right.'

But for once there was no acrimony in this. They swam down river until the trees closed in on either side and the water became cold, dark, deep. There they floated on their backs, looking up at the leaves. The sun, only now reaching its full height, knifed its way through.

Peter screwed up his eyes against the glare. 'I can't stand this,' he said. And dived.

Edward waited. A ribbon of bubbles floated to the surface. He began to get anxious: the water seemed calm, but there might be currents underneath. When, finally, Peter's head burst the surface, Edward was angry enough to push him down again.

He rose for the second time, spluttering. 'What was that for?'

'You know bloody well what it was for.'

They started to play as if they were children again, splashing each other, diving between each other's legs, jumping from an overhanging branch into the river. The feel of this branch under his bare feet, as he clung to a twig to steady himself, brought Edward more joy than he knew how to account for. He let himself drop, and this time when he came to the surface, he said, 'We ought to be getting back. It's not fair leaving Liza on her own.'

As a little girl she'd always trailed after them, more like a lad than a lass. But he'd never minded that.

'Stay just a bit.'

Edward looked surprised. 'All right.'

For a long time they found nothing to say, floating like two pale starfish on the cold, brown water.

'What's it like at Wynyard's?'

'Hot. Dusty.' Edward's face hardened. 'Do you remember Paul Batey? His father got killed there last year. Fell into the furnace while they were lowering the bell. They tried all morning to get him out, but they couldn't. Your Dad came in the end and read the burial service. Then they shoved the next load of ironstone in and went back to work.'

'Yes. Dad told me.'

'No doubt the Wynyards gave the widow a few bob.'

'So you don't like working there?'

Edward hesitated. The truth was he loved it. He looked at Peter and found him laughing.

'What about you?'

'Oxford.'

'Next year?'

'This.'

'You don't sound overjoyed.'

'I'm not.' He started to swim. 'Come on. You're right about Liza. Let's get back.'

Something had been left unsaid. They crawled out onto the bank, Peter pulling a face as his toes squelched in the mud.

'I hate mud.'

'You're ovver fussy.'

They walked back in silence, white bodies streaked with mud and goose-pimpled, nipples wizened with cold.

When they came out onto the sunlit bank where Liza waited, their mood lightened again, though a slight hostility remained. They began to tease Liza, persuading her to wade further and further out into the river. But she wouldn't be drawn. She'd felt Peter's going away to school almost as much as Edward, and was less prepared to forgive the change that had followed. Also, she was hurt by being left so long on her own.

Suddenly, she said, 'All right, then.'

She went behind the bushes, and came out wearing only her drawers and petticoat.

'*Liza* . . .' said Edward.

She didn't even look at him. Just ran straight across the grass and plunged into the river.

Peter stood on the bank and clapped.

'Don't be daft,' said Edward. 'She can't swim.'

Liza had gone in where the water was deepest. She felt her

feet touch the cold slime at the bottom. Then something hard and tight closed round her chest. She thought, *Air*, and with all her strength thrust up towards the fractured and rocking light.

Her first breath came in with a screech. Edward appeared beside her, his head as sleek and unsurprising as a seal's. She stretched out her hands towards him.

'Don't let her!' Peter shouted. 'She'll drag you down.'

It was too late. Liza's arms twined round Edward's neck. The water surged and foamed around a knot of struggling blackness. And then they sank, leaving only ripples and bubbles behind to show where they'd been.

Silence. Somewhere quite close, a bird sang.

Peter waded in as deep as he could, and waited. The water boiled, and their heads burst through. Peter held out his shirt, and Edward grasped it. Slowly, he began to tow them towards the bank, Liza's head lolling back over Edward's arm.

They laid her on her stomach on the grass. Peter sat astride her, rocking rhythmically to and fro, pushing his weight down hard at the end of every swing. Liza's head was turned to one side and her cheek, distorted by the pressure of the ground, looked blue and swollen. Peter worked on, jagged spikes of hair jerking across his forehead as he rocked.

Edward thought, *It's no use. She's dead.*

At last, when Peter was almost on the point of giving up, Liza writhed, and tried to lift her head. Her eyelids flickered open, though only the whites showed. She gagged. Water and vomit spewed from her mouth and ran down her nose.

They rubbed her with their shirts to get her warm, and dressed her, after a fashion. Then she lay in the sun, coughing and retching. Edward was so shaken he could hardly think. All he could do was imagine the walk home, not as it would be now, but as it might have been.

Liza sat up and wrapped her skirt more tightly around her. She wondered how much Peter had seen, and wished she had real breasts like Harriet, instead of silly knobs. At the same time she was shy and blushed when he looked her way.

'Well, Liza,' he said. 'That was quite a performance.'

'Me Mam'll kill me.'

'I don't see why. You've done the washing for her.'

Of course he knew her Mam took washing in. They'd taken the Grahams' washing in before now.

'I think we'd better be getting back,' she said.

She tried to stand and eventually succeeded, though she was white-faced and wobbly on her feet. 'You've got your shirt wet as well,' she said.

'It doesn't matter,' Peter said. And obviously it didn't. To him.

His hair was dripping wet, and the hairs on his chest and thighs stuck to his skin, forming strange patterns. He looked very naked. She met his eye and this time they both blushed.

'Do you think she has any idea how close she came?' Edward said, as they walked home.

'No, I don't think so.' Peter looked at Liza, who'd insisted on walking on ahead. 'I think she's more worried about getting her drawers wet.'

'You'd understand that if you knew me mother.'

But Liza needn't've worried. As they turned into their own street a man ran towards them, waving his arms and shouting. 'War! We're at war with Germany!'

She stood, wet and bedraggled, on the steps of their house, watching Peter and Edward run to join the other young men. They were all talking and shouting and nudging each other. And then two of them broke away from the rest, and started to shadow box, laughing at each other over their clenched fists.

Liza shivered in her wet dress, and looked up at the sky.

Eight o'clock. Liza walked down the muddy lane to the factory. A group of steelworkers coming off shift, white-faced under the red dust, whistled and called out after her. She turned round and whistled back. God knows what they find to fancy, she thought. Just be grateful they still do.

She went down the steps to the basement, where a long line of girls waited to clock on.

'All right, Lena?' she said.

'Aw, not so bad.'

Lena was a tall girl, head and shoulders above the rest. She might have been attractive if she hadn't crept around bent almost double to disguise her height.

'Doesn't get any quicker, does it?'

Ellen Parker turned round. 'Why? Are you in a hurry to get there, like?'

Liza was about to reply when a soft voice said, 'I'm sure we all want to get there as fast as we can.'

They stared at her. This was Miss Elizabeth Wynyard, 'doing her bit'.

Ellen, who, before the war, had worked as the Wynyards' maid, opened her mouth to speak, only to have the breath knocked out of her by Liza pushing her in the back.

'Bloody get a move on, will you? We're all gunna lose our place.'

The queue shuffled forwards a few steps.

'Well done, Liza,' said Lena. 'I don't think I could stand another row just yet.'

In the dressing-room they put on fireproof overalls and caps, pulling the caps low and tucking away every hair. There was a smell of sweat in the room, and rubber from the rubber boots lined up under the pegs.

'Get that hair in, Jarrett,' the supervisor said, and tweaked a strand of Liza's hair.

'She loves pulling my hair,' Liza said, looking at the supervisor's back.

A cracked mirror hung in the corner of the room, but none of them liked to look into it. The crack produced deformities in even the prettiest face, and the sour light from the window overhead increased the yellow tinge in every skin. 'Canary girls' they were called, and that was what they looked like. Badly kept canaries. Caged, moulting, songless, much given to the pecking of their own and each other's breasts.

'Are we all ready then?' asked Lena.

Elizabeth Wynyard was waiting by the door.

'Some of us are straining at the leash,' said Ellen.

'Well, we might as well get on with it,' said Liza. 'It'll not go away.'

The women lined up facing each other across a long trestle table. A few of them continued to talk, carrying on conversations they'd started in the dressing-room, but most fell silent as the supervisor walked past.

'Mrs Merton,' she said, stopping just behind Liza. 'Would you mind moving further up the table, please?'

Madge got up, lifted her boots clumsily over the bench, and resettled herself further along. She wasn't daunted at all: there was a smile just below the surface of her face, and the supervisor gave her a long, hard stare before she moved on. It was one of her rules that married women should be kept separate from young girls. In her experience, the conversation of married women – at least married women of this class – was seldom of an elevating nature.

'She's frightened we'll put you off it, girls,' Madge yelled, when the supervisor had moved almost out of earshot.

'And we would'n'all!'

The older women laughed. The supervisor's shoulders twitched, but she gave no other sign that she had heard.

Miss Forster, her name was. She was supposed to be a lady, but Ellen, watching her talk to Elizabeth Wynyard, had noted the tell-tale sagging of the knees. She had Miss Forster exactly placed.

The four girls at the end of the table: Liza, Ellen, Lena and Elizabeth Wynyard worked in silence. Their job, this week, was to check through boxes of brass parts used in the assembly of fuses and reject those which fell below standard. The job was purely mechanical and yet required total concentration, particularly since some of the parts were sharp. Looking along the table, you saw bandaged fingers sticking out like sausages. It was rare to get through a shift without one or more of the girls going to have their fingers dressed.

This job was a rest from their real job: the testing of fuse springs. In the spinning room where they normally worked the air would by now be full of powder and dust, it would reek of chemicals, and the throats and nostrils of the girls working there, even the passages through their lungs, would already have begun to hurt.

'I must say,' said Ellen, 'it's a relief being able to breathe.'

'Oh, I don't know,' said Elizabeth, 'I rather like the spinning-room.'

'You would.'

'I only meant . . .'

'We know what you only meant.'

'Well, I don't,' said Liza. 'You never give her a chance to finish.'

Elizabeth blushed. 'I meant the work there is very important.'

'It's also very bloody hard,' said Ellen.

'I don't think that should matter. Do you?'

'Not to some perhaps. Them that can go home and sit on their big fat arses till the start of the next shift. When I go home I've got a week's washing staring me in the face.'

'For heaven's sake', said Lena, 'give it a rest.'

But Ellen couldn't let it rest. There'd been trouble ever since Elizabeth arrived.

'This is . . .' Miss Forster had swallowed hard, 'Wynyard. She'll be working with you.'

It was a brave attempt, but 'Wynyard' could no more be said casually here than 'Plantagenet' could have been in medieval England.

Elizabeth had sat down, looked across at Ellen, and blushed. She had looked, then, startlingly fair against the yellow complexions of the other girls. 'Why, Ellen,' she said. 'I didn't know you worked here.'

'I've been here ever since I left service.'

'I'm sure my mother was very happy to let you go. This is much more important.'

'Pays better too.'

Elizabeth learned quickly. Asked for – and got – no privileges. Volunteered for all the overtime there was.

'What have you got against her?' Liza asked.

'She's playing,' said Ellen. 'It's not real to her, it's just a game.'

'Some game,' said Liza, taking off her respirator and shaking out the powder that had collected inside it.

So that, today, while up and down the line women leaned

53

towards each other and whispered, or even, some of them, sang, there was silence at Liza's end of the table. She was sick of it and so was Lena, but neither of them could think of anything to say. There weren't many topics Ellen and Elizabeth couldn't disagree on.

'You see her up there,' said Lena, talking to Liza across the table, 'she's supposed to be on.'

'What do you mean, "on"?'

'Expecting.'

All four of them looked up the table at this girl, who looked no different from anybody else.

'How do you know?' asked Elizabeth.

'I heard her talking to one of the women. She says her courses have stopped, she hasn't seen for months.'

'You get like that in the spinning-room,' said Ellen. 'Tell her not to be soft.'

'She seemed pretty definite she was on.'

'Do you know onceover,' said Ellen, 'I thought I was on. It was the first position I went to and I didn't see for a full four month. I was worried sick and, at the finish, I told the other girls, and they said, "Come on, own up, you've been with a lad, haven't you?" I didn't know what they meant, I just thought, *Eeh, I went to the dance with that lad and he put his arm round me.* I thought that was it, I thought that had done it. Oh, I was terrified, I thought, *I'll lose me situation, me Mam'll go hairless.* Then it just started again. And when I finally did what I should've done to begin with and told one of the married women, she says, "Why didn't you come to me before, honey? You'll be upset with leaving home. A lot of girls are like that when they first leave home." Just think the worry I could've saved meself. Just for a bit of common sense.'

'How old were you?' asked Elizabeth.

'Fourteen.'

For once the silence that followed wasn't tense.

Elizabeth leaned forward. 'Why do you dislike me so much?' she asked.

Ellen looked startled, but only for a second. 'Because you were such a snotty-nosed little bugger as a kid. I try not to hold that against you, because we all do things as kids we wouldn't do later. And because . . .' Ellen waited for the supervisor to walk past. 'Because you're playing.' She jerked her head to indicate the roomful of working women. 'Because all this is just a game.'

'You've no right to say that. I work every bit as hard as you do. Harder. I know I don't do the week's wash when I get home, but here in this building . . .' She rapped the table with her forefinger. 'Here in this building I work harder than any of you.'

'It isn't that,' said Liza. 'You're a volunteer and we're not. If we didn't *choose* to do this then we'd *have* to do something else. Something that mightn't be as well paid . . .'

'Like working for the Wynyards,' said Ellen.

Liza ignored this. 'You don't *have* to do anything.'

'Of course I have to do it,' said Elizabeth. 'All you think about is money. I've got three brothers at the front. Or perhaps you think they're playing, too?'

'No,' said Ellen. 'I don't think they're playing. But I do think what they're fighting for, what they really mean when they say *England*, is your little playground. All right, you've been let out for a bit, but as soon as the going gets rough you'll be back in. Look.'

The others stared as Ellen put her hands quickly under her skirt and rolled her stocking down.

'See that?' she asked, jabbing her finger into the swollen ankle. 'You don't get that till you've been in the spinning-room for months. And as soon as *you* get that,' she jabbed again, repeatedly, and her finger left little potholes in the skin. 'As soon as you get anything like that, your father'll have you out of here.'

'What makes you think I'd go?'

Ellen leaned back from the table and smiled. 'You'll go. We all do what *Mr Wynyard* says, don't we?'

'She was only trying to be friendly, you know,' Liza said, as they sat over a meal in the canteen.

'I know she was.'

'So why can't you meet her halfway?'

'Because she wouldn't know where halfway was.'

They ate in silence for a while. Then Liza said, 'You know I don't like the Wynyards. Edward hates them, but it's one thing to hate the idea of them, it's another to take it out on a real person.'

'I don't hate the idea of them. I hate them.'

'I don't see why. Me Mam says there has to be people who give orders and people who take them.'

'And people who eat and people who starve? And people who work their guts out and people who get the profit? She must be a happy woman, your mother. If you think like that nothing'll upset you.'

Liza laughed. 'Every bloody thing upsets her.'

Ellen put her knife and fork down. 'I don't mind *her*, Elizabeth. I mean, actually I think she's all right. I just want her to face the truth.'

'And the truth is that she's playing?'

'Yes!'

'I wouldn't like to say that about anybody. She has got three brothers out there.'

'But she doesn't *see* us. Haven't you noticed? She looks at you, but her eyes never quite focus. She's used to not seeing people. You know, up there, I don't know whether you remember, you had to wear these caps pulled down right low, so that you all looked alike, and you all looked gormless. Didn't matter how much you'd got on top, you still looked gormless. And you always had to make sure your cap was pulled right down before you went in to see the Missus. You used to stop by the mirror at the foot of the stairs and pull it down. Well, one day . . .' Ellen paused and made an odd little sound in her throat that might have been a laugh. 'One day, I looked in that mirror and there was nothing there. Nothing. Not a bloody thing. I could see the wall behind me. I ran like hell back in the kitchen and Mrs Hayes said, "Don't be so soft, you're imagining things." But I knew I wasn't. That was an awful moment. It was like I didn't exist at all.'

After the meal there was always a half-hour singsong around the piano in the corner of the canteen. Mainly they sang songs from before the war. Even Miss Forster joined in, standing sedately at the back of the group, her hands clasped in front of her as if she were in church.

> Now Johnny Jones he had a cute little boat,
> And all the girlies he would take for a float.
> He had girlies on the shore,
> Sweet little creatures by the score,
> But Master Johnny was a wise 'un, you know.
> His steady girl was Flo.

To begin with, these singsongs had been frowned on by the supervisors, who felt that the girls, many of whom were exhausted by the long shifts, should use their dinner hour to get as much rest as they could. But you only had to look round the circle, at the linked arms and swaying bodies, to realize it did them good.

> And every Sunday afternoon,
> She'd jump in his boat and they would spoon.
> And then he'd row, row, row!
> Way up the river he would row, row, row!
> A hug he'd give her,
> Then he'd kiss her now and then,
> She would tell him when.
> They'd fool around and fool around,
> And then they'd kiss again.
> And then he'd row, row, row!
> A little further, he would row-o-o-o-ow!
> Then he'd drop both his oars,
> Take a few more encores,
> And then he'd row, row, row!

As soon as they'd finished, the women burst into applause. Then somebody shouted, 'Howay, Lena.'

The girls at the back pushed Lena forward. She bent down to whisper to the girl at the piano, and silence fell as she played the opening notes of the song.

> Keep the home fires burning,
> While your hearts are yearning.

57

Though the boys are far away,
They dream of home.
There's a silver lining,
Through the dark cloud shining.
Turn the dark clouds inside out . . .

Here she raised her arms for them all to join in.

Till the boys come home!

There was a moment of silence after Lena had finished. Then Miss Forster clapped her hands and said, briskly, 'Come along now, girls. There's work to be done.'

They streamed back to the fuse-checking-room, in groups of two or three, all chattering, and this more relaxed atmosphere lasted for the first hour. There was a persistent hum of tunes, fading away whenever Miss Forster looked in the culprit's direction. Not that it mattered here, but in the spinning-room, where the girls spent two-thirds of their working lives, any lapse of concentration was dangerous. Miss Forster had seen an explosion in a munitions factory once, faces cut by flying glass, and at the centre of the explosion, worse – oh, much worse.

'Quiet, ladies! Let's all settle down now.'

The girls smiled at each other, but worked more quietly after that.

Liza reached for another box of brass parts and took off the lid. She was miles away, back on the river on a summer day, three years ago, when Peter Graham had been a young man with wet hair on his chest and thighs and not, as he was now, a name on a plaque beneath a memorial window in the church. She sighed and raised a metal edge to the light.

Everybody heard him before she did. The squeak of his new boots on the floor. At the end of the table, just behind Lena's chair, he stopped.

Elizabeth Wynyard had gone very white.

'Miss Jarrett,' he said.

More even than his presence the 'Miss' told her why he came. But still she looked round at the other girls as if, by some miracle, the message might be for one of them.

58

'Could I see you in my office, Miss Jarrett?'

Liza got up to follow him, keeping her eyes fixed on the squeaking boots as they were pressed down, one after the other, on the floor. A blur of white on either side, faces looking at her, pitying or frankly relieved. She saw Miss Forster with her mouth open, her fingers making little twitchy movements in front of her chest.

Then they were out in the corridor, whose white tiles and stone floor struck a welcome chill. She put one hand on the cold wall.

'It's all right,' she said, wanting to spare him. 'I know what you're going to say.'

He looked down at her, at the pinched yellow face under the fire-proof cap, and hoped she wasn't going to faint or cry, as so many did.

'I've got my motor waiting for you at the front gate,' he said. 'I'll take you home.'

Three weeks after Edward died, they got a letter from him. This letter convinced Louise that he was still alive. It was months before she could be persuaded that he was dead, and even then she fought against accepting it. She began to go to spiritualist meetings, not once or twice, but three or four times a week.

Liza went with her, since she could not be allowed to go alone. But she went in silent, absolute disbelief, a long, thin stick of a girl in a shabby, black dress, red hair scraped back into a bun.

One Sunday afternoon they went to the hall where the spiritualists met. Louise had heard that this meeting would be taken by Frank Wright, a remarkable young man, himself just back from the war, with a throat injury that seemed likely to keep him out of it for good. Liza trailed up the path after her mother, into the dusty hall. Groups of people, almost all of them wearing black, stood around and talked. Here and there the black was broken by khaki, where a dutiful son accompanied his mother, but the audience was minaly women. In the corner a paraffin stove squatted on its own shadow.

As the time for the meeting drew near the women stopped talking and drifted to their seats. An elderly man came in and pulled the blinds down, so that the hall was in near darkness. You could hear the breathing of people all round you. As Liza's eyes became accustomed to the light, she saw the pale, moist foreheads of women blooming in the darkness like the rounded caps of mushrooms.

A lamp was brought in and put on the small, green baize-covered table at the front of the hall. Frank Wright, who had been waiting in the shadows, came forward and stood immediately behind the light. Illuminated from below, the pouches under his eyes bulged out like lids.

After the first shock of seeing his face wore off, she realized she knew him, or rather she remembered that he'd gone to the same school. He'd been a little thin boy with a head too big for his shoulders and sharp, dark eyes, sharp enough to prick. He was always getting left behind. Liza remembered him running down the street after the other boys, calling, 'Wait. Wait for me.' But they'd never waited. They'd gone off: to the playground, the river, the slag heap, the sea. And he was left to follow.

He began to speak. He asked the congregation to pray with him, and led them in the usual petitions: for rest eternal and light perpetual and, of course, victory – he didn't forget to pray for that. Then his voice lapsed into silence. At first it was the usual silence of people in a crowded room: coughs, breathing, tummy rumbles, a belch politely smothered, the rasp of wool as women crossed and uncrossed their legs. Liza's leg developed pins and needles and she shifted cautiously in her seat, grimacing with pain as the blood flowed back.

Then, without warning, the silence deepened, became something that was not merely the absence of speech, but a positive force. Positive, or perhaps negative, she couldn't tell. At any rate a source of power, binding them together, drawing them in, and it was easy to believe, in that silence, that the white-faced women were no longer alone, that other figures crowded in the doorway and stood in the shadows at the back of the hall. Liza felt the hair on her neck prickle. She wanted to turn round, to stare hard into the darkness, but she didn't dare.

He began to speak again. Or rather he opened his mouth and voices poured out. One voice after another, and all different. Not as different, perhaps, as they had been in life, because there is a limit to what one damaged set of vocal cords can do, but different enough to be recognizable, and woman after woman leaned forward and strained to hear the voice of her son.

These were the voices of young men who had died; he was resurrecting an entire neighbourhood, because the attack that gave him a bullet in his throat had wiped a battalion out. He'd lain for three days in a shell-hole before he managed to crawl back to the British lines and ask for his regiment, only to be told that they were gone. Almost to a man. Gone. And as he was carried to the dressing station behind the lines perhaps he'd said, *Wait. Wait for me.*

His face shone with sweat. A snake-like vein appeared on his forehead, wriggling down from hairline to temple, the sort of vein you see only on the foreheads of old men. And still the voices poured out. Mouths, silent, mud-stopped, gaped open and spoke. Lungs, gas-blistered, blood-frothed, drew in air again. They gasped for air and for life.

Liza had no idea how long this went on. She only knew if she went on sitting there she would eventually hear Edward's voice, and she could not bear it. Already Louise was sitting forward in her seat, her hand, as thickly veined as *his* forehead, grasping the back of the chair in front. Liza got up, not caring how much disturbance she caused, and ran from the room.

The door breathed shut behind her. She walked down to the fence and stared out across an allotment where ghostly cabbage stalks reared up, ringed mysteriously like ancient stones, and the snow-speckled earth was hard and black. She held on tight to the rotten fence and breathed in the smell of wet wood and cabbage stalks, and waited for the pain to pass.

Nothing supernatural in what she'd just heard. He'd gone to school with them, to church, to work, to war. Knew every inflection of their voices: in laughter, anger, weariness, joy, pain. There was nothing he didn't know. If he chose to reproduce what he knew, that was his business, but he had no right to pass it off as more than it was. He was a parrot, that was all. A parrot.

From inside the hall came the sound of chairs scraped back. Liza turned to look back. Her mother came towards her down the path, and there behind her was the medium, looking normal again and smiling.

'This is my daughter,' Louise said.

Liza looked at him, reluctantly.

'This is Frank Wright, Liza. You remember Frank?'

Their hands met.

'You're cold,' he said.

'Yes. I was holding onto the fence. I didn't see the snow.'

Louise was flushed, but looked happier than Liza had seen her look for months. 'Frank knew Edward, Liza. They were in the same platoon.'

Liza nodded and turned to follow them down the path.

'You'll come and have a cup of tea with us, won't you?' Louise said.

'Yes.' His voice was faint. He looked ill.

'And tell us about Edward? As much as you can.'

'Yes.'

He looked at Liza then, but Liza had turned at the gate and was looking back across the empty ground to the allotments. He thought he saw her lips move.

'I'm sorry the service upset you,' he said.

'I wasn't upset.'

'Liza doesn't believe in spiritualism, I'm afraid.'

'You'd find a lot of consolation in it. If you could believe.'

'I doubt that.'

They walked on together. After they'd gone a few yards, Louise raised her hand and rested it lightly in the crook of Frank's arm.

'You must come and see us often,' she said, 'while you're at home. You know any friend of Edward's is a friend of ours.'

He turned and looked at Liza then, as if for confirmation, but she walked on in silence with her head bent.

5

Stephen had a couple of hours at home in the late afternoon, before going to the youth club in the evening. He had a shower, then wandered back into the living-room where he poured himself a gin and sat looking out of the window. An orange cat from next door peered at him from the under-growth, and he promised himself yet again that this weekend he'd get out and do something about the garden. The truth was he preferred it like this: the light in the room green, the window heavily shaded, because the honeysuckle and rambling roses that surrounded it had not been cut back for years.

He stretched out on the sofa, letting the gin glass rest in a cold ring on his belly, and closed his eyes.

When he'd first moved back to the area, he'd lived in one of the high-rise blocks in the city centre, on the same estate as many of his clients. He'd intended to live there a year, until Gordon returned from America and they could choose a flat together. But the weather that autumn had been foggy: sea-fret clung to the land for days at a stretch, and when he looked out of his window, on the tenth floor, he couldn't see the ground. No sounds reached him either. No cars. No voices. Nothing.

'Look, you'll never stick this for a year,' Gordon had said the week before he left. 'Why don't you find somewhere decent?'

'I just think we should choose it together.'

'I don't mind where we live.'

'I do.'

'Well, if you get fed up, for heaven's sake *move*. Don't wait for me.'

The silence outside the tower was not matched by silence inside. Rows, reconciliations, parties, people pacing up and down the floor. And yet in the lifts . . . Again, silence. You knew too much about people to talk, and too little. Did that quiet little man in number thirty-three *really* beat his wife's head against the wall? That's what it sounded like. You met him in the lift and said nothing.

In the end, Stephen hated the tower, the constant chafing of people against each other, without intimacy, without community. He could understand the slogans, the graffiti, the vandalism, the red paint daubed everywhere.

He'd gone out one day, taking time off from work, and found this place. He liked everything about it, even the darkness of the rooms, though the estate agent had apologized for that. He could see the place had faults: the walls were damp; house spiders, which he hated, lay in wait for him in the bath; and the bath itself was streaked yellow, where the cold water tap dripped. None of it mattered. Or at least none of it mattered to him. He wondered sometimes what Gordon would think, but then Gordon was almost indifferent to his surroundings. 'I can settle anywhere,' he said.

Outside the main entrance was an impressive, double-fronted staircase. When Liza told him about her childhood visit to the Wynyards he'd wondered at once whether this could be the house, and a subsequent visit to the library had confirmed that it was. In this room, on this polished floor, ten-year-old Liza had danced. It had stuck in his mind, the image of the little girl dancing, all alone, and it pleased him enormously to discover this was the house. He would have liked to bring Liza here for tea. If he could persuade her to come. She hadn't been out for years.

The place might be a shock though: names of people on little plaques outside the front door, a hall that obviously belonged to nobody, a garden that had run wild. He wondered whether she would mind. Or whether there might even be a kind of triumph in seeing what the Wynyards' house had come to. The Wynyards had moved out in 1919, to a bigger house in the country. The old man was said to have become some-

64

thing of a hermit in his last years, perpetually grieving over the loss of his eldest son.

In a few minutes he'd have to get ready for the youth club, especially since he'd agreed to call for Jan and drive her there. He opened his eyes and looked down at his stomach, pinching his skin for signs of surplus fat and finding it. *Have to do something about that.* He looked further down. *And that.* Three months since Gordon left and he wasn't due back for another eight.

Stephen rolled over onto his stomach and thought *Hell.* Time he did something about it, but not tonight. Tonight would probably end, as Friday nights tended to do, in a pub with Jan. Pleasant enough, but not exciting.

'Do you find yourself dreading this?' Jan asked, as they turned onto the estate.

'Yes,' Stephen said, 'and I don't know why. I mean, the afternoons are OK now. It's just . . .'

'Friday nights. Yes, I know. I feel just the same.' She waited until he'd turned into the next street. 'Does Zit turn up on your afternoons?'

'No. None of that lot do. They all lie in bed and get their strength up for Friday night.'

They got out of the car. 'You'd better bring that tape recorder in,' she said. 'You'll not see it again if you don't.'

They'd taken to bringing only one car with them and leaving it some distance away from the club. It meant a long walk at either end of the evening, but at least they didn't get slogans painted or, worse still, scratched, all over their cars.

As they turned into the drive, they could hear the younger kids already hammering on the front door. Tony appeared on the roof, urging them on. There was a surge forward, followed by the tinkle of breaking glass.

'That didn't take long,' Jan said.

'Pointless mending it.'

'I don't know why we don't let them in. Officially, I mean. Perhaps if we started with Tony we might get somewhere.'

'Oh, I doubt that. Tony's a real hard case.'

'You think he's marvellous.'

Stephen laughed. 'Yes. *And* he knows it. *And* he exploits it.'

'*And* you don't mind.'

'No, but I should mind.' He smiled at her. 'Shouldn't I?'

They got to the door to find Colin struggling with three or four boys who swung on his arms and refused to let go. Stephen and Jan tried to wriggle past him without opening the door too far, but failed, and the horde of youngsters swept into the club behind them.

'Popular tonight,' said Jan.

The hall was crowded. Stephen looked around for Whitey, who was the easiest member of the gang to pick out. There he was, in the far corner, his white hair catching the light. Beside him, the dark, narrow, intense face of Zit.

'I wonder what the attraction is?' Stephen asked.

'I think it's the new dartboard,' said Colin.

Stephen and Jan looked at him. 'I hope you're right,' said Jan.

They watched as Whitey and Scrubber cleared a space round the dartboard. Zit took no part in these preparations, though he threw first. Within a few minutes, the gang had started to quarrel over the score. A dart, thrown by Scrubber, landed just short of Kevin's feet.

Colin started to walk towards them.

'Leave them,' said Stephen. 'They know what they're doing.'

'They could hit somebody,' said Colin.

Young kids were charging round everywhere, weaving in and out between groups of teenagers, though none of them went near the dartboard. You'd've thought there was an electric fence round that.

'Perhaps we should make Zit a youth leader,' said Jan.

'Too late, I'm afraid. He already is.'

Stephen went into the kitchen to check they had enough cups and mugs to provide coffee for the horde. The kitchen was dark at the best of times and when he tried switching on the light he found the bulb had gone. Too bad: he wasn't going round to the caretaker again. It was somebody else's turn to fight that battle. He got the cups out and the coffee and started counting.

'Should've invited Jesus,' said Tony from beneath the sink.

'What are you doing here?'

'Behaving meself.'

He was, too. There wasn't a sign of damage anywhere.

'Are you feeling all right?'

Tony glared at him. 'Sarky bugger.'

'No, I meant it.'

Tony struggled, visibly, before he would admit to weakness. 'Me throat hurts,' he said at last.

Stephen got him out from under the sink and felt the lumps in his throat. His forehead was hot, too.

'I think you should go home,' he said. 'Come on, I'll give you a lift.'

'No!'

'You can't stop here.'

'I'm not bothering anybody.'

'Will there be anybody at home if you go?'

'No. Me Dad works at the off-licence.'

Stephen nearly asked where his Mam was, but stopped himself in time. 'I'll make you a coffee,' he said.

He saw Tony relax as the expected question didn't come.

'I haven't got any money.'

'It's on the house.'

Back in the main hall, there was more noise, more running about, and, here and there, bottles of cider had appeared. Nothing constructive was happening, no games were being played. Except darts. The darts players seemed to float on the surface of the evening, separate, self-contained, like an oil-bead on water. Menacing, though it was hard to say why, since their dart-throwing was strictly controlled and aimed only at each other.

Far worse things were happening in other parts of the room. Somebody had produced a can of aerosol paint, and huge purple cocks and gaping cunts were spreading over the far wall. Stephen went across to get hold of the can, but it and

67

its owner had disappeared into the crowd. A ring of faces surrounded him and grinned.

A scuffle broke out at the other end of the room. Colin had decided to intervene between the darts players, whose shots were edging closer to their targets. Whitey shouted something and one of the girls laughed. By the time Stephen got there, Colin's hands had been pinned behind him, and he'd been dragged into the open to face Zit. Hands scrabbled at his thighs. 'Here you are,' Scrubber shouted. 'See if you can hit this.'

Stephen glimpsed Colin's stricken face. The girls giggled and nudged each other, or frankly stared.

'Let him go,' Stephen said.

He found himself facing a boy with orange hair and pale gold eyes, who stared back at him, without blinking.

'I think it's time you left,' Stephen said.

'Make me.'

They'd let go of Colin, who was zipping himself up again, though he looked close to tears.

'I don't want to have to make you. I think it's best if you just go.'

A long silence. The boy looked round the circle, until his eyes met Zit's, who, almost imperceptibly, nodded.

If Stephen had waited a second longer, it would have been all right. Instead he touched the boy's arm and began moving him towards the door. After a few steps he broke away, and turned on Stephen, spitting and scratching like a much younger child. He was almost unrecognizable: face chalk-white, lips flecked with foam. He started to run round the circle, arms and legs jerking in all directions. He picked up and threw any object that was light enough for him to lift, including the darts. The circle backed away from him as he ran from side to side, then closed in again. At last he stopped and stood in the centre, arms hanging by his sides. He was crying.

No jeers or laughter now. Only silence.

Brian Jackson came out of the crowd, put his arms round the boy, and said, 'Howay, now. Howay.' He went on talking to him gently, as he led him across the hall. They disappeared into the porch and, a second later, the outside door closed.

Stephen was left alone in the centre of the circle, looking from one hostile face to another.

'What do you want to pick on him for?' Whitey asked.

'I wasn't picking on him. He was picking on Colin.'

Zit laughed. 'Gerraway, man, they were having him on. Do you really think I couldn't hit *that* – little as it is – if I'd been aiming for it?' He stared at Stephen. '*Well?*'

When Stephen didn't answer, Zit turned to the dartboard, and, without seeming to take aim at all, put three darts, one after the other, in the bull's eye.

The sound of their flight feathers brushing against each other, as each one struck home, seemed to echo through the room for a long time after Zit and his gang had walked out. Most of the older boys, and some of the older girls, followed them. The owner of the spray can left a final message on the wall:

STEVE IS GUNNA GET FUCKED TONITE.

'Do you think that's a threat or a promise?'

'I think we're in trouble,' said Jan.

'Not *you*. Listen.'

A crowd had gathered by the door and were. chanting his name.

'I think we should stick together.'

'I don't. I think you should take him home.' Stephen nodded in the direction of Colin, who was doubled up in one of the chairs, hugging himself as if he'd been kicked. 'Do whatever women do to reinflate the male ego.'

'I don't see that as my role in life.' She walked across to Colin. 'Come on, Colin, we're closing up.'

'Jan's driving you home.'

'Jan isn't,' said Jan. 'No, really. There's no way we're letting you walk out of here on your own.'

Stephen sighed. 'All right.' He started to walk towards the kitchen.

'Where are you going?' asked Jan.

'Get Tony. I've just remembered him.'

He was asleep under the sink.

'Come on, Tony, time to go home.'

Tony staggered into the hall, rubbing his face. He stared at the mess.

'There's been a fight and I've missed it.'

'I don't think you have,' said Stephen.

Tony ran to join the crowd outside.

'Well,' said Jan. 'Here we go.'

They walked out of the hut together. Stephen was taller than any of the boys facing them, which ought to have been reassuring, but wasn't. He tried to make them meet his eyes, to force each of them to be an individual again, but it didn't work. Their eyes slid away and they pushed and jostled the harder to avoid having to look at him.

The three of them linked arms and began to push against the wall of faces and bodies surrounding them, seeing freckles, spots, spittle on teeth, feeling denim, wool, hair, skin. Smelling breath. The crowd backed away before them, but not from fear. Scrubber fell in beside Stephen, bumping against him at every step, like one car trying to force another off the road. All the shouts and threats, and most of the punches and kicks, were directed against him.

Stephen turned to Jan and whispered, 'Look, it's me they're after. Take the car.'

He started to run towards the group at the end of the tunnel, aiming for the end of the line where a knot of very young boys had gathered. He burst through them and up onto a grassy bank that led to the main road. The whole crowd turned and gave chase, throwing stones and bottles at him as he ran.

He saw a bus in the distance and ran for it. But just as he came within reach of the platform it began to pull away. He ran along behind, pleading with eyes and outstretched hands for the bus to stop. The conductor, a small man with a wispy, grey moustache, regarded him placidly and would not ring the bell. Stephen's fingers closed around the pole, but he stumbled and had to let go. By the time he'd recovered his balance, the bus was out of reach.

70

But he wasn't being followed. He looked back and there was a police car, parked about two hundred yards up the road. He knew he ought to go back, but he was too tired and too sick of it all. Instead, he climbed the bank to the fence that divided the main road from a pedestrian way. He sat down with his back to the wire, legs trembling, lungs heaving. He could smell the sweat in his armpits and it smelled different. Not like ordinary sweat at all. The details of the evening sank temporarily beneath the surface of his mind and hung there, a confusion of fear, shame and failure that would have to be sorted out, sometime, when he had breath. There was a pain in his chest, very sharp and localized, like a spike stabbing, and he wondered whether he could possibly have strained his heart on that final stupid run for the bus. He unfastened his shirt and flapped the edges of cloth to dry his skin, but soon even that became too much and he simply sat back with his mouth open and stared at the sky.

Late the following night Stephen parked his car on the outskirts of town and walked the last few hundred yards to the pub. It was almost opposite the entrance to the fairground, which had just opened its gates for the new season. He paused outside the pub and looked across the road, smelling the mingled smell of sweat and beer. The cars on the waltzer whirled round and a girl's scream sliced the air.

He gulped the first half of his pint quickly, then slowed down, not wanting to face the crush at the bar again. Young men, mainly, short, heavily muscled, skins dead-white. Dole-queue wallahs built like their steel-making and ship-building fathers, resembling them in this, if in nothing else.

Tight jeans, boots, skinhead crops, out for their Saturday night piss-up before the long week at home, stretched out on the bed, with a porno mag and a stiff towel for company.

He noticed the tattoos on their arms. Girls' names, a rose, a dragon, a heart with 'Mam' underneath: all this on boys who, staggering home tonight, full of northern macho and New-castle Brown would strike terror into anybody who crossed their path. He remembered boys like these at the baths: the smell of wet bodies, slapping, jostling, the greens, reds, purples of their tattoos, and his belly stirred with a mixture of lust, loneliness and nausea.

Two pints of beer appeared on the table in front of him. He looked up and saw Brian Jackson.

'I thought you could do with another,' Brian said, indicating Stephen's almost empty glass.

'Thanks. Cheers.'

He sounded neither grateful nor cheerful, and Brian's smile acknowledged as much. 'Had a spot of bother then?'

'You know I did. You were there.'

'I arrived late to find what looked like a riot, *already in progress*, poured my little ration of sweetness and light onto the scene and departed.' He raised his hands, palms outwards. 'Clean.'

'Yes, well. Thanks for getting the boy out anyway.'

'I didn't do it for you. I did it for him.'

'I gather he's the one you don't tangle with.'

'He takes fits.'

'Oh. It would've been nice to've known that.'

'Maurice knew.'

'He hasn't been well enough to talk to anybody.'

Brian hesitated for a moment. Then said, 'I can tell you most of it.'

'I want to know what we're doing wrong.'

'Everything,' Brian said, cheerfully. 'Well, not *everything* . . .' He shrugged, feeling the pressure of Stephen's continued silence. 'Look, they fancied a punch-up. It was nothing personal.'

'It bloody was, you know.'

'No, it wasn't. They'll all be back next Friday.'

'Well, unless I can find out what's going wrong, I won't be.' He waited. 'The afternoons are all right now.'

'So I hear. Woodwork, basic literacy, dress-making, bike workshop.' He grinned. 'All *very* constructive.'

'Is that why you stopped coming?'

Brian opened his mouth to say something, then laughed instead. 'No. I got a job.'

'Good!'

Brian shook his head. 'Just over there, on the fairground. It's nothing much.'

'Are you still claiming?'

For a moment, it looked as if he wouldn't answer. Then he nodded. 'Yes.'

A brief pause as Stephen registered the beginning of trust. The lights had started to change: a pattern of red and green rippled across their skins like transitory tattoos. Stephen looked down and saw a real tattoo on Brian's arm, a snake twisted round a staff. Its head disappeared under his rolled-back sleeve, but the thick body rippled with the movements of his arm.

'Does it hurt?' Stephen asked.

Brian looked down. 'Why, aye. That's the point.'

Stephen bought another round of drinks, and tried to draw Brian out. It was hard going, at first: then, suddenly, he started to talk, in a torrent that Stephen couldn't've stopped, even if he'd wanted to.

He lived alone with his mother, didn't know where his father was, didn't think his mother knew either. He'd left home when Brian was ten. 'I was glad when he went, he was always threatening her. I used to lie upstairs and hear them scream and shout and carry on. Once I had to go for the next-door neighbour to come and pull him off her. I used to walk home from school counting lampposts, stuff like that. You know, if it's more than twenty he'll be gone when I get back. And if it wasn't twenty, I used to cheat, I used to count the ones up the side streets as well.' He laughed. 'She was jealous to death of him. We used to go every night and stand outside some bloody pub to see if he was on his own when he come out. She used me to spy on him. I used to have to go to places he worked. Even at work, she thought he had somebody. I mean, he was a *welder*! At the finish, I think he hated me worse than he hated her, and that was saying a lot. The day before he left home, he beat the shit out of me, I mean, really bad. He'd've got time for it, if she'd reported him. But of course she didn't. As far as she was concerned, the sun rose

73

and set out of his arsehole. I think she hated me after he left, because I should've been able to hold him for her, you see, and I couldn't. I don't know what sort of son he wanted, but it wasn't me. You should see her now. She's only turned forty, but she's a wreck, she is, she's pathetic, she just sits with her feet in the gas oven and moans on, her feet, her tits, her knees, her womb, they're all dropping off. God, I can't *stand* it.'

'So why don't you move out?'

'Where to?' He looked down at his glass. 'I can't afford anywhere.'

Probably true, but not the real reason. He looked startled, as if the idea had never occurred to him. 'Oh, there's ways round that.'

'I'll think about it.'

'Well, if there's anything I can do . . .'

Brian nodded. Stephen waited for him to drink up and then they wandered out into the street together. The wind had freshened. They walked across to the sea-wall, feeling the sand gritty underneath their feet. Far out to sea, a ship waited, motionless, marked only by her lights. An oil-tanker, perhaps. The tide was out: the sand lay clean and wet and shining in the moonlight.

'Do you fancy a walk then?' Brian asked. There was a new thickness in his voice.

Stephen looked at him, at the Adam's apple quivering in the young neck, and said, awkwardly, 'No, I don't think so. I think I'd better be getting back.'

'All right.' Brian smiled, almost maliciously. 'See you Friday night.'

Stephen walked away quickly and didn't look back.

6

'You look a bit rough,' Liza said, catching a glimpse of him from the corner of her eye.

'I feel rough,' Stephen said. 'I had a bit of bother with some lads at the youth club. Ended up with them chasing me down the dual carriageway.'

'Peter Taylor was it? Zit?'

Stephen nodded.

'He's a right little bugger, him. Lives next door to Mrs Jubb, you know. You want to take her with you. She'd sort him.'

He laughed. 'Yes, I think she would. She sorts me.'

'Oh, she likes you.'

Did she, indeed? Well, like Nelson, she had a funny way of showing it.

'The other thing is, Mam rang last night and apparently Dad's worse. But he won't go to bed. Says if he lies down he'll die.'

'There's a lot like that. Trouble is they do. They get it into their heads, and then . . .'

He looked at her curiously. 'Do you really think dying's like that? I mean, that it's how you feel? Not how ill you are.'

'No, not always. Wouldn't be all these old people in nappies, would there, if it was like that? But for some people it is. I do believe you can make up your mind to die, and none of this plastic bag nonsense.'

'*You* wouldn't do that, would you?'

'Why, no. We were brought up to think it was a sin. The Lord took you when He wanted you. I just wish I could think of a way of whetting His appetite.'

'I'm glad you're alive.'

She looked at him, and nodded. 'Yes, son, I know you are.'

It was the first time she'd called him 'son', the first time she'd allowed herself to say the word, and it went on murmuring, in the room or in her head, for a long time after he'd gone. He was like Tom. She'd never told him that, and probably she never would. In any case, he wasn't like Tom as Tom would have been now. It took all the effort of her imagination to realize that Tom would have been an old man.

Meanwhile she got on with her dying, since that was the task in hand. She hadn't known it would be like this: so much like *work*. Like labour. When she became impatient as the night hours passed, staggering from breath to breath, she remembered the births of her children, how long she'd had to wait for life. You couldn't expect death to come rushing in like a skivvy because you'd rung the bell.

You'll be worse before you're better.

She heard the words spoken aloud, as if her mother was with her in the room, easing this transition, as she had the other, with gentle hands and bitter words.

'Mam,' she said, and on the rim of her vision a shadow moved.

'It's all very well you saying that. It's bad enough now.'

'You should've thought of that, Liza.'

'What do you mean, I should've thought of that? I knew nowt.'

'You knew right from wrong.'

Louise reached for her crutch and Liza flinched. But she was only going to the scullery, to fill the kettle.

'To hear you talk, Mam, you'd think I wasn't married.'

'To hear you talk, you wish you weren't.'

Liza looked down at the bulge and wondered how it got out. Through the belly-button, she'd thought as a girl, and a few weeks ago that had still seemed possible. Her belly-button jutted out of her stomach and looked as if it was going to pop. But then she met Mrs Brady outside the Co-op and she said, 'Don't worry, pet. It's just like having a good shit.' So perhaps it came out of your bum?

76

Louise came back into the room with the kettle.

'Where does it come out, Mam?' Liza asked.

Louise stared. 'Well, you daft little bugger, it comes out where it went in.' She set the kettle on the fire. 'Putting it in's the good bit.'

Liza tried to grasp what she'd been told and failed.

'Is that to wash it with?' she asked.

'No. It's to make me a cup of tea while I sit and listen to your yattering. You'll be hours yet, Liza. You've hardly started.'

They sat in silence for a while until the kettle boiled.

'I've never said I wished I wasn't married.'

'You turn up on the doorstep with a big belly and a black eye, what else are we to think?'

'Me Dad was furious, wasn't he?' Her voice deepened. '"I'll hang for that bugger in York!"'

'I'm glad you think it's funny. I told him straight, he's not worth hanging for.'

'*You*'ve changed your tune. Wasn't so long ago the sun rose and set on Frank.'

'Yes, well . . .' Louise sighed. 'It's no use going on like that. You should let the dead rest.'

'They get bugger-all rest in our house. Seances in the living-room now.'

'You should put your foot down.'

'And get the other eye blacked.'

'One thing you never saw in your own house.'

'They're not all like me Dad.'

'They're not all like Frank, either.'

Liza leant back in the chair. 'Nobody's like Frank, Mam.' She bared her teeth in a grin as the next pain started. 'You know he's faith-healing now as well?'

Louise said nothing.

'Oh, yes.' The pain ebbed. 'Up all night with them. I wouldn't care, but his chest's bad and yet he'll sit up night after night with somebody dying of consumption. And he'll hold them and he'll pray with them right till the very end. Then he comes back home and he's too shattered to go to work.'

'How much work does he lose, Liza?'

Liza looked down at the fire. 'A lot. I can't even say I wasn't warned. His Mam warned me. She says, "You think I don't want you to have him 'cause I'm jealous, don't you? Well, I'm not. You could have any one of my other lads, but not Frank. He's peculiar."'

She held onto the arms of the chair as the next pain started.

'His Dad's the same. No room for him at all. Between you and me, I think they wish they'd lost him instead of Robert.'

'You can't choose.'

Liza could've kicked herself. A whole morning with no mention of Edward and she had to go and open her big gob.

'If Edward had lived you wouldn't be in this state.'

'If Frank had died, I wouldn't be in it. Like you say, Mam, you can't choose.'

Louise looked down at her hands. 'Have you thought any more what you're going to call it?'

'Tom,' said Liza, steadily. 'After me Dad.'

Liza didn't know why she was so determined not to call the baby Edward. She'd loved Edward. Missed him, if anything, more, now, than when he first died . . . And yet . . .

'Might be a girl, Mam. Have you thought of that?'

'God forbid.'

It was always difficult to rouse her once she'd started thinking of Edward, but Liza did her best. 'You know, Mam, there's one thing bothering me.'

'What's that, flower?'

Liza bent close to her mother and whispered.

Louise hit the roof. 'Calls himself a Christian? A dog in the street knows better than that.'

'It won't hurt the baby, will it?'

'No. No, I shouldn't think so. But it doesn't show much respect for you. I'll tell you one thing, Liza. That's finished your husband with me. He can come and see the baby, but that's as far as it goes. Nobody in this house gets up to make a cup of tea for him.'

Liza was left feeling she'd overdone the change of subject. Not that it wasn't true. Only she didn't know if she resented it, or not. Oh, yes, she resented it! The preaching, the praying, the Bible reading, the seances, the faith-healing, the always being made to feel inferior, and then at night he swung his leg over and pounded away as if you'd no more feelings than the mattress.

The woman hadn't been born who could live with Frank. 'He's like his Dad, you know. For all they can't stand each other. He led Frank's Mam a merry dance. Oh, not hitting her, nowt like that. But she had a bairn in the workhouse, before she met him, and he's never let her forget it. That's Frank.'

By mid-afternoon, Liza was ready for bed. She lay back against the pillows and closed her eyes.

'You're bad, aren't you?' said Louise.

Liza gritted her teeth. *'I'll be worse before I'm better.'*

The afternoon wore on. For a time Liza slept between pains. When she opened her eyes again, a fire had been lit and shadows flickered on the wall.

'Oh, that's nice,' she said.

'Frank's downstairs.'

'Oh, is he? Well, I suppose he'd better come up.'

He stood by the bed, white faced, ill at ease with the female smell of the room.

'You've had your tea, then?'

'Yes.'

'And you're going to your Mam's for your dinners?'

'Yes.'

She closed her eyes, withdrawing from him as the next pain started.

'How are you?' he asked, wanting to pull her back.

'She's not so bad,' said Louise. 'Be here by midnight, I should think.'

At that moment, the clock on the stairs chimed. Liza counted eight. Years ago, when she was a little girl, eight was bedtime. The clock had called her in from the street then, as now it marked out the hours of her labour.

Two hours later the pain was bad. She could never've imagined pain like this existed.

'I was going to pop round home,' said the midwife, Mrs Wilson. 'But by the looks of her I don't think I'll have time.'

'You go downstairs and tell Harriet to make you a cup of tea,' said Louise. 'I'll stop with her.'

Liza felt rather than saw Mrs Wilson leave the room.

'It's not going wrong, is it, Mam?'

'Why, no! It's a big baby you've got in there. You can't expect it to pop out.'

Louise pulled the bedclothes back.

'Just lift your knees up, flower. There, that's right.'

Her mother's hand slid inside her, while the other hand came down and pressed gently, but firmly, on the white mound. A minute later, she put the sheet back.

'You'll be better now,' she said.

She was, too. Instead of lying there crushed by pain, she dragged herself up onto the pillows, and began to feel she was in charge. The idea that her body might stretch to let out a full-size baby didn't seem like a bad joke now. She felt it could. She felt its softness, its flexibility and its power. Now, when the pains broke over her, she rose to meet them. Like a strong swimmer in a heavy sea, she was exhilarated by waves that from the land must look like a fury of boiling foam. She raised her eyes to her mother and laughed.

'You don't often see *that*,' said Mrs Wilson.

Louise looked down at her daughter. 'That's Liza.'

Half an hour later, the head crowned. Liza groaned once, and then again as the shoulders wrenched their way out. Then there was no more pain.

'It's a boy!' said Louise.

Liza struggled to sit up. 'Let me see him.'

They gave him to her. Heavy, slimy, floppy, curled up on himself like some creature without a skeleton, a slug, perhaps, or a snail. She put him to her breast, not caring that he left trails of blood and slime. He sucked hard, fingers waving like the tendrils of a sea-anemone as his cheeks worked.

'Well, she got him on all right, didn't she?' said Mrs Wilson. 'You'd think she'd been doing that for years.' She nodded approval at the young girl in the bed.

But Liza turned to look at her mother and saw how hungrily she looked at the baby, as if she wanted to eat him, or put him to *her* breast.

Liza had to lie in bed, belly bound tightly with strips of torn-up sheet, for fourteen days after the birth, and during all this time she was not allowed to wash herself below the waist. Except when he was brought to her to feed, she hardly saw the baby. Louise took charge of him.

'I want him bathed in here, Mam,' she said. 'Where I can see him.'

'You can't expect me carrying water upstairs.'

Her legs were better than they'd been immediately after the birth of the twins, but she still needed a crutch to get around.

'Then don't bath him till Harriet gets in. It won't hurt her to carry it up.'

Louise grumbled, but agreed. Liza turned restlessly on her pillow, disturbing the smell of hot blood.

'God, I'll be glad to be out of this.'

'You'll be grateful for this after,' said Louise. 'You wait till you've got four or five and you've *got* to get up. Then you'll know.'

'Frank says we're only having one more.'

Louise grunted her contempt. 'Way he goes on it'll be twenty.'

Harriet brought the bath and saucepans of warm water upstairs. Louise followed with the baby.

'Over here,' said Liza. 'I want to see him.'

Louise lowered him into the water, swishing little waves and ripples into the creases of his arms and groin. He hiccuped with surprise, but stopped crying. She was talking to him all the time, a murmur of endearment in which no words were clearly audible. Liza lay back against the pillows and watched.

Suddenly, she sat up.

'What did you call him?' she asked.

Louise looked up, with an odd, fearful, waking expression, like somebody coming out of a deep sleep into a day she can't face.

'You called him Edward,' Liza said, 'didn't you? Well, he's not Edward. He's Tom.'

81

She held out her arms for the child. With one last look down at him, Louise handed him over. Then she hauled herself up on her crutch and limped out of the room.

Liza held her son in her arms, one hand underneath his buttocks, the other cradling his head. She could see, through the gap in his skull, the throb of blood under the thin membrane that protected his brain from the world. The cool air moved over him and his scrotum tightened. Inside it, she could see his testicles, looking like tiny crushable eggs. She held in her hands the potential power of a man's body, and also its weakness, its total vulnerability.

Already the cord that had bound him to her was withering away. They could take him away and kill him for no reason she would ever understand. They could fill his head with dreams of adventure and glory and make him want to go. Her son was no different from the rest.

When her mother came back into the room, Liza said, 'Thomas Edward.'

Louise looked down at her daughter and her grandson and, slowly, nodded.

The young man stirred in his sleep and tried to push the quilt away from his face. A narrow shaft of sunlight lay across the bed and he almost woke; but then a white hand, moist, damp and cold, like a pad soaked in chloroform, came down over his face and pushed him down into the nightmares.

A yellow smell, the smell of rotting bodies and mustard gas, the smell that lingered on men marching back from the line, but they were marching towards it, slipping and slithering on the duckboards, each man holding onto the pack of the man in front. They came to a place where the duckboards had vanished altogether and a corpse had been used to plug the gap. It belched gas as the first man trod on it.

On either side of the track were shell-holes full of water and in one of them a trapped moon stared at the sky. Nothing moved except the line of men, shuffling forward. No trees, no grass, and the water that looked so pure would blister the skin that touched it. A film of grease floated on its surface, where the dead of previous battles had dissolved into the mud. And around the rim of every crater the more recent dead swelled up like bladders, until a practising sniper burst them.

Ahead of him, on the side of the duckboard, was a small lump. He looked at it as he went past and saw a hand, gripping the edge of the track. Just the hand, a wrist, the cuff of a sleeve – everything else had gone.

You couldn't get a man out of the mud, once he fell into it. Once they heard screaming coming from a crater and ran towards it. A young man, fair-skinned, blond, was floundering in the mud, up to the shoulders already by the time they reached him. They formed a chain and tried to pull him out, but he was too far gone, and so they had to watch him sink. It took a long time. He kept begging them to shoot him, but none of them could, not point-blank, like that, into his living face, and so the mud swallowed him. For a few minutes after he sank it went on quaking and puckering, like porridge coming to the boil.

Frank's eyes flickered as a finger of light reached him. The curtains were thin cotton and skimped in the making. However hard you pulled them, they would not close.

The morning light tormented him, drawing him out of the darkness. He was cold all down one side where he'd thrown the blankets off. He didn't open his eyes, but he knew he was awake and cold, and that what lay around him was not mud and desolation but a bedroom with a patchwork quilt on the bed, and a thin dagger of sunlight on the floor. He moved his hands and felt the roughness of the sheets. No warmth on Liza's side of the bed – he was alone.

He had a son. He knew that, remembered, but still he did not want to wake, enmeshed as he was in the darkness of his dream, afraid that if he moved too quickly the bedroom would vanish and he would find himself back in a hole in the ground. It wasn't easy to know which was dream and which reality. Out there he'd often dreamed he was in bed, cosy and warm, only to wake in a dugout, cramped and stiff, on a bunk made from chicken wire.

He opened his eyes and lay for a while watching the shaft of sunlight lengthen. Then he got up and pulled the curtains back. A small sun, silvery and distinct, lay above the horizon. Another day had started, whether he wanted it or not.

He remembered he didn't have to work today, so he could take his time over breakfast. He wasn't expected at his mother-in-law's until late afternoon. He thought about the baby, how it cried and stretched out its curled fists, and how Liza had looked in labour, that utterly withdrawn, inhuman look. It was too much for him to grasp, all at once, too much to take in. He was tired.

Permanently tired. Sometimes it seemed to him, terminally tired. Liza blamed his faith-healing, but it wasn't that. It was the anguish of his nights, the nightmares that wouldn't stop, but gargled up in him, black and sour, like the taste of his own bile. He woke every morning with the taste of nightmare on his tongue.

He straightened the bedclothes, poured water into the basin and splashed his face. No shaving today, or not until later. It was reassuring to pull on clothes, to feel cotton and wool against his skin. When it was bad he clung to the small things, to the details of life, moving cautiously from one moment to another, until it passed. It did pass – he knew that now.

The first week after he came out of hospital, he'd gone into the town centre and seen people treading on dead faces, prosperous men with moustaches and cigars, girls with parasols to protect their skin from the sun, treading on dead faces. They couldn't see the corpses that sprawled there. But Frank had walked among them, recognizing faces, naming names, remembering voices. And the voices had packed together in his throat, a hard lump pressing on his damaged vocal cords, hardly distinguishable from the pain of his wound. *Speak for us*, they said. *We cannot speak.*

He had doubted his sanity, then. Not now.

He went downstairs, rejoicing, though he didn't know it, in the emptiness of the house. It was a treat to him to have the place to himself, to have silence, and space around his limbs. Liza, though she was so thin, crowded him. He wasn't used to her yet.

Once he'd got the fire going, he put the kettle on and made tea. He liked it strong and sweet, but the moment when he clasped his hands around the mug and felt the tingle of opening pores was always a moment of danger. His memory boiled and a black bubble burst. He waited for the moment to pass and, then, squatting down with his back to the fireplace, drank his tea and was happy.

What did it matter that once he'd crouched in a shell-hole and drunk tea with men who laughed as if they hadn't a care in the world? Little Paddy Mason, crawling out, under cover of darkness, to bring back water from the flooded trench behind them. Billy Turner, crouched at the bottom of the trench, wrapped in his gas cape, coaxing the kettle to boil. The tea was lukewarm and tasted of iron, but it kept them going. When dawn came they looked down into the flooded trench and saw dead bodies floating in water streaked with blood. Nobody bothered to retch.

'Well,' Paddy said, 'it didn't kill you last night, did it, lads? How about some more?'

They drank another cup, while they waited for the whistles to blow.

Billy, one foot on the firestep, as they crowded to face the guns, said, 'Cheer up, lads. Least you know you're not anaemic.'

He'd laughed then. He could laugh now, or forget – which might be easier than laughing alone.

He went out as soon as he'd finished his tea, walking up the steep path that led to the top of the cliffs. Now the town was spread out below him, a miniature Sheffield, crammed in between moors and sea.

On the opposite cliff the steel works stood, and he remembered how many of the shells that exploded in France had been made here. By day a column of smoke rose into the air, by night a column of fire. Day and night, summer and winter, spring and neap tide meant nothing here. The movement of the tides was marked in lines of rust on the sea-wall, because the river flowed through old iron-workings and carried iron with it to the sea. Time was the clocking on and clocking off of shifts. He hated his bondage to this artificial clock that often made him sleep by day and eat his dinner in the middle of the night. Other men got used to it, as Liza never tired of pointing out. But he could not.

All the more reason, then, to enjoy today. On the top of the cliff he paused, bracing himself against the wind. This was the highest cliff in England. At its foot the sea chafed, probing the rock pools obsessively, like a tongue exploring the cavities in a tooth.

Further on was a pool, set a little way back from the edge of the cliff, and he flung himself down beside it. Newts lived here, great-crested newts, and if you kept still long enough you could see them. The pool itself was strange, isolated in its cliff-top setting, and perfectly round, so it looked man-made. A local legend said it was bottomless.

He took off his shirt and plunged his arm into the water, shivering as it reached his armpit. His groping fingers encountered nothing. One day, perhaps, mad or despairing, he might dive into this pool and swim down, deep, deep, until the light faded and underwater currents winnowed his hair. Neither fish, nor man, nor any living thing, but a plumb line sounding the depth of England.

He pulled out his arm and shook silver drops onto the grass. Then he lay back and looked up at the sky. Somewhere quite close a skylark sang.

Twice today he'd thought of dying, once back there on the edge of the cliff and again just now by the pool. He didn't often think of suicide. As a solution it seemed to be ruled out for him, not by faith, but by the fact that he'd already died. Three days he'd lain in no-man's-land. Drifting between light and darkness. Hardly aware of the pain in his throat. Rain fell. The hole filled with water and he scrabbled at the slippery sides to save himself, but his fingers loosened and he drifted down into the dark.

On the third day, in the final hour before dawn, he knew he was awake, though he had no desire to open his eyes. He was cold and numb, and the blood had stiffened on his neck. He reached up and put his fingers into the wound and they came away dry.

86

He had the strength to crawl, but he lacked the will. Who but a fool would want to come back from the dead, and to such a place as this? Across the water, sprawled on the rim of the crater, was Paddy Mason, or what was left of him. His head lay some distance from his body. At times during the night Frank had talked to him and Paddy had replied. But now it was day and he could see that Paddy was beyond speech. It was lonely lying there, now that he was no longer one of the dead.

He closed his eyes, hoping to be one of them again. But in spite of himself his feet scrabbled in the mud, searching for firmer ground.

It took him eight hours to crawl to the British lines. When he got there he heard Scottish voices and knew his regiment had been withdrawn. He never doubted he would see them again. Even going back to the dressing-station he expected to meet them, and looked eagerly into the faces of other wounded men.

He could still recite their names.

Later, in the grounds of the hospital, he endured an English spring: snowdrops, grape hyacinths, crocuses, daffodils, anemones. He was alone in a world that hadn't died. He looked at the Resurrection window in the chapel and wanted to laugh, it was so obvious this Christ had never died. He began to search for pictures of the Resurrection and found none that satisfied him, until he borrowed a book from the free library and found a painting by Piero della Francesca. Then, at last, he could rest. For there He was: white body, wafer-thin against a blood-red landscape, a flag of triumph in His hand, death in His eyes. Finding this picture was the most important event in his life, though he told nobody. Somebody else *knew*. He was not alone.

He knew he couldn't go back to ordinary life. He was set apart from other men, 'hid with Christ in God,' and his mission was to give the dead breath, to preach the word of God and to heal the sick. He knew some people thought him mad, but it didn't worry him. The same people had thought Christ mad, before it became fashionable to think otherwise.

Everything other men hoped for was barred to him: wife, family, home. He knew that, too, and accepted it. Then, shortly before the end of the war, he met Liza Jarrett, got her pregnant and married her. *For I delight in the law of God after the inward man: but I see another law in my members, warring against the law of my mind.*

'Fucking hypocrite,' said Tom Jarrett, lacking St Paul's way with words. No inner divisions *there*.

He'd lain on the edge of the pool so long the newts had grown accustomed to his presence and came out onto the grass. The nearest of them, a big male with a high, serrated crest and fire spots on his belly, clambered over the stones like a prehistoric monster. Frank waited. It came right up to his hand and then, finding this stone no more alarming than the rest, walked across it.

The sun was warm on his back. After a while he closed his eyes and slept, and this time there were no nightmares.

Frank found the presence of a small baby in the house well-nigh unbearable. He was a light sleeper at the best of times, and the slightest sound from the child woke him. Then the following day's work exhausted him. He came home bad-tempered: nothing seemed to satisfy him. The dinner was late, or there were nappies drying in front of the fire. If the baby cried, as it did every evening between seven and twelve, he could not bear it. He began by being patient, but ended by shouting and clenching his fist. More than once Liza snatched the baby up and ran out of the house with him, afraid that this time Frank's self-control would snap. Then the baby, startled by the rain or the wind on his face, would stop crying and fix his wandering eyes on the sky.

'Aye, it's all very well,' Liza said, 'but I bet you'd soon yell if I took you back in.'

Frank began staying out late at night. The spiritualists were a thriving group and there was generally an evening meeting of some kind: faith-healing, for those well enough to come to the hall, Bible study, or prayer. And if all else failed, Liza thought bitterly, he could always visit the sick.

One Saturday night he stayed out later than usual. The baby was fretful and cried whenever Liza tried to put him down. She was trying to wean him because she believed herself to be pregnant again and felt too weak to cope with the double burden of pregnancy and breast-feeding. She'd begged an old medicine bottle from the chemist and put a teat on its neck. But Tom screwed up his face at the taste of rubber. He kept letting go of the teat and screaming, and the more he screamed the more air he swallowed. Soon he was in real pain.

Liza felt close to tears. She was still weak from the birth, and the prospect of another baby, when she could hardly cope with the one she'd got, filled her with dread.

If only Frank would come. At least, then, she could go to bed and snatch a few hours' sleep before the next feed.

The baby quietened at last. She put him down in the drawer that served him as a cot and gently tucked the blanket round him.

Frank would be sitting up with the Dawson child. She knew she ought to go to bed, but she was too tired to move, and afraid that if she stirred the baby would wake.

'You're lucky to have a husband that doesn't drink,' her sister-in-law had said, only the other week. 'A lot of women'd give their eye-teeth for that.'

'I wouldn't take their eye-teeth off 'em. They can have him for nowt.'

Liza stiffened as she heard Frank's footsteps in the street outside. His boots sluthered up the passage, he was so tired. She gazed down at the sleeping child, in order to avoid looking at Frank, but she was aware of him all the same.

At last, she looked up. He was white and drained, with two red spots on his cheeks.

'Is it over?' she said.

'No.' He came across to the fire and stood warming his hands. Then his face kindled. 'I think he'll live.'

There was pure, disinterested joy in his voice. He looked to Liza for a response, but none came.

Instead she got up, and started to lay the table for a meal.

'I don't want anything,' he said, quickly.

89

'You've got to eat. You're working a double shift tomorrow. Or had you forgotten that?' She could see from his face he'd forgotten. 'I can't help it if the taties are mushy,' she said. 'They've been on hours.'

She watched bitterly as he ate a few spoonfuls of the stew, then pushed the plate aside.

'Look at you,' she said. 'What kind of state is this to come home in?'

'I had to stay with the child.'

'You've got a child of your own.'

'But he's not ill.'

'How do you know? You're never in to see whether he's ill or not.'

Frank smiled, patiently. 'Is he ill?'

'No.' She caught the flicker of amusement and her blood rose. 'No thanks to you if he's not. Look at you.' She tapped her own cheeks to indicate the flush on his face. 'You've got it on you now.'

'I can throw it off,' he said.

'Oh, well, that's you all right then, isn't it? What about us?'

'There's no danger to you, or the child.'

'And if there was? Would you stop?'

He didn't answer. Instead, he clasped his hands in front of him until the knuckles showed white, and said, 'You're being childish, Liza.'

'Childish!'

'Yes. It *is* childish to be jealous of God.'

'I don't see why. He gets most of your time, all your strength, and I get what's left.'

'I couldn't love you at all, if I didn't love God more.'

'You'd have your leg over whether you loved God or not.'

'Liza!'

'Oh, don't mind me,' she said. 'I'm coarse. I'm just the swamp you crawl out of every morning.'

'Liza, we're both very tired. I think we'd be better off in bed.'

'Oh, you're always ready enough to go there.'

He looked at her. 'Still no sign, then?'

90

He looked down at his clasped hands. 'God doesn't lay more burdens on us than we can carry.'

'Arseholes!'

'Liza. You didn't hear language like that in your own home, did you? I bet you never heard your mother say that.'

'She didn't have you to live with.'

'If you find it so unpleasant, why don't you go?'

'Because if I did I'd lose me bairn.' She waited. 'You wouldn't let me take him, would you?'

'No. He's mine.'

'You've only got my word for that. Come to think of it, that's all any man's got.'

He put his knife and fork together, neatly, in the centre of his plate. '*You* can go, Liza. Anytime you want.'

'With another bairn inside me to remember you by? Thanks. Why should me Dad keep your git? You might not have noticed this, Frank, but *men* look after their own children. Not just any kid in the town. *Their own.*'

She took the baby and went upstairs to bed. After she'd got undressed, she went and stood by the window. A full moon was spilling itself on the sea. She stood there a long time, watching the lights of the town go out, one by one.

Frank came into the room behind her. She heard the soft thud and click of his clothes going off, and then felt his hand on the nape of her neck.

'I'm sorry,' he said.

'There's no need.' She turned to face him. 'It's as much my fault as yours.'

Frank shifted his hand to her cheek and she closed her eyes. They stayed like that by the open window, and the moon threw their linked shadows across the baby's drawer. He snuffled in his sleep and Liza laughed. 'I think he's going to snore like you.'

'I don't snore.'

'Not much!'

A pulse throbbed in her neck. She raised her head and they kissed each other on the mouth. Then drew apart. Liza's skin gleamed in the moonlight.

'Come to bed,' Frank said, and Liza let him take her hand and lead her towards it.

After a long time, she felt his fingers in her hair, and looked up.

'You'd better get some sleep, Liza. He'll be awake soon.'

She looked across at the drawer. 'I know he will,' she said.

They lay together in silence. Then Liza said, 'Frank, you will go to work in the morning, won't you?'

'Yes,' he said.

When he was sure she was asleep, he got up and sat by the window. The hair in his groin was still wet. He got a towel and rubbed himself dry, and only then felt comfortable. He was a passionate man, but not sensual.

He looked at Liza. Her hair, which she wore long, was spread out over the pillow. In the moonlight it looked black, but it smelled red. When he first met her, the strong, almost foxy smell of her hair had startled him. He hadn't been sure, then, that he liked it. He wasn't sure now.

He remembered a brothel in France. A queue of young men shuffling forwards along a corridor lined with white tiles, like a lavatory. Whenever one of them came downstairs, smiling shyly or brazenly buttoning his flies, a chorus of jeers and catcalls went up from those whose turn was still to come. But they weren't as confident as they sounded. Adam's apples jerked in young throats because there wasn't enough spit to make swallowing easy. When you looked at them closely, their eyes slid away.

The woman – there was only one – lay on a mattress, legs spread apart, the tuft of dark hair wet. He'd slid into her on other men's spunk, and it sickened him, though not enough to make him stop. It had been the first time for him, and, he thought, for many of the others. He'd looked at her for a second before he was pushed out of the room. Dark eyes, ringed with shadows. An infinite weariness. He'd forgotten her now, but he remembered *them*. Eager young faces looking up at him as he came downstairs. Timid, excited, determined to have *it* once at least, before they died.

He turned and looked out across the bay. The moon rose steeply, trailing wisps of black cloud. From this window you could see the steel works, visible as a reddish glow under a bank of cloud. He ought to sleep. He had sixteen hours of that to face in the morning, and the baby would be awake before dawn.

In the room behind him, Liza stirred and stretched out her hand to the empty place where his body ought to have been. But Frank wrapped a blanket round himself for warmth and sat for a long time at the window, looking at the sea.

Liza was not pregnant. When she knew this, she went to see her mother, and cried.

'You want to be thankful,' Louise said. 'You're getting a year off.'

'Yes, but I've weaned Tom! I thought when I didn't see, it meant I was on.'

'You daft little bugger. You don't see when you're feeding.'

'Mam, why didn't you tell me?'

Liza looked at the medicine bottle with its rubber teat, and then at the baby. *I'm sorry, Tom*, she said, silently. *I liked it too.*

But Tom seemed to thrive whatever he was fed on. He grew into a strong, sturdy little boy, who sat up, crawled and walked early, but talked late.

'Stop worrying,' the neighbours said. 'He's thinking.'

But Liza did worry. As her relationship with Frank soured, she poured herself without stint into her son.

Frank had no idea how to approach the child. He had bouts when he would come home early and play with his son, but he expected too much of him. He tried to play cricket with Tom when he was only three, and then gave up in disgust when he cried. Liza was not sorry to see the distance between father and son: it made her own position more secure. Without letting herself realize what she was doing, she stood between them.

Eventually Tom started to say a few words. Liza took him with her everywhere. She would walk for miles with the child in her arms rather than leave him with one of the neighbours. Every Saturday, they went to Woolworth's. This was the climax of the week for Tom. Just above the level of his eyes were rows of soldiers with horses, flags, trumpets, drums. Row upon row of them. Scarlet, green, gold, purple, black.

'Just one, Mammy,' he said, holding up a finger.

They cost a penny and pennies didn't come easily. Frank had been out of work, on and off, for months.

'Well, just one then.'

Tom received the soldier into his hand and for a few minutes was happy, looking inside the paper bag to admire his treasure. But then he thought how much better it would be if this man, who was scarlet, had a green man to fight.

'Just one, Mammy,' he said, holding up his finger again. 'Just one.'

As often as not he would get the second, before Liza finally managed to drag him out of the shop.

Liza, like many women, put off the breeching of her first born as long as she could. At four, Tom had long hair in ringlets and still wore dresses. This was not unusual, but it worried Frank. One day Liza went out to sit with a neighbour whose labour had started early, and father and son were left alone.

'Howay, Tom,' Frank said, and led the boy by the hand into the kitchen, where he lifted him onto the draining board.

Tom stuck out his legs obligingly, assuming his knees were going to be washed, since this was what the draining board normally meant. Instead his father got out a pair of scissors. Tom looked at him, frightened, though he didn't know why.

'I want me Mam,' he said.

'Your Mam's with Mrs Walker.'

'Can I go and see her?'

'No. She's helping Mrs Walker get ready for their new baby. But *you're* a big boy now, aren't you?'

He had a comb in his hand now and was wetting it under the tap. Tom looked round the kitchen, but he was alone with his fear.

'I've got you some new clothes,' Frank said. 'We'll try them on after, shall we?'

He came towards Tom with the scissors and the wet comb. Tom shrank away from him and started to cry. 'I want me Mam,' he said again.

He couldn't've said anything worse. 'It's too much *"I want me Mam"* that's got you into this state. Look at you.'

He got hold of the boy and started to chop at his hair. Tom went still for a moment, in sheer terror, but then saw coils of hair dropping to the ground, and howled.

'Shush, now. It doesn't hurt.'

Tom was screaming too hard to know whether it hurt or not. Frank felt his brain twist inside his skull. Screams were a dreadful thing to him, he'd heard so many. He shook the child, not realizing the force in his hands. Tom went quiet and watched his father with a new depth of fear.

'I want me Mam,' he whispered.

His father's face twitched with disgust. 'A lot of lads wanted their Mams, son, and they couldn't have 'em.'

By now most of Tom's hair lay in coils and half-moons on the kitchen floor. Frank lifted him down.

'Howay, come and see your new clothes.'

Tom couldn't take it in. His father held out a jersey, a shirt, a pair of grey trousers, but they didn't seem to have anything to do with him. Frank was hurt. But he merely said, in a voice tight with anger, 'I'm afraid you've got to wear them whether you like them or not.'

Tom's ears and neck felt funny. He raised his hand and the unfamiliar bristly feel of his head made him cry again.

'Oh, for God's sake!'

Frank pulled the child to him. He stripped off the little dress and threw it to one side. The child stood between his legs, white and skinny, in his vest and pants. Frank pulled the shirt on clumsily over his head and tried to make him smile by saying '*Boo!*' loudly, when his face appeared. Tom screamed again. He was stiff with fright, and Frank had to force his arms and legs into the clothes. At last, though, he was dressed.

Frank, who all this time had kept himself apart, withdrawn, as if the sobbing child had nothing to do with him, now looked at him and was shocked by what he saw. Tom's face

95

was tear-stained, blubbery. He looked not merely frightened, but beside himself with fear. His eyes were fixed. Even when Frank picked him up and rocked him, they didn't alter, his expression didn't change.

'There, there. It wasn't so bad, was it?' Frank said, rocking all the time.

But the child went on crying. He was stiff and unresponsive against Frank's chest, and would not look at him. Frank felt his self-control begin to crack. He wanted to break the little body that rejected him. Above all, he wanted the noise to stop.

He looked round for something to pacify the child, and saw the box of soldiers by the hearth. He knelt down, still holding the child, and pulled the box towards him.

'Here, look,' he said.

Tom didn't stop crying, but he caught his breath as if, momentarily, the soldiers had attracted his attention.

'Hey, c'mon,' Frank said. 'You show me how you set them up.'

He put Tom down on the floor and started to set the soldiers out in two long lines, the red and the green. Tom sucked his thumb, and went on crying, but he looked interested. Then, deliberately, Frank put a green man in the red line.

'No!' Tom stretched his hand out to correct Frank's mistake.

'You show me then.'

Soon they had a game going. The line between fantasy and reality was as blurred for Frank as for Tom. Soon the crackling of the fire was a village burning. A timber roof collapsed sending showers of sparks into the air. Smoke, black and strong, drifted towards them, and through this smoke the sun went down. Men sat around and waited, and then, as dusk fell, you could see steam rise from the latrines as they peed. And a mile away other steam rising from the German lines.

Paddy Mason ran a lighted cigarette down the seams of his trousers. Passchendaele for lice. Billy Turner read the letter he'd read every day that week.

'By heck, she writes a good letter, your Missus,' said Paddy.

96

'She does 'n' all.'

Paddy winked. 'I can see the scorch marks from here.'

'There'll be scorch marks on your bloody balls if you don't shurrup.'

A shell burst, sending showers of earth and stones into the air. Billy was down. Frank ran to help, only to find his hand caught and held.

'You can't do that, Dad. He's *dead*.'

Frank stared. 'Oh, yes. Yes,' he said, 'I'd forgotten that.'

His fist was clenched. Slowly, he lowered it and forced the fingers to uncurl.

When Liza came back she found them playing with the soldiers.

'Has she had it yet?' Frank asked.

'Popped out like a greased piglet,' Liza said. 'Half an hour ago.' She came further into the room. 'My God, I wish I had the knack.'

Then she saw Tom sitting at his father's feet.

Frank smiled, nervously. 'I thought it was time he had his hair cut.'

'*Cut*? You've bloody shaved it, man.' She ran to Tom and picked him up in her arms.

Frank was uneasy, but determined to fight back. 'You can't keep him tied to your apron-strings forever. He's a man.'

'*A man*? Frank, he's four years old.'

'High time he stopped looking like a lass. You don't want to make a Nancy of him, do you?'

Liza knelt with Tom in her arms and cried into his shorn hair. After a few minutes he got bored with this and wriggled off her knee to go back to the game, but his father didn't seem to want to play anymore.

Later, Liza went into the kitchen and picked up the coils of hair from the floor. She got an envelope and wrote on the flap: *Thomas Edward Wright, 23rd Nov, 1921.*

Then she sat in her armchair by the fire, and laughed at herself for being so silly.

7

Stephen heard the phone ring as he walked up the steps to his flat. At first he tried to hurry, fumbling with the key and swearing because the lock was stiff, but then he made himself slow down. There'd been a number of post-mortems on the youth club fiasco, and he was in no hurry to get another load of that. If they wanted him badly enough, they'd try again.

But the phone went on ringing. It'll be nothing, he thought, and his voice as he gave the number was more crisp than encouraging.

It took him some time to recognize his mother's voice. She was still afraid of the phone, and tended to hold the receiver at a safe distance from her face. It had been no loss to her when, in the second year after his father was made redundant, they'd had to give up the phone. Stephen had tried hard to persuade them to keep it and had offered to pay the bills.

'You'll do no such thing,' his father'd said.

'I'll feel happier if I know you can contact me.'

'We'll manage on what we've got coming in.'

The offer was less than generous, and perhaps Walter had known that. Somewhere at the back of Stephen's mind was the idea that frequent phone calls might mean fewer visits. And yet he loved them.

Now he listened intently and, as he listened, his expression changed.

'All right. Look, Mam,' he said. 'You go on home now. Who's there with him?' He listened. 'Well, go on home then, I'll be over . . .'

He listened again.

'Look, if I get cracking now I can be with you in half an hour . . .'

She went on talking, yapping rather, and the fear in her normally quiet voice tore at his nerves.

'Go home now,' he said, firmly. 'Christine'll be worried.'

At last he heard the line click. He glanced at his watch and wondered whether there was time to phone Jan. No. Get there first. He could always phone in the morning.

This second return was as peaceful as the last. The streets were dark and empty, his father's garden present only as a raw, damp smell that caught at his throat as he went up the path. His mother was waiting for him this time. She started to cry as soon as she saw him. He bent down, intending to calm her with a quick kiss, but she clung onto him and wouldn't let go.

'It's bad, is it?' he said.

'Yes. It's bad.'

They moved together into the living-room.

'The doctor's been?'

'Oh, yes. Lad next door ran for him. Hospital, he says. But you know your Dad.'

'He won't go?'

She shook her head. 'Says they'll have to carry him out.'

'I'd better go up and see him.'

'No, not yet!' She said, more quietly, 'He's asleep. Sit yourself down and have a cup of tea first.'

She went into the kitchen to make it.

'Where's our Christine?'

'She had to go home to see to the bairns. Mike's on nights, otherwise he'd've seen to them for her.' She appeared at the door of the kitchen again. 'She's been here off and on all day.'

'Yes.'

He was abruptly aware of himself as a stranger again, an intruder, though until now the urgency of getting here, the drive through the rain, had stifled that feeling. Now, for a minute, sitting by the fire, he just felt awkward.

He was aware of a cup of tea being pushed into his hand. He looked down. Family china this time.

'I've made you a sandwich,' she said, 'in case you didn't have time for your tea.'

'I'm not hungry,' he said. But then he looked at her, and saw how the small jobs were holding her together. 'All right. Put it down here.'

In fact, after a few gulps of tea, he picked up the sandwich and wolfed it down, almost not noticing what he did. His mother watched him and smiled.

She sat on the arm of the sofa, glad to see him, though worried to shaking point for the man upstairs.

'What happened?' he asked.

'He was working in the garden. You know he frets himself to death if he thinks it's getting on top of him. And he'd been having pains on and off for a few days. But he wouldn't give in, he would dig. And he'd promised himself he was going to get the bottom bed dug over, no matter what. I knew he was in pain, but you can't talk to him when he's like that. You just have to let him get on with it. Then I heard this shout. I'd just that minute switched the Hoover off, so he could've been shouting before that, and I ran down the garden, and there he was. He looked awful, he was . . .' She dragged her cheeks down with the fingers of both hands. 'Anyway, Mr Thorpe put his head over the fence and I says, "Help me lift him." But he says, "No, leave him where he is. I'll send our Michael for the doctor." But, anyway, after a bit your Dad picked up. He says, "Get us inside, woman. I can't stop here." So Mr Thorpe come round and he helped us carry him in. It was a bloody good job their Michael was in, because the phones round here, it's a disgrace, there's never one that works. As it was, the doctor was here within half an hour. He was a nice young chap, very easy to talk to, but I think I'd rather've had Robinson. You know, he's got the knack of talking to your Dad. He could mebbe've put it across better. I mean, nobody likes hospitals, but you just have to put up with them sometimes.'

'I'll see if I can talk to him.'

This was so obviously improbable that he thought they were both left wondering why he'd said it.

'Well . . .' He put the cup down. 'I'll just have a look round the door. If he's asleep I won't go in.'

'He's mebbe a bit drugged. The doctor give him something for the pain.'

'I won't disturb him.'

'I'll be up in a minute. I'll just put these in the sink.'

The back bedroom was smaller and colder than the front, but Stephen's father preferred it because it overlooked the garden. The front garden he took no real interest in, beyond seeing that it looked neat and presentable. But the back garden, with the patch of common land behind it, and the stream, was a view he loved.

The room was dark, and crowded with old-fashioned furniture. Stephen had known all these objects since childhood, and yet they seemed strange, as unfamiliar as his father's Christian name. Walter. He didn't think he'd ever said it.

He pushed aside his father's gardening trousers and sat down. He couldn't tell whether his father was awake or not. His eyes were closed, but there was a drawn, intent look on his face that suggested pain rather than sleep.

The face looked older than it had looked on his last visit. The lines that grooved the thin cheeks had deepened until they looked like scars.

'Stephen?'

'Yes.'

Walter's eyes opened, but independently of each other, giving him for a moment a look of idiocy.

'It's good of you to come.'

'It's not good of me at all.'

Walter's lips were drawn back momentarily from his bottom teeth. 'You know what I mean.'

But that, thought Stephen, withdrawing mentally from the crumpled bedclothes and the smell of sick flesh, was something he'd never known.

'I can't talk much,' Walter said. 'Me mouth's that dry.'

'Can I get you a drink?'

'In a minute.' His eyes flickered. 'You'll stay with your Mam?'

'Yes.'

101

Walter's eyes closed. He slid further down the bed as if the assurance had given him some comfort.

After standing awkwardly for a minute, Stephen went back to his chair and sat down. He watched his father's face, feeling the effort of resisting pain as a tension in his own muscles. At least at the moment they *couldn't* talk, physically couldn't, so they were spared the routine embarrassment of finding nothing to say. Usually it was a few stiff sentences about the weather, then football – which Stephen knew nothing about – then silence. Yet at moments of crisis in his life, Stephen found himself carrying on long, unspoken conversations with his father, and this dialogue was passionate, bitter, unrelenting in its intensity. Then they met again, and again – silence. The only positive effect of their meetings was that the interminable, unspoken conversations stopped. For a few weeks at least. *God help me if he dies*, Stephen thought. *I'll never be able to shut him up again.*

And then he caught his breath, because for the first time he'd been brought face to face with his father's probable death.

Walter's breathing had grown a little quieter and he was a better colour, as if the latest spasm of pain had begun to pass. Then there came the sound of Margaret's footsteps on the stairs and Stephen got up to open the door for her. She was carrying a tray with the teapot, a cup, and a feeding beaker with spout and lid.

'Mrs Thorpe let us have a lend of that,' she said to Stephen. 'Wasn't it kind of her?'

He took the tray off her and put it on the dressing-table. She was just going to pour the tea out when the doorbell rang.

'Aw, no. They know when I'm up here, I'm bloody sure they do.'

'Tell them to leave us alone,' Stephen said.

'Oh, I couldn't do that.' She sounded shocked. 'They're bound to want to know.'

She ran downstairs, and Stephen heard her talking to the neighbour. Their voices were cut off, suddenly, as the passage door closed.

'Tea, is it?'

Walter opened his eyes. His pyjama jacket had come unbuttoned at the top and his ribs stuck out beneath the yellowish skin.

'Here, I'll lift you.' By forgetting it was his father he could do it easily. 'There. Now do you think you can manage the cup?'

'Cup's for you.'

Stephen poured the tea into the beaker and added two heaped-up teaspoonfuls of sugar. He raised the spout to his father's lips. 'Can you hold it?'

But it was obvious that the effort of sitting up had exhausted his strength. Stephen pushed the spout between his lips and tilted the beaker. Tea dribbled down Walter's chin and Stephen wiped it away on the back of his hand.

Walter stared resolutely out of the window, refusing altogether to look at his son. The wasted throat wobbled as he drank.

Stephen was aware of the bristles growing on his father's chin, black and grey mingled, with a particularly stubborn tuft just below the bottom lip. He could see the spines below the surface of the skin, smell the lingering smell of soil on his father's hands. When Walter raised one hand to steady the beaker, his fingernails were black.

'There. Is that better?'

Walter lay back against the pillows.

'I think I'll have a little sleep now,' he said.

Stephen took it as a dismissal, and carried the tray downstairs.

Next morning Stephen woke late and lay for a while looking at the ceiling, before he remembered where he was. The room looked strange, though for many years it had been his. His spine knew every inch of the not-very-comfortable mattress and, there, by the window, was the table where he'd done his homework. Other kids had played in the street outside. He could hear their shouts, but in this room it had always been quiet.

Now the room was denuded of personal belongings. A box full of old books stood in the far corner, waiting, he supposed, for Christine's children to be old enough. The only other thing that belonged to him was the suitcase into which he'd thrown an almost random selection of clothes, not knowing how long he'd have to stay. Between them, he thought, the box and the suitcase said everything about his present relationship to the house. In it, he was a stranger passing through, and the only other self he encountered was a pale-faced, scholarly, acne-ridden boy. He couldn't accept either role, or be accepted in it, and yet to speak honestly as himself . . . That was impossible, too.

Abruptly he remembered why he was here and jumped out of bed. He paused on the landing outside his parents' room. Knocking on the door of a sickroom seemed ridiculous, and yet he couldn't just go in. Then he heard his father cough, a dry, cautious cough. He relaxed, and only in the moment of relaxation registered how tense he'd been.

He went downstairs and found the living-room full of watery sunlight. His mother was busy in the kitchen. Stephen sat down on the sofa and picked up the local paper for a glance at the headlines. It was a fortnight out of date and this puzzled him, until he remembered that Auntie Vi saved her newspapers and brought them round for his mother to read.

It was very cold, despite the sunlight, and he rubbed his ankles together, not wanting to light the fire, since he suspected the economy was a necessary one. No sounds from the street outside, the estate seemed dead, and this gave him a Sunday-morning feeling. It was Thursday, but very few people on this estate worked. He glanced at his watch. By now the advice centre would be packed and Jan would be wondering where he was. He wasn't on duty in the mornings, but he generally looked in. He'd ring her later on and then go in for the afternoon session. After all, he was only a half-hour drive away.

His mother appeared at the kitchen door. 'Here's your breakfast. Bacon sandwiches all right?'

'Weetabix would've done, Mam.'

Margaret sat at the table with her arms folded and watched him eat.

'Aren't you having anything?' he said.

'I've had as much as I want.'

'Which was nothing.'

She didn't deny it. With the sunlight full on her face she looked desperately tired.

'What kind of night did you have?' he asked.

'He had a bad do about one o'clock. I didn't sleep much after that.'

'You should've woken me up. I could've sat with him.'

'You've been working. You need your rest.' She took the empty plate away from him. 'The doctor's coming in this morning. You'd best get dressed.'

He'd forgotten about doctors' visits, the scouring, the cleaning, the putting out of soap and towels, the tension in the house over and above the tension caused by the illness. When finally, about eleven o'clock, they heard the sound of the car, his mother stood up and said, breathlessly, 'That'll be him now.'

She went out to wait in the hall until the doorbell rang. Stephen stayed in the living-room: it was her job, not his, to take the doctor upstairs. He walked up and down, listening to his mother's voice, the doctor's voice, and then a low rumble that must be his father. Then there were footsteps coming downstairs, and a light, amused voice saying, 'He's a very stubborn man.'

Stephen went out into the hall, but too late. His mother was just closing the front door.

'What did he say?' he demanded.

'He said he should be in hospital, and your Dad said no, he'd go tomorrow, but he wasn't going today. But it'll be the same story tomorrow. He says, "He's a very stubborn man." I says, "I know he is."' She was pink and a bit breathless, but relieved to have the visit over.

'What's the matter with him?'

Margaret looked blank. 'Oh, I don't know. He never said anything about that.'

Stephen turned to look out of the window. His mother followed him, her pleasure in the success of the visit fading.

'He just said to keep him quiet. Little drinks when he wants them, but nothing to eat.'

'And how long *for?*' He walked towards the stairs.

'Now don't you go upsetting him. I've just got him settled back down . . .'

Her voice died away to an ineffectual wail as Stephen turned the corner of the stairs. But he checked himself before entering his father's room.

He found him stretched out, his hands placed on either side of his swollen stomach.

'Be born any minute now,' he said, through stretched lips.

Stephen waited in silence for the spasm to pass. His father's jacket was open, his trousers pushed down to where a line of grizzled hair showed. Stephen had never seen his father so nearly naked before, and the sight shocked him. The belly, what he half-derisively thought of as his father's 'pot', clearly didn't belong with the rest of the body. If anything, Walter was too thin. His ribcage seemed to flare out like a chicken's, bones, sinews, muscles pushing up beneath the skin.

Walter relaxed and seemed momentarily to drift off to sleep. Perhaps the doctor had given him something for the pain.

'I wish it was labour,' he said. 'At least I'd know it had an end.'

His hands twitched at the covers. Stephen started to make him more comfortable, pulling up his trousers, buttoning his jacket, straightening the sheets, arranging the pillows behind his head. He was angry with himself for being so ineffectual. As soon as he'd finished this, he'd go to see the doctor, find out what he needed to know, and stop behaving as if he were an adolescent, leaving everything to his mother.

Margaret was very quiet when he went downstairs. She hadn't forgiven him for making her feel incompetent.

'I'm going to see the doctor,' he said.

'You'll need an appointment.'

'I'll wait till the end of the surgery. They'll pop me in then.'

Outside he hesitated, wondering whether to take the car. But the day was fine and a walk would help calm him down. He still hadn't phoned Jan and he made up his mind to do that as soon as possible, but though he passed two phone boxes on his way to the surgery neither of them worked.

He waited two hours for the doctor to be free and was then told what he expected to be told.

'How long?'

The doctor spread his hands.

'Can I go back to work? I haven't been able to arrange anything.'

'Oh, yes, I should think so. Nothing's likely to happen in the next few days. And if you *can* persuade him to come into hospital . . .'

'I don't think he'll do that.'

'Then we'll have to manage the pain relief at home. I'll arrange for the district nurse to call in.'

Stephen stood on the steps outside the surgery, looking across the shopping centre. The sun shone, but it was cold enough for most of the women to wear gloves and scarves. He watched them hurrying along, heads bent into the wind, belts pulled in tightly around non-existent waists.

Two telephone boxes stood on the other side of the square. He went into the first and found that the phone had been ripped out altogether. The other looked all right. He rang the advice centre, and waited. The box stank of urine and when he looked down he saw a puddle on the floor. Jan answered and the pay tone began, but when he tried to put his money in, the coin jammed in the slot. He pushed and swore, hearing Jan's voice at the end of the line, but unable to speak. When the line clicked dead, he pounded the box with his clenched fist.

After a while he stopped and looked round, afraid somebody might have seen him, but there was nobody about. He leant against the wall of the box and put one hand to his forehead. It came away wet. He tried to laugh at himself, but not very successfully: he was too frightened to laugh. The loss of control had been total and unexpected. It was the waiting, he supposed, the waiting, the walking, the drabness of everything, and then the frustration of not being able to *get through*. He didn't attribute his sudden rage to the shock of hearing about his father, because he didn't yet know it had been a shock. He'd heard what he expected to hear.

As he walked back, he thought of his mother trying to ring him to tell him about his father. How impossibly difficult it must have been, and how little he'd understood at the time.

He arrived home to find her at the foot of the stairs with a bowl of water in her hands.

'I thought he might feel better for getting his hands and face washed, but he says he doesn't want to be chewed about.'

'I'd let him rest.'

She walked past him. He realized she wasn't going to ask what the doctor had said.

'I saw Robinson.'

'Oh, yes. He's nice isn't he?'

She looked at him almost pleadingly.

'He said it might be a long job.'

When she was sure there would be no more, she said, 'Yes, well, we know *that*. He won't be properly on his feet again . . . Oh, not for a good while.'

The danger past, she became very busy again.

'Our Christine'll be round in a minute. She was going to call in after she'd collected Ian from the playgroup.'

'I can't stop, Mam. I've just got to go in to work. I couldn't even get through to tell them I wasn't coming.'

'I know. Isn't it awful? You just think if you were trying to phone an ambulance!'

Stephen went upstairs to say goodbye to his father, but found him asleep. He stood for a few minutes by the bed, but though Walter stirred several times, he didn't wake.

Stephen thought he'd be late for the afternoon session, but in fact the queue was only just beginning to shuffle forward when he arrived. He walked straight through into the office and found Jan on the phone. She put her hand over the mouthpiece.

108

'What happened to you?' she asked.

'My father's been taken ill. I tried to phone, but I couldn't get through.'

'Is it serious?'

'Yes. I'll tell you later.'

Stephen went to his first client. In the waiting-room every chair was occupied; the queue overflowed into the corridor. Some of them would have hours to wait.

'Well,' he said, turning with a smile to the first. 'What can we do to help?'

Normally he enjoyed the advice centre sessions. He was honest enough to admit that what he enjoyed most was the sense of competence, of knowing how to cope with situations that left other people floundering. This afternoon was different. He explained benefit rules, made telephone calls, drafted letters, listened, reassured, advised, but all the time he was aware of another person in the room: the man who only that morning had hit a jammed telephone with his clenched fist. For once, he'd known what it was like to be helpless.

It made him sensitive to the signs of helplessness in others. He picked up from the diffident way a woman held a letter that she was illiterate, and read it aloud before she could feel humiliated. He didn't know, but he suspected he might have missed that on another day.

The next client was a surprise.

'Hello, Brian. What can we do for you?'

His best professional manner, friendly but reserved.

'I've been thinking about what you said. You know, about leaving home?'

'Yes.'

'Well, I was just wondering how much help I'd be entitled to. You know with the furniture and stuff.'

Stephen went to consult the files. It crossed his mind that this visit had very little to do with furniture or housing or anything like that. He was flattered, but not tempted.

'In order to qualify for any kind of help with furniture, you'd have to prove there was no suitable furnished accommodation

109

available, and the onus of proof would be on you. I don't personally think you'd get very far with that. So that brings us to housing benefit. Now if you can tell me a bit more about your circumstances I can give you a *rough* idea of what you'd be likely to get.'

Nothing like a pocket calculator for dampening the ardour. By the time Stephen had finished working it out, Brian was looking dismayed.

'Is that *all*?'

'Well, yes. It is *cheaper* to live at home.'

'I'll say.'

Stephen pushed his notebook away. 'Are things bad at home?'

'She goes on at me a bit.'

He did look tired.

'Actually, if anything, things have looked up a bit. We're not on top of each other so much now I've got the job.'

'You're still working at the fairground?'

'Yes.'

'And still claiming?'

'Yes.'

Stephen smiled. 'Mightn't be the best time to attract their attention.'

'Well, no. I had thought of that. They come round snooping anyway.' He looked up. 'I thought you might've been round.'

'What, snooping? Not my job.'

'No,' Brian said, steadily. 'Not snooping.'

An awkward pause.

'I've been busy.' Stephen gathered up his notes to indicate the interview was over. Then surprised himself by saying, 'My father's ill. I'm living at home at the moment.'

'What's the matter with him?'

'Cancer.' It was the first time he'd spoken the word aloud, and it shocked him. 'Well, everything's wrong. You know, his chest's bad, his heart's bad . . . But I went to the doctor this morning and he said: cancer.' Stephen stopped, abruptly. 'We've never been particularly close.'

'I don't suppose that makes it easier.'

'No,' Stephen said, 'it doesn't seem to.'

They walked to the door together.

As Brian was leaving, he said, 'Well, I'll see you, then.'

It was almost a question.

Stephen hesitated, then nodded. 'Yes.'

When Stephen got back home, Christine and her three children were there. He picked Ian up and swung him round, patted Sharon on the head, and pretended an interest in the new baby. He tried to put Ian down, but the child's arms and legs wrapped tightly round him.

'Let your Uncle Stephen be,' Christine said. 'Come on, now.'

'Oh, he's all right.'

'He wants to go and see his Grandad, but I don't think so, do you?'

'No. Best left.'

Margaret said, 'Well, how was it?'

'Packed. Just as well I went in. But Jan says she can fix something up for tomorrow.'

'She sounds nice, Jan.'

'Oh, she is. Pity she has to be separated from her boyfriend, but he's doing a course in Leeds.'

Christine smiled at him behind their mother's back. '*Oh, well played!*'

'How is he, Mam?'

'Well, he seems a bit better. He had a little sleep and then when he woke up I poached him an egg. But he still gets tired pretty quick.'

'Well, I'll be off,' Christine said. 'Howay, Ian, you'll see him again tomorrow.'

'Do you have to go?' Stephen asked.

'Oh, I think so. His lordship wants his feed. They've been ever so good.'

'They've been little smashers,' Margaret said. She bent down to speak to Sharon. 'You gunna come and help your Gran again tomorrow?'

Sharon nodded. As Christine was leaving, she said, 'You'll send round, won't you, Mam, if you need me? I can always ask one of the neighbours to pop in for an hour.'

'Oh, don't worry, I'll let you know if anything happens. But I don't think it will. I think we might have a better night.'

'I hope so.' She kissed her mother and then hugged Stephen. 'I aren't half glad you're here.'

They stood on the doorstep to wave goodbye. As Christine and her children turned the corner into the next street, Margaret said, 'You know it's lovely having them, but it's a relief when they go.'

'Did she get up to see Dad?'

'Oh, yes. I think she was a bit offended I wouldn't let Ian go up, but you know your Dad can't stand the chewing.'

'Oh, I think she knows that.'

They went back into the living-room.

'You sit down,' Stephen said. 'I'll get the tea.'

She looked as if she was going to argue, but he pushed her gently into a chair. As he switched the kettle on, she called through to the kitchen, 'You've never mentioned Jan's boy-friend before.'

The evening passed quietly. When Stephen went in to say goodnight to his father, he found him sitting up, looking livelier than he'd looked all day.

'You don't look as if you're going to settle down.'

Walter pulled a face. 'I feel sticky.'

'I'll get you a wet flannel.'

'Aye, go on.'

Stephen took the flannel and wiped his father's face, concentrating on the nose and mouth. What he had thought were shadows in the creases of the nostrils turned out to be tiny, rusted scales of blood, left over from the haemorrhage of the previous day.

Walter beckoned Stephen to bend down. His breath was strong and sour.

'Look, I don't want your Mam sitting up tonight. She needs her rest. Will you stop in here?'

Stephen straightened up. 'I'll try. But you know what she is.'

'You'll do more than bloody try! I don't want her to see, you know . . .' He made a vague gesture towards his mouth. 'If it happens again. She's had enough.'

'I'll sit up with him tonight, Mam,' Stephen said when he went back downstairs.

'You will not.'

'Yes, Mam. Just this once. For one thing, it's easier for me to lift him on the bedpan than it is for you. I don't know how you've managed.'

'No,' she said, 'neither do I.' She seemed to be considering. 'All right,' she said at last. 'But the slightest change and you call me, mind.'

'I'm not having you sat in yon chair,' Walter said.

And so Stephen undressed and got into bed beside his father, who tried to turn away, but the effort of rolling over onto his side was too much. Stephen lay on the edge of the bed and stared into the darkness. He turned to look at the window and thought that in these circumstances he would never be able to sleep, though on a chair, with a blanket over him, he might have managed to nod off.

'Wake me if you want anything,' he said.

Walter grunted in reply.

In fact Stephen did sleep, though his father's breathing echoed through his dreams, being at one moment a car that refused to start, at another something nameless that pursued him down a dark corridor, at another the sound of the sea rasping on a beach. When finally he woke he had no clear recollection of the dream, only the remembered presence of water, endlessly shifting, cold, dark, deep, and the soughing and rasping of the waves which, as he rose towards consciousness, resolved itself into his father's harshly-drawn breath.

He was wide awake.

After a while Walter said, 'Could I have a drink, son?'

'Yes.'

It was a relief to move.

'No, don't put the light on. You'll have your Mam up. Just pull the curtains back.'

A full moon, strong enough to see by. He held the beaker to his father's lips and waited while he drank.

'I hate this thing,' Walter said, between gulps. 'Back to the bloody nipple.' Some of the water dribbled down his chin, but he dabbed it away himself.

When he'd finished, Stephen said, 'Is there anything else you want? The – um.'

'No, I don't want the – *um*. Thank God. I'll tell you what I do want.' He leaned forward and whispered, 'A cigarette.'

'You know you shouldn't.'

'I don't think it's gunna make a lot of difference now, son.'

So he knew. Stephen got up and opened the top drawer of the dressing-table where he knew his father's cigarettes were kept and took the packet out. Not only did Walter know he was going to die, he had dared Stephen to acknowledge it too. But to do that was to step onto untried ground, or worse, the marshy, shifting, unstable waters of his nightmare.

Walter made his own cigarettes, a concession to the dole, and the little stick of paper was so fragile Stephen was afraid of breaking it as he put it between Walter's lips. His hand and his father's face leapt up through the darkness. Walter's hand came up to steady his, and the flare died down. Their linked flesh shrivelled into darkness.

'Do you know, I've tried everything to give these buggers up. I even went and got stuff off the doctor. It was supposed to make you feel sick whenever you smoked, but I only felt sick when I didn't. That's one thing I was glad of. You never started.'

'Oh, I did. We used to make a den under the bushes down there and smoke.' Stephen waved towards the window. 'But I only pretended to like it. I was as sick as a dog really.'

'After I knew I couldn't give up, I used to smoke with a pin stuck through the end, so you could get right down. Bloody near fell apart in your hand.'

He laughed, and the laugh turned to a fit of coughing. After it was over he said, 'Well, anyway, I shan't have to worry about making this lot last.'

114

He lay for a while in silence.

'Your Mam'll feel it. But I know I don't have to tell you to look after her. You've been a good son.'

This was so far from Stephen's idea of himself that he suspected sarcasm, but there was no trace of it in his father's voice.

'You must be tired,' Walter said. 'We'd better get back to sleep.'

There was no more than a hint of regret in his voice, but Stephen caught it.

'I'm not tired,' he said.

They sat in silence for a while. Walter's eyes were closed and his breathing was so quiet that Stephen began to think that he had, after all, gone to sleep.

'They never give us any warning, you know, and they must've known, mustn't they? It stands to reason they knew. You don't close a place that size down and not know. Twelve hundred pounds in one pay packet, I'd never seen so much money in me life. There was blokes running round, you'd've thought they'd won the pools. But by heck you bump into them a year later and it's a different story. But you do, you know, you think you're rich.' He held out his hands as if they were full of money, then slowly clenched them. 'And it's all . . . *Shit!*'

A long silence.

'Oh, for a long time after I was finished, I used to jump out of bed. Grab me trousers. Be halfway downstairs sometimes before I remembered there was nowhere to go. Your Mam'd be yelling down the stairs after me, 'Walter, where are you going?' Then I used to crawl back into bed and pretend to doze off again, but I never did. I just used to lie there with me eyes shut, I was that frightened. Frightened?' He laughed. 'I was scared shitless, because I knew I'd never work again. And I didn't know what to do.

'I couldn't talk to your Mam. She doesn't know it's not funny looking for a job when you're past fifty, and I haven't the heart to tell her. I used to get the paper every morning and write off for jobs, and I used to go out and tell her I was

115

looking for work, whereas half the time I was just wandering round. You get you can see the look in people's eyes. You know, you get the card out off the board at the job centre and you take it to the girl and . . .' He laughed. 'You tell her how old you are.'

'Don't wear yourself out talking, Dad.'

Walter smiled. 'I'll have time enough to be quiet.'

A long silence. Stephen felt his father's tension, and understood, for the first time, that he was working up to something quite specific, something he found difficult to say.

'I got very restless. I got I couldn't stop in the house. I was under your Mam's feet all the time. You know, she's got her own way of doing things, she doesn't want me sat there . . . Half the time I was in her way. So I just used to get out and wander. And then . . .' He swallowed. 'And then I found I was starting to look at girls a lot. You know, young girls, bits of lasses.' He glanced quickly at Stephen, and away. 'I used to go and get a loaf of bread for your Mam, and I realized I was timing meself so I'd be outside the comp round about four, when they were all coming out. I used to go and sit on the bench behind the bus shelter, so if anybody saw me they'd think I was waiting for the bus. I never said nowt, but I think some of them knew. I think one or two of them must've twigged it, because they used to giggle and go on as they went past.'

Stephen had begun to sweat. He didn't want to hear this and yet he couldn't bring himself to say, 'Stop'.

'I couldn't live with it. I used to do all kinds of things to try and stop meself, I'd go for a long walk in the other direction, I tried everything, but somehow or other when four o'clock came, there I was. I thought the old people in the flats behind'd notice me hanging about and phone the police. There was one old biddy kept looking out and I thought, *She knows. She must know.* I really did, I thought I was gunna be picked up.

'I couldn't even work out what it was I wanted. I kept thinking all the time: *Only one woman.* Because, you know . . . When I started going with your Mam I'd never been

116

with anybody else. And after we were married . . . Well, mebbe I'm old-fashioned, but I don't believe in promising one thing and doing another. But it got it was like a fever. *Only one woman*. On and on. And I honestly don't think it was sex I wanted. I didn't want to be a mucky old man hiding in a bus shelter. *I wanted to be their age*. To start over. I wanted to be a lad with them.

'I went from one extreme to the other. I got I stopped in all the time, I told your Mam I was bad. I remember there was this film on the telly about a werewolf. You know, he was a normal man most of the time, but every full moon he used to change and kill people. Real kids' stuff, and I was that bloody frightened I couldn't go to bed. Because, you know, I was thinking, my God, that's me. Not wanting to kill people, but the *change*. Like there was another man inside me and he was trying to get out. I started going to church, oh, not to services, but I used to go and sit. You know St Columba's? That's a lovely church, and it used to help me a bit. And then I thought, I'll go to the doctor. There's bound to be summat he can give me. When I was in the RAF they were always on about the stuff they put in your tea. Bromide. That was it. It was supposed to damp down your urges. But anyway when I got there I just couldn't bring meself to tell him. *No way*.' He laughed. 'I come out with a jar of cream to rub on me back.

'I never did nowt. I don't want you thinking that. I never said a word out of place to one of them. It was all here.' He tapped his forehead. 'You get to thinking. You've got too much time to think. People don't know about time, when they're working, it's all neat and tidy for them. You talk about *passing* time, *killing* time, and you don't know what you're on about. You don't kill time, time kills you. It gets your head like in a pair of nut crackers and it *squeezes*. Some afternoons I used to look at the clock, and I swear it didn't move. Afternoons is the worst time. I used to walk miles. At the finish your Mam says, "I wish you'd stop looking for work, it's costing me a fortune in shoe-leather."' He laughed. 'The best thing was walking along the beach, on a nice windy day. Windier the better. You walk ten or fifteen miles and you

117

can't think, all you can think about is taking the next step, and you're leaning into the wind. And when you come back home you can sleep.' He lay back against the pillows. 'I haven't had a walk like that . . . Oh, not for a long time.'

Stephen waited to see if there was more, but Walter lay with his eyes closed.

'I think we'd better get to sleep now, Dad.'

One leg had gone numb where he'd been sitting on it. He felt it tingle as he stood up and straightened the counterpane.

'You don't mind me talking to you like that, do you, son?'

'Of course not, Dad.'

They lay in the darkness together, but it was a long time before either of them went to sleep.

Stephen woke to the sound of his mother's voice, and the sight of a cup of tea being put on the table beside him.

'You've slept in,' she said, and sounded pleased.

Stephen struggled to sit up. 'What about you? Did you have a good night?'

'Yes. I didn't think I'd be able to sleep, but I did. And your Dad says he slept well.'

Stephen turned to face his father. 'How do you feel?' he asked.

'Fine.'

Stephen was still half asleep, and only the embarrassment in his father's voice made him remember.

'I'll have this while I shave,' he said.

He got out of bed and reached for his dressing-gown.

'I don't suppose you fancy anything to eat, do you, Walter?'

'Oh, I don't know.' His voice sounded stronger and there was a little colour in his cheeks. 'Bit of bacon and egg mebbe.' He rubbed his hand down the side of his face. 'Will you help us get shaved after, Steve? I feel like a tramp with this.'

'Yes, of course.'

'I wish you would,' Margaret said. 'I dread doing it.'

'*She* dreads it. What about me?' Walter cowered in mock terror.

Stephen went into the bathroom and got on with his own shaving, which he did angrily and as quickly as he dared.

The more he thought about last night's conversation the more he resented it. Perhaps he should have been flattered, or at least pleased, that his father had chosen to confide in him before he died. Well, he wasn't. He knew what had been at the back of his father's mind.

Not once had his father referred to what he must know to be the truth of Stephen's life. The evasion had started when Stephen was in his teens. When visiting relatives, bored or bewildered by academic success, had asked about girlfriends, Stephen had never had to answer them, because his father had rushed in so quickly with some little joke about 'playing the field', 'too much sense', 'time for all that later'. At the time he'd been grateful. Later, when he'd've been quite prepared to answer the questions, they stopped coming, as people presumably drew their own conclusions. Only his father's determination to ignore the truth did not change.

It came to a head, predictably, with Gordon. He and Walter had only met once, and that was by accident in the street. A few days later Gordon had suggested that the three of them go for a drink together.

'No,' said Stephen.

'Why not?'

'I don't think it's a good idea. He's always made it perfectly plain he doesn't want to know. I think I'd rather keep it that way.'

'I wasn't suggesting a floor show.'

'I just don't think you've got the right to force awareness on people when they've made it perfectly clear they can't cope and don't want to cope.'

They hadn't gone out together, and Gordon never suggested it again. Walter referred once to 'That bloke . . . What's his name? Bloke we met in . . .' And that was all.

Until last night. And last night, running through the entire conversation, had been one unspoken sentence: *You can't afford to judge me.*

Stephen was ashamed of himself for thinking this way. Even to himself it sounded paranoid, and yet he couldn't shake it off, the impression that his sexuality had been used, without being acknowledged. It left a sour taste in his mouth. Something he couldn't describe or define.

You don't mind me talking to you like that, do you, son?

'You bet I bloody do.'

He went back to the bedroom and found his father sitting up, cradling a cup of tea in his hands. The rather bulbous, orange-peel-textured tip of his nose looked coarser than ever in the rising steam.

'Are you really going to have bacon?' Stephen asked.

'Yes.' He leaned back and patted his stomach almost boastfully. 'It feels a good bit easier today.'

His mood seemed to have lightened. He looked happy, though he avoided Stephen's eyes.

'I'll see if it's ready.'

As Stephen went downstairs he could smell bacon frying in the pan. Perhaps he needn't sleep here tonight. Perhaps alternate nights would be enough. He'd reached the bottom step when he heard a glugging sound and stopped. His first thought was he must have left the tap running, because it sounded like water gurgling down the overflow pipe. But then he realized it was coming from his father's bedroom, and ran.

He burst into the room and there was Walter, his eyes frenzied and rolling above a black hole, blood spreading down over his neck and chest. He stretched out his hand to Stephen. The glugging had stopped, but only because a clot of blood, like a lump of black liver, was stuck in his mouth. Stephen got his finger behind it and hoicked it out. It came away with a dreadful sound, like the plop of an unblocked sink, and red blood gushed out after it. Stephen put his fingers to his father's lips and pressed, as if he could keep the blood in.

He hauled him into an upright position and he crouched there, gasping for breath.

'Mam!'

She came running. She didn't cry out or anything like that, but he saw how extreme fear smoothes out the face.

'Who's got a phone?' he asked.

120

'The Wilkinsons.'

'Get them to ring for an ambulance. Not the doctor. *The ambulance*. Dial 999.' When she still stood there he reached out and grasped her arm. 'Come on, Mam, there isn't much time.'

She turned and ran.

No time at all, he thought, turning back to the bed. His father's fear was terrible. He was choking on his own blood. 'Steady now,' he said. Walter slumped forward over his arm, as floppy as a new-born child. A second eruption began. Stephen cleared the clots of blood from his throat, found one stringy enough to twine his fingers round, and pulled. The gush of frothy, red blood that followed looked almost festive against the whiteness of pillow case and sheets.

He could feel his father's life slipping away. He lowered him onto the pillows and his face looked greyish-black. The darkness, tightness, hardness of the face was so extreme that at first Stephen thought, *He's dead*. But then a slight moan came from the stretched lips.

Shock, Stephen thought, and went to get blankets off the bed in the other room and piled them on top of his father, thinking as he did so that he could smother him now and nobody would know. Even as the thought formed, he took his father's teeth out and turned his head to one side so his mouth and nostrils were clear.

His mother came into the room closely followed by Mrs Thorpe. Margaret knelt by the bed, put her hand, almost timidly, on Walter's arm, and said, 'Don't leave me. I couldn't live without you.'

A sound came from the open, blood-smeared mouth. No words.

Walter died in hospital, three hours later, without recovering consciousness.

When they got back to the house, Mrs Thorpe was at the gate and seemed to know already that Walter was dead. Christine wrapped a coat round her mother's shoulders and sat her down in the armchair. Margaret was shivering and rocking herself backwards and forwards, greyish with cold and shock.

'Do you know what we've gone and done?' she said. 'We've gone and left his things at the hospital. You'll have to go back and get them, Steve.'

'Later.'

'No, you go, son,' Mrs Thorpe said. 'I'll stop with them.'

It was obviously important to his mother to have his father's pyjamas back home. 'All right,' he said. 'I'll be as quick as I can.'

The sister, a plump, dark woman with a line of moustache hairs on her lip, handed over the parcel and he signed for it.

'Can I see him?' he said.

He expected the request to be refused, thinking they wouldn't've had time to do whatever it was they did, but she immediately said, 'Yes,' and summoned a young nurse to show him the way to the mortuary.

Stephen expected something very modern, clinical, the kind of thing you see in American thrillers, but this looked like an old-fashioned dormitory. The nurse walked across to a cubicle on the far side of the room and pulled the curtain back. She lifted a white cloth and immediately, without any warning it seemed, he was looking down into his father's face.

He stood beside the slab and touched the cold skin. This was nothing like sleep. The mouth was tight, blackish-looking, as if even in life it had never spoken. There were two lines of force scored into the skin between pinched nose and clenched mouth and they had never looked deeper. But the strongest impression was of silence, as if he were bonded into silence, welded to it, and this final speechlessness revealed a truth about his life that Stephen had never recognized till now.

He stood for a long time by the slab, and then touched his father gently on the hand, and left.

It was very strange. He had no desire to cry and yet there was a pain in his throat that became more severe as they retraced their steps. As he followed the nurse along the corridor the strip light unwound before him, like thread from a bobbin. He said goodbye at the entrance to the ward where his father died, and his voice sounded faint.

122

More than once as he walked across the car park he had to stop and swallow, as if something was stuck in his throat.

To calm himself, he opened the parcel containing his father's things and checked through them. Pyjamas, soap, comb, slippers – all packed hopefully by his mother in the last frantic minutes before the arrival of the ambulance. He dreaded giving them back to her.

He reached the car and put the parcel on the roof while he dug in his pocket for the key. It slid towards him down the slope, and he put up a hand to stop it from falling. As he did so, one of his father's slippers fell out. The sole had come loose, and as he bent to pick it up, it flapped like a tongue.

He remembered the clenched mouth, the pact with silence, and found himself gripping the edge of the roof. He let his head hang down between his outstretched arms. The pain in his throat had become unbearable. There was a sense of enormous pressure, as if his father's silence had somehow got in and impacted there, a lump he could neither cough up nor swallow. He thought of Liza's husband, of the bullet in his throat, the dead voices packed inside, and he thought that after all Frank Wright had been sane, or if not sane, that it was a madness he might come to share.

He put both hands to his throat like a surgical collar, and coughed.

In the days before the funeral, relatives and friends came to pay their last respects. Stephen went to collect his Great-aunt Clem, and found her in bed with her fancy man.

'Eeh,' she said. 'Is that the time?'

He waited in the living-room while she got dressed. It didn't take long; she wore her wig and make-up to bed. Joe appeared at the door of the bedroom, grinning nervously.

'How's your Mam bearing up then?' he said.

'I don't think she's taken it in.'

'No, well, you don't,' said Clem.

Joe went back into the bedroom to get dressed.

'He's upset because I won't let him come to the funeral.'

'He'd be welcome. You know that.'

123

'Aye, but if I let him start coming to funerals, he'll think he's got his feet under the table. He's bad enough as it is.'

'He just wants to make an honest woman of you.'

'That's how it starts.' She looked round from the mirror, waving her lipstick. 'I've got nowt against him. There's not a better man breathing, as men go. It's marriage.'

'I'd marry you tomorrow,' said Joe.

'Yes, love, I know you would. And how long would we be happy?' She lowered her voice. 'A man gets his feet under the table, he *changes*. You mark my words.'

Stephen held her coat while she put it on.

'You see, love, I didn't start living till I buried your uncle,' Auntie Clem said, as they walked towards the car. 'Before that I had no life at all. I didn't know what it was to put me foot over the threshold. Now I get out. I go every Friday and I sing at the Rose and Crown. I'm not going to let a man take that away from me. I remember when we buried your uncle, the vicar got hold of my hand and he says, "Don't cry, my dear. You'll meet in heaven." I thought, *My God, I hope not*. I was crying with relief.'

She bent down to get into the car, and her red wig slipped sideways. Stephen righted it for her.

'Thanks, flower. I enjoy my life. I enjoy sex. Never liked it while I was married to your uncle. Until I was sixty all that side of life was a closed book to me. But I'm making up for it now. There's nowt nicer on a Sunday morning after the pub. You come in, you smell the gravy . . . And up he goes.'

They turned out of Auntie Clem's road.

'Has she had your Dad brought back?'

'Yes.'

'That's nice.' She looked at the passing streets with interest. 'You can't always do that now. What with the central heating, and all that. But I always think there's nothing looks worse than a corpse being turned away from its own front door. There's a bloody awful going-on over in them flats. The door at the back of the lift's jammed. Friend of mine passed over the other week and believe me or believe me not she set off to her funeral *standing up*. And I wouldn't care, but she was a martyr to her feet.'

She was silent for a mile or two.

'Dignity,' she said. 'That's what's lacking. Dignity and respect. People used to know how to deal with death. They don't now. Too busy running round the park munching rabbit food. They say they do it for their health, but they don't, you know. They do it to be immortal. And what a hell of a shock they've got coming.'

Stephen drew up outside the front door.

'Well,' said Auntie Clem, looking doubtfully at the house. 'Wonder what sort of reception I'll get. The black sheep returns.'

Stephen steadied her wig as she got out of the car. 'Not black. Titian.'

'Burnished mahogany, you cheeky sod.'

Stephen settled Auntie Clem among the small group of relatives in the living-room, and took refuge with Christine in the kitchen.

'Who are they all?' he said.

'God knows.'

She stopped buttering bread and giggled with nervousness and grief.

'Auntie Clem's on form.'

'Why on earth didn't she bring Joe?'

'Thinks it'll give him ideas. About being family and all that.'

'Well, I hope she doesn't go on too much about the joys of widowhood, because I don't think me Mam's quite ready for it.'

'I don't think she will. She was fond of Dad.'

'It'd mean a lot to me Mam if you went up and saw him, you know.'

'I've seen him, Chris.'

'Wouldn't hurt you to see him again.'

'I can't go on like this,' he said. 'She wants me to have his best suit. She wants me to have his ring.'

'Well of course she bloody does. Don't be such a wilting lily, man. Get yourself up there.'

Margaret sat in her chair by the fire, looking lost, Stephen

125

thought, as if nobody owned her. All around her, relatives grimaced and talked and the noise lapped round the edges of her silence. When she sensed him in the doorway, she looked up and smiled.

He nodded his head in the direction of the stairs.

'I'm glad you changed your mind, Stephen. He looks lovely. I wanted you to see how nice he looks.'

They went into the small back bedroom together. The bed had been pushed back against the wall and the window was open. The coffin stood just inside the door.

'It's better in the old-fashioned houses,' she said. 'Where you've got the frontroom. These houses aren't meant for it. But I couldn't just have him brought to the door.'

'No.'

She went to the head of the coffin and pulled back the cloth.

Stephen looked down at the shrunken face and felt nothing but relief. This yellow doll in its white satin cot was nothing to do with him. He put his arm round his mother and held her while she cried.

'They've done a good job, haven't they?' she said, sniffing and wiping her nose on the back of her hand.

'Yes.' His tongue weighed like lead. 'Yes, yes, he looks . . . nice.'

'I wanted his ring left on, but they say they can't do that. You might as well have it, Steve. It's a good ring.'

'Yes.'

She bent down and kissed the cold face, running her fingers down his cheek. 'Goodnight, love,' she said.

When she turned to Stephen her eyes were bright, but she didn't cry again.

'I'll leave you with him for a bit,' she said.

Stephen stood by the coffin and looked down. He ought to be moved by this final parting, but he wasn't. He waited in the room long enough to satisfy his mother and then joined her on the stairs.

'It does look like him, doesn't it?' she asked.

'Yes.'

126

'It's just . . . Last night I thought it didn't look like him. I had to keep getting up to see.' She turned to him. 'I keep thinking they've sent the wrong body.'

'It's him, Mam,' Stephen said, gently. 'He's dead.'

She nodded, and walked downstairs.

'I wish they'd all piss off!' he said to Christine. 'She's in no state for this.'

'No. Did she tell you she thinks he isn't dead?'

'Not in so many words.'

'Last night she was trying to get him out of the coffin. I just got there in time.'

'Well, she'll sleep tonight. That stuff the doctor's given her'd lay anybody out.'

'You don't think I should stay?'

'No. My turn. You've done enough.'

That evening, after the relatives had gone, they watched television. Stephen glanced at his mother from time to time and saw her eyes were focused on a point two or three feet in front of the screen. The singing and dancing figures must be a blur.

When it was switched off, they sat in silence for a while.

'It was through your Auntie Mavis I got to know your Dad,' Margaret said, suddenly. 'His Dad had just died and his Mam had bought him a new suit out of the insurance, and I says to your Auntie Mavis, "Eeh, look, there's Walter in his new suit. Doesn't he look smashing?" And she says, "I'll tell him you said that." I says, "Eeh, no, don't." But she did, she went right up to him and told him, and I could see his mates laughing and I thought, *By heck, he won't thank me for that.* But then as we were going home he comes up and says, "Do you fancy going to the pictures next Saturday?" I was that embarrassed I didn't know what to say. But, anyway, off we went to the pictures, and that was how I got on with your Dad.' She looked up at him and laughed. 'He was a smashing-looking lad. You won't remember him like it, but he was tall. He was straight.' She stretched up and straightened her own shoulders to show him. 'He was a grand man.'

127

But she was too tired to talk for long. She pushed her cup of tea aside while it was still half-full and said, 'I'll be up and down all night if I have that.'

At the foot of the stairs she hesitated and said, 'I hope you don't mind, Stephen, I've put you in our room. I don't think I could face sleeping in there just yet.'

'I don't mind,' Stephen said.

'I'll just pop in and say goodnight to your Dad.'

He was afraid she might press him to come with her, but she didn't. He went into his parents' bedroom and closed the door. After a few minutes he heard her cross the landing and go into her own room.

It was strange, he thought, the three of them under one roof. Each in a separate room. He sat on the edge of the bed and started to unfasten his shoes, looking round him as if he'd never seen the room before. In fact, he'd slept in it with his father only two nights ago. But now his father's death seemed to leave it open and vulnerable to his gaze.

The overhead light was weak: his parents couldn't afford to burn a powerful bulb in a room where no close work was done. The light had the impersonal, alienating quality of the light in station waiting-rooms. His father's personality had gone, leaving only odds and ends behind: his false teeth in a glass, a paperclip, a postage stamp, a brush.

Stephen picked up the brush and saw a wisp of white hair trapped in the bristles. He pulled it out, held it lightly for a moment between thumb and forefinger, then let it drift down slowly into the bin.

He switched the light off and lay in the darkness, knowing he wouldn't be able to sleep. His father's death pressed in on him, a physical force, boring through the jelly-filled sockets of his eyes and into his skull. He fought it, mind and body together, denying the right it seemed to be asserting over him. His hand crept down to his cock, which was small and moist. He forced it to respond, calling up images, switching from one to another as time and again they failed, forcing life into the limp flesh until at last it started to swell, throbbed, swelled again, stood up proud and curved and hard in his hand. Then

128

with grinning teeth and labouring breath he set to work to expel the death from his body, jerking it out of himself in spasm after shuddering spasm, until at last it fell, hot and thick and creamy, on his arched belly and slackening hand.

When it was over he lay back and thought, *Christ!* He was surprised by what he'd done, but not disgusted or ashamed. Now when he closed his eyes he saw a swirl of warmth and colour, not the endless corridor leading from darkness into deeper night.

When he woke up he could hear voices in the living-room. He got dressed quickly and went downstairs.

Christine was having breakfast, but she got up as soon as she saw him.

'I'll get your breakfast,' she said.

'Sit down, woman. I can get me own.'

'It's already cooked,' she called into the kitchen after him. 'I've put it to keep warm on the grill.'

'Have you had anything, Mam?'

'Not yet. I'll have something later.'

She sat at the table while Stephen and Christine ate. It was curiously unreal, like a film with a bad sound track. Jaws chomped, cutlery clattered, but their voices were muffled. More than once he had to ask Christine to repeat what she'd said.

It was a relief to everybody when she stood up and declared the meal over. 'They'll be here at ten,' she said. 'We ought to start getting things put straight.'

After that everything seemed to happen very quickly. The house was full of relatives, all talking and exchanging news at once.

'It's like a wedding in there,' Stephen said.

'No, it isn't,' said Christine. 'Weddings aren't that cheerful.'

The party was going with such a swing that nobody noticed the arrival of the hearse. Eventually they were persuaded to go into the kitchen until the coffin had been removed. Among the ham sandwiches and buttered scones, an uneasy silence fell. Then the undertaker appeared in the doorway and nodded to Stephen who put his arm round Margaret's shoulder and led her out to the car.

As they drove away he looked back at the house, and felt a wrench so sharp it seemed to come from outside himself. Christine got hold of his hand. Margaret looked straight ahead.

The service was simple. A priest met them at the door, and walked before them into the chapel:

I am the resurrection and the life, saith the Lord: he that believeth in me, though he were dead, yet shall he live: and whomsoever liveth and believeth in me shall never die.

A rolling sound as the coffin disappeared. The curtains closed behind it and the service went on.

Afterwards, the mourners walked out onto the lawn.

'Thank God that's over,' Stephen said.

'There's still the tea.'

Stephen turned. From the chimney above the crematorium a column of smoke rose into the sky and gently dispersed, drifting down across lawns and rose beds like a wisp of white hair.

8

Liza arrived in Walker Street on a blustery day, with big splashes of rain falling on her face and bare arms. She held onto her son with one hand and with the other pushed a pram so heavily laden with carrier bags and parcels of various kinds that you couldn't see underneath the hood. She had become a thin, freckled, sharp-looking woman with a smile that promised anything you liked, friendship or a fight, whichever suited you. She wore a brown jacket that had been made for a bigger woman and a skimpy dark-blue skirt. Her legs were bare and, unlike her face and arms, a blue-veined, sunless white.

Beside her walked her husband, pushing a handcart. There was a general air of refinement about him, in spite of his frayed cuffs and the patch in one knee of his trousers. The handcart was laden with odds and ends of furniture, and several times, in pushing it up the steep cobbled street to number twenty-nine, he had to pause for breath, turning his head a little to one side to shield his mouth from the wind.

The boy walking by Liza's side was about four years old, perhaps a little more. His hair was close-cropped in a pudding-basin style and his little grey trousers drooped down past his knees. He was whining and rubbing his face with his free hand, partly from tiredness, but partly because in the excitement of the move Liza had taken her attention away from him for once.

When Liza turned to hush the boy her jacket fell open and it was possible to see she was four or five months pregnant.

A man walking past on his way to work took in the

131

combination of small boy, pram and pregnancy and said to his companion, 'By heck, she's getting good yeast!'

Liza spun round. 'You cheeky bloody sods,' she yelled. 'I'll have you know it's saucepans in here.' And she rattled the pram to prove it.

They burst out laughing.

'That'll do, Liza,' Frank said. 'You're showing yourself up.'

She flushed and for a moment looked like a young girl again. But then her face kindled. She turned round again, and yelled, 'But you're right. It is 'n' all!'

The men laughed again, but with her this time.

'There you are,' she said. 'Nice lads.'

Liza and Frank walked on in silence.

When she could stand the tension no longer, she said, 'You should be flattered. It's not every bloke arrives in a new street with a testimonial like that.'

'It's not every *bloke* wants to.'

She was no longer frightened of him. Something, whether the experience of being a mother or the hardship they'd endured since he got the sack, had given her the strength to fight back.

Number twenty-nine was a hell of a mess. It had, until recently, been known as Dirty Dick's after the old man who lived there, and the filth that lay thickly everywhere accounted, in part, for the low rent. The women of Walker Street watched with dour approval as Liza got down on her hands and knees and worked her way through the entire house, top to bottom, front to back, with a bar of carbolic soap, a bucket of water, and a strip of sacking to kneel on. Once the initial cleaning was over, they watched to see how much work she did on a week-by-week basis, and again they could find nothing to criticize. She scoured the front doorstep daily, cleaned her windows twice a week and put up clean curtains which, although faded, were neatly pressed. She spoke to none of them, which displeased them greatly since it gave them no opportunity of ignoring her.

Strangers were not welcome in Walker Street, or anywhere else in the neighbourhood for that matter. Once, immigrant labour had flooded in from all over the country and abroad. But that was more than a generation ago. Nobody came to the town looking for work now. Grass grew in the shipyards, and even the steelworks had started to lay men off. And so the streets that had welcomed Scottish, Irish, Welsh, Germans and Swedes, as well as workers from all other parts of England, became closed and clannish communities, suspicious of outsiders. Invisible boundaries lay between apparently identical streets, boundaries that were fiercely defended, by ostracism of those who tried to move in, if you were an adult, or by unrelenting gang warfare, if you were a child.

Liza had been born less than four miles away, but far enough to count as a stranger.

The husband hadn't got a job, though he always went out dressed smart and with his head held high. He didn't drink, he didn't smoke, he didn't gamble, he didn't chase other women, and at first the women were inclined to feel envious. Then they noticed the drawn curtains and weird noises that came from the house every Thursday evening, and sometimes on Sundays as well. Seances. If you could believe that. Mrs Bower's Maude crept up to the drawn curtains one night and looked in, and according to Mrs Bower came back *dumbstruck*. You couldn't find out exactly what she'd seen because Mrs Bower wouldn't let you get near her. The child, she said, was *in shock*. After that the women of Walker Street looked at their own men staggering in from the pub on a Friday night with as much as they could carry, and thought that perhaps they weren't so bad after all.

She called her little boy Tom. By Walker Street standards he was coddled. He actually wore a coat and this made him an object of scorn to the Walker Street children who went out bare-armed, and sometimes bare-arsed, in all weathers. He was classed immediately as a Mammy's pet, and, when he ventured out into the street alone for the first time, had the coat ripped off his back by the two Dobbin boys who then, for good measure, rolled him over and over in the nearest puddle until it was difficult to tell the colour of his hair.

Liza appeared on Mrs Dobbin's doorstep.

'What's this?' she asked, holding up the remains of the coat.

Mrs Dobbin pretended to examine it. 'Looks like a bit of mucky old rag to me.'

'It's what's left of my lad's coat after your lads had finished with it.'

'And how do you know it was my lads?'

'I saw them.'

'Oh, did you now? I'll ask them about it when they get in.'

'You don't need to ask them. I'm telling you.'

'I don't chastise my lads on anybody else's say-so.'

'Well, mebbe it's time you started. The buggers are running wild. Look at the pair of them, laughing behind your back.'

The two Dobbin boys had crept along the wall to listen to the row. Suddenly they took to their heels and ran. Liza looked round and saw Harry Dobbin walking up the street.

'Now then,' he said.

'Now then.'

'Anything the matter, Missus?'

Men liked Liza. Another good reason for their wives not to.

'No,' said Liza. 'We were just passing the time of day.' She nodded to Mrs Dobbin. 'I'll be off then.'

Mrs Dobbin nodded, and watched her go.

'What was she on about?'

'Oh, some story about our lads ripping her lad's coat. I told her they hadn't.'

'Oh, no, they couldn't, could they? Bloody little plaster saints.'

'They're no worse than anybody else's.'

'No, and no better either. You watch it, you little sods. Hey, I'm talking to you!'

The youngest Dobbin boy froze at the foot of the stairs. 'She's after us, Dad.'

'*She's* the cat's grandmother. Say who you mean.'

'Mrs Wright.'

'Well, don't come to me and say she's belted you. Because if she belts one side I'll belt the other.'

'That's a nice way to talk to your own children.'

'You'd be the first to yell if somebody ripped their clothes.'

'They'd not get the chance. My lot rip their own.'

Liza kept Tom in for a while after that. But he got bored staying in the house all day, and slipped out. He wandered along the street to where the two Dobbin boys were playing alleys. They looked up.

'You got any?' said Wally, noticing that Tom kept his hand in his trouser pocket.

'Yeah.'

Wally glanced sideways at Ned. 'Give you a game.'

They expected to take all his alleys away from him, without effort, but they got a shock. He not only kept his own, he virtually cleaned them out. He even took Wally's King, a big cream-coloured marble with pink swirls that had conquered every other marble in the street.

A great wail of anguish went up as the King disappeared into Tom's pocket. 'Hey, that's not fair.'

'I'll give you it back for ten little uns.'

By the time the swop had been haggled over and agreed, they'd forgotten the fight and went back to Mrs Dobbin's together, caked with dirt and hoping for a doorstep of bread and dripping to keep them going till tea-time.

As Liza's pregnancy became more obvious, she became an object of interest. Women who had walked past her a few weeks before now paused and said, 'Doing all right then?'

Liza would smile back and say, 'Oh, not so bad. Can't complain.'

She gave back as much warmth as she received. Never more, never less, and so gradually they got into the habit of speaking to her, though never more than a few words and always in the street.

One day, very close to her time, Liza did a full day's wash. By early afternoon she'd filled the line in her yard and had started on the line that stretched across the alley at the back.

Seeing Liza with a mouthful of pegs about to reach up and hang a shirt on the line, Mrs Dobbin came running.

'Hey up, Missus, I'll do that,' she said, taking the shirt out of Liza's hand and a peg out of her mouth. 'You shouldn't reach above your head, you know, while you're like that. You'll have the cord twisted round the bairn's neck.' She looked closely at Liza. 'Didn't your Mam ever tell you that?'

'Yes,' Liza admitted.

'But you knew better?'

'I didn't see how else I was gunna get it on the line.'

'Well, in future, you ask me. There was a girl used to live up there . . .' Mrs Dobbin gestured vaguely towards the top of the street. 'She *wouldn't* be told. She used to sit with her leg bent up under her, all the time she was carrying, and do you know it used to go through me. I used to tell her, "You'll rue the day," but you couldn't get it into her. She just laughed. But you believe me when that bairn was born it had a twisted leg and it was the same side as she used to sit on.'

Mrs Dobbin was breathless with effort, for the sheets were wet and very heavy. 'You go and get the rest of the washing, love, and I'll fetch a chair. We'll have it up in no time.'

'I wasn't sure what day the rag and bone man came. I'd got him worked out to a Tuesday, but it was a Wednesday last week.'

'They suit themselves. I've had many a day's work ruined by the buggers, but what can you do? They've got their living to earn same as everybody else.'

First one line was filled and then the other. Soon the two women were encircled by flapping and billowing white sheets. A snapping, cracking, big-bellied, sunlit world.

'There's nothing like seeing it hung up, is there?' said Mrs Dobbin.

'No. You can see what you've achieved, can't you? Whereas housework . . .'

'Oh, housework.'

Mrs Dobbin stood back and gave a final tug to the leg of Frank's long johns. 'There,' she said. 'Don't they look nice?'

Within minutes the clothes would be speckled with red dust from the steelworks, but for the moment they looked beautiful and the two women stood back to admire their work.

'Would you like a cup of tea?' Liza said.

'I wouldn't say no. And you look as if you could do with one.'

'I'll put the kettle on.'

Liza took Mrs Dobbin inside the house. She glanced round her living-room quickly, not ashamed of its bareness but ready to defend it if need be.

'You got straightened out then,' Mrs Dobbin said, looking round. 'You've had a job.'

'I wouldn't like to think I had to do it again.'

Liza made the tea and they drank it, sitting on either side of the range.

'Nice gap you've got between your two.'

'It isn't two yet,' Liza said, and touched the wooden arm of her chair.

'Better than poor Mrs Taylor. She's had four in four years, and she thinks she's on again.'

'Some don't have the luck, do they?'

'Luck?' Mrs Dobbin looked intently at Liza.

'Me Mam had no luck,' Liza said. 'Fifteen. And she reared nine.'

'Is she still living?'

'Oh, yes. Crippled, mind. She doesn't get about much. You know, she had the white leg and it turned to ulcers so she has to have her legs bandaged all the time. She's supposed to change the bandages every morning but she's that busy most of the time she puts it off. Then when she does get round to it her skin's stuck to the bandages, and she has an awful job.'

'So you won't be going to her to have the bairn, then?'

'Oh no, I want to stop in me own home this time. I went to her when I had Tom.'

'Well, you don't look as if you're going to take after her in one respect. Fifteen kids.'

'My God, I hope not. You should see the state she's in. It isn't just her legs, it's her womb as well. She has to wear one of them rings, but every now and then it slips out of place and then she has to lie on the floor till the doctor comes and puts it back in. And the whole lot's hanging out, you know. You'd just think it was a turnip stuck between her legs.'

'You'll miss her this time.'

137

'I know I will.'

'Well, if you need anything, just bang on the grate. I can be over that wall in two seconds flat. You'd be surprised.'

After Mrs Dobbin had gone, Liza went into the front room, which had been turned into a kind of study for Frank. He was reading his way through the encyclopaedias he'd bought from a travelling salesman, and had reached the third volume. Not being in work gave him plenty of time to read. He didn't look up when she came in. It was his practice to read to the end of the page before he spoke to her, so that over the years she'd had plenty of time to observe him. He was fair and slight, almost girlish-looking by some standards, and not strong. She had to keep reminding herself that he wasn't strong.

They'd been married for more than five years now, and for the last year he'd been out of work. When he first lost his job she'd asked if she could go out to work. Their Harriet was willing to mind Tom: he was only two years older than her son. Frank wouldn't hear of it. He wasn't going to have it said he couldn't afford to keep his wife. She could *work*, but not outside the home, and not at a proper job. Taking in washing, butchers' bloody aprons that made you sick to smell them, that was all right. Half a crown a week, but it was all right. No security, but it was all right. Nobody could see her doing it and so his precious masculine pride was safe. When she rebelled and insisted on looking for work, he got her pregnant. Of course she couldn't prove he'd done it deliberately, but there'd never been a slip-up before.

Well, after this little lot was over, he was in for a shock. No more bloody butchers' aprons for her. If she could see her way clear at all she was going for a proper job. She hadn't told him that yet. No sense getting punched until you had to. To look at him, to listen to him even, you'd never've thought him capable of that, and yet he was. She'd had many a black eye off him, though to be fair always when his voice gave out. As long as he could lecture and preach and make her feel knee-high to a grasshopper that was fine. But when he couldn't . . . Wham! Out came his fist.

She looked at him as he went on pretending to read. A

pale, clear, clever profile. Thin lips, with a bluish shadow round them that only came when he was tired. She'd seen a shadow like that round the mouth of a baby sister who'd died, and as she thought of this her heart clenched. In spite of everything she still loved him.

And he her?

No.

She'd asked him once whether he would still have married her if she hadn't been pregnant. He thought about it for a moment and then said in his gentle, precise voice, 'No.'

Now he looked up from the book and waited for her to speak.

'That was Mrs Dobbin from next door. She seems quite nice.'

'Yes, well, people are if you approach them in the right way.'

His voice was always quiet, except sometimes at the height of a seance. An educated voice. He'd passed the scholarship for the high school, but his parents hadn't been able to do without his wage.

'Will you have your tea now?' she asked.

'Whenever you're ready.'

She withdrew, feeling rebuffed. As she sliced and buttered bread she thought it wasn't fair of him to imply that her problems with the street were all of her own making. His head was so far up in the clouds, most of the time he didn't even know what was going on in the next room.

When the time came she went about her work as long as she could, not even mentioning to Frank that her labour had started, though it was a relief when, after dinner, he went into the front room to read his encyclopaedias. She was ironing. Her back always ached when she ironed so it made little difference that today it ached more. Tom played on the hearth with marbles he'd won off the Dobbin boys. It was the thought of being parted from him that kept her going. He looked up once, just as a pain reached its peak, and she raised the shirt she was ironing to her face and held it there, as if she were just testing to see how damp it was.

When she'd finished the ironing she sat in the armchair for a few minutes and then rattled at the back of the grate with the poker.

She'd expected Mrs Dobbin, who was certainly no fly-weight, to come round to the front door and knock. Instead, first her head and then one stout, gartered leg appeared over the wall of the yard. She swung herself from the top of the high wall and landed lightly on the ground.

'Started have you?' she asked. Her arms were floured half way to the elbow and looked, in their meaty rawness, ready for the oven.

Liza nodded. 'If you could just pop round for Mrs Fisher . . .'

'I'll send our Maggie.' She went to the yard end and yelled at the top of her voice until the girl came running. 'There, I've sent her off. And don't you worry, she won't come back without her. Our Maggie's a sensible lass.'

'If you'd like to put the kettle on . . .'

'Are you bad enough for bed?'

'Why no.'

'Well, don't make a martyr of yourself now. We don't want it popping out on the carpet.'

'I'm afraid mine don't pop.'

'Nor mine. Must be nice though, mustn't it?'

Mrs Dobbin made the tea and brought it in. 'There,' she said. 'Plenty of sugar.' She put the cup in Liza's hand. 'They do say you should keep moving, you know.'

'Aye.'

They laughed, and settled down to their tea.

Liza was in the middle of a contraction when Mrs Fisher arrived. She took her coat off and stood in front of Liza's chair, looking down.

'Was that a pain?' she asked.

'Aw no,' said Liza. 'It was a bloody tickle. Good God, woman, what do you think it was?'

'Upstairs with you, me girl,' Mrs Fisher said. She looked at Mrs Dobbin. 'When they start losing their tempers there's not long to go.'

Tom's face puckered as he watched Liza stand up. He had

no idea what was going on, but he knew he didn't like it. He stiffened when Mrs Dobbin tried to get hold of his hand.

'You've got to, flower,' said Liza. 'It'll not be for long.'

'Howay, son,' said Mrs Dobbin. 'I've got some jam roly-poly for tea.'

Tom squared his mouth and howled. In the end Mrs Dobbin had to unpick his fingers from Liza's skirt one by one and carry him out screaming. 'Don't worry,' she yelled above the din. 'He'll be all right with me.'

Liza went upstairs to bed. The midwife helped her to undress and then she was under the coverlet and beginning to get warm.

'All right, honey?'

'Fine,' she said.

Mrs Fisher bent over and pinched her cheeks. 'You've got nice rosy cheeks,' she said. 'That's what I like to see.'

Well, at least this time she *knew*. None of that nonsense about your belly-button opening.

'They should tell girls more,' she said.

'I quite agree with you,' said Mrs Fisher, though she seemed a bit surprised. 'But you know sometimes their mothers think they're doing it for the best. They think, *Why spoil her girlhood? She'll know soon enough.*'

The pains were strong and regular, but Liza seemed to make little progress. She kept her eyes closed, and opened them only once when she felt a breath of cold air by the bed. It was Frank who'd realized what was going on at last.

'Are you all right?' he said.

'As right as she can be,' said Mrs Fisher, and Liza felt a little sorry for him as he turned away and would have liked to call him back only the next pain swelled to a climax and claimed all her attention.

This was a strange labour, quite unlike the other, slow and heavy and peaceful like a calm sea. Each wave gathered itself together for an assault upon the shore, broke in a sharp line of foam and fell back. A moment of peace, and then the dark muscle began to swell again, knitting together, flexing itself, focusing always on the single task.

141

Liza was absorbed in her long labour and yet not divided from the life of the street that went on all round her. The tramping of feet of men who had work to go to, the squatting on haunches of men who had none, the skitter of a stone over the pavement as children played hopscotch, the hanging-out of washing, the billowing of sheets, the snap and crackle of shirts blowing on the line, women with open-pored, harassed faces chasing a little bacon round and round the frying pan, always asking, *Will it be enough?*, a cat slinking down the alley, dogs barking, smells of meat and cabbage, the crackle of flames in a grate as fires were lit for the men coming home, then dusk falling, lights going on one by one, windows glowing the colour of their curtains, red and blue and green: all these things and many more revolved around the periphery of her vision, and she felt as her labour went on that she was giving birth to them all.

She was reluctant to break into this peaceful, strenuous, attentive mood, but the pains became more urgent and she began to cry out as each one reached its peak and then, just as she felt like saying, *I can't bear this*, except what would have been the point, they changed their character, not rising to a peak and breaking cleanly, but as it were collapsing in upon themselves, dissipating themselves in the swirl and eddy of a rock pool, and the midwife, sensing the change from a look at Liza's shuttered face, whipped back the covers and said, 'Not long now.'

Liza had a moment of regret for the long, dark, absorbed hours but then she struggled to sit up and turned with renewed energy to this different task. Between pains she felt Mrs Fisher's hand pressing against the stretched skin. Then, at the peak of the next pain, there was a cry and a gush of warm water drenching her buttocks and thighs. Another pain and then Mrs Fisher said, 'It's a girl.' She lay between her mother's legs, purple, shrieking, perfect and so *heavy*, heavy and purple like a fruit, and the next thing was Mrs Dobbin's voice on the stairs saying, 'Is she all right?'

'Why, aye. Come on up,' Mrs Fisher winked at Liza. 'There's somebody here we'd like you to meet.'

142

Liza held the baby on her suddenly soft and doughy belly. It was odd, she thought, how the baby came as a shock even after the longest labour. One minute there was just you and the midwife in the room, the next there was this new life screaming for its share of the world. Nothing really prepared you for that. She touched the baby's cheek and its head swung round strongly in search of milk. When Liza put it to the breast it got the idea at once and sucked strongly.

'She knows what she's about, doesn't she?' Mrs Dobbin said.

'She looks as if she wants a knife and fork,' said Mrs Fisher.

'Feels as if she's bloody got one,' said Liza, whose toes were curling up.

The three of them were silent for a minute, admiring the baby. Her hair was starting to dry, and though it had looked dark, almost black at first, there was a hint of bronze in the curls behind the ear.

'Pity she hasn't got your colour,' said Mrs Fisher.

'Oh, I wouldn't wish this on her,' Liza said. 'She's all right as she is.'

'Your husband'll be pleased,' said Mrs Fisher.

'He wanted another boy, I think.'

'Then want must be his portion,' said Mrs Fisher.

The day after she'd been churched, Liza took Eileen to see her mother. She knew it was no use going sooner. Her sister Harriet, while still weak from childbirth, had walked three miles to see her mother, carrying the baby in her arms, only to be turned away.

'Have you been churched?' Louise had asked.

'No,' said Harriet. 'I'm going on Sunday.'

'Then bugger off back home. You can come here on Monday.'

Liza was not turned away from the door, but she was very quiet when she came home.

'What did your mother think of her then?' Frank asked.

'Barely looked at her,' Liza said, bitterly.

They sat down together and ate in silence. Frank insisted

on absolute silence at mealtimes. It'd been his father's rule, and he couldn't imagine eating in any other way. He never realized how foreign this seemed to Liza, whose own memory of childhood mealtimes was of a noisy, chattering crowd gathered round the kitchen table, many of them standing up since there'd never been enough chairs to go round.

After the meal was over and the table cleared, Liza said, 'Are you going to read?'

'No. I think I'll have a walk out.'

Since Eileen's birth, Frank had spent more and more time outside the house. The arrival of a new mouth to feed increased the pressure on him to find work. So much so that at times the baby's crying sounded like a personal reproach. He wanted to hit out, though he always managed to control his feelings until he was away from the child. If it was too late to go for a walk, he would go out and stand in the backyard, rocking a little from side to side, at times beating on the wall with his clenched fist.

Everything seemed to be disintegrating around him. When he'd first lost his job at the steelworks he'd embarked on a daily timetable that was almost military in its discipline. He rose early, shaved, washed, dressed, put on the boots he'd polished and left ready the night before, and set out to look for work. He looked smart, but he was slightly built with a persistent blue shadow round his mouth. Not the man a cautious employer would pick out of the crowd. Consequently, all his attempts to get a job ended in disappointment, and some in humiliation.

One place in particular he dreaded going to. The word would go round that there were jobs to be had and all the unemployed men of the neighbourhood would troop up the hill, chatting to each other as they went, but with a certain reserve, a tension in the talk, because they would shortly be pitted against each other and only one or two could win.

They queued for hours outside the gate, the weaker sinking down on their haunches as the day advanced, the stronger leaning against the wall or walking up and down, always with a weather eye open for the place they'd left.

144

Not that it mattered. The owner paid no attention to who was at the head of the queue but walked along the line, flanked by his deputies, looking the men up and down. When he saw a man who looked reasonably strong he would call him out from the line and feel his biceps and shoulders. If these were satisfactory he would sink down to his knees and feel the calf and thigh muscles, running his hands down the leg as grooms do when testing the soundness of a horse. Then, if the man was lucky, he would be told to go in at the gate. Otherwise, he was waved back into the queue.

Frank was surprised when the owner called him out of the line: he was so obviously not the equal of men who had already failed the test. He felt the owner's fingers close round his biceps and bite in, probing the strength of the muscle. He held himself rigid, withdrawing his mind from what was happening, since this was the only way he could survive. He looked out across the fields, over the owner's head, and made himself notice the curve of a hedge, the precise details of a rabbit scree, the way the smoke of a farmhouse curled up and dissolved against a greyish-white bank of cloud. The view was obscured, momentarily, by a face he tried not to see and then his thighs and calves were squeezed, the owner grunting a little as he bent down because he was a heavy man with an unhealthily high colour.

The owner straightened up and waved Frank back into the line. He would have moved off without a word spoken, but Frank grabbed him by the shoulder and swung him round. A gasp of indrawn breath from the men in the line, but Frank didn't hear it. He searched the owner's face, and the owner stared back at him, unflinching. They held each other's gaze for a full minute and then Frank fell back into the line.

'No use getting your dander up, mate.'

Frank had gone very white.

'He goes through this bleeding routine over and over again and I'm bloody sure half the time there isn't a job there.'

'That's right,' another man said. 'Picks nobody sometimes. Just says, "Come back tomorrow."'

'And you do?' said Frank.

They stared at him. 'Well, what else can you do, mate? You have to try.'

Frank didn't reply. He was trying to absorb what he'd seen when he looked into the owner's eyes. He was still thinking about it as he walked back down the hill, in silence, separate from the other men. When he forced the man to look directly at him, he'd expected to see lust, perversion, shame. He couldn't think of any other reason for a man to behave in that way. Instead, he'd seen the conscious, naked and deliberate enjoyment of power for its own sake. He'd backed away from it, knowing this was something he would never understand. It wasn't just that the owner had power and Frank had none. That was a mere social fact, though a fairly intractable one. No, the crucial difference was that Frank couldn't *imagine* that kind of power. He couldn't imagine having it, or even wanting it. The difference, in the end, was in their souls.

'*Arseholes*,' said Liza, when he confided this thought to her. 'You should've clocked him one.'

'And do you really think that's the answer?'

'He shouldn't be allowed to go on as if he owns people,' Liza said.

'He can't own anybody who isn't willing to be owned,' said Frank. 'Freedom's something you have inside yourself.'

It sounded good, he thought, but he didn't know if it was true. It would have been nice to talk to Liza, really talk, but how could he talk to a woman who said 'arseholes' every time he mentioned the soul? For him the soul was the supreme reality. Poverty, sickness, the daily humiliations of life on the dole: none of this really mattered. Oh, it could scratch the surface of his mind, irritate, drain, but it couldn't, finally, damage or destroy him. He couldn't explain any of this to Liza. He had never managed to interest her in things of the spirit, or even of the mind, and had long since given up trying.

One evening he arrived home after a particularly bad day. Eileen was in her drawer by the fire, red-faced and screaming inconsolably. Tom, who'd been sitting beside her, got up as

146

soon as he saw his father and trotted off to join his mother in the kitchen. This instinctive, silent avoidance hurt Frank, who tried hard to be a good father, played with the boy, talked to him, did everything in fact that his own unapproachable father had not done.

He followed the boy into the kitchen. 'Isn't tea ready yet?' he said.

'No, I'm sorry, Frank. I've only just put Eileen down. I can't seem to settle her.'

'You should let her cry,' he said. 'The more you pick her up the more she expects it.'

He went back to the fire. The baby, as she wriggled and screamed, looked about as attractive as a lump of raw meat. He had so much looked forward to his own children, to the *idea* of children, that he found it difficult to admit, even to himself, how very much he disliked the reality, the screaming and puking, the yellow-stained nappies, the endless broken nights. Even the smell of milk and blood from his wife that made her seem not Liza at all but a different, rather intimidating, form of life. The human body is beautiful, he reminded himself, not merely in some postures and activities, but in all. It was one of his dogmas, framed in defiance of his father who had taught his children that the body was shameful, a thing to be hidden, all its functions, in varying degrees, disgusting.

He so much wanted to believe the opposite. But it was not always possible to break clear of the past, and sometimes in trying you sank deeper into the mire.

For a second he was again looking into the eyes of the man who had drowned in France, but then he blinked and the image vanished. They didn't come so frequently now, these memories.

Liza came into the living-room with the teapot.

'I expect tea to be on the table, Liza. *Not* when it happens to suit you. *When I come in.*'

Liza opened her mouth and then shut it again, firmly. This was mild. There were worse rows, much worse, rows when blood was drawn and Frank stormed out of the house and walked the beach for hours, his face tight with rage and shame.

Liza wanted to go to the pictures with some of the women she'd known before she was married. 'No,' said Frank. 'There won't be any men there,' said Liza. 'No,' said Frank. Liza was offered a job. 'It's only twenty hours a week,' she said, 'and our Harriet says she'll take the kids.' 'No,' said Frank. 'I could still get all the housework done, and I'd be in for your tea.' 'No,' said Frank. Liza wanted to join the Labour Party. 'It'd only be a Thursday evening. You've got your seance then anyway.' 'I need you to make the tea,' said Frank.

'You don't seem to understand, Liza,' he said. 'Your job is to keep the house and be a good wife and mother. Time enough to think of other things when you've made a success of that.'

'I'd like to see you make the money go as far.'

Then she was quiet again, going about her work silently, aggressively, keeping house against him, straightening cushions as soon as he stood up, pushing the broom between his legs when he sat down to read, drying nappies in front of the fire on the rare occasions when he joined them in the living-room.

Once a week she took the children to see her mother. Sometimes she had a bruise to show and her father, who was getting old now, would be beside himself with rage. Her mother was less concerned.

'I daresay she asked for it,' Louise would say. 'She doesn't tell you what she did.'

'It doesn't matter what I do, Mam. He wants a doormat.'

'A man likes to be master in his own house, Liza. Especially if he's master nowhere else.'

In the end she began to oppose him openly, unthinkable in the first few years of the marriage. She'd never liked the seances, but as time passed she began to find them intolerable. Some of the people who came were genuine believers, many of them recently bereaved, but there was another group whom she called 'the ghouls'. The nickname was an attempt to pretend that these people were merely ridiculous, but they weren't. Every Thursday evening they invaded the house. Every Thursday night there was a row and these rows, coming as they did when Frank was drained after a long seance, were particularly likely to end in blows.

Usually the rows started about something trivial. Frank would forget to collect the money for tea and biscuits because his mind was on higher things.

'I don't know how you think I can afford to feed that lot on what you give me. I'm fed up with you and your bloody seances. And what that Esme wants with raising the dead, God alone knows. She's only got to look in the mirror.'

'She's anaemic.'

'Anaemic? She looks like a vampire's droppings.'

Liza turned to go upstairs, but paused on the bottom step. 'Oh, and I've joined the Labour Party. So I won't be here next Thursday. You'll have to get one of the ghouls to make the tea. Esme'll do it. She'd like to get her hands on a few of my things.'

Frank expected Liza to give in over this, as she'd done so many times before. But no. Thursday night came. He watched her putting on her hat and coat, giving her shoes a final polish, even adding a dab of lipstick. She had, it seemed, joined the Labour Party.

'I hope you realize this'll be the death of your father,' said Louise. 'He'll not be long for this earth now.'

'Well, tell him to hang on a bit. Frank'll go with him.'

At first Liza sat on the back row of the meetings and said not a word. Then, a few weeks after she joined, a woman came to address a public meeting. The married name meant nothing to her, but when she looked up at the platform she saw Ellen Parker, her old friend from the munitions factory.

Liza waited for the meeting to begin almost as nervously as if she'd been giving the speech herself, but Ellen didn't seem nervous at all. After she'd been speaking for a few minutes, Liza glanced round and saw nods of approval here and there. She relaxed then, and started to enjoy herself. Ellen seemed to have an answer to everything, and when a man at the back shouted something out, she turned the tables on him in no time at all.

After the meeting Liza hung about, not sure if this new

Ellen would want to know her, but Ellen came straight up to her and said, 'Well, Liza Jarrett! I thought it was you.'

Through Ellen, Liza became more deeply involved with politics than she'd ever been before. She needed an explanation for the mess she saw around her. Everywhere you looked men wanted work; everywhere you looked, work needed doing. And yet nothing happened, the men and the work weren't brought together. Year after year machinery rusted, men rusted, women wore their lives away making one penny do the work of two. Or ten. Why? As soon as Liza knew of the existence of other people asking the same questions, there was no holding her back. She read, talked, argued, canvassed, marched, even, eventually, spoke, though only on street corners. Frank was staggered by the change in her.

Thursday evenings were always a problem, even when the children were older, because Eileen was frightened of the seances. She sat at the foot of the stairs, afraid to go into the living-room, but even more afraid of the darkness upstairs. All she could do was look at the clock and count the minutes until Liza came back from her meeting.

Once, Liza came back to find Eileen even more frightened than usual.

'What's the matter, flower?'

'The lady,' Eileen said. 'There was a lady on the stairs.'

'Be one of the ladies from your Dad's meeting.'

Eileen shook her head. 'No.'

'That child's psychic,' Frank said.

'Is she hell.'

'A lot of children have buried gifts.'

'Well, hers are stopping buried.'

She expected him to argue, but he didn't. She sensed that a change was coming over Frank. He seemed to have less confidence in his ability as a medium, and once or twice she thought she detected a dislike of the hysterical atmosphere of the meetings. But when she tried to probe he refused to talk to her about it, and he always defended Esme and the others whenever Liza dared to criticize them.

Nobody in the street understood about the seances. A lot of

people thought it was all fraud or self-deception, and of course a lot of it was. But not all. She'd lived too closely with spiritualism not to be aware of events that couldn't be explained, and some of these events had been frightening. Eileen mustn't be involved.

One night Frank lay awake longer than usual, sighing heavily at intervals in the way she detested.

At last, he said, 'Well, there'll be no more meetings, Liza.'

'Oh. Why not?'

'You obviously don't like them.'

'I've not liked them for thirteen years. It's never been a reason for stopping them before.'

'Esme says we can use her front room. It'll be more convenient.'

'For what?'

'Oh, Liza.'

The Thursday meetings stopped, and Eileen gradually lost the rather timid and strained expression that everybody, including Liza, had come to take for granted in her. Frank went out on Thursday evenings, came back late and went straight to bed. Liza watched his comings and goings without interest. She was absorbed in her work for the Labour Party, and so the lives of the two adults in the house slid past each other. Tom and Eileen turned to each other for warmth and became very close. Watching them together, Liza would sometimes be reminded of herself and Edward, but all that seemed a long time ago.

There weren't so many rows now. Liza and Frank hardly met and when they did they were polite, even gentle to each other. Liza could afford to be generous, and Frank, who was locked in his own struggle, had no energy to spare.

He spent a lot of time walking by the river, past empty wharves and chained and padlocked factory gates. The men who'd worked in such places lived by the clock. Clocking on, clocking off, time anaesthetized, vivisected. He remembered something he'd read in one of Liza's books, something about the working class selling the carcase of time. Most of what

151

Liza filled her head with was rubbish, but that one image stayed with him.

Time was not a carcase for him now. It roared in his ears and threatened to devour him. Or slowly, day by day, picked the flesh off his bones.

He was a fraud. That was the thought he couldn't escape. There had been a time in one seance when the inspiration had failed. He'd looked round at the waiting, expectant faces and rather than say, 'There's nothing there, I can't do it', he'd gone on. To his relief and horror they were all taken in. One woman even came up to him afterwards and said, 'You know, you've really helped me this evening.' And Esme, before she went into the kitchen to wash up, had whispered, 'That was the best meeting yet.'

If *they* couldn't tell fraud from reality, how could he be sure? Perhaps it had all been fraud, or self-deception, right from the beginning, even the voices of the men in France. Dead. All dead. No returning. And himself a madman with a bullet in his throat.

He stopped going to the meetings. On Thursday nights he got washed and dressed as usual, but he spent the evening wandering round the town. He tried to pray, but it was no use: his faith was gone. He even tried going back to the Baptist faith of his childhood, but the God of the Baptist chapel looked so much like his father that though he might believe in Him, he could neither love nor serve Him.

He started to walk. Anywhere, mile after mile, sometimes not coming back to the house till after midnight. He became shabby-looking. His shoes were worn through and his trouser legs whitened with the dust of the roads. Liza asked him what was wrong, but he couldn't talk to her. He no longer cared what Liza thought, and perhaps had never cared. She and the children seemed remote now, remote but brightly coloured, like pictures in a book he would have to close before long.

On one of these long walks he went into St Columba's church and sat down. It was dark inside, though lozenges of emerald, sapphire and ruby lay on the stone floor of the aisles and fell across the reddish backs of the pews. When he looked up at the window, the sunlight falling through stained glass dazzled him. Christ risen from the tomb. He saw beauty in the window, but no hope. It was like the beauty of a summer evening that derives more than half its poignancy from the approach of night. Men go down to the grave and do not rise again. The mouths of the dead are stopped forever. They cannot speak.

After leaving the church he walked for an hour by the river and the wind coming up from the North Sea scoured his mind clean. The tide was out, the river shrunken, exposing bare, sloping banks of mud, streaked with opal and amethyst where oil had leaked from visiting ships.

Frank came to the transporter bridge and, pausing often to get his breath, climbed the staircase that led to the walkway at the top. The water crawled away from him as the wind wrinkled its surface. Far below, the transporter platform lurched and began to move. It was a pleasant feeling, to be so far above everything, to be a speck in the sky, looking down on toy cars and men like matchsticks walking around.

He leaned against the rail and looked out across the river. He could remember this place as it had been in the boom years before the war, the clanging of hammers, the cries of men, the sudden roar and rush of flame as a furnace was charged, the columns of smoke by day, the pillars of fire by night, and everywhere the sound of men's boots, tramping along the pavements, striking sparks from the cobbles on frosty nights. As a small boy coming home from school, he'd watched for the sparks.

Now it was quiet and the few men who moved around below him did so almost furtively, as if they'd lost all confidence in what they were doing.

Two men were walking along the gangway towards him. He flattened himself against the railing to let them pass.

'Now then,' one of them said.

'Now then.'

Frank's voice seemed to come from a long way back in his head and the bones of his skull went on vibrating after he'd spoken, like the casing of a bell.

One step forward, and it would be over forever. He'd never learned to swim and the river in the central channel was deep, with God knows what decaying wreckage trapped underneath the brown and oily water. He imagined the river closing over his head, the instant dark, the chest-tightening, eyeball-bursting struggle for air, and then the water rushing in. A quick death, or so they said. He remembered a boy in France who'd slid into the water and drowned. Not wounded, not even awake. He fell asleep and the water closed over him. His unmarked face and floating hair had lived in Frank's mind long after more terrible sights had been forgotten.

He had walked so many miles in the course of his lifetime, and all his walking had led to this one place. He looked back over the years, searching for something that would stay, leaning his weight now here, now there, and stone and brick crumbled wherever he stood. Staircases twisted and turned and led up into the blankness of the sky or down into the darkness of the earth. Doors opened onto closed doors. Nothing could be found that would connect with anything else.

He knew that if he could make himself move away from this place, he would be safe. But his hands grasped the gangway railing as if they'd been welded on. Hours passed. The transporter platform swung to and fro, and the passengers looked up at the man who stood there, a dark speck framed by the bridge and the sky. They squinted up at him, then looked quickly away, dizzied by the height on which he stood.

It was dark when he got home. His dinner had been put to keep warm on the hearth and had dried up round the edges. He expected Liza to ask where he'd been, but she said nothing. There was a good fire in and he huddled close to it as if he would never get warm again. The life of the family went on around him, but it didn't include him except once, for a few minutes, when Eileen came and sat on his knee.

When the time came to go to bed, Liza raked the fire and pulled the hookey mat well back so that no chance spark could jump out onto it during the night. Frank sat, staring into the embers of the fire.

'Are you coming to bed?' Liza asked.

'No, not yet. I'll stop up and have a read.'

He leaned forward and picked up a book from the table beside him, but he didn't open it.

'All right then. Don't forget to lock up.'

After she'd gone he relaxed, stretching his feet out towards the fire. He was remembering a story his mother had told him about her childhood, a story about a magic tree. She'd been born and brought up in the deep countryside, though as a child she'd stood and looked across fields of ripening corn to where the steel works smudged the horizon, and the houses crept down along the brow of a hill. A little nearer every year.

As a woman she'd married a labourer from the steel works and lived out all her adult life in one of those houses on the hill. And yet, Frank thought, the town had never become real to her. The countryside was real, the rhythm of seedtime and harvest, the terrified rabbits in their dwindling citadel of hay, breaking cover at the last moment, only to be caught by her brothers, sunlight and sky ending in one expert chop of the hand. Not idyllic, this countryside of hers, not sentimentalized, but real, and in her scullery you had been able to touch and smell it, in the bunches of dried herbs she kept pinned to the rafters and the pig's bladder that hung there, revolving in the draught from the open door.

Her father had told her the story of an apple tree, a tree that shook by magic when there was no wind, so that if you stood underneath it at the right time, when the moon was full, the apples would fall into your pinafore without you even trying, and they were the juiciest apples in the world. She and her brothers believed him and went in search of this tree, but however hard they tried, it was never the right time or the right place. The apples had already fallen and were lying, brown and maggoty, in the grass, or else it was too soon, and they hung in hard green clusters, tantalizingly out of reach. But they went on believing in the tree, and although his mother had laughed, telling her father's story to her son, he thought she'd gone on believing it to the end of her life.

He was glad he'd told Tom and Eileen this story. It was an

important story to tell, more important than many of the things he'd gone out of his way to tell them. He'd suffered so much under his father's relentlessly critical, hectoring voice, and yet he'd never succeeded in finding any other voice in which to speak to his own children. He was glad that at least he'd managed to pass on his mother's story.

A thought struck him. He'd been thinking of Tom and Eileen as if they were dead, or he was, and when he realized this, he stood up and stared at the fire.

Liza lay in bed, glad to be alone. She moved her legs from side to side, enjoying all that cool space, and listened to the children who were whispering to each other through their bedroom wall long after they should've been asleep. She waited for the sound of Frank's footsteps on the stairs. There were times now when she was oppressed by the closeness of his body, which only seemed to emphasize the division and absence of his spirit. He seemed to have wandered off into some desert where she couldn't follow him, and now when he clung to her she wanted to cry out not with passion but with horror, as if his flesh had the power to chill or curdle hers. He wasn't making love to *her*, she knew that. Any woman's body would have done as well or better.

It had been a strange evening, she thought. One of the very few in recent months that they'd spent in the house together. Yet even tonight Frank had seemed distant. She and the children formed a unit, and he was outside. She would have to try harder to reach him, but even as the thought formed, the hand she'd thrown out across his side of the bed relaxed, and her fingers loosened in sleep.

She woke early, while it was still dark, but Frank was already up. That was a surprise because generally he was a poor riser. Even when he had a job, it had been a struggle to get him up for the morning shift. She touched the other side of the bed, and the cool, unused feel of the sheet frightened her.

She went downstairs in her nightdress, expecting to find him asleep on the sofa in front of the fire, but the room was empty, the ashes blue and cindery in the grate. Thinking he

156

might be on the toilet, she went to the back door and called, 'Frank?' No reply.

As soon as she came back into the room she saw a note pinned to the cushion of the sofa where he'd been sitting the night before. She wondered how she could have failed to see it when she first came downstairs, since once seen it reduced everything else to shadow. She unpinned it, but did not open it.

Instead, holding the note in her hand, she wandered round the room, straightening the chair covers, twitching the folds of the net curtain more neatly into place, tidying the hearth where a lump of dead coal had fallen out of the fire. These are the last moments of normal life, she thought. And she tried to conserve those moments as simply and naturally as the body tries to conserve heat. Then a faint cry from upstairs brought her back to the grey and waking world. She opened the note quickly and read:

I have gone to find work and will send for you and the children as soon as I can. Till then take care of them, and yourself. I will send money as often as I can. Frank.

She pushed the net curtain aside and stood with her cheek pressed against the window pane, watching, while the street, stale after its long sleep, stretched and came slowly back to life.

She tried to get money on the pancrack, but they took a lot of convincing before they'd give her any.

'Find your husband,' they said.

She stood there, holding her little girl by the hand.

'How the bloody hell am I supposed to do that?' she said.

'That's your problem.'

They thought he'd got a job somewhere else and was sending her money. She couldn't prove he wasn't.

'Well, where do you think he is?' asked Louise. 'You must have some idea.'

'I haven't. He's gone on the tramp.' Liza outstared her mother's scepticism. 'There's plenty doing it, Mam.'

'You mark my words, he's got another woman.'

'Well, it isn't Esme. I bumped into her the other day and she's still the life and soul of the local graveyard.'

'He's gone to look for a magic tree,' said Eileen.

They stared at her.

'My God,' said Louise. 'He's got that bairn as daft as he is.'

Meanwhile winter was coming on and there was no money to buy coal. Liza did what many a one had done before her: she went to the slag heap and scratted for it.

It was a long walk to the heap, and the last mile or so was down a country lane. There were hawthorn bushes on either side and the red berries glowed in the grey air. Masses of them. This was supposed to be the sign of a harsh winter, and you could only hope it wasn't true. But the birds were gorging themselves. In one bush alone there were hundreds of them, clustering along its branches as dark and bright as leaves.

Liza slipped along between the hawthorn hedges, a thin woman, moving quickly, head wrapped in a black shawl. As she got closer to the heap, the red, damp earth became grimed and streaked with black which gradually became so thick and powdery that puffs of it rose up in front of her and settled on the toes of her boots.

She climbed the gate at the end of the lane. The slag heap was ahead of her now, bigger and blacker than it had looked from the fields. The wind swirled the coal dust round and round the peak, so that it looked not merely black in itself, but veiled in black. As she came closer she could see figures, crawling or staggering round the hill.

She began to climb. It was harder than it looked: the rubble crumbled away beneath her feet and rattled down to the bottom of the hill, sometimes carrying her with it. She was soon on her hands and knees, crawling up. Right at the top, on the other side of the brow, was the place where the coal dust was emptied, the buckets coming in along the wires and opening to release what looked even at this distance like a shower of black rain.

All around her there were people, whether men or women it was impossible to tell, sifting through the black dust with hands as black as colliers' and transferring tiny nuggets of coal

158

to bags that were slung on their backs or balanced on their hips like babies. Liza thought she probably knew some of them, but under this black it was difficult to tell. Nobody paid any attention to her.

Getting a bag of coal – even a small bag – took longer than she'd thought. By the time she'd finished the sun had slipped down below the level of the hill and each dark figure pinned down a shadow many times its own length. She wrapped her shawl round the bag to hide it and set off back along the lane.

Blades of grass stood out as if etched in gold, the thorns and twigs of the hawthorn bushes glowed like filaments of electric wire and her own face was transfigured, blackish gold, as she walked along, a slight, dark figure, haloed in burning light.

On the third day a man raised his cap to her with incongruous courtesy as she struggled up the hill, and she nodded in acknowledgement.

On the fourth day a woman spoke to her, briefly, holding her hand, as they steadied each other on the scree.

On the fifth day a figure ran towards her down the slope, balancing effortlessly, though it was harder for him than for many, since one arm of his greatcoat was pinned, empty, to his chest.

'Welcome!' he said. 'Welcome!'

This was Ben, the centre of what Liza gradually came to recognize as a tightly knit and tenacious society. His arm, and some said half his mind, had been left behind in France, but he loved to laugh, and laughed more often and more joyously than anybody else she'd known. Some of his jokes were so well known that his listeners shouted out the punch lines for him and laughed long before the end, but these were the best jokes of all. Laughter bound them together and stiffened their courage on days when hailstones slanted across the heap and the coal dust turned to black sludge and you had to shield your mouth with your hands to be able to laugh at all.

'Lloyd George,' he said. 'What did he promise us? A land fit for heroes to live in.' His arm swept out to embrace the plumed slag heap and the stooping figures. 'This is it. What did he promise us? An acre of land and a cow. We got the cow

159

all right. She was waiting at the station. But where's the bloody land?'

Many of his stories were about France. One night he'd gone out with a burial party and this was the fourth year of the war when burial for those who died in the front line was rare. But on this night off they went, picking up pieces of bodies and assembling them into the rough shapes of men.

'"Hey up, this'n's got three arms," said the sergeant. "That's nowt," I said. "Bugger back there's got three heads and one of them's a Jerry." I wouldn't care, but they hadn't been buried two minutes when a ruddy great shell come over and dug 'em up again.'

'You know,' he said, bending close enough to Liza for her to catch the moonshine on his breath. 'When men get their heads shot off they don't stop running. Now many a one doesn't know that, but it's as true as I stand here. One poor lad I knew saw his mate's head shot off and the legs went on running. What does he do but he picks up the head and starts chasing the legs. "What you doing, son?" said the sergeant. "I'm putting it back on," he says, but just then the legs and body fell. That lad, he was in an awful state. At the finish the sergeant belted him, and then he put his arms round him and rocked him till he cried. And when we had to go on again he kept that lad by him and he was still with him when he died. He was a good man, that sergeant. Worth fifty of the officers, and they knew it. Aye, hard times.' He stood up and looked at the slag heap, with its bent, patient, revolving figures. 'A land fit for heroes to live in.' He looked down at Liza and, with an expression half-mocking, half-tender, offered his remaining arm. 'Howay, lass.'

She managed to keep what she was doing from the pancrack. Once, within her hearing, the man from the pancrack came and asked where she was. She was staggering home with a bag of coal underneath her shawl, and was only a few yards away from him when he spoke.

'Liza who?' Mrs Robinson said. 'Eeh, naw, sorry, son. Doesn't ring a bell. Does it with you, Missus?' she called up the street.

160

'"Wright" does he say? Eeh, naw.'

'How about you, sonny?'

Mrs Dobbin's Wilf, eight years old and as fly as a bag of monkeys, put on his best adenoidal expression. 'Eeh, naw.'

The man was about to turn his attention to Liza when Mrs Dobbin's back gate flew open, and Mrs Dobbin appeared.

'Where the devil have you been?' she said. 'I'm waiting for them taties.'

She hauled Liza in through the back door, leaving the young man to meditate on the idiocy of the lower classes, none of whom seemed to know who their neighbours were.

But the pancrack wasn't always so easily avoided. It was Eileen's birthday, and Liza, who had managed to sell two bags of coal, decided to give the kids a treat and bought a punnet of raspberries and a tin of condensed milk for their tea.

They were just sitting down to the feast, when there was a knock at the door. It was the man from the pancrack, and of course there was no hope of keeping him on the doorstep. You had to let them in. The raspberries and condensed milk were on the table, there were red stains round the children's mouths. Guilt was plain for all to see.

'What do you call that?' he said, looking down at the table.

She didn't answer.

'We don't give you money for such as that,' he said.

'Me Mam bought them,' Liza said.

'If she can afford to buy raspberries mebbe she can afford to help you with other things as well.'

'Of course she bloody can't,' she said. 'Me Dad's retired. Takes them all their time to manage.'

The presence of the children did nothing to shut him up.

'Have you heard anything from your husband?' he said.

'No.'

'Has he sent you any money?'

'Not a sausage,' she said.

Oh, and Tom's face.

After he'd gone, Liza sat down and said, 'Finish your teas.' She made herself take a bite of bread and spooned up a mouthful of raspberries, but it was no use.

161

'Look, I'm not hungry,' she said. 'You have the rest.'

She was often 'not hungry'. Sometimes she remembered her mother who always used to say, 'I've had mine', or 'I feel a bit bilious' whenever Liza's Dad asked her where *her* food was. As a child Liza had believed it. Now she understood.

Her mother ranted and raved on about Frank. 'You should never've married him.'

'I was pregnant,' Liza reminded her. 'There wasn't much choice.'

'And what if you were?' Tom Jarrett put in. 'I could've worked for what bit of food the bairn ate.'

'I can't understand you, Liza,' said her mam. 'You played your mouth plenty while he was around. Now he's buggered off and left you, you won't hear a word said against him.'

'He did what he had to do. I'm doing what I have to do.'

Only sometimes, hauling coal along the back alley, she would stop and lean against the wall and remember the jobs he'd forced her to turn down, and then she'd say, 'You really buggered me up, didn't you, Frank? You really buggered me up.' Then she picked up the sack of coal and went on. She refused to give way to bitterness, not out of any sense that it would have been unjustified, but because she knew it would be an extra burden to carry, and there was no room for surplus weight on this trip.

She was given an old pram and used this to carry the coal. By selling a bag here and there she just managed to keep above the bread line. She could be seen in all weathers and in all seasons pushing the pram along the rutted lane that led to the slag heap and then, five or six hours later, with much more difficulty, pushing it back home.

She'd forgotten any claims to good looks she might once have had. Her skirt was replaced by a pair of Frank's old work trousers that she found hanging up behind a cupboard door. She wore Tom's cast-off boots, and a woollen balaclava thick enough to protect her mouth from the wind. People got used to seeing her like this and quickly forgot that she had ever looked different.

Once, pushing a more than usually heavy load back from

the heap, she got stuck at a kerb. Only a few yards further on the kerb was lower, but she'd reached a stage of exhaustion where she could only persist blindly in doing what she was trying to do by the most direct, and hardest, route. There were two men talking on the corner of the street, respectably dressed men, with coats and hats. One of them came across and said, 'Give you a hand, mate.' His voice had the put-on roughness of the upper classes, but Liza was in no mood to quarrel with that.

'Ta,' she said, when the pram was on the pavement.

His jaw dropped. He stepped back and involuntarily raised his hat. *Oh God, he thought I was a fella.* She turned and smiled, but he just stared at her, his hand frozen to the brim of his hat.

When she got home she went to the mirror. At the corners of her eyes and round her mouth, where she screwed up her face against sun and wind, there were white wrinkles. The rest of her face was black.

She sat down at the table and started to laugh, remembering the look of horror on his face. But the laugh got out of control. Her ribs began to hurt, and she was amazed by the dry sobs that erupted from her throat.

When the kids came in from school they found her sitting there with the coal dust on her face, and they were surprised. Generally she got stripped off in the scullery and washed before they came home and their tea was ready for them on the table. Eileen stared at her. She could see the white marks on Liza's face had been left by tears and this disturbed her because she had never in all her life seen her mother cry.

It's all right, Liza thought, as she lay in the big double bed that night, *it's all right as long as you plod on day after day, never thinking where you're going or what you've become. And then something happens and you have to think. Like a pit pony that works all its life underground and when it comes up it's so dazzled it can't see, and so it stumbles along, smelling grass and never seeing it, lost to the light, until finally its eyes are not hurt by darkness at all, but only by the sun, and it starts to long for the pit, for the darkness where it feels safe.*

She cried herself to sleep that night, but then put the incident behind her. She was hardening all the time, becoming tougher, more able to stand up for herself. There were children to protect, in a world that cared no more about them than it did about her.

Tom was a cheerful, active little boy, always in some kind of scrape, but with a centre of darkness in his life, so that sometimes, in the middle of a game, his face would change, would become pinched and thin. His eyes would darken and he would leave the game and go home. But as soon as he saw his mother in the house, washing or sewing by the fire, he would start to smile again.

'What do you want?' she would ask.

'Nothing,' he would reply. 'I just wondered where you were.'

'Well, you can see where I am. I'm here.'

Then he would nod gravely and go back to his game. A few minutes later she would hear his voice shouting and laughing, as if the moment of fear had never been.

Eileen was a plump, stolid little girl, the sort of child teachers are apt to dismiss as unimaginative, though in fact she had rather too much imagination for her own good. She was useless at games, being inclined to puff along, breathing noisily through her mouth, and for all these reasons had a tough time at school. When she was nine she developed erysipelas, which resulted in the loss of most of her hair. When she went back to school, Liza gave her a cotton bonnet to wear and a note for the teacher explaining why it was necessary. Eileen's teacher, who was noted for the strictness of his discipline, made her take it off. The other children burst out laughing and at break Eileen was pursued round the playground by a big crowd shouting, 'Baldy! Baldy!' At dinner time, she ran home and burst into the house, crying with shame. 'You'll have to go down,' Mrs Dobbin said.

'Don't you worry, I'm going!'

Liza set off for the school, and a few minutes later the women of Walker Street stood on their steps and cheered, as Liza, brandishing a broom, chased Mr Lumley the full length of the street.

'I thought it might've been a mistake,' she said afterwards. 'But it wasn't. The only mistake he made was thinking he could get away with it.'

One day Liza, feeling more than usually tired, had decided to stay away from the heap, and get on with her washing instead. There was a knock on the door and she went to answer it, dreading another visit from the means test man. Her hands were bleached white and pleated from their long immersion in soda, her face shiny and open-pored from the steam. She brushed her hair back from her eyes and opened the door.

The man standing there wore the workhouse uniform, and for one terrible moment she thought they'd come for her and the kids, and started to close the door.

'Mrs Wright?' he said.

'Yes.' She peered round the closing door.

'We've got your husband,' he said. 'In the infirmary.'

There was time only to wrap the old black shawl around her shoulders, which with its cindery smell of coal-dust seemed to shroud her in the years of work and misery she'd lived through since he'd gone.

The sun was setting behind the workhouse as she approached, so that as she walked towards it she walked also towards its shadow, which came out to meet her and enveloped her in cold.

She knew as soon as she saw the screens round the bed.

'Half an hour ago,' she was told. 'After a nice bowl of soup.'

She sat down heavily beside the bed.

'He spoke about you before he died.'

'How long had he been here?'

'Just since last night. They found him collapsed outside the gate. It was only this morning he come round enough to tell us who he was.'

So he'd been trying to get home, trying to get back to her, only his legs had failed him on the last mile.

She looked towards the bed and the attendant went out and pulled the curtains across behind her.

He lay stretched out, his head raised on pillows, with the light from the frosted glass window behind him casting deep shadows over his face. Only his arms, lying bare on the coverlet, were in full light. She reached out and touched his hand, searching for the fast fading warmth that was still detectable there. The hand felt different from the hand she had known. There was a hard ridge of callouses across the palm and, when she looked more closely, she saw the tip of the index finger was missing.

The tears might have come then, but she controlled herself. He looked so remote in death. She was aware of the mystery, the gulf that divides one human being from another, the gulf that no amount of love or longing can cross, that is absolute, final.

Her mouth was dry. She licked her lips and looked around at the stone floor, the frosted glass, the green curtains that surrounded the bed and stained the light green. When she moved her hands they looked like small creatures scurrying across the ocean floor.

He had been coming back to her. She held onto that, which was fact and not dream, a fact that not even this final silence could destroy.

Far away there was a murmur of voices. A trolley clanked and rumbled across a stone floor.

There was a trolley on the other side of the bed, with a big yellow cake of soap, water, bandages and, side by side in a small saucer, two pennies. Then Liza knew what she had to do.

She approached the bed. Close to, his skin looked transparent, stretched so tightly over the bones of nose and cheek, that he had, even in death, a surprised, slightly reproving look.

She stripped back the sheets. He wore only a cotton shift, tinged yellow with age and fastened with tapes at the back. She unfastened them and pulled the shift away from his body. His skin was yellow-white like ivory, except for the dark hair between his breasts and in his groin. This hair curled so vigorously that it seemed to have nothing to do with the cold, translucent flesh from which it sprang.

She began to wash him, cleaning inside his mouth, his eyes, his nostrils. She lifted, sponged and dried each heavy limb. She wiped away the urine and faeces that had leaked from his dying

166

from his dying body. She cradled his feet, one by one, in her hands.

Finally, she closed his eyelids and weighed them down with pennies. It was time to go.

'Goodbye, Frank,' she said, and her tongue felt big and unused, as if the silence that bound the two of them together had lasted not minutes but years.

She looked back at him from the gap between the curtains. So bad was the light coming in from the fast dying day beyond the window that the pennies looked like black holes in his face. Letting the curtain fall, she left him there.

She walked home through the centre of the town, the longest way, but she needed time to prepare herself to meet the children. Day was ebbing in a thin, acid light that couldn't compete with the multi-coloured lights of shop windows, though it etched the faces of the shoppers, making them look thinner and more worried than perhaps they were. Liza carried her pain home with her, carefully, as if it might spill. A tram rattled past and jetted sparks into the dusk. Liza stood on the kerb, one of a crowd of people waiting to cross the road.

Suddenly she started to cry and the tears, once started, streamed down her thin face without stopping. She was crying not for herself but for Frank. It seemed the people hurrying past denied him: his life, his death, the terrible stone-breaking struggle of his final years. She wanted to shout his name, to silence the roar of traffic, so the people who ignored and jostled her would have to stop and listen. She needed words powerful enough to ignite the silence that was densely packed in her, a voice that, fanned by the bellows of her lungs, would stream out of her mouth like a living torch.

The crowd, seeing a gap in the traffic, surged forward, carrying her along with it, and in the struggle to keep her feet she stopped crying, though her eyes still glittered with a hard, brilliant, angry light and her forehead jutted out and gleamed as if it were made of some substance more durable than bone. For one second the chance flare of headlamps caught her and she stood out from the surrounding darkness. Then the crowd surged forward again and she disappeared into the hurrying, anonymous grey.

9

'So who's with your Mam now?' Liza asked.

'Oh, she goes round to my sister's to sleep, but she's on her own during the day.' Stephen shrugged. 'That's the way she wants it.'

'It is better to stay put, you know, if you can. There's only one way to get used to an empty house and that's to stop in it.'

'I'll be back there at the weekend.'

'I'm glad you come round. I was wondering what'd happened to you.'

Stephen looked at the clock and realized how long he'd been talking. 'I ought to go,' he said. 'You'll be wanting your tea.'

'No hurry.'

The fire burned grey in a shaft of late afternoon sunlight. No sound but the ticking of the clock, and the soft, almost furtive, rustling of Nelson's wings.

'And you had him cremated?'

'Yes. Apparently that's what he wanted.'

'I don't know what they'll do with me. Put me on top of Frank, I expect.' She laughed. 'See if we get on any better dead than we did living.'

Death's different for her, he thought. *So close, so long expected, she doesn't feel the fear I feel. The fear he must have felt.*

He saw his father in the perspective of the generations, and realized, for the first time, that he'd died young.

'You know, it isn't his death that hurts,' he said. 'It's the way he was made to feel *useless* for so long before he died. I don't forgive this country for that.'

'No,' she said, and a flash of recognition passed between

them. 'Neither did I. I was very bitter . . . Oh, for a long time after Frank died. Not for myself. For him.'

Stephen waited for her to go on. She opened and closed her mouth several times, before eventually she began to speak.

'When we were first married we lived on the coast, and he worked at the steel works. But of course it'd been a fishing village for centuries before that, and most of the local legends were about the sea. The old wife next door told me a story about some fishermen who went fishing and caught a man in their nets. A young man. Naked. But although they'd pulled him up from the depths he wasn't drowned. They brought him back to the village and they locked him up in a little room behind the church, and this room had bars on the windows and bolts on the doors, and they tried to make him say the Creed. But he wouldn't speak. Or couldn't speak. He wasn't a foreigner – he didn't seem to have any language at all. When they couldn't make him say the Creed, they tortured him, with branding irons and knives. Then one night he escaped, he crawled back down the hill and into the sea. They were all running into the waves after him, but just as they got their hands on him, he changed. He was a silkie, and as soon as the salt water touched him, he turned back into a seal and swam away.'

'That's a terrible story.'

'Yes, isn't it? But he escaped. He didn't come back.'

Stephen put a hand to his throat and coughed.

'I'll get some coal in,' he said.

'It's all wet. That daft bugger left the coalhouse door open.'

'Well, it won't be wet if I dig for it, will it?'

He coaxed a smile out of her.

'I won't be a minute,' he said.

Outside in the yard, he looked at the boarded-up windows of neighbouring houses. The occupants were dead or scattered, but he could have named them all, for in the months he'd been coming to see Liza she'd talked about them often, weaving their stories in and out of her own.

He filled the bucket with coal and went back inside the

house. Coming in from the needle-sharp brightness of the day, he was struck by the darkness and stuffiness of the room.

'You know you ought to get out,' he said.

'Out?' She looked startled.

'Yes. I could take you. We could go in the car.'

He could see her mind feeling its way round the idea.

'I don't know,' she said. 'I wouldn't know anywhere, would I?'

'Course you would. The house you were born in's still standing, you know.'

'Is it?'

'Yes. That's one of the streets where they knocked down one end and left the other.'

'Like Hitler.'

'Yes,' he laughed. 'Like Hitler.'

Silence.

He prompted gently, 'You will come?'

'I'll think about it.'

He saw that he'd gone as far as he could go on this occasion and turned his attention to the fire.

Liza, lying on the bed, though outside the coverlet, watched him work. She thought again how like Tom he was, though when she'd shown him her photograph of Tom in uniform he hadn't seemed to notice any resemblance, and she'd feared to prompt him in case this cherished discovery should turn out to be a delusion. The resemblance had struck her, no, more than struck, had startled her to the depths of her being when he'd first come to see her. Of course you were anxious for resemblances, but it was years since she'd seen one. Now she looked at Stephen and thought that Tom might have turned out like this.

Stephen turned round and smiled, and her heart bumped against her ribs, the resemblance was momentarily so strong.

He said, 'There you are. That ought to be all right now.'

He stood on the doorstep, disconcerted by the locked door and wondering whether he could have mistaken the day. But then a woman's voice called, 'Stephen!' and he saw his sister

170

hurrying along the pavement, a plastic bag stuffed with shopping in each hand.

'I was expecting you a bit later,' she said. 'I thought you'd come on from work.'

'I did. We close at four on Fridays.'

They smiled at each other and, a little self-consciously, embraced. He was aware of her breasts pressing against him and thought how extraordinary it was that Christine should have turned into this plump, matronly, capable woman. As a child she'd been skinny. As a girl she'd been so thin her headmistress had suspected anorexia.

'Anorexia!' Walter had spluttered when he understood what it was. 'They want to get themselves round here and watch her tuck in.'

'Mam went off all right, did she?'

'Yes,' Christine laughed. 'Just about. She started getting the willies at the last minute, but Mike said, "Mam. You're going." So that was that.'

'It'll do her good.'

'It's what she's been needing for a long time. And she'll get out and about, you know. Auntie Mavis'll see to that. She's not one for stopping in.' She unlocked the front door. 'Anyway, come in. I'll put the kettle on.'

Stephen sat down. He felt uneasy, almost guilty, as if they were children again and had somehow usurped their parents' roles: himself in his father's armchair by the fire, Christine in the kitchen making tea.

'She'll be all right once she's there. They'll look after her.'

They were here to sort out their father's clothes. Margaret had been intending to do this ever since the funeral, but each time she attempted it her courage failed. Finally she'd agreed to stay with her sister until Stephen and Christine had finished the job.

The back bedroom was freezing. The bed, made up under its white coverlet, looked very big and blank in the middle of the room.

'She's still sleeping in the front,' said Christine. 'She won't come back in here.'

'I don't blame her,' said Stephen, remembering his night in that bed.

They were uneasy, both of them. Stephen remembered an incident from their childhood. They'd come into this room while their parents were out at the pictures and on top of the wardrobe they'd found their father's secret condom store. They giggled over the packet, and speculated, and then Christine'd blushed suddenly, and told him to put it back. Evidently their father was aware of the disturbance, fingerprints in the dust perhaps, because the next time Stephen looked there was nothing there.

'Well,' said Christine. 'I'll start on the wardrobe. You have a go at the drawers.'

They worked in silence. Christine, who was allergic to house mites, sneezed now and then as she sorted through the clothes.

'You know this suit's got a lot of wear in it,' she said.

'Of course it has. When did he ever wear a suit?'

'It's a shame to throw it out. You ought to try it on.'

Stephen looked up. She was holding a dark grey jacket against herself, fingering the cloth.

'Wouldn't fit. I'm taller than he was.'

'Oh, I don't know.'

'OK. Put it on the bed. I'll try it on later.'

Their breath congealed on the air. It must be colder in this room than it was outside, and yet neither of them suggested bringing the electric fire upstairs. They needed to keep things as they were, to do as little violence as possible to the white silence of this room.

'How you doing?' Christine asked, a little while later.

'Winning. I think.'

Stephen was beginning to wish he'd opted for the wardrobe. The top drawer was still full of the bits and pieces he'd seen on his last visit. He wasn't ruthless enough to bundle them together and dump them in the bin, and so, slowly and meticulously, he sorted through them.

'Do you know, I get on better with Mam now than I've ever done,' said Christine.

Stephen looked surprised. 'I never realized you didn't get on with her.'

'No. It was always you and Dad, wasn't it? On the surface.'

'We never rowed.'

'It might've been better if you had.'

The next two drawers were much easier: underwear and sweaters. Underwear couldn't be given to anybody, so that went in the bag; the sweaters were all in good condition, so they went on the bed.

'The kids help. Which is funny because to begin with that was one of the things we rowed about. As soon as I started going steady, there was me Mam: bootees in her eyes. Oh, and I thought, *No way. I'm not getting saddled with that.* "Oh," she says. "You'll change your mind." She seemed as if she couldn't grasp it. That actually you might not want one. Oh, she tried, she used to say, "It's your business. You know your own mind." And I used to say, "That's *right*!" But the trouble is, it *is* their business, in a way, and when I seemed not to want it, it was like slapping her in the face. It was like I was turning me back on her whole life. Because that was her life wasn't it, you and me, and Dad, and the house. It was only after Ian was on the way that we really started talking to each other again. And even then not much. I never wanted her with me when I was in labour. The only person I could bear near me was Mike. But it's a funny thing, labour. Your Mam's there whether she's there or not. And then afterwards we got a lot closer. When you're bringing up kids you realize . . .' She glanced sideways at Stephen. 'You realize education isn't everything.'

'I never thought it was.' A long silence. 'You're lucky. You could get back to them through the kids. I can't.'

'She hasn't given up hope of you getting married yet.'

'She will.'

'Is there anybody . . .?' She was blushing. 'Anybody special?'

'You mean a girl?'

'*No.*'

'Yes,' he said, looking up from the drawer. 'Yes, there is.'

'Good.'

173

They smiled at each other.

'He's in America at the moment. But perhaps we could all get together and have a drink when he comes back?'

'Yeah. That'd be nice.'

A few minutes later she said, 'Well, that's that then. I'll go and get the dinner on. We might as well have it here, mightn't we? Mike won't be back yet.'

'I've got a bottle of wine in the car.'

She hesitated. 'Well, yes, why not? It's not the world's most cheerful job.'

No, it wasn't, he thought. Sifting through the past, trying to decide which things served a useful purpose still, which were worn out or useless. Simpler by far to throw the whole lot away, to make a clean sweep and start again with all the surfaces blank. But to do that would be to show a lack of respect for the dead, or an arrogance about the capacity of the living to create from scratch, and sustain, a civilized life. So you went on, testing the worth of what was left, though often it seemed like the contents of this drawer: the random accumulation of a life lived unreflectingly.

On the bed was his father's suit. He'd have to try it on sooner or later. Neither Christine nor his mother would rest till he did. He slipped the jacket on, expecting to tense his shoulders and feel constricted. Instead, there was almost too much room. Refusing to believe what his skin told him, he walked across to the mirror. The jacket was too long: the sleeves drooped down over his wrists.

Well, at least there was no doubt that he couldn't wear it. He took it off and laid it carefully on the bed. He could have sworn his father was three or four inches shorter than he was. It disturbed him that his perception of his father, literally what he saw when he looked at the man, should have been so quietly and persistently and devastatingly wrong. He had seen a small man. Only the evidence of this cloth, drooping over his wrists, could have made him doubt that the perception and the reality were one.

174

10

Liza fought hard to preserve something good in Tom's memories of his father. It wasn't easy, because he'd absorbed a lot of his grandmother's bitterness. Whenever Frank was mentioned he would shake his head, as if he'd've liked to erase his father, not merely from the present, but from the past as well.

After the funeral, Liza let Tom lead her away, pretending to lean on his arm. As they were going home she said, shyly, 'You know, Tom, your Dad was never meant for a labourer. He hadn't the strength for it. He was meant for a scholar.'

Tom shook his head, but she thought he seemed curious and that evening she gave him his father's encyclopaedias, which she'd kept wrapped up against the damp. She told Tom how Frank would always wash his hands and scrub his finger-nails before he opened a book. She half expected to see Tom do the same, but no. He held the books gently, but she thought it was her feelings he was being gentle with. After a while, seeing the encyclopaedias remained unopened, she put them back in the cupboard with Frank's paintbrushes and his stringless violin.

Tom never had to be asked to do things for his mother. While he was still at school he came and helped her back from the heap with the pram. They got used to seeing him, the fair, close-cropped head bobbing along the lane with something purposeful, almost dogged, in the movement that didn't belong with his age, but sprang from his anxious, strained determination to be the man his mother needed, to make up to her for the absence of his father.

'There's your lad, Liza,' the others would say, and she would start pushing the pram down the path to meet him.

'Did you have a good day at school?' she always asked when they met.

'Naw.'

The reply was so unvarying Liza sometimes wondered why she asked. Tom did very badly at school. More than once Liza had to go down to the teacher, when he'd been caned for not understanding. Tom, himself, never complained. He seemed to know, instinctively, that the world of school and books was not *his* world.

One thing Tom did get from his father, and that was a way with girls. *They* didn't seem to mind that he was slow and gentle and didn't talk much. The other lads teased him about his success, speculating loudly on the reasons for it. 'Eleven inches?' 'Brass balls?' Tom smiled.

Liza was delighted when girls came to the house after him, though she always pretended to disapprove.

'I don't know,' she said. 'When I was a lass it was the lads did the courting. You didn't use to go banging on their doors.'

'You're old-fashioned, Mam.'

'Aye, and glad of it.'

He picked her up and swung her round, to show he could.

'Mothers are supposed to be jealous of their sons,' he said.

'Are they?' asked Liza, innocently. 'I never heard that. All I want is for you to find a nice lass and settle down. The day you walk through that door and say, "Here she is, Mam," I'll be over the moon.'

'She means it, you know,' said Eileen. 'She's got a big can of peaches stuck at the back of that cupboard. That's not for us, you know. That's for her daughter-in-law.'

'Eeh,' said Tom. 'Pushing a poor young lad out of his home. With down on his chin.'

Liza's fingers rasped along his jawbone. '*Down*,' she said.

Tom worked for a year after leaving school, then got the sack. The firm took on another fourteen-year-old boy who could be paid the same pittance he'd been paid.

176

'You'll find another soon enough,' said Liza, pretending a confidence she didn't feel.

In fact there were no jobs, and she had to watch him kick his heels on street corners or wear out his shoe-leather in the hopeless search for work. He had to go to the dole school, mornings one week, afternoons the next, but so many of the tasks were self-evidently useless that it became a greater humiliation to Tom than school had ever been.

One week they decided to teach the boys basic sewing.

'That'll come in handy,' said Liza. 'You want to think: you mightn't always have a woman to do it for you.'

But Tom wasn't convinced. He was angrier that night than she'd ever seen him.

The following afternoon Tom came home earlier than usual. Liza was at the kitchen sink getting washed after her return from the heap. She was blind with soap and felt rather than saw him come in. His silence made her nervous.

'Tom? Is that you?'

'No, it's the milkman,' he said, and grabbed her round the waist.

'Daft bugger!'

She groped for the towel and felt him hand it to her.

'What's the matter?' she said.

He stood there with a look on his face as if he pitied her. It made her afraid.

'Mam,' he said, 'I've joined up.'

Liza felt the room recede. 'Well,' she said breathlessly, and got hold of the cooker for support.

'I'm fed up of the dole school. I'm fed up of depending on you, and if our Eileen gets a job when she leaves school they'll expect me to live off her as well.' He paused, and when he spoke again his voice cracked. 'That's no life for a *man*.'

It seemed strange to her to hear him use that word, standing there so raw and gawky with a moustache that was no more than a shadow on his lip. But she could hear how the word was torn out of him.

'You do what you think best, son,' she said.

She turned away, emptied the bowl, folded the flannel and

177

started to wash the sink. His eyes were on her back all this time.

'If it came to a war I'd be called up anyway.'

'Oh, yes.' She laughed. 'They'd find a use for you then.'

He went into the living-room and a few minutes later she heard him talking and laughing with Eileen.

Liza had been hesitating over whether to have carrots as well as potatoes in the stew, but now she thought: *Bugger it. It's not every day your son joins up*, and tipped in carrots and potatoes and peas as well.

Tom came to see her in his uniform, and she stroked his shoulders and didn't cry. After he'd gone she and Eileen crept round the house, too stunned with misery to speak.

In January 1940 Liza's mother arrived to live with her. She'd been a widow for three years and was finding it difficult to manage on her own. She chose Liza, rather than one of her other daughters, because Liza's husband was dead. In Liza's house, Louise might still hope to rule.

Her legs were so badly ulcerated there was no question of her managing the stairs. Liza and Eileen carried a bed downstairs and put it under the window in the living-room. Here Louise could keep an eye on what was happening in the street, and still be within shouting distance of Liza in the kitchen.

It was not, after the first few hours, a happy arrangement.

Liza felt that Louise should show some affection for Eileen, who was the only girl among the twenty-two grandchildren so far born. In fact, Louise disliked Eileen and made no effort to hide it. This reawakened Liza's memories of her own childhood.

Eileen did her best. Coming in from work, she would go straight up to Louise and kiss her. Or try to.

'Wash that muck off your face before you come near me.'

'It's not muck. It's lipstick.'

'Painted whore,' said Louise.

'I wish I was. I'd make a damned sight more at it than I make washing-up.'

'*Liza!*'

'You'd better go in, Mam,' said Eileen. 'She wants to tell you what a mess you made of bringing me up.'

After dinner Louise slept, though always, as Eileen said, with one eye open, like a cat. They washed-up quietly, so as not to disturb her.

'You let her get you down, Mam.'

'One thing she could always do.'

'You want to stand up to her more.'

'Aw, it's easy said. She ruled us with a rod of iron, and if you didn't just jump to do what you were told, she cracked you over the head with her crutch. I've had many a bruise off that.' Aye, and many a squirt of milk in the eye, but you couldn't tell Eileen that. 'She's old. We'll be old ourselves one day.'

'Well, I hope you don't turn into a bloody old witch like that.'

Eileen began to avoid her grandmother by staying out late every night, though she always managed to get home when the sirens went.

'You should've stopped in the air-raid shelter over there,' said Liza. 'There'd've been room.'

'You'd've worried yourself sick.'

'I'd've been a damn sight more worried if I'd known you were running through it!'

But nothing you said made any impression on Eileen.

'That girl hasn't the sense she was born with,' said Louise.

'She's only thinking of me.'

'She doesn't *think* at all.'

The raids became more frequent. Louise's legs were too bad for her to be moved so Liza stayed with her in the house. Eileen was sent to the shelter, though she protested at having to leave her mother and grandmother in the house.

'Let me stop with you, Mam. Or you go in the shelter and I'll stop with her.'

'You can both bugger off,' said Louise. 'I can stop on me own.'

But Liza was firm. Eileen went; she stayed. She missed the cheerfulness of the shelters, the teasing that went on, Mr and Mrs Bower with their box of 'keepsakes' that everybody knew was money.

'By heck, you mean to take that with you, don't you?' said Mrs Dobbin.

You could tell they were offended, they took to staying in the house after that.

'Why, I meant nothing by it,' said Mrs Dobbin.

She was a great favourite in the shelter with her flasks of soup and tea and her Victory jigsaw that never got any nearer completion.

'God help us if that's how long it takes,' said Harry. 'The kids'll happen live to see it.'

Louise required a lot of nursing. Her legs were so bad now that her bandages had to be changed every day. When she saw Liza coming with the bowl and the clean bandages she would go white. But she made no sound, just lay there with her black, burning eyes and her clenched mouth that had never – in sickness, in weariness, in childbirth, in pain, in grief – had never let out a single cry. Liza wrapped the bandages and held her own face rigid, because not the least sign of disgust must show, though the smell of rotten flesh churned her guts. She wished more than anything that her mother would cry out. She wanted to tug the bandages off the black skin. She never did, of course, but unpicked the mattery cotton as delicately as if it had been the finest embroidery, feeling every twinge of pain in her own flesh. And yet the urge to cause pain, to do something that would break that clenched, stoic, iron will was there. She couldn't hide it from herself.

Liza had cleared out and whitewashed the cupboard under the stairs intending to use this as a shelter, but after the first few nights Louise refused to leave her bed. They sat together in the darkness, Louise in bed, Liza in the cupboard, while overhead the bombers droned and the air shook and flakes of whitewash from the ceiling drifted down and lay on Liza's head, so that in the morning, when they could see each other clearly again, it was Liza who looked old.

At first Liza could think of nothing but the bombs. Walker Street was close to several steel works, all now converted to the production of armaments, and the area was an important target. Liza listened for the whine and told herself again and

180

again that you don't hear the one that kills you, though how the bloody hell could anybody know that, she wondered, since nobody came back to tell.

Later, as fear diminished or became habitual, Liza came out of the cupboard and sat by the fire, which they kept burning as late as possible in order to have a little light. The flames flickered and played tricks with their faces. In Louise's face a skull could be seen, rising closer to the surface night by night. Liza's face, too, was transformed by the flames, seeming, sometimes, in the warm steady glow, to be a child again, but then a ridge of cinders would crash and in the blue bleakness of the flare a woman sat, as stripped of youth and beauty as her mother was, and whenever this happened each was aware of resemblances they didn't see by daylight, or welcome now.

On one of these nights when the surface truths of skin and mind were being stripped away, Liza heard herself ask her mother, 'You never loved me, did you?'

There was no animosity in her voice, or she was aware of none. Though when she'd finished speaking she picked up the poker and battered the black crust of cinder till it collapsed in the heart of the fire, and new flames leapt up.

Louise struggled to sit up in bed, while outside a long whine began, threatening less real forms of pain and loss. '*What* did you say?'

'I said, "You never loved me, did you?"' Liza turned away. 'Water under the bridge. It doesn't matter now.'

'It matters enough to bloody say it.'

'I suppose I just want to get things straight.'

Louise lay back against the pillows. 'It's me should be getting things straight, not you. You've half your life ahead of you yet.'

There was a long silence. Then Louise picked up a strand of long, black hair and held it across her mouth, like a veil. It was a young girl's gesture, and Liza had never seen Louise do anything like it before.

'No,' she said, in a new, uncertain voice. 'I don't suppose I did love you. I tried . . .'

Liza waited. 'And . . .'

'Then life caught up with me and I stopped trying.' The voice was hard and decided again.

'Oh, well, that's that then.' Liza felt raw, skinned alive, though for some reason the pain made her think not of herself but of her own children, of the way Eileen had clung to her when she was small. 'It's nice to know where you stand,' she said.

'You mean you'd rather I'd lied to you?'

'Of course I don't.'

'Yes, you do. I'm too old, Liza. You get past everything but the truth.'

They listened to the darkness outside, to its minute breaths and rustles. Then another whine started, and each unconsciously held her breath, waiting for the thud.

'Close,' said Louise.

'Wellington Street.'

'They've hit everything but the bloody steelworks. You know them new bungalows by the aerodrome? They were giving them away before the war. Harriet says there's not one been touched. I wish now I'd gone in for one.'

'There's air-raids every night there.'

'There's air-raids every night here. They'll be worth a fortune after the war, and I wouldn't have had to go upstairs with me legs.' She lay for a while in silence with her eyes closed. 'You never went hungry.'

'I never said I did.'

'None of you did. The first time you knew hunger, the first time you didn't have a decent pair of shoes on your feet was when you married *him*. It used to break your father's heart seeing you come up the street. Lads' boots on, wore out, thin as a rake, all them years never a decent coat on your back. It *hurt* your father seeing you like that.'

'I know it did.'

'You never had any of that. You were fed, you had shoes. If I went without meself I made sure you got.'

'That's not what I'm talking about, Mam.'

'Oh, I know what you're talking about, Liza. I'm not stupid. Here, give us me bag.'

182

Liza passed it across the bed to her.

'There,' said Louise. 'That was me when I was sixteen.'

Liza held the photograph close to the flames. A serious, dark-haired girl, holding some kind of flower, lips slightly parted, eyes staring into the camera with a kind of grave sweetness.

'I was sixteen when I was married. He saw me dancing, he was thirty-six and I thought the sun rose and set on him. I wouldn't listen to a word anybody said against him. I found out different, I found out they were right, but there was nothing I could do. I had four children by the time I was twenty, and then the diphtheria came and I lost them all in a week. All I can remember is walking behind the coffins to the grave and coming back home and sitting up with the next one, and then that one died and the next one died. Harriet was born three weeks later. She doesn't belong to your father. She was to me first husband.

'I was sat feeding her, dazed, you know, and all of a sudden the door opened and in walked this woman. "Get out, you whore," she says. "I'm his wife." I don't know why I believed her, but I did. When he come in from work I says to him, "Is it true?" Oh, and the look on his face, he didn't know what to say. I just picked up the bairn and walked out. Didn't take a change of clothes or anything, and I left me wedding ring on the table. Got home, me Mam took one look at me. "What do you want?" she says. Well, you know. Screaming brat, no wedding ring, me brothers were getting on in the world. She says, "I think you were too hasty, Louise. You should've stopped and seen what he'd do." But I couldn't go on like that. I was too proud. Anyway, they packed me off up here, there was supposed to be an auntie on Cannon Street, but they never said how long it'd been since they heard from her. When I got here nobody even knew the name. Anyway, after that things went from bad to worse. I was stood outside this pub on Cannon Street waiting for a man to come out, because he'd said he could find me cheap lodgings, when along comes your Dad and he says, "What's a young lady like you doing here?" I says, "I'm waiting for . . ." and I told him the name,

183

and I says, "He's going to find me cheap lodgings." "Oh," says your Dad. "Is he? I know what kind of lodgings them'll be. You come along with me." And he took me to a woman that ran a corner shop in Calthorpe Street, and he says, "You'll be all right here." Anyway she give me a bed and the next day I got a job scrubbing at the infirmary. It wasn't until your Dad and me were married that it hit me. I hadn't had time to grieve for them bairns or anything. But my God, when it did hit me it hit me hard. I used to think there were men coming to take Harriet away. I didn't know who they were, I didn't know anything about them, but I knew they were coming. And I used to shove her out of sight anywhere I could. In the blanket box, under the sink, in the coal hole. I even put her in the midden. Your Dad was always running back from work and dragging her out of something. It was a wonder I didn't suffocate her, because I used to pile the blankets on top of her. He was patience itself, your Dad. And do you know, Liza, when I married him I didn't love him. I was in no state to love anybody. But when I saw how good he was to that bairn *then* I loved him. And then Edward come along, and somehow he seemed to be the end of all that darkness. I idolized him. And then you, and I suppose I should've felt the same about you. But I didn't. Oh, I tried, I really tried. They kept giving you to me and I kept saying, "No, put her where I can see her, put her in the drawer." I didn't want to hold you. Oh, you were fed, you were kept clean, when you were bad I sat up with you, but no, I didn't love you, not in the way you mean love.'

Louise was crying by the time she'd finished. She looked down at the photograph of her younger self and ran her fingers across it. Then she looked up at Liza and said simply, 'I don't know why.'

Liza felt herself picked up and swung around till she had no clear sensations left except the smell of warm khaki. He seemed to have grown, which was impossible: he'd surely been fully grown when he left. It must be just she'd forgotten how tall he was.

'Put me down, you daft bugger,' she said.

'There you are, you see, that's all the welcome I get.' He walked across to the bed and knelt down beside it. 'Hello, Gran,' he said, and leaned across to kiss her.

Louise held onto his shoulders, her fingers felt the familiar cloth. 'Hello, Eddie,' she said. 'Hello, my son.'

Liza opened her mouth to speak, but a glance from Tom silenced her.

'How you doing?' he asked.

Louise started to cry. 'Not very well. You've been gone such a long time.'

Liza went everywhere with him during the day, hanging onto his arm like a young girl. When people stopped them in the street and asked, 'How long has he got?' or 'When are you going back?' she said, 'Oh, he doesn't want to think about that yet! Good heavens.'

She lived in the present. When she woke up she thought of what she would give him for his breakfast, of what they would do that morning; never of the end of his leave, scarcely even of the end of a day. The end would come and she knew it. But she would not give it power by naming it or even thinking of it. So, second by second, his leave passed.

He had ten days. There was an air-raid every night: they sat under the table in the living-room and told each other stories. 'You know Jim Wheeler?' Liza said. 'Well, he's an air-raid warden now. Oh and you should see him, he doesn't half fancy himself. He's fighting the bloody war single-handed if you listen to him. But anyway, the other week they were coming out of the shelter and there he was on his hands and knees with his backside in the air, sniffing the railings. "Keep back!" he says, "It might be gas." "I don't know about gas," says Harry Dobbin, "but our dog had a piss there a bit back." He didn't know where to look.'

Once, when the windows rattled more sharply than usual, Tom and Eileen pulled Louise's bed further into the centre of the room. 'I don't know, Mam,' said Tom. 'I've seen more action here in a week than I've seen in six months back there.'

One night Tom unearthed a game of snakes and ladders

from his bedroom and they all joined in the game, he and Eileen squabbling like a pair of kids over whose turn it was to throw the dice. 'Six!' Eileen shouted, banging the board, and then they heard it: the long scream, and nobody said, *That's close* because there wasn't time. There was a thud that jolted the brain against the walls of the skull, and then the crack of breaking glass, and silence. Liza opened her eyes to find herself lying on the floor with her cheekbone pressed hard against the leg of a chair. She tried to speak, but there was dust in her mouth.

At least she could move. Slowly, she worked out where her arms and legs were.

'Mam?'

'Mam?'

Eileen's voice, then Tom's.

She managed to sit up. 'I'm all right. What about your Gran?'

Louise was shaking fragments of glass from her shawl. 'The buggers,' she was saying. 'The buggers. The bloody bleeding sods.'

'Hey up, Gran, I thought you didn't swear,' said Tom, crawling across to her.

'I've been provoked.'

Liza's voice came and went with shock. She opened her mouth now and found she couldn't speak at all, but Louise was as clear as a bell.

In the street outside there were sounds, voices, heavy boots slurring over cobbles.

'Who's in there?' somebody asked.

'We are!' Eileen yelled.

They heard Mrs Dobbin's voice, cracked and yelping with fear. 'Liza Wright. Her mother and the two kids. Her son's home on leave.'

'Poor bugger! He'll be glad to get back.'

'If he's alive, he will.'

'They can't hear us,' said Eileen.

'They'll hear me,' said Louise and, lifting up her voice, she roared, 'Get us out of here!'

The strange thing was that while they waited for the men to free them she never once called Tom 'Eddie'. He was always Tom.

'It hasn't half cleared her head,' said Eileen.

Liza lay in the darkness, aware for the first time of a pain in her leg. 'Do you know, I think I've busted me ankle,' she said. The words stuck in her throat. She hunted round for spit to clear the dust, but there wasn't any.

All around them the silence boomed and roared with the memory of the bomb. It was a relief when the rescuers smashed what was left of a window, and they heard the tinkle of falling glass.

Suddenly the room was full of people. You felt them in the darkness.

'Where's the old lady?' a voice asked.

'I've got her,' said Tom.

A stranger's hands started prodding Liza.

'It's just my ankle,' she said.

'You don't know how lucky you are. Howay.'

She felt herself lifted up. Her face was pressed against the rough serge of a jacket, and she heard his boots crunch on splintered glass as he carried her outside. There was Mrs Dobbin, her mouth a round, dark O in the puddingy white of her face. 'You all right?' she said. 'You can put me down now,' said Liza. She knew from the greasy feeling of the pavement under her bare toes that it'd been raining. Mrs Dobbin wrapped a blanket round her.

'It fell up there,' she said, pointing.

The light had thinned sufficiently for them to see the cloud of dust that hung over the end of the street. The silence was what you noticed. Liza looked at the shattered houses and saw the patterns of the wallpaper in the bedrooms, the beds where sheets and coverlets had been pushed back, a lavatory with the door ripped off and the stairs leading up. It felt indecent, somehow, as if you were prying into the neighbours' business. At the same time she remembered the dolls' house she'd had as a child: you lifted the front off and there were all the rooms, with tiny furniture and pictures on the wall.

187

They peered into the semi-darkness, afraid of what they might see. Suddenly, there was a sound of footsteps, running, and then, staggering towards them out of the dust, came Mrs Bower. Her hair, which she kept so neatly curled, stood up in shock waves of dust and blood. One wrinkled dug had escaped through a rent in her nightdress and swung from side to side as she ran. She was trying to say something, but no sound came out. 'Howay, honey,' Tom said, and folded her in his arms.

They found Mr Bower under a pile of rubble. His head looked quite peaceful, still lying on the pillow where he'd slept. But of his body and the box of 'keepsakes' that had meant so much to him, there was no sign.

Walker Street got off lightly: all the other houses destroyed were empty. Stunned people came and looked at the wreckage, moving around the fallen timbers like ghosts or scavenging in a haphazard way for their possessions, but at least, with the exception of Mr Bower, there were no dead to mourn.

The rest of Tom's leave was spent helping to clear up. With so much rush and confusion Liza had no time to dread his going. Only at the station she thought: *This may be the last time I see him.*

As the train pulled away, she wrenched herself out of Eileen's grasp and ran along beside it. On the other side of the glass were khaki shadows, thin as reflections in water. One of them leaned forward and pressed his hand against the glass. Then a cloud of smoke and steam blew across the platform and hid him from her sight.

Liza and Eileen moved in with Mrs Dobbin until their own house was repaired. Louise went to live with Harriet. She grumbled a lot about this, but in fact her nightly fights with Harriet's husband increased her zest for life. When Liza went to see them she found her sitting up in bed, looking young and strong. Harriet seemed rather subdued.

One night that winter Liza was walking home from the corner shop when Maggie Dobbin came rushing up to her.

'Mrs Wright! I've just seen Tom.'

188

'Where?' asked Liza. She knew he was not due home on leave.
'At the pictures. On the *Pathé News*. I'm sure it was him.'

The next night, and every other night that week, Liza went to the pictures. The first film was a musical, girls kicking their legs up and down in time with the beat, all lying on their backs in the shape of huge daisies. She didn't see any of it. Then the cock crew and a clipped, rousing voice began to speak. She gripped the back of the seat in front, leaning forward so that she would miss nothing. A group of young men were getting ready to go on board ship, and five of them were photographed on the gangplank, with bundles on their backs. They were all smiling, and jostling each other a bit to make sure they got their faces in the picture. That one, two from the back, leaning over the shoulder of the man in front. Was that Tom? It was impossible to tell. The smile was his, but the eyes were in shadow, and before you could be sure the young men had turned and walked up the gangway and were gone.

She sat through the patriotic film that followed, and then went home and dreamed of young men whose faces dissolved into dots and shadows.

A week later she heard that he was dead.

11

This would be Stephen's first weekend in his own flat for a long time. He told himself he was looking forward to it, but in fact he rather dreaded it. He'd grown used to the constant company and the emotionally charged atmosphere of his mother's house, and the silence and emptiness of the flat bothered him.

He missed Gordon more now than at any time since he'd left. In the first weeks after his father's death he thought, *Bugger the expense*, and phoned America, but you couldn't go on like that for long. The time came when he had to wait for the post. He tore open the letters as soon as he got them, but then flicked through the words. What Gordon wrote meant less than the physical presence of a letter. Stephen carried them round with him in the inside pocket of his jacket and, at intervals during the day, slipped his hand inside to touch them.

He was happiest at work and, fortunately, he was busy. The mornings were spent at the advice centre where there was never time to think about his own problems, the afternoons at the club for the young unemployed or, failing that, writing letters and reports.

At night he went round the bars drinking, bumping into people he knew, or not, it hardly mattered. He talked to anybody he met who looked interesting, but there was a strained look in his eyes, as if he was hungry for something that mightn't be easy to provide, and people tended to avoid him. He came home from these outings tired, but it wasn't the kind of tiredness that results in sleep.

He scarcely knew he was grieving for his father, since the

emotional emptiness that had affected him at the funeral continued and even increased. Nothing seemed to have any meaning or connection. Only in Liza's house did he feel a kind of peace, but he rationed the time he spent with her, for her sake. He sometimes felt he was draining her, squeezing her dry, though he knew, too, that she looked forward to his visits. But she was old. There were times when all she wanted to do was to turn her face to the wall and sleep.

He was continually troubled by a feeling of constriction in his throat, and sometimes his voice came out hoarser or fainter than he'd expected. He thought about visiting the doctor, but decided against it. The link with his father's death was too obvious for that.

On Saturday afternoon he drove to the coast, telling himself a long walk in the fresh air would do him good. It wasn't until he parked the car and saw the lights of the Ferris wheel flashing that he knew why he'd come. Fresh air, indeed. He crossed the road to the fairground gates and went in.

He wandered from stall to stall, watched phlegmatically by a big, blonde woman who sold tickets and gave change. Most of the rides were looked after by boys, some of them so young they must still be at school. One of them, a dark, curly-haired youngster who couldn't have been more than twelve or thirteen, was in sole charge of a large and dangerous-looking mass of machinery, which whirred and jetted sparks and surely needed guards of some kind, though Stephen could see none. The boy smiled at him and let a stream of coins trickle from one practised palm into the other.

'Tenpence a ride,' he shouted. 'Roll up!'

Stephen heard the crack of rifle fire and walked towards it. By a green-and-white-striped awning he saw a head and shoulders he recognized.

'Hello,' he said.

Brian turned round. 'Hello.'

They hadn't spoken to each other since Brian's visit to the advice centre, and Stephen was already wondering why he'd come.

'Not a lot doing,' he said.

'It'll hot up a bit later. The afternoons are always quiet.'

'Are you on this evening?'

'Yes, God help me. But I go off for a few hours first. When *he* comes back.' He nodded in the direction of a bald-headed, middle-aged man who was sitting on the steps of the waltzer, drinking tea from the top of a thermos flask. 'I won't be sorry to get off either. I've had enough of this.' A moustache of sweat glistened on his lip. 'Feels like thunder.'

'It *is* close, isn't it?'

Brian grinned, as if Stephen had said something amusing. 'Yes. We'll have a walk along the front, shall we? When he comes back.'

'You look as if you could do with a drink, not a walk.'

'Naw. I'm sick of people.'

The man took his time. Stephen and Brian stood around awkwardly, neither of them finding much to say.

'You could always have a go on the rifles, you know,' Brian said at last, smiling as if in enjoyment of a secret joke.

'I wouldn't be any good.'

'They aren't meant for crack shots. The sights are wrong.'

The ducks bobbed along against a background of painted reeds. Stephen took aim and fired. The duck quivered, but didn't fall.

'Ducks are pretty solid, too.'

The man on the waltzer steps poured the dregs of his tea onto the ground. The drops became dust pellets and bounced on the ground, until he rubbed them into the earth with his foot.

'Howay, Grandad,' said Brian, under his breath.

The man levered himself upright and came towards them. He nodded to Stephen. 'Now then.'

He looked suspicious. Perhaps he was signing on too.

'He's all right,' Brian said, quickly. 'I know him.' A brief pause. 'He's me social worker.'

'Oh aye?' The man sounded half scandalized, half respectful.

Stephen watched, irritated, as Brian got his jacket from underneath the stall.

'What's wrong with the truth?' he asked, as they walked away.

Brian shrugged, 'Got to explain you somehow, haven't I?'

'I don't see why.'

'Oh, sure you do. Anyway it is true, isn't it? In a way.'

'No,' said Stephen. 'It isn't.'

If they'd hoped for cooler or fresher air along the front, they were disappointed. Not a breath of wind came off the sea and the flag outside the lifeboat station hung limp from its mast. Sand, blown over the sea-wall in the spring storms, padded their steps.

They walked by mutual consent to the sea-wall and hung over it, looking at the sea. It lay in a thin silver line about half a mile away, the sand still wet and shining from its withdrawal. Just below them, a man was covering up the last of the swings, and the few families left on the beach were calling their children in from the sea. Stephen remembered being dried at the end of the day, how the sand hurt. 'Go and give it a rinse.' But however often you washed you were always sandy again by the time you got back. He saw the top of his father's head as he rubbed away with the towel, while Stephen rested both hands on his shoulders and watched the swings and the roundabouts close down.

'You sure you don't want a drink?' he said. 'They'll be open in a minute.'

'Aye, and packed too. No, I'd rather be down there.'

They walked down to the water's edge. Above the town, on the cliff top, the half-demolished steelworks pointed an amputated finger at the sky.

'I'm sorry about your father.'

'Oh. Yes. It was . . . very quick.'

They began walking along the sea-edge away from the town.

'Who told you?'

'Jan. The little wifie with the . . .'

'Yes, I know Jan.'

'She had to say something. She was taking your weight-training class.'

193

They'd reached the end of the foreshore. The lights of the Ferris wheel were just beginning to assert themselves against the curious yellow-grey of the sky.

'We'll be busy tonight. If this holds off.'

'Do you have to go back?'

'Yes. Put in a couple of hours. Mick likes to be off by ten. He likes his pint.'

They turned and walked on, leaving the fairground lights behind. The tide had turned and was pushing a line of coal dust up on the beach, a thick fringe of black, like the lashes of an opening and closing eye.

'Do you like it? The fairground.'

'I don't mind. When I left school I used to work along here, on a YOP scheme. We were supposed to clean the beach. It was daft, a machine could've done it in half the time.' He laughed. 'Before you started you had to go and pick your boots, make sure you got the right size. That was the training element.'

'How long did you do that?'

'Not long.' He glanced sideways at Stephen. 'I packed it in the first month.'

'I suppose you don't get offered anything now?'

'No. Too old.' He laughed. 'I wouldn't take it anyway. I'd rather do the fairground. At least it's a proper job.'

They picked their way between heaps of rubbish. The tide brought in lollipop sticks, plastic bottles, Coke tins, French letters. Mulled over them, and then abandoned them, further up the beach.

'We used to play along here when we were lads.' Brian's voice was raw with the kind of nostalgia you expect to hear only in old men. 'We used to play in the dugout up there. Come on. I'll show you.'

They left the beach and started to climb the cliff, slithering on hands and knees up the sandy path. Near the top the ground bristled with jagged spikes of concrete. These were dragon's teeth, the tank traps of the last war, but as the dry ground crumbled around them they seemed to Stephen more like gigantic seed pods that a few days' rain might burst.

He clambered over them, following Brian along the path to where a box of dirty grey concrete squatted on the cliff edge, staring out to sea through the letter-box slits that were its eyes.

The entrance, almost choked with gravel and mud, was at the rear. Brian, without hesitation, bent down and wriggled inside. Stephen followed, not liking what his nose told him. The place stank of pee and, in the far corner, was a crumpled piece of paper caked with shit.

None of this seemed to worry Brian. He leant against the far wall, peering out through one of the slits. Stephen joined him, pressing his face hard against the concrete. He was hoping for a breath of fresh air, but he was disappointed. This bay was too sheltered for the wind to reach.

'This used to be headquarters,' Brian said. 'It was Zit's idea. We were all going to come and live here after the Bomb fell. We were going to get guns and dig holes to store food, and we were going to mount guard and shoot anybody who tried to steal it. He got the idea from the telly. Apparently, some people in America are really doing it. He used to make us practise all the time. Living off the land. We baked a hedge-hog once and ate it. It was awful. Oh, and you had to crouch for hours in all sorts of funny positions, till your legs ached. That was supposed to increase your endurance. Zit's got a brother in the SAS and he gets a lot of his ideas from him. Worships his brother, does Zit. God knows why, beats the shit out of him every time he comes home.'

'You used to hang around with them a lot, didn't you?'

'I still do.'

'But not as much?'

'Naw, not really. I see 'em around.' He turned back to the past with an old man's hunger. 'We used to nick tins of baked beans from the supermarket and bury them. Then we'd get hungry and dig 'em up again.' He laughed. 'We ate that many baked beans you'd've thought the Bomb *had* fallen. We used to light a fire and stop here till midnight. It was smashing. We used to bake potatoes, fry sausages, stuff like that, and you could catch fish off the end of the jetty, little things, codlings, but they didn't half taste good. We used to just stick 'em on a fork, and you know . . . Burnt one side, raw the other. Didn't seem to matter. There was an old bloke used to come and sit with us, he used to sleep in here, I think, and he was as mad as a hatter. Nobody knew who he was or where he come from, or anything. I don't think he knew. But we used to give him a sausage and a baked potato and he was as happy as a king. I don't know what happened to him. He wandered off one night and never come back. Me Mam read in the paper that somebody'd been dragged out of the river, and it sounded a bit like him, but whether it was or not I don't know.'

There was a long silence. Brian looked down, found a Coke can near his feet, and broke its back. 'Come on,' he said. 'Let's go.'

At the top of the path they stopped and looked down onto the beach. The sun had broken through the clouds, and the sea glittered for miles out, in ridge after ridge of silver.

'It needs a war,' Brian said. 'That's the only way they'll ever sort this lot out. That's how they did it last time, isn't it?'

He stared at Stephen, as if daring him to contradict.

'You lot think, because of the Bomb, it can't happen, but it can. Look at the Falklands. The lads round here lapped it up. Why else do you think they voted for Thatcher? They loved every minute. It was the only *real* thing that'd ever happened to them.'

'*Real*. They watched it on the telly!'

'People know what they're doing in a war. They know they're alive.'

'A lot of them aren't.'

Useless to argue. The dirty grey box on the cliff, the boy's eager face, his thin, taut body balancing on the dragon's teeth as if he'd grown out of them: these were images more powerful than words, images that belonged here, to this time and place.

Stephen turned silently away, and faced the sea.

12

The telegram that announced Tom's death slammed into
Liza's face like a trap-door closing. For days she sat in the
house and didn't speak. Eileen tried to rouse her, tugging at
her attention as once she'd tugged at her skirt. But Liza would
listen for a minute or two and then turn away.

Take each day as it comes, people said. But at first it was
more like living from minute to minute. So many steps from
the draining-board to the cupboard. Pick up the plate. Walk.
Open the cupboard door. Put the plate down. Turn. Walk
back. Her body performed the familiar tasks, but her mind was
lost in a white land. Fields of snow broken only by the
footprints of small animals, animals that you never saw, but
only heard or felt, pitter-pattering along, somewhere close
behind.

When she could bear it no longer, she went out and walked
up and down the street, head bowed, arms folded across
her body. The neighbours let her alone, though they were
always aware of her, pausing in their washing of bedroom
windows or looking up from the front door-step as she passed.
Then somebody would go to fetch Mrs Dobbin and she would
run out and put her arms round Liza and lead her back to
the house. 'Howay in, love,' she'd say. 'Look, it's gunna
rain.'

Liza looked up at the sky.

'I've got a nice bit of pie left over. We'll warm that up, shall
we, and have it for us teas?'

Liza shrugged off Mrs Dobbin's arm and walked on alone.

'You know, Liza, if you don't buck your ideas up a bit it's
going to be St Luke's for you.'

This from Louise.

'Life's got to go on, you know. What do you think your Tom'd say if he could see you now? He'd be horrified.'

Liza learned to avoid comment by walking to the churchyard where her father was buried. It helped to have somewhere to go. She had Tom's name added to the stone, and this gave her a focus for her grief.

She needed to remember Tom clearly, but at first she could remember very little. On bad days it was difficult even to recall his face, except as a blur of grey and white dots on a screen. Then, as time passed, as walk succeeded walk, the memories became clearer. She'd found the way back, past grief. Tom was a boy again, playing in the street. The murdering armies had gone home.

If she tried hard she could keep him alive in her mind for days at a time. He was at school, or asleep in his room, or out poaching with the lads.

They took him on that winter when she had pneumonia and couldn't go to the heap. She didn't like it, she was frightened for him, but there was nothing she could do.

One night he'd stayed out so late she couldn't sleep at all, but lay awake hour after hour convinced he'd been caught. At last she got up and sat downstairs in the dark, coughing quietly. She didn't hear the kitchen window open, only the slight squeak of the washer as he climbed down from it to the floor.

'Is that you, Tom?'

'You're in trouble if it isn't.'

She went across to the kitchen and switched the light on. 'Where have you been till this hour?'

'Courting, Ma,' he said, and tapped the tip of his nose to warn her to keep hers out.

She put her hand inside his jacket. 'Aye, I know,' she said. 'Posh tarts you go with. They've all got fur coats.'

He grinned and put two rabbits down on the table. Their glazed eyes and bloody mouths gaped up at her.

'Eh, Tom, you shouldn't.'

'I bloody should, you know.'

She stroked the blood-spiked fur.

'Got the veg as well.' He pulled a turnip out of his pocket. 'I'll skin 'em for you in the morning.'

'You will not. I'm not that far gone I can't skin a rabbit.'

She kissed him then and went upstairs to bed.

The memory ran out at the end of a rutted lane. Liza rested her arms on the gate and looked down at the church, which lay in a wooded hollow on the other side of the field. Slack-bellied rain clouds hung over the tower. As she set off across the field, the first drops fell.

She found the grave and stood before it, her fingers cold and wet around the stems of the daffodils she'd brought with her.

Three names: Edward Jarrett, Thomas Jarrett, Thomas Edward Wright.

The grass around the stone grew long and coarse. It reminded her of the grass in an orchard where she'd gone scrumping as a child. Edward climbed high into the branches, but she was afraid to soil her dress and so went looking for windfalls in the grass. Sharp and sweet, she remembered them. But you had to be careful. Some had lain too long against the soil and when you picked them up your fingers sank into brown mush. Specks of white fungus sprouted from the rotting skin.

Her father had been dead for five years. It didn't horrify her: the thought of his decay. It was right that he should return to the earth, that he should fade, gently, into the soil. Tom's death was another matter, a wound that wouldn't heal. Nothing was worth it, she thought. She would never be brought to say that his death had been worthwhile.

As she turned to go, the drizzle thickened to a downpour. She ran back along the path meaning to shelter in the church, but as she rounded the corner, she came to an abrupt halt. A woman stood there, a tall woman wearing a mucky old mackintosh. Her stillness was uncanny, as if she'd been waiting in the porch for years. A lifetime, perhaps. She turned, hearing the crunch of Liza's footsteps on the gravel, and the light fell full on her face. It was Lena Lowe.

'Hello, Lena.'

'Liza.'

They stared at each other, noting change. The skin round Lena's eyes was brown and shrivelled. The skin of her cheeks hung loose from the bone.

'I heard . . .' Liza said. 'About your lad.'

Lena nodded. 'You lost yours too, didn't you?'

'Yes.'

'I didn't know who it was at first. I couldn't remember your married name. But then a woman further down the street says, "Oh, that's Liza Jarrett."'

They sat down on opposite sides of the porch. From the open church door came a smell of mould and sanctity.

'Is your husband still living?' Liza asked.

'No. He died just before the war broke out. Heart attack.'

'I'm sorry.'

'Oh, I thought at the time it was cruel, but not now.' She looked straight at Liza. 'He couldn't have stood this. He was only a little fella. I used to tell him "Good stuff comes in small parcels." And it did. I never once regretted marrying him.'

'More than I could say about mine.'

'Do you remember that song you used to sing? "*I need a ladder to kiss Lena Lowe . . .*" One thing I said to me Mam when I was getting married, "I'm glad Liza Jarrett isn't here." Because you'd've sung it, you bugger, you know you would.'

'Well, if he was that little . . .'

'They're all the same length in bed.'

'Not where it matters.'

They giggled, teeth glinting in the light that dyed their skins yellow.

'First laugh I've had for months,' said Liza. She didn't feel guilty because her laughter belonged to the past, to the years before Tom was born.

'I think it's going off a bit, isn't it?' Lena said, looking at the rain.

'Yes. I suppose I'd better be getting back.'

'And me.'

They walked down to the gate together. Although Liza

knew this graveyard so well, it had come to have for her the slight unreality of a place visited frequently in dreams. She saw, as if in a vision, how the roots of the elms reached down like a net to catch and hold the gleaming dead, while high above the topmost branches the rooks wheeled and cawed, drifting like scraps of burnt paper on the wind, or flapped down, black and ungainly, to fight and copulate and rebuild their nests.

The rain was washing away the snow: there was a smell of damp earth. And at that moment, when for the first time since Tom's death she ceased, momentarily, to grieve for him, she felt him restored to her.

The moment was quickly gone, but it gave her hope. She turned to Lena.

'Come on,' she said. 'Why don't you come round our house for your tea?'

Six months later Liza was sitting by the fire when she heard the front door open. It was unusual for the neighbours to come to the house in the evenings, and even Mrs Dobbin, who did come and sit with her occasionally, always knocked. It must be one of her sisters, she thought.

But when the living-room door opened, it was Eileen. She went straight up to Liza and kissed her. 'Oh, it is good to see you,' she said.

The texture and smell of the uniform brought Tom back. But the sloping shoulders, the height, the barely perceptible curve of Eileen's breasts: all these were wrong. Gently, Liza pushed her away.

'I wasn't expecting you for another fortnight.'

'I got away early. They've been chopping and changing us about.'

'They're not sending you abroad?'

'Oh, I don't think so.' She laughed. 'Wouldn't tell us if they were.'

'I'll just pop the kettle on,' Liza said. 'If I'd known you were coming I could've wangled a bit extra meat.'

'I thought you couldn't do that?'

'You bloody can, you know.' Liza looked round the kitchen door. 'It's been an eye-opener to me, working there.'

'Do you like it?'

'It's all right. He just wants somebody to hump the carcases around. He can't do it himself, he's got a hernia.'

Liza came to stand in the doorway while she waited for the kettle to boil.

'Do you really like working there?'

'I don't mind. His son's a butcher, you know. It's a reserved occupation.'

'Is it? I didn't know that.'

'You should've seen the old man when he got his call-up papers. He was shitting himself. All you could get out of him was, "Will they take me instead?" I says, "Of course they bloody won't." And his wife was as bad. The son's wife, this is. She says, "If he goes, it'll be the end of us." And I wouldn't care but they know I've lost my son, and I have to sit and listen to it all. I don't mind the old man. He's done his bit. He got a bayonet wound in his belly. Apparently the bloke stuck it in, and then somebody shot him before he could twist it.'

'You seem to know a lot about him, Mam.'

'Yes, well, he's lonely. I stop behind sometimes and cook him a bit of dinner.'

'He's not after you, is he?'

'Mebbe. Question is: Am I after him?'

Eileen came to the kitchen door. 'I wouldn't mind, you know, Mam. It's your life.'

'Ah, but he's a tight-fisted old sod.'

'Well, you wouldn't be marrying him for the money, would you?'

'Course I bloody would. I tried love the first time.' She reached up and got two cups from the top shelf. 'Anyway, what about you? You shouldn't have time to think about your mother's love life.'

'Oh, well, you know . . .' Eileen looked down. 'Mine's a washout, Mam, you know that.'

More trouble, Liza thought, and who was it this time? Bad enough at home when you knew the man.

The kettle began to boil, filling the kitchen with woolly steam. Quickly, Liza made the tea and carried the tray through into the living-room. Eileen sat down on the sofa, feet stretched out towards the fire, hands clasped between her knees.

Liza could never say why, but at that moment she knew Eileen was pregnant. Carefully, holding her breath, she put the teapot down on the hearth.

'No biscuits, I'm afraid.'

'That's all right, Mam. I'm not hungry.'

Dear God, let me be wrong. 'Well, love, aren't you going to tell me?'

'Oh, Mam.' Eileen covered her face with her hands.

'How far on are you?' Liza's voice seemed to come from somewhere behind her head. She knew there were things she had to know, questions she had to ask, but she couldn't think what they were.

'Four months.'

'Well.' Liza swallowed hard and tried again. 'Is he in a position to marry you?'

'I don't know what position he's in. He got posted to the Orkneys. I wrote to him twice, but I got no reply.'

'And how long ago was that?'

'Two months.'

'Well, for all you know he's abroad. They could've shifted him on.'

'For all I know he's dead. That'd shift him a damn sight further.'

'Oh, Eileen.'

'I'm sorry, Mam.'

'There's no point being sorry.' Her mind was beginning to work again. 'Have you took anything?'

'Dr Witte's female pills.'

Liza laughed bitterly. 'If *they* brought it on there'd never be a kid born.'

'It was all I could get.'

Liza picked up the teapot. It had stood too close to the fire and the handle burnt her hand. She gave no sign, but the pain released her anger.

'You thought you knew the lot, didn't you? Oh, it could never happen to you.'

'I thought he was taking precautions, Mam. I thought he had something on.'

'Didn't you *know*?'

'It was dark, I couldn't see. And then afterwards when I realized, I says, "Oh, you *bugger*."'

'And what did he say?'

'Nothing. He just laughed.'

'He'll be laughing like a sick cow when I get my hands on him.'

'I don't want him bothered, Mam.'

'Not bothered? For crying out loud, who do you think's gunna keep it?'

'Me.'

Liza stared at her. Eileen met her gaze for a few seconds, then looked away.

'Aye. Me,' Liza said. 'Well, think again. Not bloody me.'

The tea was cold by the time they got it. As she stood up to take the cups away, Liza rested her hand, briefly, on Eileen's shoulder. 'You think I'm hard, don't you, pet? Well, I'm not. It's just I know what it's like bringing up bairns on your own. I don't want to see you get saddled with it.'

'There's a woman round Lawson Street does it,' said Mrs Dobbin.

Liza wasn't prepared for this suggestion, coming from Mrs Dobbin of all people. She stared at her, coloured, and said nothing.

'Liza, she doesn't know *who* he is, she doesn't know *what* he is, she doesn't even know if he's still alive. Don't let yourself get stuck with it. You've had enough.'

Liza didn't commit herself one way or the other, but she took the address.

They went to see the woman that afternoon. Her name was Millie Porter and she lived in the Crown and Anchor, rent-free, in return for cleaning the bars. Though she did little enough of that, Liza thought, looking round. The blinds were drawn, but they let in one long column of light, enough to show the tab-ends on the floor.

They sat down, the two of them, at separate tables, and waited, breathing the smell of stale beer.

There were sounds of footsteps and muttering from the floor above their heads. Eileen looked up. 'She doesn't half take her time.'

Eileen's face was cut in half by the column of light. This light had a curious effect on the half-face it exposed. At one moment she looked childish: drooping lip, rounded cheek; and then not childish at all, as the light stripped skin down and sharpened bone.

The scufflings became louder, descending the stairs. Millie came into the room, dressing-gown wrapped tightly across a chest as flat as an ironing-board. Liza looked her up and down: thin, brown hair; doughy face; black eyes stuck in like currants; fluffy, turquoise slippers, daubed with grease.

Millie's eyes darted from Eileen to Liza and back again. She smiled at the girl. 'Well,' she said, in an unexpectedly deep voice, 'this isn't much fun, is it, flower?'

Eileen shook her head.

'Well, howay then, let's have a look.'

Rather shyly, Eileen pushed her skirt down. Millie's hands crept across the exposed stomach, like small, brown animals.

'She's three month gone,' said Liza.

'Pull the other bugger, it's got bells on.' Millie straightened up. 'She's four month if she's a day, mebbe more. It's no tiddler she's got in there.'

'Can you still do her?'

'I've done them at six month before now.'

Liza twisted the strap of her bag. 'Her father's dead.'

Millie nodded. 'They're not a lot of use living.'

'I wish my Dad was alive,' Eileen said.

'He couldn't make your mind up for you, love.'

Eileen looked, if possible, whiter than before, but she said, steadily, 'I've made me mind up. I just want to get it over.'

Millie looked down at her feet and said nothing. Her

stockings drooped round her ankles, like the folds of an elephant's backside.

'I just don't want anything to happen to her,' Liza said.

'It already has.'

Eileen's face was no help. It seemed to crumble away, as you looked at it, and other faces peeped out through the cracks. Eileen, five years old, sitting on the draining-board while Frank cleaned the grit out of a grazed knee with the twisted corner of a handkerchief. 'Big girls don't cry,' he said, and Eileen hadn't, then or since. She saw the two faces, the profiles so alike, bending towards each other in the light from the kitchen window. Then she looked up and there was another Eileen, watching her.

You can never see your own child clearly, she thought. *Not the way other people see her, because inside that face are all the other faces, hiding and revealing younger faces still, until eventually the line disappears into the one face that is like no other: the convulsed, bloody, purple face of a baby immediately after birth.*

'What do you want to do, Eileen?' she asked.

'I've told you, Mam.'

Oh, she wouldn't flinch. She'd see no danger, though Millie's fingernails looked as if she scratted in the earth with her bare hands.

The bar of the pub, the eyes she could feel watching her, receded. All around was a mesh of shadows, but immediately in front of her the tree pulsed and gleamed. She reached out her hand and touched the bark. This was as far as she could come and still remain herself, but her self seemed a small, weak creature, a skin to be sloughed off and left behind. Soil closed around, cool and dense, nourishing the roots of hair. Wind moved in her branches. Her fingers, resting on a beer mat, were twigs bursting into leaf.

Something hard and white pushed itself into her face.

'Hey up,' said Millie. 'If you keel over like that you'll have me thinking you're on too.'

'God forbid,' said Liza, and laughed.

'One good gulp, go on, you'll be all right.'

She was a dab hand at bringing folks round. Had to be, of

206

course. She'd get them over the threshold, no matter what state they were in.

Liza pushed the bottle away. 'Howay, Eileen, we're going home.'

'You'll regret it, you know,' Millie said. She looked small and drained in the light from the open door.

'Yes,' said Liza. 'I know I will. Part of the time.'

'Why, Mam?' asked Eileen, as they walked home.

'I've lost one bairn. I'm not risking another.'

That *was* the reason, or one way of putting the reason. She only knew that in the end every nerve and muscle and vein in her body had said, *No*.

Did you see her fingernails?

As the time of her confinement drew near, Eileen retreated in on herself, moving around the house as unobtrusively as her vast bulk would allow. She refused to go outside.

'You want to get out a bit more,' Liza said. 'You're doing yourself no good cooped up in here. Howay, put your coat on, we'll have a walk round the block.'

'I'm all right where I am.'

'You'll have to take the bairn out, you know. You can't bring it up in a cupboard.'

'I don't even know if I'm keeping it yet.'

Liza sat down. 'What do you mean?'

'I could have it adopted.' She stared at her mother, defiantly. 'There's plenty of people'd give it a good home.'

'This is its home.'

'Why should you be the one to decide? You never asked me, did you? "Howay, Eileen, we're going home." You never once asked me what I wanted to do.'

'And what did you want?'

'I don't know.'

'Well, it's just as well I saved me breath, then, isn't it?' She thought back for a second. 'Anyway, I did ask you.'

'You'd made up your mind. I was nowhere.'

'Eight months ago you were on your bloody back. Let's not forget who got you into this mess.'

207

'Oh, don't start all that again.'

'Why the hell should he have his pleasure for nowt? I don't understand you, Eileen. All I can think is you don't *know* who it was.'

Eileen flinched.

'Well, what else am I to think?'

Liza was glad to get to work, away from it all. Not that the work was easy. Dawson watched her hoist the side of a pig onto a hook and his eyes gleamed with admiration. She was his kind of woman and he pinched her bum to show his approval.

'Do that again you mucky old sod and I'll hang you on the hook.'

A few mornings later Liza came downstairs to find Eileen sitting at the kitchen table, her hands clasped round a mug of tea. She was wearing her pink dressing-gown, bought when she joined up and left home for the first time.

Liza looked closely at her. 'You're bad, aren't you?'

'I'm all right.'

She'd still be saying she was all right when they nailed down the coffin lid.

'Have you started?'

'Yes.'

Liza felt momentarily helpless. She'd gone through all the preparations for the birth, booked the midwife, cleared out Tom's room, without ever allowing herself to imagine the event.

'Have I to stop off work?' She heard the helplessness in her own voice and was frightened by it.

'No, you go.' Eileen got up and put her mug in the sink. 'I'll be all right.'

Liza hung about, not knowing what to do, until eventually a glance at the clock convinced her she had to go. She tied the headscarf round her head and said, 'You will rattle on the grate for Mrs Dobbin, won't you? She'll be up in half an hour.' Liza remembered rattling on the grate for Mrs Dobbin when she was in labour with Eileen. Time went so quickly, flooding past you like a stream that tugged at your legs and threatened to pull you down. She put a hand on the sofa, to steady herself. 'Don't you worry now. I'll soon be back.'

All morning her head was full of Eileen, so much so she gave the wrong change twice.

'What's up with you?' Dawson asked roughly, on the second occasion.

'Our Eileen's bad.'

'She's about due, isn't she?' asked the woman whose change had been wrong.

'Yes.'

'I bet you'll be glad when it's over.'

'I'll say. I think I'd rather be having it meself.'

The woman laughed and pocketed her change. 'You get like that. I wore a hole in the carpet when our Margaret was having hers.'

At dinner-time, Liza put on her coat to go home.

'Mind, I'm not coming back if she's bad,' she said.

'It's Friday, think on. We've got the orders to get out.'

It had come on to rain. Big drops pelted her as she ran, soaking the shoulders of her coat. By the time she reached Walker Street, her hair was plastered flat to her skull. She burst into the house, not knowing what to expect.

Eileen lay on the sofa, another mug of tea gone cold by her side.

Liza started to speak, but stopped when she saw Eileen's face. She waited for the pain to pass, then said, 'How long has it been like that?'

'All morning.'

Dear God. Liza knelt down and rattled the poker in the grate. 'I thought you said you were going to call Mrs Dobbin?'

'I would've done if there'd been owt happening.'

'You don't have to wait till you can see the colour of its hair, you know. You're meant to be in bed a bit before that.'

Mrs Dobbin came rushing in, her arms white with flour. 'Your ruddy family,' she said. 'You always start when I'm baking.' She looked down at Eileen. 'Chin up, pet. Soon be over.'

'If you stop with her I'll fetch the midwife.'

209

'No, I'll go. You get her to bed. And make yourself a cup of tea, Liza. You look done in.'

'I've been running, that's all.'

As they reached the front door they heard a groan from the living-room, quickly stifled.

'I'll be as quick as I can.'

'I don't suppose you could pop into Dawson's on your way back?' said Liza. 'He'll be fuming.'

'Let the old sod fume,' said Mrs Dobbin. 'He gets more than his pound of flesh out of you.'

Eileen went to bed in Tom's old room. The bed had been pulled out into the centre of the room and there were towels tied to the headposts, for when the time came to bear down. Eileen touched the towels as she got into bed, but didn't ask what they were for.

Liza had seen many children born. Some slipped into the world easily, some were torn out. She'd seen women laugh as the baby's head crowned, and other women beg for chloroform. She'd sat up with women who fussed over trifles, and women who endured agony in silence, but she had never, until now, seen a woman go through her labour indifferently, as if it were happening to somebody else. She was afraid for Eileen, knowing that she couldn't go on like this to the end.

The midwife arrived, examined her, and promised to come back in a few hours' time.

'Don't worry,' she said. 'She's a long way to go yet.'

Mother and daughter were left alone. Liza lit the fire and sat by it as the long afternoon wore on.

'She said I'd be better walking around.'

'Would you like to try?'

'Mebbe later. I'm a bit tired. I was up all night.'

'You should've woke me.'

'You had to go to work.' She turned on her side. 'Was he all right about you taking the afternoon off?'

'I'm taking the week off, not the afternoon.'

Another pain started. When it was over Liza said, 'There's no law against having a little moan, now and then.'

'Pain's the same whether you moan or not.'

The afternoon darkened. The wind howled round the house, spattering the glass with sleet. Liza shivered and put more coal on the fire.

'Bringing bad weather with him,' she said.

'You don't know it's a him.'

'I do, you know. I can tell by the way you're carrying.'

The wind tugged at the flames. Bits of soot caught fire and sparked up the chimney. You could imagine them whirled away on the wind, far away over the housetops.

'You'll have the chimney on fire if you don't watch out.'

Liza peered into the darkness. 'Do you want the light on, flower?'

'No, I like it like this.' She hoisted herself up on the pillows. 'She'll switch it on soon enough when she gets back.'

The sky darkened; night closed in around the woman and the labouring girl. As the hours passed, Liza felt herself merge into the girl on the bed. *She* had laboured to give birth like this, in this room, this bed. She became afraid of the vanishing boundaries and turned to the fire, only to feel it strip the flesh from her face and reveal her mother's bones. Eileen was not Eileen, Liza was not Liza, but both were links in a chain of women stretching back through the centuries, into the wombs of women whose names they didn't know.

Perhaps Liza drowsed a little, because she jumped when she heard the midwife's footsteps on the stairs. Nurse Hardcastle bustled in and switched on the light.

'Good heavens. Sitting in darkness,' she said. She bent over the bed and waited for the next pain to pass, before examining Eileen. 'Progress. We're winning.'

'You're stopping then, are you?' Liza asked.

'Oh, yes, I'm stopping.' She looked down at Eileen. 'That's what I like to see – nice flushed cheeks. Come on, Mrs Wright, let's have a cup of tea.'

'I could do with a bloody cup,' said Eileen.

'It's not for you, love. It's for us.'

'Bloody hell.'

Liza and the nurse looked at each other and smiled.

The baby, a girl, was born shortly after ten. Eileen was

disappointed it wasn't a boy, the hurt showed in her face, but she took it in her arms and cuddled it. Then she handed it over to the nurse and sipped the scalding tea she was allowed at last.

'She'll need stitching, I'm afraid. I'll have to get Dr Ritchie.' She looked down at Eileen. 'Now no getting out of bed.'

'I wasn't thinking of it,' Eileen said, and they all laughed.

After she'd gone, Liza sat by the fire and nursed the baby. 'Isn't she lovely?' she said.

'I wanted a boy,' Eileen said. 'I was going to call it Tom.'

Liza, who until that moment had shared Eileen's disappointment, looked down at the baby and thought, *Thank God*.

They sat together in the firelight, hardly aware of the smell of blood and clean linen that filled the room.

Dr Ritchie arrived an hour later. 'Sorry,' he said, 'it's been one of those nights.'

He made Eileen wriggle to the edge of the bed, got a chair and sat between her legs. But whichever way he moved the chair, he was working in his own light. Liza got a torch and held it for him while he stitched. 'There, there,' he said, when he'd finished, and pinched Eileen's cheek. 'You've been a brave girl.'

On the way downstairs he turned to look at Liza. 'You've been fretting yourself sick over this, haven't you? Well, *stop it*. She's one of thousands.'

Liza closed the door after him and leant against it. From upstairs came a small, mewing sound, the scarcely human cry of the newborn. She smiled, and went upstairs to join her family.

There was a party in the street on VE day. Eileen went out early to help with the preparations, but Liza stayed inside the house. In the afternoon she decided to take the baby out for a walk, though only as far as the bombed site at the end of the street. They walked down the alley together, slowly, because Kath stopped every few yards to examine bits of grass or stone.

'By, she hasn't half come on,' said a woman, hurrying past with a jar of jam in her hands.

'Oh, she's a grand bairn.'

The bombed site was overgrown with weeds. Tall, purple flames of rose bay willow herb flickered, where only five years before the houses had burned.

Liza sat with her back to a half-demolished wall and closed her eyes, while Kath toddled about, playing in the rubble of ruined buildings. The day was warm. Butterflies rested on heaps of broken stone. From far away came the sound of singing, muffled by the heat and heaviness of the afternoon. Walker Street celebrated and Liza did not begrudge it, though she preferred to spend this day alone with her memories, and, when these became too sharp, to look up and watch her granddaughter play. Kath came back frequently, with scraps of coloured wallpaper or the spring from a broken chair.

'Ideen,' she said, on one of these trips back.

'She's gone to the party. She won't be long.'

Kath seemed to accept it, and wandered off to play again. But a few minutes later she was back. 'Ideen.'

'*Howay*,' said Liza, and held out her leg.

Kath sat astride it. Liza held her hands, and sang.

> She'll be coming round the mountain when she comes!
> She'll be coming round the mountain when she comes!
> Coming round the mountain,
> Coming round the mountain,
> She'll be coming round the mountain when she comes!

As she sang, Liza jiggled her leg up and down and Kath shouted for joy.

> She'll be riding six white horses when she comes!
> She'll be riding six white horses when she comes!
> Riding six white horses,
> Riding six white horses,
> She'll be riding six white horses when she comes!

Liza stopped, breathless, and said, 'Howay, now, let's go home and have our tea. Eileen'll be back soon.'

She got up and, taking her granddaughter by the hand, walked home across the blitzed ground.

13

'I dreamt about Lena Lowe last night,' said Liza. 'She come to me in that mucky old mackintosh she used to wear. And she had something in her hands, something very bright, and I couldn't understand what it was, because I knew they were jewels, and yet they seemed to be alive. Sapphires, rubies, diamonds: but brighter. And they were all moving about, and making this little squeaking noise, as if they were singing. And then I woke up, and I heard a voice say, "The souls of the faithful are in the hands of God." And I lay there and I thought, *Well, how daft. That wasn't God, it was Lena.*'

To the very last Liza had resisted this trip. When she did finally emerge, she looked like a small animal coming out of hibernation, sniffing the air, lifting almost blind eyes to the sun.

Now she was settled in the front seat of the car with a rug wrapped round her. But still she wanted to talk about her dream, in order, Stephen thought, to postpone the moment when she would have to face the world.

'It's almost like the bright things in her hands were death, although they seemed to be alive, and she was saying to me, "Look, don't worry. It's not the way you think."'

'Do you always dream in colour like that?'

'Oh, yes. Beautiful colours. And I dream a lot about animals. I dreamt about a seal the other night. You know how sometimes you have dreams that colour the day? Well, my seal dream was like that. Like a blessing.' She risked one cautious glance out of the window. 'Do you have dreams like that?'

Stephen laughed. 'No, I'm afraid my dreams are much more mundane. I thought we'd go down to the river.'

'Yes, all right.'

Another quick glance. He wondered what she made of it: the three blocks of flats, rising from the earth like clenched fists.

'Is Wynyards still standing?'

'No. They knocked that down three years ago.'

Neither of them spoke again until they reached the transporter.

'I thought you might like to go across,' Stephen said.

She stared at the arc of sour blue that spanned the river. 'Yes,' she said.

'You lived on the other side, didn't you?'

'In the end we did. You had to serve your time to get one of them houses. Generally, you had to work for the Wynyards oh, ten, twelve years to get one of them. There was no ferry money to find, you see. You were practically living at the works.'

Stephen drove onto the platform and parked the car.

'I think you should stay inside,' he said.

'Not likely. Not now I've come this far.'

He helped her out of the car and she hobbled across to the railings. The bridge juddered into life.

'I always used to love this,' said Liza. She pointed at the pedestrian gangway high above. 'I walked across that with Edward the day he joined up. Oh, he was going to do this, he was going to do that . . . And he'd've done it, too, you know. He wouldn't've let anything stand in his way.'

The river crawled away from them, streaked blue-purple, like cigarette smoke unfurling. The wind wrinkled its surface, a cold wind off the North Sea, and Stephen was afraid for Liza and tried to shield her body with his own.

'It's colder than I thought,' he said.

'Oh, it's always cold by the river.'

A man in a peaked cap came to collect their fares.

'Can you still walk across?' Liza asked, craning her head back to see the walkway.

'No, love. Shut that off a few year back.' He winked at Stephen. 'Ovver many buggers topping 'emselves.'

215

The platform clanged to a halt: the barricades swung open. Liza got back into the car and Stephen drove a few hundred yards up the road.

High, barbed-wire fences enclosed work yards that would never work again. The wires throbbed and hummed as the wind blew through them. Bits of cloth and polythene clung to the barbs and snapped.

'Come on,' said Liza. 'I want to get out.'

She walked a few steps, holding on to the side of the car. In her mind's eye she saw this place as it had been. Tall chimneys, kilns and furnaces loomed up through the brown smoke of a winter afternoon. Trains rattled, hammers banged, furnaces roared, and always, day and night, columns of flame rose up into the sky.

'There's nothing left,' she said, and, although she'd known that it must be so, her voice was raw with loss.

Tansy, dog-daisies, rose bay willow herb grew and flourished where the houses had been. Here and there, half-hidden in the grass, was the kerb of a forgotten road.

The wind keened across the brown land, and it seemed to Liza that it lamented vanished communities, scattered families, extinguished fires. Mourned the men who'd crowded to the ferry boat, at each and every change of shift, their boots striking sparks from the cobbles as they ran.

She saw her father among them, and his voice echoed down the road that was no longer a road. Ginger-black, afraid of nobody. Men spilling out of the pubs to watch him race.

– *You're never gunna race like that, are you?*

– *Course I bloody am. I can beat you buggers wi' me boots on.*

'Dad?' she said, aloud.

Silence. Silence from hearth and road, from pub and church, from foundry and factory yard.

'I oughtn't to have brought you here,' Stephen said.

'I wanted to come.'

She'd been crying, he saw. But the tears had already dried to a white scurf at the corners of her eyes.

'Come on,' she said. 'I could do with a cup of tea.'

He sat her down on the sofa and switched the fire on. She'd scarcely looked at the room.

'I heard from our Eileen this morning.'

'Oh? Everything all right?'

'As all right as it ever is. She's coming down to see me in December.'

'You don't seem to be looking forward to it.'

'It's nice seeing her. But she drives me scatty, nattering on. She never had much sense you know, Eileen. And she was a fool with men. Still is, and she's gone sixty.'

She was looking round the room now. He waited.

'I know where this is!' she said.

He laughed. 'I wondered whether you'd recognize it.'

'It is, isn't it?'

'Yes.'

'Well, I never did.'

She looked round the room, smiling.

'There used to be a big mirror over there. Still the same floor, though. Eeh, I remember Ellen Parker cursing this floor. Because, you know, she had to polish it till she could see her face in it, every single day. And not just any old time either. Before the family got up.'

'Did she ever go back into service?'

'Did she hell. She rose to be a big woman in the Labour Party. I used to go and listen to her speak. I didn't know who it was at first because she used to speak under her married name, but as soon as she walked onto the platform, I knew her. And she was a wonderful speaker. I was surprised she was married, mind, because . . . Well, let's put it this way: she wasn't the world's best-looking lass. But anyway, she must've had something, mustn't she, because he absolutely idolized her.'

She was enjoying her tea.

'I'm sorry I was such a wet blanket, down by the river.'

'I'm sorry it upset you.'

'You see you get old, you look back. You're bound to think

them days were better, aren't you? But I try not to slip into that, I try to remember what it was really like. Women wore out by the time they were thirty. Because they were, you know. You were old at forty.'

She stared into the fire.

'I met Ellen again, you know. Oh, a good while after. Be in the sixties sometime. She was a good age by then, but she was still working for the Party. I passed her in Boots, and I thought, *Oh, she won't want to know me.* But she says, "*Liza.* Howay and have a cup of tea." She was always the same, Ellen. Never changed.'

'Would you like another sandwich?'

'Aye, go on. I've ate more here than I eat in a week.'

'You know I've been thinking about you joining the Labour Party.'

'What about it? We all did. Even Elizabeth Wynyard did, and that caused a stir.'

'No. I meant, how natural it was for you to do it. And yet I look at the kids I work with, and I can't see any of them doing it. That . . . *link* seems to've gone.'

'Well, they're only young. I wouldn't've given you tup-pence for the Labour Party at that age.'

'I don't think it's just that.'

Liza held out her cup for more tea. 'You know you put me in mind of something Ellen said. We were sat in the new shopping centre and it wasn't long before Christmas and they were all going mad. Spend, spend, spend. And you know we looked round at all this, and it was like a different world. I said, "Ellen, where are we going?" And you know there was a lot of good going on. New hospitals, new schools. She could've pointed to all that. But, no. She put her cup down on the table and she says, "Liza, I'm buggered if I know."

'I've thought about that a lot since. Because that's where it went wrong you know. It was all *money.* You'd've thought we had nowt else to offer. But we *did.* We had a way of life, a way of treating people. You didn't just go to church one day a week and jabber on about loving your neighbour. You got stuck in seven days a week and bloody did it, because you knew if you didn't you wouldn't survive and neither would she. We had all that. We had pride. We were poor, but we were *proud*.'

'It's all gone though, hasn't it?'

'No, I don't think it has. You've only got to look at Connie Jubb, she'd go out of her way to do a good turn for anybody. There's thousands like that. Shut people up in rabbit hutches and what are they supposed to do? But give them a chance and it's still there.'

Stephen didn't reply. It startled him to realize that Liza had more faith in the future at eighty-four than he had at twenty-nine. He looked round at the people he worked with here and on the Clagg Lane estate, and it seemed to him that he was witnessing the creation of a people without hope.

Liza, meanwhile, wetted her forefinger to pick up crumbs of chocolate cake. 'That was a lovely tea,' she said.

'Would you like to see the garden?'

She looked across at the French windows. 'Aye, howay.'

Outside, she looked back at the house. 'It's a big place,' she said.

'Yes.'

'You'll be glad when Gordon gets back.'

'Well, I haven't got the whole house, you know. It's just the ground floor.'

'Even so. Big rooms.'

They walked down to the lily pond.

'No fish?'

'No. I thought I might get some next summer. No use putting them in now.'

Looking round the garden, he felt for the first time a real interest in it. He would, this weekend, clear the weeds that choked the surface of the pond. The next time he brought her here it would look more like the garden she remembered.

At the door of her house she turned for a last look at the sky. Stephen thought, *She's saying goodbye*, but immediately pushed the thought aside. There was no reason, now she'd got used to the idea of going out, why they shouldn't do this again.

'Take the cover off his cage, will you, pet? Just for a few minutes.'

Nelson had been protected from loneliness by the premature descent of night. When Stephen lifted the pillowcase off his cage, he stretched his legs, looked through the bars and screamed.

'I don't think he likes me.'

'Oh, he does. He talks more to you than anybody.'

'You know there's a superstition about parrots? That they don't rot when they die.' He tried to remember a poem he'd read that said something to that effect, but failed. 'They're supposed to symbolize the soul.'

Nelson produced his perfect imitation of Liza's laugh. 'Drop 'em, dearie,' he said, and poked his beak through the bars.

'But whoever thought that hadn't met Nelson.'

Liza sat down on the edge of her bed. She looked exhausted.

'Is there anything I can get you?' he asked.

'No. Just put me a bit of coal on the fire.'

She lay back against the pillows and closed her eyes. Within a few minutes, she was asleep.

Stephen held the newspaper up to the hearth, until it began to brown. Then whipped it away in a cloud of acrid smoke. The reawakened flames flickered over Liza's face, giving life to features that might otherwise have been drained into a semblance of death.

'Goodnight,' he said, as he left her.

She stirred in her sleep, but didn't wake.

14

Three women shuffled backwards on their knees down a long corridor, leaving the floor in front of them wet and gleaming. Liza looked up at the clock as they crawled underneath it. Twenty minutes to go.

Ethel Whittaker, a thin, sallow woman with a long, drooping, inquisitively twitching nose was telling some story she'd read in the paper about a bride who'd died in a car crash on the way to her wedding.

'Our Pauline was going on you know, "Oo, isn't it awful?" I told her, I says, "You want to think what she was spared."'

Ethel, beneath the bawdy relish, nursed a deep dread of life, a dread she'd instilled into her daughters so conscientiously they crept about like ghosts.

'Shouldn't think she was spared anything,' said Nance Claypole, with one of her raucous laughs. 'They try before they buy these days.'

'They always did,' said Liza.

They'd almost reached the end of the corridor when Nance looked up and said, 'Oh, look, Liza, isn't that your bairn?'

A small face peered round the door at the top of the corridor.

'Howay in, flower,' Liza said.

Kathleen started to walk down the corridor, then stopped abruptly seeing the marks her feet left on the wet floor.

'Don't bother about that, pet,' said Liza.

'Can't fly over it,' said Nance.

Kathleen reached the end of the corridor and stood looking down at the women. She had dark eyes, surprisingly dark in

221

view of her fair hair and skin, and these eyes looked older than
the rest of her face.

'I won't be a minute, love,' said Liza. 'Here go and get
yourself some sweets. The canteen'll still be open.'

Kathleen took the threepenny bit and left.

'Got old eyes that bairn,' said Ethel. 'Been here before.'

'Yes,' said Liza. 'And I know who as. She was only a couple
of weeks old when me Mam took bad.'

It was half a joke, but only half. She was aware in Kathleen
of Louise's continued life, a presence that lurked in those dark
eyes like a fish at the bottom of a pond.

At last the floor was done and the three women were able to
stand up. Buckets clanking, they walked along the corridor to
the caretaker's cupboard where they left their overalls and
signed off for the weekend. Liza lagged behind the others: she
was older by ten years and it took longer for her joints to
unlock.

Kathleen was waiting at the door of the canteen, a smear of
chocolate round her mouth.

'I thought you were going to wait at home.' Liza said. She
didn't like Kathleen coming to the factory after dark: the lane
leading down to the industrial estate was long and badly lit.
'You don't want to come down that lane on your own, pet.
Anything could happen.'

'Such as what?'

'Such as never mind.'

They went home on the tram. Men lined the aisle, smelling
of oil, bait tins slung across their shoulders, lurching from side
to side as the tram swayed. There was a smell of wet wool and
the slatted floor was puddled with damp. No sound, except
when one briefly greeted another.

Liza took Kath on her knee so the man standing next to her
could sit down. Kath pressed her nose against the window and
Liza, too, stared out, waiting for the flash from the cable
overhead, and when it came they turned to each other and
smiled.

Liza sat back, feeling the girl's light bones and remembering
the day she'd taken her to see Louise, who was dying.

The whole family had been there, her brother and six sisters, all gathered at Harriet's house around the mother's bed.

It turned into a family conference on what was to be done with Eileen's child.

'You want to put it in a home,' said Harriet. 'At least for the first few years. Till it's out of its shit.'

Harriet had never forgiven Liza for being bombed and landing her with Louise.

'You'd be better off getting her adopted,' said Jimmy, the sole surviving son. 'You can't bring a kid up properly without a father.'

Liza looked at him, remembering how she'd squeezed her small chest together to get enough tit to push into his mouth.

'You can all shut your gobs,' she said. 'She's mine and I'm keeping her. Time enough for you to play your mouths when you're asked for help. And that'll be never.'

'Liza's right,' said a voice from the bed. Louise raised her braided head, in which even now not one grey hair was visible. 'You don't give your own flesh and blood to strangers.'

Liza carried the baby across to the bed. 'It is a girl you know, Mam,' she said, thinking Louise must be too far gone to have taken this in.

'I know it's a girl,' said Louise. 'I'm *dying*, Liza. Not *daft*. And I wish to God you'd all bugger off and let me get on with it.'

This was her last coherent speech. Later that night they gathered round her bed again, the living son and the daughters, but Louise did not speak to them, but recited, over and over again, the names of her dead children. Edward. The twins: Elizabeth and Rachel. Then, as she turned towards death, the names of her first children, names that none of the living children had ever heard before, and now would never forget. Through the long night she named them, softly, insistently, like a bell tolling.

'Look,' said Liza, and pointed. The tram had stopped opposite a toy shop, its windows brightly lit for Christmas.

They pressed their faces against the glass.

223

'We'll have to see what Father Christmas brings you,' Liza said, settling back into her seat as the tram moved on, but with a flush of excitement still on her face.

Liza played with her wedding ring, remembering Frank. Only the other week she'd gone into the front room and found Kath reading one of his old encyclopaedias. She must have opened the cupboard and found them herself, by accident, because Liza had never mentioned them, or even thought about them for years. She was curled up on the floor, so intent on the book she didn't hear Liza come in, and when finally she looked up there was the same fixed, dreamy look in her eyes that Liza remembered in Frank. She kept her finger in the book, marking the place. It brought back so many memories that when Liza tried to speak she choked on the words. In the end she simply closed the door and went away.

'Are we gunna see me Mam tomorrow?'

'Not tomorrow, love. Next weekend.' Liza hesitated, then said, 'She's got the new baby now. It's a girl.'

She watched Kath for signs of jealousy or unhappiness, but there were none. Kath simply turned and stared out of the window, her face expressionless. Not like the day her Mam left, when she'd held onto Liza and screamed as if every tooth in her head was being pulled out.

Mrs Dobbin came in as Liza was getting the tea.

'I've brought you a plaited loaf,' she said. 'Was that right?'

'Aw, yes, thanks. That'll save me having to go out.'

'What's wrong with the bairn?' Mrs Dobbin jerked her head towards the sofa where Kath was curled up. 'She looks a bit mopey.'

'She thought she was gunna see her Mam.' Liza shook her head. 'Do you know I love our Eileen, but there's times when I could wring her neck.'

'Hello, Mam.'

Eileen came running down the stairs of the pub to meet them. Mother and daughter kissed, then Liza stood to one side while Kath buried her head in her mother's apron-clad stomach, flat again now, and clung on.

'Hello, pet,' Eileen said casually, ruffling her hair. 'Howay upstairs and see the new baby.'

A smell of milk and shit hung over the room where Eileen, her husband and the new baby lived. In one corner, between the double bed and the wardrobe was a small chair. Eileen lifted it over the cot and gave it to her mother. Kath sat on the bed.

'Don't wake her up,' said Liza. 'I can see her from here.'

'Oh, no,' said Eileen. 'You must hold her.'

The baby looked raw: skin and hair both red. Liza said the right things, but failed to feel them.

'Bet the hair was a shock.'

'Oh, it was. And you know all the lasses were having me on. You know, "What colour hair has the milkman?" All that kind of thing. Then when Leonard come in and they saw how dark he was they says, "Bloody hell, it was the milkman." I says, "*No*, it's me Mam."'

'Just as well I couldn't get,' said Liza, pulling a strand of her grey hair. 'They'd've thought you were having them on.'

Eileen got a teapot out of the wardrobe and said, 'If you hold the bairn for a minute, Mam, I'll make us a cup of tea.'

The kettle stood on the floor by the bed. As it came to the boil they had to move their legs to avoid being scalded by the steam.

'Were you all right in the end then?'

'Oh, not so bad. You know I went in a week early? Oh, and the sister on duty, she wasn't half rotten. She says, "A woman your age should know better than this." And she says, "Of course you haven't started." But you see I think she knew I had *her*.' Eileen nodded at Kath, who sat beside her on the bed, holding onto her waist.

'She shouldn't do. Unless you've gabbed.'

'Oh, it gets around. I used to think you could bury the past, but I know now you can't. Howay, love,' she said, unclasping Kathleen's hands. 'I've got to make the tea. Anyway, after that I was determined I wouldn't give her the opportunity to be nasty again so I waited till I was well on before I went in. And I did, you know, I damn near had her in the corridor. They didn't have time to shave me or anything, and afterwards when she was taking the stitches out, she says, "What's this? I'm not used to working in a jungle, you know." And I thought, *Aye, you old bag, if you'd been a bit more reasonable you wouldn't have to*. Oh, but there was one poor lass she had a bairn with no mouth. Like she'd had German measles and oh it was such a bonny bairn, you know. Its eyes and its nose and then down below there was just this hole and what a hell of a job she had feeding it. I don't know how she'll go on.'

'Oh, they can work wonders these days. Plastic surgery.'

'I hope so. She come out the same day as me and you know I took *her* round and showed her to everybody and this lass says, "I don't suppose any of you want to see my baby." And they says, "Oh, don't be so daft, of course we want to see him." And they passed him all round the ward and everybody give him silver. The carry cot was weighed down.'

Eileen poured the tea and took the baby back.

'Well,' she said, turning to Kath. 'How you doing at school?'

'All right.'

'Do you like school?'

Kath shook her head. 'No.'

'She's doing all right,' said Liza. 'I don't suppose any kid likes school.'

The baby began to cry and Eileen unbuttoned her blouse. 'I thought she wouldn't be long. She knows when it's tea-time, don't you?'

The baby's red hand pressed into the white, blue-veined breast and she sucked vigorously. Liza watched Kath and saw how, unnoticed by Eileen, she reached up and touched the collar of her blouse.

'Why don't you go out and play?' Liza said. 'Look, the sun's shining.'

Kath got up reluctantly and went downstairs.

'She doesn't want to be sat here listening to us,' Liza said.

'No, well, I know it's boring for her.'

Oh, you bloody fool, thought Liza. *She'd look at you till her eyes dropped out*. Aloud, she said, 'Any news of a house?'

'Not yet. I thought when I told them I was pregnant we might get one, but they haven't said anything, and Flo – that's me landlady – she's getting very awkward. It was all right when I was doing the cleaning for nowt and out at work all day, but now there's a bairn . . . She says, "I can't have it crying, you know. The customers won't like it." I say, "It's bound to cry sometimes, Flo." She says, "Well, I don't know. I can't have the customers upset." I says, "It's the other way round. I just get her off to sleep and they wake her up." Oh, and she's awkward about the nappies too. I have to try and get them dry in here in front of the fire because she won't let me have the kitchen and then she comes waltzing in and complains the wallpaper's damp. I threatened them, you know, down at the council offices. I says, "I'm going to write to my MP." I thought if they got a letter from the House of Commons that'd shake them up a bit, but he says, "Honey, we could paper these walls with letters from the House of Commons." Leonard says, "You want to tell them you'll write to Gilbert Harding. They'd take more notice of that."'

The baby, feeling her mother's tension, let go of the nipple and screamed.

'Don't get yourself upset. You're filling that bairn with wind.'

'I'm bound to be upset, Mam. Here I am . . . Three bairns . . .'

'*Two*,' said Liza.

'Counting Leonard's . . .'

'*Four*,' said Liza.

Eileen looked puzzled.

'Remember Kath?'

'That's right!' Eileen said. 'Four.'

Liza took a deep breath.

'Ah, but Kath's got you. Leonard's bairns've been knocked from pillar to post.'

'Yes, they have. And no credit to Leonard.'

'Oh come on, Mam. Keith was nine days old when his Mam died. What could Leonard've done?'

'More than he did.'

227

'You're against men, aren't you, Mam?'

'On the contrary. I've got a higher opinion of men than you seem to have, because you think they're bloody useless, and I know they're not. There's many a man lost his wife sets on and keeps house as good as a woman . . . And they're not left to do everything on their own. People rally round.'

'Not now they don't.'

'And why did she die when the kid was only nine days old? She was a young, strong woman. You know what they say, don't you? He never give the midwife time to put her hat on.'

'It was her kidneys, Mam. I've seen the death certificate.'

'And that lad. Keith. One foster home after another, and all because Leonard won't pay.'

'*Can't* pay.'

'He doesn't stint himself when it comes to drink and cigarettes.'

'It's not that anyway. Keith's a right little bugger. His last foster mother had a nervous breakdown. She had to go in the Retreat. And it wasn't that Leonard didn't try. He used to go down every weekend and leather the kid.'

'Oh well. What more could he do?'

'I'm sorry you don't like me husband, Mam.'

'I'd put it stronger than that.'

'But I am married to him. And it doesn't matter how hard the bed is, I'll lie on it.'

'I'd think more of him if he'd waited till he could offer a home to the kids he's got already. *Before* . . .' Liza waved her hand at the baby.

'I had to have her! I needed the points.'

Liza closed her eyes. 'Poor little bugger.'

'When we get a house, Mam, I'll take Kath. And you needn't worry. Leonard says he'll treat her like one of his own.'

'Yes,' said Liza. 'I know.'

'There's no need to say it like that.'

'Look at the way he leathers Keith.'

'He needs a firm hand.'

'Not that firm! You want to get that kid into a proper home.

It's no use farming him out onto private foster homes. They're only doing it for the money, and Leonard *won't pay*.'

Silence. Eileen wasn't an intelligent woman, but she was Frank Wright's daughter and she believed, beyond any shadow of doubt or turning, that the care of her step-children had been entrusted to her by God.

'Sheila isn't much better off, is she? Sleeping on the floor of a pub.'

'It'll be better when we've got a house.'

Liza looked at her, at the white face and shadowed eyes, and asked, 'Is he good to you?'

'He loves me, Mam.'

'Yes, well,' Liza sighed. 'That makes up for a lot.'

Downstairs Kath sat on the doorstep of the pub. A sharp wind blew dead leaves along the street, but the sun was shining and it wasn't a school day. She screwed up her eyes and light splintered on the lids.

When she opened them again, Keith was there. Keith was eleven, three years older than Kath, and beautiful, with brilliant, shallow amber eyes that never seemed to think or feel anything.

'Hello.'

'Hello.'

He came and sat beside her on the step. 'Is your Gran with you?'

'Yes.'

She was pleased to have Keith: he was a bonus, a ready-made brother, and the first few times they'd met they'd talked about their parents' coming marriage and looked forward to being together. They didn't do that so much now.

'Is me Dad back?' asked Keith.

'No. Not yet.'

'Are you stopping?' he asked.

'No, I'm off back. What about you?'

'I'm off back too.'

They sat on the steps for a while until Eileen shouted down to them. 'Tea-time!' She sounded happy, but then she always did. They went upstairs and looked at the new baby together, until Keith got bored and wandered back down to the bar. He took a slice of bread and butter with him.

'He won't half get wrong if Leonard sees him,' Eileen said. 'He can't stand kids that won't sit up at the table for their meals.' She looked anxiously at the clock.

'I think we'd better be going,' Liza said.

'Won't you stop and see him, Mam?'

'No. It gets dark so early, I think we'd better be getting back.'

Mother and daughter looked at each other over Kath's head.

'All right,' Eileen said. 'You know you're welcome to stop if you want.'

Keith came running up to them to say goodbye. When Liza kissed him he started to cry, though he'd forgotten about her before she reached the end of the street.

A year later Eileen moved into her council house, and three months after that gave birth to a son. Liza gave her six weeks to get settled, then sent Kathleen to stay. She worried about the girl all week, counting the minutes till Saturday when she could go and get her back.

Eileen came to the door, so quickly she must've been waiting for the knock.

'Hello, Mam,' she said.

Her feet and arms were bare. She looked worried and older than Liza remembered, but then she had Keith in trouble with the police . . .

The house seemed dark after the brightness of the day. At first Liza thought the living-room was empty, but then she saw Keith curled up on the end of the sofa, sucking his thumb.

'What's up with him?' she said.

'He's not been feeling well.'

Keith looked up, suddenly, and grinned.

'See you got your front teeth back,' Liza said.

'Yup.'

'That's because you've stopped kissing the lasses.'

Keith laughed. He had a charming smile and in his shallow

230

eyes no emotion was visible except hunger. He sat close to Liza and snuggled in.

Eileen said, 'He's been off school all week with a bad cold. Haven't you?'

Keith nodded and leaned forward to pick up the baby's rattle from the floor. As he did so his shirt and trousers – both too small – parted in the middle, to reveal weals on his back.

Liza said nothing, but caught her breath. Eileen went across to the pram in the corner of the room and lifted the new baby out.

'Well, Mam,' she said, in a voice throbbing with emotion, 'you've held two daughters in your arms and now I want you to hold my son.'

It was a bad moment for the violins to come in.

'What the bloody hell do you call that?' asked Liza, ignoring the baby and yanking Keith's shirt up to show his back.

'He's been a bad lad, Mam,' said Eileen, flushing.

'*That* bad? He'd get gaol for that, Eileen, and if he wasn't your husband I'd see he got it. There's no need for that. *No* need.'

'His nerves are bad, Mam.'

'Oh, don't give me that. Your father's nerves were bad when you were born, he'd been out of work for three bloody years. But I've seen him go out in the backyard and punch a brick wall till his fist bled before he'd raise it to a child. So don't come that with me. *His nerves are bad.*'

'I notice you don't ask what Keith did.'

'No, I don't. It's matterless.'

'He took the money his Dad give him for the football pools, to buy the postal order, and Leonard won. I knew something was wrong, because Leonard was over the moon, you know, reckoning up how much it was gunna be and that little monkey was just sat there. Grinning.'

'*Did* you take it, Keith?'

'Aye.'

'It's afterwards, Mam. He doesn't seem to know what he's done. All he does is sit there and grin. And that really gets to Leonard. I had an awful job with them when the baby was

231

born. I could hear him shouting and then the kid screaming and I come downstairs, and I got the buckle end of the belt instead of him.' She pointed to a mark on her cheek. 'Another inch and it'd've been me eye.'

Liza looked at Eileen's cheek and asked, 'Where's Kath?'

'Oh, she took Jenny across to the playground. He didn't mean to hit me, Mam. He's never once raised his hand to me.'

Liza looked at Eileen's blubbery face and said, 'Howay, give us the bairn. You go and put the kettle on.'

Left alone with Keith, Liza remembered the kind of thing visiting adults usually say to children, and asked, 'What you gunna do when you grow up, son?'

Keith took his thumb out of his mouth. 'I'm gunna kill me Dad.'

Liza looked down at the new baby, which was a miniature version of Leonard. Only wizened.

Kath came into the room, carrying Jenny.

'Hello, Gran,' she said.

'Hello,' said Liza. 'Are you all right?'

'Fine. *She's* tired.'

She put Jenny down on the hearth-rug, and tried to amuse her by shaking the rattle, but Jenny whinged and tried to crawl towards Eileen.

'She can walk really,' said Kath. 'She just goes back to crawling when she's tired.'

'That's another thing,' said Eileen, coming back in with the teapot. 'They won't let us have Sheila out of the home. They more or less said I only wanted her to help me look after these two, but you know that's not it, Mam. I want them *together*. There's no point being a family if you're not together.'

Liza looked round the crowded and chaotic room. She thought: *One child in care and the other battered. I can't let Kath live here.* But then she looked at Kath, and thought, *I can't stop her. Not if she wants to come.*

The children watched the telly while they had their teas. Liza hadn't seen it before, and she was fascinated. There was this young couple and they had to answer questions and every time they got it right they got some money. But then they had to choose whether to take that money or double it and risk going home with nothing. At the end, the girl was put in a cubicle by herself and she had to watch things passing by her on a conveyor belt. She had to remember as many as she could, and as many as she remembered she got. Some of the things were really valuable: a washing-machine, a fridge, a vacuum cleaner, an electric drill, a dinner service. Others were just silly: a banana, a pink teddy bear. But it was the silly ones that stuck in your mind. You couldn't blame the girl for remembering the teddy bear and forgetting the drill. Her husband laughed and said it didn't matter, but you could see it did. He'd wanted that drill.

The children ate with their eyes fixed on the screen. Keith got really carried away, shouting out the names of things and pounding the table, until in the end he knocked a bottle of milk over and Eileen yelled at him, in a voice that didn't sound like Eileen at all.

After the tea things were cleared away, Liza bent down and touched Kath's shoulder.

'I've got to go back tonight. You know that, don't you? But you don't have to. You can stop with your Mam.'

A long silence.

'No,' said Kath. 'I'll come home with you.'

Eileen took a deep breath. 'All right,' she said. 'If that's what you want.'

'It's not what I want.' Kath looked from one to the other. 'What I want doesn't matter.'

'Of course it matters,' Liza said. 'If you want to stay with your Mam, stay.'

'I want both of you.'

Kath hid her face in her hands, while Liza and Eileen looked at each other over her bowed head.

Liza had just started to wash the kitchen floor when Kath came in from school. She hopped across the wet lino and sat on a corner of the sofa, her hands clasped round her knees.

'I've passed,' she said. 'I'm going to the grammar.'

'Well,' Liza said.

'Liz didn't.'

'No. Well, I'm not surprised.'

'She went white when the names were read out.'

Liza got up, slowly.

'Well,' she said again. 'Your Grandad would've been pleased.'

Kath couldn't attach any meaning to that: her grandfather was a pale young man in a photograph that Gran kept in a box under her bed.

'Liz's Dad promised her a bike.'

'Then he should know better.' Liza picked up the floorcloth and began squeezing it dry. 'It'll mean a lot of expense. There'll be a uniform.'

'They give us a list.'

'What, already? They didn't lose much time.'

She took the list and read through it, holding it at a slight angle because the dimness that seemed to be encroaching on one eye narrowed her field of vision.

Kath saw her expression change.

'Is it a lot?' she asked.

'No,' said Liza. 'Not more than I expected.' She went back to wiping the floor. 'You know your Mam draws the children's allowance for you. She says she doesn't, but I know for a fact she does. And I get nowt.'

'You should make them pay.'

'Aye, and get our Eileen into trouble. No, I'll manage.'

'You should tell her it's yours.'

'It's not her, is it? It's him.'

'Him then.'

'She won't question anything *he* says. If he says, "Keep the money," she'll keep it. If he said, "Rob a bank," she'd rob it.' Liza sat back on her heels. 'Do you know, I sometimes wonder what I did to deserve your mother.'

'Oh, she's not that bad.'

'She's not bad at all. She's a fool.'

They went to a shop in Wellington Street to buy the clothes. Before they went in they stood outside and looked at the uniform on a dummy in the window. The dummy had silky golden curls and a small, upturned nose. Liza stared at it, doubtfully.

'Well, we won't get any further stuck here.'

She pushed the door open and they went in. Liza was shy of the quiet, expensive shop, though not so shy that she didn't insist on value for money, fingering cloth and tugging at seams in a way that made Kath want to die.

'She's into women's sizes now, you know.'

The assistant nodded. 'Oh, they aren't children long these days,' she said.

She stared at Kath, who felt more than ever like a freak. She hoped she wouldn't have to get undressed because then the assistant would see one breast was bigger than the other. It happens like that, Gran had said, when Kath brought herself to mention it. But Kath didn't see why it should. After all if people's legs started behaving like that nobody'd be able to walk.

'You don't think she could do with the bigger size?'

Liza was on her knees measuring the hem of the raincoat against Kath's legs.

'I don't want the bigger size,' said Kath. 'This'n's too big.'

'The way you grow? You'll be out of that in a year.'

'Oh, I don't know,' said the assistant. 'She's got a good bit of room in that.'

She tightened the belt buckle and the tongue went all the way round and back to the front again.

'She'll fill out,' said Liza.

'I'd need twins to fill this lot out.'

'Shush,' said Liza, looking around her, anxiously.

Kath hated her for being in awe of the place and then loved her again, passionately, as she watched her open the worn black purse and fumble for the money. It came out in coins and twisted notes, exact to the last penny. Liza pushed the heap of notes and coins across the counter and said, 'There. I think you'll find that's right.'

A couple of weeks before the beginning of term Liza went to the new school for parents' night and Kath, who hated having to explain that she had no parents, waited anxiously for her return.

'What was it like?' she asked.

'Oh,' said Liza, 'it was very nice. They showed us round and explained everything. By heck, it's a big place.' She sat down. 'I can see what you mean now about finding your way around. Oh, and the PE teacher had a word with us. About periods and all that. She said we had to make sure you knew before you come, because apparently a few girls've found towels in the bins and got upset. I thought, *Well, our Kath's all right*. But she was, she was very sensible. I thought she put it across really well.'

Kath made the tea and they sat by the fire to drink it.

'Do you know how I found out?' Liza said. 'I was sixteen and it started while I was at work and I ran all the way home and I burst into the room shouting, "Mam, Mam, I've busted!" And she was sat there with the curate from All Saints and she says, "Don't be so daft, of course you haven't busted." And as soon as he was gone she got her crutch and she belted me with it. Right across the face. "There," she says. "That'll teach you to mention that in front of a man." There I was – bleeding both ends – and that was the only explanation I ever got. Then when our Winnie started I found her on the sofa in the front room crying and I went through to me Mam in the kitchen and I says, "Haven't you told her?" "Told her what?" she says. Oh, I was disgusted with her. I went through to our Winnie and I explained to her as best I could, but you know the damage was done. It's beforehand you need to know.'

Before she started at the new school Kath went to stay with her mother again.

'I want to know who me father was,' she said to Liza, the night before she left.

'I can't help you there,' said Liza. 'Because I don't know.'

'No, but she does!'

'Now don't you go upsetting your mother. She's got enough on her plate with him.'

Kath was old enough now to make the journey on her own, and increasingly Liza, worn out by the attempt to disguise her failing eyesight, was content to let her go alone.

She arrived back on the Monday, looking amused.

'How's your Mam?'

'Oh, fine. Dad's not so good.'

Liza said nothing. She couldn't bring herself to believe in Leonard's illness, though he'd been on the sick for more than a year.

'Keith's in trouble again. Broke into the Conservative Club and pinched the whisky.'

'Well, if you must pinch . . .'

'Dad took the belt to him, and do you know what he did? He just lifted his hand like this and caught it. And he says, "*No.*" You should've seen Dad's face.'

'He's lucky that's all he got.'

'Me Mam says she's gunna put Keith in the army when he leaves school. She says it'll give him a trade.'

'Stop him murdering Leonard more like.'

'Oh, and I found out about me Dad.'

'She *told* you?'

'Not who he was. Where he's buried.'

Liza stared. 'First I knew he was dead.'

'He's underneath the hedge at the bottom of the back garden. Dad killed him, and they buried him together. On their wedding night.' Kath made violin-playing movements with her right arm. 'You know what she's like.'

Liza did, but it could still come as a shock.

'And is that what she told you?'

'Yes. And she's told our Sheila and Keith that too. So it's all over the estate.'

Liza shook her head. 'No wonder his taties grow.'

At first Kath seemed happy in the new school, but gradually, as the year passed, she became tired, irritable.

'It's all right if you can't do it, you know,' Liza said, timidly.

'I can do it.'

One day Liza came in from work and found Kath at the table in the living-room, writing lines. Liza was too far away to see what the line was. She sat by the fire and waited.

237

When the silence had gone on a long time, Kath said, 'I got wrong for saying nowt.'

'You must've said summat.'

'No! I said *nowt*.'

'Oh. Well, you know that's wrong. You know you should say *nothing*.'

'Actually, that's wrong too. It's *nuthing*.'

'Is that what they said? Oh, tell 'em to get stuffed!'

Kath started another page. 'I did.'

Liza looked at the bent head. She was putting together a lot of small changes in Kath's speech. In her manners, her interests, her attitude to life.

She said, uneasily, 'Kath, you won't . . .'

Kath looked up and waited.

'Oh, nothing,' said Liza. *'Nuthing.'*

Kath smiled. *'Nowt.'*

Liza's eyesight, particularly in the left eye, was now very bad and at last she gave in and agreed to go into hospital to have the cataract removed.

She was in hospital six weeks, longer than planned, because the operation went wrong. For the first few days she had bandages round her head, and it was doubtful whether she would be able to see with her left eye. When the bandages were taken off she could see, though not clearly: just light and dark and shapes moving round the room. Slowly, her sight improved.

But it was difficult to eat: she was self-conscious about the mess she made. And the business of peering into people's faces isolated her. By the time she was ready to go home she was deeply depressed, but hid it, afraid that she might not be allowed to go. At least at home she would know where everything was.

She went home on a Thursday. The following Monday Kath came back from Harriet's, and life returned to normal.

On the surface, at least.

While Liza was in hospital a man in one of the houses opposite had killed himself. The street mulled over the event in its usual way, and Liza heard the fading echoes of its gossip.

238

'Wife buggered off and left him.' 'Aye, and took all the furniture. I saw the removal van come and I thought, *Eh, that's funny. I didn't know they were moving.*' 'Put the gas poker in his mouth. But he must've changed his mind because his cheek was torn where he'd tried to pull it out again.' 'Bloody fool.' 'Oh, you can't say that.' 'Course you can. She was rubbish.' 'Ah, but he loved her.' '*Love.* Catch me killing meself for love.'

From her bedroom window Liza could look down into the front room of the house where the man had killed himself. A sandy-haired man, she remembered. Nothing remarkable. She spent hours at the window, looking down. *Eh, fancy doing that*, she would think. This was the only conscious thought she brought back with her from the long hours of watching. The words tinkled in her head, a small sound in the vast silence.

Kath got used to going upstairs after school and seeing her Gran, a dark shape against the window, cutting off the light.

The familiarity of things in the house, which Liza had so long looked forward to, failed her. Her eye could not slide past any detail, however trivial. She stared at the wallpaper and lost herself in the intricacies of the pattern, which was not a pattern at all, for where there should have been only ordered repetition there were minute differences, divergences from the expected, and each one had to be traced to its source.

Everything was dark, heavy. She felt the pressure of the furniture on the floor, how the minute particles of dust were ground beneath its weight, how solid it was, how sharp-edged and dense and final.

She was not deluded, or not at first. The real world had become more real; it pressed in on her and left her no space. But then the noise began. A whisper that slithered across the floor of the room and died before she could hear what it said.

For a few days there was silence. The whisper didn't return, though she found herself listening for it. She would sit with her head on one side while the wireless played and seem to listen, but always she was listening for something beyond music or words. She felt a sense of loss, of dying almost, for the whisper, though terrible in itself, had eased her isolation

239

among the hostile furniture, these shapes that swelled and fattened on darkness. Then, just as she was beginning to accept that she was alone, it came again. And again. Soon it was her constant companion: a whisper that always promised speech, and always slithered into silence.

At times it seemed to be the echo of all the sounds she'd ever heard: the clock that chimed midnight on the night of her birth, Frank's voice dying in his throat and the other voices glugging out, the birth cries of her children, Ben's laughter on the heap, the tinkle of glass in that great silence after the bomb. The worm uncoiled again. She strained to listen and, as she listened, Tom's voice, Louise's voice, Frank's voice shrivelled into silence. Only the whisper was left, and in the silence it had created all around itself, she heard it speak for the first time, and it said: *Kill*. She waited to know who it was she had to kill, and the whisper came again. *Kill Kath.*

Liza waited for her to come in from school. She heard the front door open, then the sound of her satchel dumped on the floor.

'Gran?'

Liza waited. She heard the living-room door open, and close again. Kath was coming upstairs, expecting to find Liza in the front bedroom, but Liza wasn't there. She was in the cupboard at the top of the stairs, waiting, and as she waited she giggled and the giggle spread all over the walls and joined forces with the whisper, so the worm became a bigger and bigger worm.

'Gran?'

She was walking across the landing now. Liza stepped out of the cupboard, put her hands round Kath's neck and squeezed.

Kath choked, but she was thirteen now and a big girl for her age. She grasped Liza's wrists and, after a slight struggle, lifted her hands away.

They looked at each other.

'Howay, Gran,' said Kath. 'Come and sit down.'

Still holding Liza's hands, she led her downstairs. Liza stumbled after her, her head so full of blood and pain she couldn't hear whether the whisper was there or not.

Kath pushed her gently down onto the sofa and sat beside her. Silence. Liza looked round the room, waiting for the whisper to start again, but though the furniture bristled at her in the familiar way, there was no sound.

'I tried to kill you,' she said.

'Yes,' said Kath. 'It's all right.'

Liza went on looking round the room, and listening. Then, when she was sure the silence would last, she raised her eyes back to her granddaughter's face.

A few days later Liza went to the doctor and told him something, though not all, of what had happened.

'You should go into hospital,' he said.

'No, I can't. I've got to get back to work.'

He looked doubtful, but drew the prescription pad towards him and began to write.

'It was the devil,' she said, watching his pen move over the page.

'No!' he said, kindly and with no more than a trace of condescension. 'Of course it wasn't the devil. You were ill.'

She accepted his kindness and his pills, but continued to believe she'd encountered a power of darkness greater than the human mind. If words meant anything, that small, infinitely dry whisper was evil.

During these months Liza developed her mother's habit of 'cutting' the Bible for guidance. She never forgot the first text she found:

Then was Jesus led up of the spirit into the wilderness to be tempted of the devil. And when he had fasted forty days and forty nights, he was afterward an hungred.

She read on to the end . . .

Then saith Jesus unto him, Get thee hence, Satan: for it is written, Thou shalt worship the Lord thy God, and him only shalt thou serve. Then the devil leaveth him, and behold, angels came and ministered unto him.

She closed the Bible. That was her own experience, not

241

tamed by pills, not trivialized by condescension, and in identifying her time of trial with Christ's she recovered a sense of her own depth and mystery.

As Frank had done. She understood now why he had become obsessed with the Resurrection. In fact, she thought, recovering her sense of humour as well, she could now, twenty years after his death, have made quite a good job of being married to Frank.

When Kath was sixteen Eileen came to stay for the weekend. She was on her way to visit Keith in Durham gaol, and Kath had offered to go with her.

'You never had to visit any of your own relations in prison,' Liza said. 'I'm buggered if I can see why you should visit his.'

Kath smiled. In the years since Liza's illness a relationship had grown up between them that was strong enough, and complex enough, to contain its own ambivalences.

'Somebody has to go with her.'

'She's got a *husband* to do that. It makes me sick the way he leaves everything to her. He's never once visited that lad in prison. One thing you can say about Leonard: he's consistent. He turned his back on that bairn the day it was born and his back's been turned ever since.'

'She says the worry of it makes him ill.'

'Only thing makes him ill is the thought of work.'

Eileen arrived later that day, and the following morning she and Kath set off on the bus for Durham. It was March and still cold. Eileen, though worried about Keith, was excited by the prospect of a day out. Since Leonard had become too ill to work, days out had been rare.

'Look,' she said, and pointed.

The dress shops had their spring displays, and in one the central figure was a bride: rapt, ecstatic, rising from a foam of lace. Eileen's face flushed.

'Isn't she beautiful?' she said.

For a moment, Kath saw somebody different from the worn-out woman she knew, and remembered a picture in Gran's box of her mother in uniform in the second year of the war. Her young face had looked like this.

'I want you to have a white wedding,' Eileen said, sitting down again. 'And our Jenny.'

'Be a long time before I'm married, Mam.'

'Oh, I don't think so. You're sixteen. And you're not bad-looking.' She peered at Kath. 'Don't know who you take after, mind.'

My father? Kath wanted to ask, but decided to leave the back garden undisturbed.

They walked up Old Elvet together and joined the queue that waited in the small square outside the prison. A cold wind blew across the open ground, and the cypress trees behind them gave little shelter. You felt exposed in more senses than one. A woman walking past frankly stared, and Kath stared back.

'He says this is the worst prison he's been in,' Eileen said. 'He says it's worse than Wormwood Scrubs.'

'It *is* tough,' a woman standing beside them said. She looked no older than Kath, though she had a year-old baby in her arms.

'He says if there's any trouble they take the bloke down the gym, wrap rubber mats round him and kick him through the rubber. He says you can be kicked half to death, and not a bruise to show for it. I don't think that can be true, do you?'

'I don't know,' said Kath. 'But you want to remember he's not in here for knocking off gas meters. He did a fair bit of kicking himself.'

Kath had expected to see Keith on the other side of a grille, but they met in a large room with tables and chairs round the walls and a warder hovering discreetly just inside the door.

Keith was as beautiful as ever. Eileen burst into tears when she saw him, and her sobs echoed across the room. Soon she and Keith were deep in their favourite 'B'-movie scene: the one where the aging mother, poor but honest, begs her delinquent son to go straight.

People at other tables turned to stare at them, but they didn't mind. Perhaps they felt acting like theirs deserved an audience. Except Eileen wasn't acting. Or was she? Kath watched and couldn't tell.

'But have you *changed*, Keith?' she was saying. 'Have you asked the Lord to change your heart?'

Say no, pleaded Kath, silently.

'Yes,' said Keith. 'I've prayed day and night. I've thought of you and me poor old Dad . . .'

Who?

'. . . and I've *prayed*.'

I don't believe this, thought Kath. She looked across the room and a prisoner sitting there caught her eye and smiled.

'Get your eyes off her, you mucky sod,' Keith yelled across the room. 'She's only sixteen.'

'No harm in looking,' the man called back, and laughed.

When the time came for them to go, Keith hugged and kissed Kath. He'd long ago cast her in the role of adoring kid sister, and nothing she ever said or did made any difference.

'I think he's repented,' Eileen said, as they walked back down Old Elvet. 'Don't you?'

'I think we should go to the cathedral,' said Kath, sourly. 'And *pray*.'

In the end Eileen prayed; Kath climbed the cathedral tower. She looked out over Durham, at church spires, college gardens, boats passing on the river. Far below, insect-size, murderers and rapists walked round in a ring. She watched them for a long time, but none of them looked up.

'I blame meself,' said Eileen, as they stood in the queue for the bus. 'Your Gran was right. I should never've let him go in the army at fifteen. But I thought I was doing it for the best. I thought he'd come out with a trade.'

'He did,' said Kath. 'They taught him to kill.'

'The guard isn't dead,' Eileen said, uneasily.

'Not Keith's fault. He did his bit.'

That's what was missing. The realization that the red stuff, left behind in a pool on the pavement, ringed by police chalk, was not actually tomato ketchup.

When they got home, Eileen tried again with Liza. 'He had his chance in the army, and he threw it away.' She looked into the fire. 'He should never've pinched that tank.'

'That's true,' said Liza.

They saw the funny side of it simultaneously, and laughed.

'What on earth did he think he was gunna do with it?' asked Kath.

'I don't know,' said Eileen. 'He says he was just bringing it home to show me. But of course the army didn't see it that way.'

After tea, Kath went to visit a school friend, something she would never once have done while Eileen was there.

'Kath's growing up, isn't she?' said Eileen. 'She'll be leaving school this year. It *is* sixteen at the grammar, isn't it?'

'Yes.'

'Leonard was saying, you know, if she wanted to come and live with us, I could get her a job in the factory. I'm pretty sure they'd take her on.'

'She's not leaving. She's staying on.'

Eileen stared. 'You can't afford it.'

'I'll manage.'

'She'd get a good job with the qualifications she has now.'

'And tip her wages up to Leonard? No, Eileen. He's got one mug working to keep him. He doesn't need two.'

'Well, Mam, I think you're mad.'

'No, I'm not.'

'And what does she think about it? Does she want to do it?'

'If she didn't want to do it, do you think anybody could make her? You don't know your own daughter, Eileen.'

'I know enough to know you've ruined her.'

'Aye, mebbe I have. But somebody had to bring her up, Eileen, and there wasn't much competition for the job.'

'You put her in front of everybody.'

'Yes, I do. But what you don't seem to understand is, it's not just *her*. It's Edward and Frank and Tom, and me pushing that bloody pram up the hill year in year out. And there's no way that's going to be thrown away on Leonard and his sodding factory. I've never said this to you, Eileen. And I'll never say it again. But you're getting it now. She owes you *nowt*.'

When Kath came in she found them sitting in silence,

Gran's eyes burning with bitter fire, Eileen's hands clasped round a mug of cold tea.

Next day, Kath set Eileen to the bus and returned to find Liza lying on the couch.

'You had a row, didn't you?'

'Not a row. I told her a few home truths I swore I'd never tell her.'

Kath sat down on the sofa. 'I don't understand me Mam.'

'Join the club.'

'But I think you do. Better than I do, anyway. You should've seen the way she was going on in that prison.' She pulled a face. 'Like somebody in a film.'

'She likes her bit of drama. So would you if you had her life, working from morning to night, cleaning the pub, cleaning the school, cleaning the house. Never a new dress, never a penny to spend on herself. If she buys herself a bar of chocolate once a year she feels guilty. She feels she's no right to it. You wouldn't like it.'

'I wouldn't do it.'

'And what else would you do? A houseful of kids and a husband that won't work.'

'Can't work.'

'Well, perhaps you're right. He finished me the way he hammered that bairn. But you don't want to run away with the idea that because it's all violins and drama it isn't real. Many a time she got between him and Keith and took the blows for the bairn. Now that's not play-acting, Kath. That's *courage*.' Liza sighed. 'Our poor Eileen. She always had plenty of that.'

On Tuesdays Mrs Dobbin and Liza went round the King Billy for a drink. At seven o'clock Mrs Dobbin would rattle on the grate, and Liza would put her coat on ready for the knock on the door.

'Where's Kath?' said Mrs Dobbin one night.

'Gone round her mate's to revise.'

'Hm,' said Mrs Dobbin. 'I suppose if that's what she wants. But it's not the young life we had, is it?'

'No,' said Liza. 'It's a damn sight easier. I was married with a bairn at her age.'

When Liza stepped out of her front door now, she stepped into a different world. The houses opposite were boarded up, and even some houses on this side of the street, which wasn't scheduled for demolition, were empty.

Liza and Mrs Dobbin set off for the pub, walking through more than a mile of boarded-up streets. Desolation and decay clung to the ruined neighbourhood like sea-fret. They moved away from the shelter of the houses and crossed a patch of wasteground, where a church loomed up out of the mist, a hulk left rotting by the tide.

'Look at it,' Liza said, waving her hand at the emptiness. 'What on earth do they think they're doing?'

'Oh,' said Mrs Dobbin. 'It's all gunna be flats over there.'

'Aye. I'll believe that when I see it.'

'But that's the attitude nowadays, isn't it?' said Mrs Dobbin, a few paces further on. 'If summat's stood the test of time, knock it down. I tell you, I'm frightened to walk past the council offices case some keen little bugger jumps out and knocks *me* down.'

Mrs Dobbin had become very fat in her old age. She did not so much walk as wallow in the wind that blew down Wharfe Street.

'By heck. I'll be glad to get there,' she said.

Liza took her arm and half pushed her up the hill. The wind blew rain into their faces, but the lounge of the King Billy was warm, so warm Liza's glasses misted up.

'Now then, ladies, what's it to be?' said George, leaning across the bar.

'A pee,' said Mrs Dobbin, and ran.

'Nay, I'd be had up if I sold that.'

'You never have been yet,' said a voice from the back of the bar.

'Cheeky bugger!'

'She'll have a lager and lime.'

'Well, I'll be buggered,' said Nelson.

'You want to watch what you're saying,' Liza told him. 'They're a funny lot round here.'

'He looks forward to you coming,' said George.

247

'I know he does.' She looked up from the cage. 'Have you heard any more about them closing the pub?'

'No,' George said. 'But I think it's pretty definite. There's no trade.'

'There will be when the flats are built.'

'Aye, and when will that be? They can't afford to keep it going like this.'

'It's history, this pub.'

'Oh, they don't care about that. It's *money* now, Liza, and bugger everything else.'

Nelson sounded a bit like George: the same slight hiss at the end of words. Not a lisp, exactly, more the result of his missing front teeth. He had some, but he couldn't get on with them and kept them in a pint glass at the back of the bar.

'*He* worries me more than anything,' said George, looking at Nelson. 'I mean who'd have him? All right in the bar of a pub, but you put him in a boarding house. And I've nowhere else to go, you know, Liza. I've no family.'

Mrs Dobbin came back, puffing and blowing, and they carried their glasses across the room to the corner, where Nance Claypole sat.

'I'll have to go and see about me bladder,' Mrs Dobbin said, as they sat down. 'Least little bit of drizzle sets it off.'

'I didn't think you'd make it,' Nance said. 'What with the bad weather and all.'

'Never seems to keep you in,' said Mrs Dobbin.

'You're too damn right it doesn't. This is the only break I get.' She looked at Mrs Dobbin. 'Some folks have all the luck.'

There was an awkward silence. Liza looked down and saw that Nance had finished her drink.

'Eh, I am sorry, Nance,' she said, and started to get up.

'No, you're all right, Liza. Next time.'

She went across to the bar and was soon laughing and joking with George. Mrs Dobbin craned round to look at her.

'How do you suppose she keeps her hair that colour?'

'Rinses it in tea.' Liza encountered Mrs Dobbin's sceptical stare. 'That's what she says.'

248

'Gerraway! Precious little of her gets rinsed in tea, inside or out.' Mrs Dobbin lowered her voice. '*Henna.*'

'You don't want to let her upset you.'

'I can't help it,' said Mrs Dobbin, gasping like a deflated balloon. 'Fancy saying I was lucky. I loved my Harry.'

Liza touched her hand. 'I know you did.'

A few minutes later, Ethel Whittaker arrived. She'd not long been out of hospital, and looked it too, poor soul.

'How are you, cock?' Liza asked.

'Middling.'

'You won't know yourself in a few month.'

'Why, aye,' said Nance, coming back to the table. 'You wouldn't've given tuppence for me two months after I had that, but by heck I'm glad I did.'

'Takes a lot out of you, mind,' said Mrs Dobbin.

'I'll say,' said Nance, and indulged in one of her raucous laughs, quickly imitated by Nelson. 'Shut your face, you!'

'Got yourself all packed then?' Liza asked Nance.

'Packed? *Packed?* I've been packed a bloody year. I'm sick of looking at packing cases. I've forgotten what I've got in some of them.'

'Well,' said Ethel. 'Just think. When you unpack, it'll all seem like new.'

'Aye, if we ever do. Bloke at the council says, "Wilson Street. All round there. That'll be the first to go." He says, "Honey, you'll be among the first out." That was a year ago, and they haven't shifted their backsides since.'

'Same down our way,' said Ethel. 'Me husband went down the other day and he says, "If you don't hurry up and knock them bloody houses down some bugger's gunna come and do it for you." Because they are, you know. They're pinching everything they can lift. There was a coupla blokes with a dustbin full of lead, and I says, "What the hell do you think you're doing?" "Oh," he says, "we're from the council." I says, "Council, my arse."'

'I see a lot of people've got notices in their windows,' said Liza. '*Still occupied.*'

'Aye, well, folks are terrified of vandals. You move out one day, they move in the next. And it's easy to make a mistake. One or two people've been broke into, because they thought the houses were empty.'

'Are you lot moaning on again?' said George, stopping by the table to pick up an empty glass.

'You'd moan on if you'd been packed a year and no sign of anything happening,' said Nance.

'You want to think,' said George, 'there's you lot moaning to move out, but there's many a one up there'd give their eye teeth to move back.'

'That's true,' said Nance. 'They put old Mrs Porter up on the fourteenth floor and as true as I sit here,' she said, looking at Mrs Dobbin, 'her legs are worse than yours.'

'Well, there's *lifts*,' said Ethel.

'When they work, there is.'

'I've heard of a lot of cases like that,' said Mrs Dobbin. 'Me sister got moved last June and she says there's not the same spirit. She says all people are interested in is what you've got, and they seem as if they begrudge you every little thing. It's, "Oh, how can she afford that on what she's got coming in? I don't know how they do it on the money." But at the same time, God help you if you have nowt. They don't want to know you.'

'And no help given,' said Nance. 'They watch Mrs Porter sweat and struggle up them stairs, and nobody says, "Here, honey, let me carry your bag." Mind you, she wouldn't dare let 'em if they did. She'd be too frightened they'd pinch it.'

'I don't think I'd like to live in a flat,' said Liza, 'stuck in all day looking at nowt.'

'And you are stuck 'n' all,' said Nance, 'because there's nowhere to go on the estate, and people can't afford the bus fare to get back into town. All right for them that are working. But what about the old people? And women stuck in the house with kids? Where's their life?'

'Well,' said Mrs Dobbin to Liza. 'I'm glad our side of the street's stopping up.'

'And how did that happen?' said Ethel. 'Knock one side down and leave the other. Where's the sense in that?'

'Bloke got pissed in the pub at lunchtime,' said George. 'Couldn't draw a straight line.'

The bell rang.

'Excuse me, ladies. Custom.'

As soon as George had gone, Nance said, 'I hear you're having Nelson?'

'If it comes to it I am.'

'Liza,' said Mrs Dobbin, 'you're mad.'

'Oh, I don't know,' said Nance. 'Be company for her when Kath goes to college.'

'Drive her mad more like.'

'She can always put a pillowcase over it,' said Nance. 'More than you can do with a man. Speaking of which . . .' She sighed, and reached for her handbag.

'You've only just come,' said Liza.

'*He* won't think so,' said Nance. 'See you next week.'

'I pity her poor bloody husband,' said Mrs Dobbin, as the door closed.

'Well, your pity's wasted,' said Ethel, 'because she's goodness itself to him and he's anything but easy.' She turned to Liza. 'He won't let her out of his sight. If she goes to the toilet, he follows her down the yard. She says it's like having a bairn.'

'She might be glad of him to follow her before she's through,' said Mrs Dobbin.

'Aye, but what puzzles me is how these women get men like it,' said Ethel. 'I could be sat on the toilet a week and mine wouldn't notice.'

'Good in bed,' said George, coming to collect Nance's glass.

'Eeh, he is a cheeky sod,' said Ethel, looking from Liza to Mrs Dobbin and back again.

George grinned gummily, and started to serenade her.

> *Are you lonesome tonight?*
> *Is your girdle too tight?*

As he sang and swayed back to the bar he wiggled his hips, pulling an imaginary girdle down. Liza choked on her drink.

251

'Eeh, he's a scream, that man,' said Mrs Dobbin, wiping her eyes.

'Isn't that awful?' said Ethel, though she waited till George was safely back behind the bar.

'I'm bloody sure it isn't,' said Liza. 'You're too narrow to live, you.'

'I've got standards.'

'Meaning we haven't? Thanks very much. Anyway, he was right, wasn't he, about being good in bed. I think that has a lot to do with holding a marriage together.'

'Well, it wasn't what held mine together,' said Mrs Dobbin. 'If we'd given it up altogether, I'd never've missed it.'

'No, nor me,' said Ethel. 'I used to think it was awful. A man dips his pen in the inkwell, and you're left reading the message for the next eighteen years.'

'Oh, at least. Doesn't matter how old they are, you still have the worry of 'em.'

'It's not like that now,' said Liza.

'No,' said Ethel, 'because they're all rotting their insides with chemicals.'

'Plenty of lasses rotted their insides with chemicals trying to bring it off. And it didn't bloody work.'

'Nothing worked,' said Mrs Dobbin, with feeling. 'Do you know, I knew a woman and she was desperate. She saw this advert in a magazine and it said if you wanted to know how to stop yourself having family you had to send a pound. Well, you know that was a lot of money . . .'

'A week's wage.'

'Aye. Anyway, she saved up and she sent off, and do you know what she got back? A drawing of a man's willie, and underneath it said: KEEP IT OUT. Well, she was stuck, wasn't she? There was no way she could get her money back. She didn't even dare tell her husband what she'd done.'

'And you talk about the good old days,' said Liza. 'What was so good about them? Women wore out at thirty. And you can't deny they were, because you *know*.'

'I don't deny it. But I still say we had something then that we've lost now.'

'*Youth*,' said Liza.

'No,' said Mrs Dobbin. 'More than that.'

Six months later, Liza and Kath were sitting on the railway station, waiting for the London train.

'You have got your money, haven't you?' asked Liza.

'Yes.'

'And your ticket?'

'Yes. I've got everything.'

The luggage had gone on ahead, so there was only a small overnight bag to carry. Liza turned and looked down the line which glistened and gleamed and led away into the distance. Until now there hadn't been time to think about it, the days had been filled with washing and ironing and pressing and packing. There hadn't been time to think about this.

'You'll write as soon as you get there?'

'Yes.'

'She sounded nice, your landlady. It's a pity it's so far out. Still, if you can't live in college . . .'

'It's not like that. It's not residential.'

Liza found it hard to grasp what it *was* like. Grammar school she'd understood. Edward had passed for the high school and not been able to go. So had Frank. When Kath went, it seemed as if she was claiming something that had been theirs by right. But this . . . She looked down the line and her imagination faltered.

'I wish me Mam was here,' said Kath.

'She sent her love.' Liza wrestled with her conscience. 'Oh, and summat else. I didn't know whether to tell you.'

Kath waited.

'Keith's been transferred to Wormwood Scrubs.'

'Oh, he'll be pleased! Well. He'll be pleased to leave Durham.'

'I suppose you'll go to see him?'

'Yes.'

'I could never see what you saw in Keith. Why you had to get so close.'

'Oh, it's all one way. Keith isn't close to anybody.' Kath looked down at her hands. 'I suppose because we were both . . . *mangled*. Only I had you. And Keith had nobody.'

A bell rang. People got up and began moving to the edge of the platform.

'This'll be yours,' Liza said.

She walked along the platform, keeping pace with the shadow of Kath inside the train. I won't cry, Liza told herself, I won't spoil it for her. After all, it should be easy not to cry. She'd seen Tom off from this station, and Edward, and she hadn't cried. Those had been endings; this was a beginning.

Kath found her seat and leaned across to say goodbye. The window was mizzled with rain, so perhaps she wouldn't see the tears, but still Liza held them back. And back. And back . . .

Until Kath pressed the palm of her hand against the glass, as Tom had done, and for a moment it was his hand. Liza reached up and covered it with her own. Then a shadow moved, and it was Kath again.

The whistle blew. Kath smiled and waved, but Liza stood with her mouth a little open, a wisp of white hair blowing across her face, and watched until the train was out of sight.

She walked back home, let herself into the house, and felt its quietness close over her, like water over a drowning head.

She'd get used to it. *I won't have to get up in the morning,* she thought. *I can have a lie in,* but it was so long since she'd even thought of such a thing . . . She wasn't sure she'd be able to do it now.

The grate rattled. Puzzled, then alarmed, Liza went to the door and saw Mrs Dobbin coming out of her house.

'You give us a shock,' Liza said. 'I thought for a minute you were ill.'

'You haven't forgotten, have you?'

'Eeh.' Liza put her hand to her mouth.

'You have. Don't worry. We're not late.'

'It's all the rushing round I've had to do.'

Mrs Dobbin saw that Liza's face was blotched with tears, but she didn't say anything until Liza got her hat and coat on and was ready to leave.

'Got off all right, did she?'

'Yes.'

Liza tried to imagine Kath on the train. She'd be halfway by now, reading a book perhaps, or looking out at drenched fields. You could imagine her on the train, but once she arrived and went out through the ticket barrier she would disappear into nothing, into a darkness so total she might as well have dropped off the edge of the world.

Easier to remember her in the days when she'd come to collect Liza from work, the small face peering round the door, her dismay at the line of wet footprints on the floor.

'You don't want to worry about her, you know,' said Mrs Dobbin. 'She's got her head screwed on the right way.'

'I know.'

'She's not like your Eileen.'

'No.'

'So don't you be thinking she'll come back like your Eileen did, because she won't.'

When Liza stepped out of her front door now, she looked out across empty space where houses had been.

'I can't get used to it,' she said.

'No, nor me.'

'Mind, the flats are coming on. Every time you look there's another storey.'

'Aye. Our Wally knows a man works on one of the gangs, and he says there isn't half some corners being cut. They'll not have to knock that lot down. Bugger'll bloody fall down.'

They walked across the wasteground, past the screened-off area where the flats were being built, and down into Wharfe Street.

'One thing,' said Liza, 'you get from A to B pretty quick these days.'

'Be A to Z soon. And bugger-all left in the middle.'

Mrs Dobbin was out of breath and a funny colour. Liza wondered sometimes how much of that bulk was really fat. She'd seen Mrs Dobbin dig her fingers into the skin of her ankles, and leave pits.

'It is good of you, coming all this way,' said Liza.

'What friends are for.'

It's odd, thought Liza. *I've never once called her Nellie. All these years: delivering babies, sitting up with people, laying them out, christenings, weddings, funerals, to say nothing of air-raids, and never once 'Nellie'. I suppose it's because she seemed such a lot older when I first moved into the street. Didn't seem older now. Couple of old trouts together, battling up the hill.*

A group of young girls came helter-skelter down the hill towards them, bare thighs flashing, stiletto heels striking the ground with a noise like rifle-fire. They scarcely saw the two old women, though they broke ranks and flowed around them, like a brightly flashing stream.

The boarding-house was ten doors further down, past the King Billy. They climbed the black and white chequered steps and peered into the hall. The smell of lavatory cleaner hit you at the door.

The landlady, all blue-rinsed hair and creaking corsets, met them on the threshold and pointed towards a room marked 'Residents' Lounge'.

Residents, Liza thought. *Inmates, more like.* Four hard chairs stood in the four corners of the room.

'Bloody hell,' said Mrs Dobbin.

'Hello,' said George. He came further into the room, looking at the gas fire as if he would have liked to switch it on. 'Well.'

'How are you keeping, George?' said Liza.

'Oh, not so bad. It's . . . quiet.'

His face and neck looked shrunken, his belly broader, as if somehow he'd melted and flowed down onto himself, like a half-spent candle.

'By heck, she doesn't believe in wasting gas,' said Mrs Dobbin, looking at the fire.

'I'll go and get him,' said George.

Left alone, the women looked round.

'He could've done better for himself than this,' said Mrs Dobbin.

'It's clean.'

'Hmm. Surface clean,' said Mrs Dobbin, settling back in the hard chair and closing her eyes. 'You'd not catch me eating shrimps in a place like this.'

'I've tied a pillowcase over him,' said George, coming back into the room.

'Aw,' said Liza, 'why?'

'Frightened old tin-knickers out there'd get a lugful,' said Mrs Dobbin.

George looked sheepish. 'I've packed his seeds and his water bowl in here,' he said, handing Liza a plastic bag.

She took it and didn't know what to say. Perhaps the kindest thing to do was go. On the other hand . . .

'I got him off a sailor,' George said. 'He come and stopped with us for a bit and then when he moved on he left him behind. He used to say Nelson got on his nerves because he'd been kept in the mess, you know, and he used to imitate all the lads' voices, and of course . . . A lot of the lads were dead.'

Bloody hell, thought Liza, looking into the cage. *It's Frank.*

'He used to say it reminded him of the mates he'd lost. He got so his nerves couldn't stand it. But I used to say to him, that's not right, you know. You *have* to remember. You *owe* it to people to remember.'

'That's right,' said Liza, 'you do owe it.'

'Well, now we've got that sorted out, can we go?' said Mrs Dobbin.

George stood up. 'I'd like to offer you both a cup of tea. But . . .'

'Oh, don't you bother yourself,' said Liza, 'Tell you what, you pop round our house tomorrow and I'll give you a cup of tea that doesn't smell of disinfectant. And you can see how he's settled in. All right?'

George helped her to her feet.

'Sure you can manage now?'

'Why aye. Shopping bag weighs more than this.'

Though it wouldn't weigh much now she was cooking for one.

'Make it midday,' she said, 'and we'll have a bit of grub.'

'My God, hasn't he gone down?' said Mrs Dobbin as they walked across the wasteground. 'Nowt left to live for, that's the trouble.'

'Oh, you can live for the sake of living,' said Liza. In the last hour or so she'd begun to realize that, although Kath's departure meant loneliness it also meant that, for the first time in half a century, she was responsible for nobody but herself.

'You know they're doing day trips to Blackpool illuminations? I've always wanted to see them and I've never got. Do you fancy a day out?'

The last thing Kath had done before she left home was to bring Liza's bed downstairs. So that night, when Liza might have been lonely, listening to the trains and wondering about Kath, she had the fire to keep her company. And when she woke up during the night, instead of the silence of the empty house, she heard Nelson's perch creaking, and a rustle as he stirred and stretched his wings.

15

Stephen closed Liza's door behind him and started to cross the wasteground towards the flats. The visit he had to do there took less than an hour, but when he left the sky was already dark. There were no windows in the stairwell, and all the light bulbs had been broken. Something brushed past him at the corner of the stair: one of the Alsatian dogs that roamed the estate. Its eyes flashed emerald in the dark.

He came out into the lobby at the foot of the stairs. The usual smell of human and animal piss lingered – the lobby was a favourite refuge for those taken short on their way home from the pub – but he thought he could smell something else, as well. Sulphur? Burnt paper? A rocket zipped into the sky. *Of course*, he thought, *Bonfire Night*.

He started to walk across the wasteground. A gang of youths had lit fires, two fires, no more than twenty yards apart. Flames and sparks whirled upwards into the darkness, but the corridor between the fires was as bright as day. Here and there, sparks fell on dry grass which had begun to smoulder and would soon burst into flame. He walked round the edge of the circle, aware of being watched by figures who were themselves scarcely visible. Even when they stepped out into the ring of light, he couldn't recognize them. The flames transformed their individual faces into masks of beaten bronze, and their shadows, thrown out behind them, were giants trampling houses down. Then two of them threw a mattress onto the smaller of the two fires and a grey twilight fell, in which they were revealed as ordinary, even rather undersize, human beings, stamping their feet and slapping their arms against the cold.

In the circle of faces were some that he knew well: Zit, Kev, Whitey, Stew, Scrubber. And Brian, standing slightly apart from the rest.

For a moment Stephen thought he might stop and speak. But he sensed the same kind of aggression here that you got, sometimes, in pubs on Friday or Saturday night. The air crackled. He walked on and felt them turn to stare at him as he passed.

Flames were already licking round the mattress: the shadows on the grass had begun to grow.

A rattling in the grate. Liza struggled to wake up, thinking that Mrs Dobbin must be calling her, but then realized Mrs Dobbin was dead, had been for twenty years, and the next house was empty. The grate rattled again. Rats? In her mind's eye Liza saw a big rat with white fur and pink eyes run across the floor. Nonsense. Her mind must be going. It'd need boots on to make that racket.

She tried to work out, from the deep blue of the sky, whether it was evening or dawn, and eventually, from its richness, concluded it must still be evening.

She was surprised how vividly her father had come back to her on the walk by the river. He'd loved her and yet, as a young woman, she'd watched him hurt and bewildered by her marriage to Frank, and she hadn't cared. Now, when she would've liked to say, 'Dad, I'm sorry. I loved you, Dad,' there was nobody to say it to.

She was older by ten years now than he had ever been, and the strangeness of this thought made her want to see his face again.

She got up, slowly, with the help of her stick, and knelt by the bed. The box was heavy for her to pull out. Whenever she felt how heavy it was, she told herself she would have to throw something away, something that wasn't valuable; but then she sifted through it again, and it all seemed valuable, even the scraps of brightly coloured material cut from dresses she'd worn when she was young.

260

Her father's photograph was near the bottom. She took it out and looked at him: one face in a row of faces. His eyes had survived the long wait for the flash, unlike the eyes of other men that looked watchful or tired or dead. She could see a blast furnace behind them, so perhaps this photograph had something to do with the union, or one of the friendly societies perhaps. The men stood with their hands on each other's shoulders, squinting into the camera. Steelworkers' hands, broad-palmed, the fingers spatulate. Hands you never saw in a pram or cradle. Hands, like the men, made at the works.

She remembered the day when her father had come home and cried. Two men had fallen into the furnace, and their bodies – what was left of them – could not be got out. Peter Graham's father came and read the burial service, there, at the foot of the furnace, and all the men stood with their caps in their hands and the great six-foot hammers lying in the red dust at their feet. Then they'd put their caps back on and charged the furnace again. She remembered how her father had cried aloud that miners would have abandoned the shift, that fishermen would have put back to port, but they, they had charged the furnace again.

In the end, his great strength gone, he'd been a weighman. A trusted position, though low-paid. Rheumaticky from his days on the gantry, wheezy from the furnace fumes and the long walk home by the shrouded river, he'd sat in his cabin year after year, weighing barrows of ironstone.

Not the good old days, but still she rocked to and fro, for the broken streets and the scattered people, for the cold hearth and the cracked furnace, for the river flowing between empty wharves.

She was glad her father hadn't lived to see it, because how could he have borne it, the wind moving across acres of blond grass and the barbed wire singing?

Gently, she brushed a film of dust from his face and put the photograph away. Then she hauled her old bones back into bed, and rested. Again it came, the rattle on the other side of the grate.

And stopped, leaving her uncertain it had ever been there.

The Clagg Lane estate appeared from a distance to be on fire, so many bonfires burned. Opposite the youth club, on a small patch of ground, a still-unlit pyramid stood, crowned by a Guy whose pink plastic face and sightless eyes stared out into the dark. Women stood on the outskirts of the group, holding small children in their arms. Round the base of the pyramid, men tried to organize the lighting of the fire.

At last one of them stepped forward with a strip of burning rag in his hand. After the long hot summer there was no lack of dry wood, and flames soon roared up through the heart of the cone. The Guy tilted a little to one side, his jacket caught fire, and the pink plastic face began to melt. Beads of moisture formed and dripped down into the flames, like sweat.

The people cheered, then turned to each other and laughed as if, the year's ritual killing over, they could enjoy themselves at last.

Stephen had expected to see lights on in the youth club, but the windows were dark. Inside, Jan sat alone, her booted feet up on the ping-pong table and a cup of coffee clasped in her mittened hands.

'Hello,' she said.

'I thought you'd've gone with Colin.'

'No. I was going to, but we decided somebody'd better stay here and mind the shop.'

'I hope he's all right.'

'He should be. They've gone to the police bonfire.'

'How many?'

'Nine. The police bonfire isn't popular with our lot. Too well organized.'

A fire engine clanged past.

'*That*'s where our lot'll be.'

'Be a bad year. Everything's so dry.'

'I've just made this,' she said, holding up the cup. 'It'll still be hot.'

He went into the kitchen, made himself a cup of coffee and carried the kettle back into the hall. 'Do you want yours freshening?'

'Please. How was Lily?'

'Charming.'

'She would be. She likes men. More easily conned.'

'She wants us . . .' He stopped and smiled. 'She wants us to collect a small debt for her.'

'Oh, yes?'

'The detective who arrested her, under the mistaken impression that she was a fence, merely because she happened to have two hundred fur coats in her bedroom, which she was taking care of for a friend . . .'

'Whose warehouse roof had sprung a leak . . . Yes, go on.'

'Still hasn't paid for his wife's fur coat. She wants us to get the money.'

'*Bloody hell.*'

Stephen raised his hands. 'That's what she said. She's a Jubb, isn't she?'

'Yes. Joe Jubb's sister. Why?'

'Oh, I just wondered.' He looked round the darkened room. 'Is there any particular reason why we're sitting in darkness?'

'No. I just got thinking, I couldn't be bothered to switch it on.'

'They mightn't be so keen burning the place down if they knew there was somebody in it.'

'Gerraway, man. Real Guys.'

'Oh, they're not that bad.'

'Do you know that in this country every fortnight somebody tries to burn an Asian family alive in its own home?'

'Yes.'

'Well, then.'

'Let's have the light on,' he said.

The single bulb hung low over the table, swaying a little in the draught from the door.

'I took the old lady out today,' Stephen said.

'Did you tell her the news?'

'No.'

'Oh, Stephen.'

'I didn't have the heart.'

'You're supposed to be talking sense into her.'

'I know. I'll tell her tomorrow.' The silence made him uncomfortable. 'They're not going to knock the house down with her in it, are they?'

'No, but if she looks out of the bedroom window and sees bulldozers move in it might be a hell of a shock.'

'She won't. She can't get upstairs.'

'Well, there you are, then. Nice little ground-floor maisonette.'

He didn't answer.

'Stephen, you've got to get her to face up to it. It's irresponsible not to.' She waited for him to say something. 'Either that, or you *fight* . . .'

'Yes, I know.'

A scuffling sound from the kitchen. Stephen went to investigate. The sound seemed to come from the cupboard under the sink. He opened the door and a white face stared out.

'Tony! What on earth are you doing here?'

'The cat's frightened,' said Tony.

Stephen looked more closely and saw two amber slits in a ball of hot black fur.

'Well, if he's frightened you'd better stay in there with him.'

Tony nodded. 'It's the bangers he doesn't like.'

Stephen put the plate of biscuits on the floor beside him and went back into the hall.

'Tony. In the sink cupboard.'

'Why?'

'Taking care of a frightened cat.'

'Oh, I remember. He got a banger shoved down his neck last year and ended up in hospital.'

'Poor little sod.'

'Whitey. Do you know, when they do things like that, I feel just like that bloke in *Heart of Darkness*. I can't remember his name . . .'

'"Exterminate the brutes."'

'Yes.'

'You need a holiday.'

'I need another job.'

Tony appeared in the doorway, nursing a remarkably phlegmatic cat.

'He feels a bit better now,' he said.

He walked confidently towards them, until a burst of crackling stars sent him scuttling under the table.

'Are you all right?' Jan said.

A small, stoic voice. 'Fine.'

'You know I've been thinking,' she whispered, pointing down at the table. 'There's a lot to be said for starting younger. His age.'

'I thought we were going to exterminate the brutes?'

'As an interim measure.'

'Oh. Go on.'

When, two hours later, Stephen drove past the end of Walker Street on his way home, the fires on the wasteground were still burning. Shadows of people flickered along the walls, seeming to struggle and grapple with each other. The fires were reflected in the glass windows of the tower blocks, like those reflections in spectacles that make their owners look blind.

Liza dreamt there was a scrabbling outside the door of her room, and when she went to open it, rats with pink eyes and twitching noses ran for cover, dragging their naked tails across the floor. She woke to find her mouth dry with fear and reached for the glass of water she kept by the bed. The room was in darkness except for a dull orange glow from the dying fire. She'd've liked to switch her torch on and see the time, but the nightmare was still strong in her.

A few sips of water calmed her. She wondered why she should have dreamt such a terrible dream, when the day had been so pleasant and when, recently, she'd had so many wonderful dreams, marvellous dreams, culminating in the vision of Lena Lowe with the living jewels in her hands – for it seemed to Liza more like a vision than a dream.

The feeling of horror receded. She wriggled down into the

bed and closed her eyes, but then she heard it again, the rattle, and recognized it as the sound she'd heard in her sleep.

This was no dream. She heard the latch of the back door rattle as somebody pressed it down. Bolted on the inside, Mrs Jubb had seen to that, but the frame was rotten. One kick and they'd be in.

Perhaps if she shouted it would frighten them off? But her mouth was dry and the shout came out as a croak. The light. Put on the light. People in the flats could see that, if anybody looked out. She hauled herself to the edge of the bed. Firelight shone on the scaly white skin of her legs as she found her stick and floundered to the door.

Too late. Even as she touched the switch, the back door burst open. A milk bottle fell from the table and rumbled to and fro on the stone floor.

She could see only a dazzle of white light and behind that a dark figure, a figure that seemed, as it came towards her, to have no face.

Other figures crowded in behind it, she couldn't see how many. She turned to the front door and tried to open it, but the one holding the torch said, 'Grab her.' Something huge and black flitted between her and the light. She felt her head pulled back by an elbow round her chin.

The man holding the torch stood in front of her, his head and shoulders just visible behind the light. He wore a balaclava, back to front, with holes cut in the wool. His eyes, inside the fraying holes, were pink.

'Hey!' the boy holding her said, and lifted his hand to shield his eyes from the light.

The man with pink eyes lowered the torch.

'Tell us where the money is and we'll let you go.'

A slight lisp. A tremor that might have been rage or fear, or both.

'*Start looking*,' the boy holding her begged.

'It'll save time if she tells us.' A third man had come into the room. He spoke quietly and his voice was calm.

She couldn't say anything because of the arm around her neck. Despite this, the arm tightened, forcing her head back

266

until she thought her neck would snap. She grunted, and it slackened enough for her to speak.

'Handbag.' She waved towards the bed.

Pink-eye went to the bed, found the handbag and tipped the contents out. Her pension book and a couple of pound notes fell to the floor. He searched through the few papers she kept in there, tearing envelopes when he couldn't get them open fast enough.

'There's nowt here,' he said, and shone the torch directly at her.

She felt the boy holding her go tense.

'That's all I've got.'

The torch swung round the room, over cupboards, chest of drawers, sideboard, bed.

'She could've hid it anywhere,' the third man said.

Until now he'd scarcely moved from the shadows, hanging back as if reluctant to come anywhere near the beam of the torch. But now he moved forward and began searching the sideboard drawers where she kept her bedlinen. He began with the bottom drawer and worked up to the top, searching not wildly as the pink-eyed boy did, but quietly and methodically.

Pink-eye came towards her.

'Now then, Gran,' he said. 'Stop playing funny buggers. We know you've got it. Just show us where it is and you can get right back in bed.'

'Tell him, love. Go on.'

The light flashed as he came closer.

'I haven't got any money. All I've got's me pension.'

'For Christ's sake!' the boy holding her said.

Pink-eye stopped. The torch swung round the room again, until it came to rest on the bars of Nelson's cage.

'No,' said Liza, thinking with him.

He walked towards the cage. Nelson, bewildered by the torch that made it seem now day, now night, gave a bad-tempered cackle. Then screeched, as a hand with no soothing preparatory words thrust through the door of his cage and grabbed for his legs.

'Right, Gran. Tell us where it is or I'll wring his neck.'
Liza crumbled. 'I can't. I haven't got any.'
Another screech.
'Got you, you little bugger.'
Nelson's wings flapped as he was dragged out of the cage.
'Right, Gran.'
The third man, in his slow, methodical search of the room, had reached the bed. As he bent down to lift the pillows his foot struck metal.
'Got it.'
'Gerraway, man, it's the jerry.'
The pink-eyed boy laughed, high-pitched hysterical giggles, and his grip on the parrot's legs slackened. With a flash of emerald and scarlet, Nelson swooped across the room and landed, beak gaping, on the curtain rail.
The third man knelt down and dragged the box into the light. Liza felt the boy holding her relax.
'Tip it out,' Pink-eye said.
The two of them bent over the box and began sifting through its contents, spilling children's hair from envelopes, tearing letters open, tossing photographs onto the floor, trampling everything beneath their feet. Finally, in disbelief, scraping the bottom of the box with their fingernails.
'Where is it?' the one with pink eyes yelled, turning to her again.
The boy holding her stiffened.
'Tell us where it is or I'll wring his fucking neck.'
She was too frightened to reply. Pink-eye walked up to her. The boy put out his arm to protect her, but a hand sent him sprawling against the wall.
'There isn't any,' the third man said. 'Look, you can see for yourself.' He picked up the scraps from the floor in his cupped hands, threw them into the air and watched them drift, slowly, down.
'There is,' the boy with pink eyes insisted. 'She's hidden it.'
He sounded like a child on the verge of tears.
'One more chance,' he shouted, but his voice broke. Then,

just at the moment when his self-control snapped and he would have broken down and cried in front of them all, his fist shot out. Liza fell back against the wall.

Silence.

'Oh Christ.'

'You bloody fool.'

'I never touched her.'

The pain in her jaw was nothing. It was her heart that bulged into her throat and would not let her breathe. She no longer cared what they said or did. She screeched as Nelson had screeched, stretched out claw-like hands, begged for air. Slowly, as they watched, she slid down the wall and sat, like a rag-doll, on the floor.

'She's dead. You've killed her, you stupid cunt.'

A scuffle, a flail of fists and feet, as they fought each other to get out. Then, silence.

They were wrong, she decided after a while. He hadn't killed her, though there was a taste in her mouth that she recognized as blood.

Slowly, she crawled across to the fire and began putting letters and photographs back into the box. Nelson, beak agape, watched from his perch on the curtain rail, as she held scraps of paper up to the fire, searching for Tom's face. Silly old fool, she told herself, as she gathered it all together. Tom's letters, the telegram announcing his death, his and Eileen's birth certificates, her father wearing the watchchain that had matched the colour of her hair, her mother's black eyes and iron jaw.

Where they'd been scattered and trampled on, the papers lay at some distance from the fire. She had to crawl to reach them, and it took a long time. Her chest did not so much hurt as house a pain that might, at any moment, need the greater space of the whole room.

When she'd found everything, even the buttons from a dress she'd been fond of, she pulled a blanket from the bed and wrapped it round her. Then, coal by coal, she built up the fire.

Perhaps they'd come back and finish the job? When people were as frightened as that there was no knowing what they might do. Well, it was all one. She wiped her fingers across her mouth, and they came away dark. But the pain had died down a little. She'd spent the night with worse pains than this.

She looked down at the box. If she tilted it towards the fire, there was light enough to see the lid. It was years since she'd looked at it, not perhaps since she was a child, lying on the sofa during one of those bilious bouts that always seemed to happen on Mondays, wash-day, the worst day of the week to be ill. Now she traced with her fingers the circle of dancers and beyond them, in the shadow of the trees, the draped figure holding something in its hands. Something you could never see because that part of the pattern had worn away. She looked again at the dancers. Almost, she felt, she could hear the music, the stamp of their feet as they turned.

Now, while the music was just beginning, she must think. Tomorrow morning, somebody would come into the house and find her. She did not now believe they would find her alive. This didn't worry her: for many years she'd been attached to life by no more than one or two easily unravelled threads. But she owed it to the person who found her to make herself as little unsightly as possible. She dragged a blanket off the bed and wrapped it round her till only her hands were visible, pulling the edge low over her forehead, like a cowl.

Now she could concentrate on the pattern, which seemed to glow and come to life as she traced it. The rhythm of the stamping feet grew louder, the clasped hands quickened, the music began to fill the room . . .

Stephen put down the book he was pretending to read and got out of bed. Rain spattered the glass, no more than a shower, but enough to damp down the smouldering bonfires. He opened his window and gulped down cold, almost liquid air. Thin leaves of willow whipped an inky blackness. Far away, between attenuated trees, he glimpsed the silver-grey of the lake. The night was full of the pressure of living creatures, coiled in sleep, or like himself, awake.

He knew he should go to bed, but he didn't feel like sleep.

He remembered Liza, and hoped she hadn't been too tired by her day out. She'd enjoyed it, he thought, in spite of her tears by the river. Though towards the end he'd noticed a hectic flush spread over her face. Her cheeks became port-wine coloured, the flesh sagged, and for once she looked every day of her age. He'd been afraid, then, for her and for himself.

He'd talked to Jan about her on the way home. They'd dropped Tony off outside the off-licence where his father worked and then gone next door to the pub. The juke box blared, the television played to an almost empty bar, and they'd sat in the corner over a pint and talked. He'd tried to explain what Liza meant to him, why his meeting with her was so important, but he couldn't find the right words. He didn't know, anyway, what he'd expected Jan to say, and yet he was disappointed when she said nothing. Only smiled, and waited for him to go on.

He knew Liza mattered, more than anything had mattered for years, but he couldn't say why. It was all tangled up with his father, with going away and coming back, with belonging and not belonging.

'You're too impatient,' Jan said. 'You want everything sorted out *yesterday*. But it isn't like that. Sometimes there isn't a solution there. Not just ready-made, like that. You have to grow into one.'

'It's important for Liza, too. It's not just me.'

'Well, of course it is. At her age, to have somebody new to love. Somebody to love *her*. It must feel like a miracle.'

He'd thought at the time Jan didn't understand. Only now, remembering her use of the word 'love', he realized she had understood, after all.

He got back into bed. As always it felt too big, and he turned restlessly, thinking of the nights he'd spent with Gordon, and wishing this was one of them. Two months. Not long, though as the date of Gordon's return came closer the weeks seemed to take longer to pass.

Stephen folded his arms behind his head and looked at the sky. The moon, now veiled, now flashing in liquid brilliance, mounted steep cliffs of silver-sided cloud. He had an abrupt,

271

powerful sense of his own physical identity, his own being in the world, independent, in the end, of everybody. On the crest of this feeling, he drifted off to sleep.

Music, thin and reedy, a pipe, perhaps, and one small drum. Loud enough to beat time, but not to cover the *stamp*, *stamp*, *stamp* of feet. They circled the bonfire, hands and arms linked, mud-clogged feet pounding the ground, keeping the rhythm of pipe and drum. The firelight glowed on their arms and faces, they seemed to be made of fire, and yet the mud claimed them. And one day, perhaps, they would crumble into it, dissolve away, like the mud dolls that children make. Meanwhile they danced around the fire, and leapt through it, too, sometimes, so the wind of their passing fanned the flames, and the sparks flew upward.

A figure stood alone in the shadow of the trees, so heavily draped he couldn't tell whether it was a man or a woman. It held something in its hands and seemed to offer it. He walked towards it, peering into the darkness of the hood.

He knew the cowled figure was Liza, and yet the hands that came out of the folds of the cloak were male. Blindly, he held out his hands. Then, just as their fingers touched, just as Stephen felt the shape and weight of the box, he woke and lay in darkness, sweating, because he had remembered whose hands they were. Somehow, in the labyrinth of the dream, his father and Liza were one.

Circling, circling. Heavy feet pounding the earth, men's feet in boots, her father's feet in clogs. That time he and Auntie May danced a clogdance on Middlesbrough station. Auntie May's skirts hoisted shockingly high, high enough to show red flannel petticoats and white knees, and her father's eyes dancing in his poker-straight face. All over the platform they clogdanced, circling round and round, while her mother and Harriet watched with prim, shocked faces. She stood, one hand clasped in her mother's, her feet tapping the ground until her father swooped down and lifted her, high, high, and put her on his shoulders, where she dug her fingers deep into his bad red hair. Her own carefully done ringlets unravelled,

as her father and Auntie May whirled round and around, and
the station, with its iron monsters, blurred into a mist, and so
they went on dancing till the train came in.

Circling, circling. Round and round the fire, like children
round a street lamp. Every night she went out to play under
the lamp and at first the street was cold, her fingers ached, it
was miserable standing there alone.

But then one small figure after another slipped out of the
houses. Lena Lowe with her boys' boots, handed down, skinny
arms, legs blue with cold, but no catching *her*, she was the
fastest of the lot. Once *she* was there the games began.

> I'll follow my mother to market
> To buy a ha'penny basket;
> When she comes home, she'll break my bones,
> For falling over the cherry stones.

That was a catching game, but Liza liked skipping games
best. The rope twinkled, you could hardly see it sometimes,
only hear the whistle as it whipped the wet ground. And then
somebody would yell, 'Too fast. It isn't fair!' because of course
they tried to trip you up, if it was your turn. The girls at the
end turned the rope and chanted:

> Mary Ann Cotton,
> She's dead and she's rotten,
> She lies in her grave
> With her eyes wide oppen.

Liza's mother said she'd worn a black-and-white checked
shawl at her trial, though after the trial you didn't see shawls
like that. But before, they'd been all the rage. And so perhaps
her mother had worn one?

'Liza! Liza!'

There in the shadows was her mother, calling. But Liza
didn't want to go in yet. It wasn't time: the clock on the stairs
hadn't struck. And the rhythm of the dancing feet was
growing stronger. Girls linked arms and danced the cakewalk,
six abreast, girls with yellow faces and respirators in their
hands. A man with one leg was forced off the pavement and

into the gutter. He looked back at them, and his lips shaped the word: *Scum*. Because not everybody liked canaries. Some people would have liked to wring their necks. But the canaries didn't care. With wages in their pockets to equal their fathers', they danced the new freedoms, the new independence. They danced the deaths of their brothers that made it possible, but here the music faltered, and, one by one, the dancers turned away.

Liza was alone in a dark corridor. There had to *be* windows because the half-light she moved through must have a source, but she couldn't see any. Rooms opened off the corridor and led into other rooms in which there were desks with nobody behind them, and filing cabinets with all the drawers pulled open, and files and papers lying on the floor. Papers littered the corridor, too, blowing along it in the draught from an open door, but the door, like the windows, was invisible. Official-looking documents too, not scraps, and yet there was no way you could avoid treading on them, no matter how hard you tried.

She came out into a hall, vast like a cathedral and cold, cold, so that her breath curdled the air. Her footsteps echoed across a stone floor. She was alone. But then, standing at the far end of the hall, she saw a man she knew. Her footsteps quickened, she almost ran towards him, wondering why he didn't turn round. Her footsteps echoed so across the floor, he must have heard them. She caught his shoulder, and he turned. He was an old man, so old his face was cracked at random like a crushed eggshell, and when she put her fingers up to his cheek they came away wet. She said, beginning to cry herself, 'But Eddie, *you* were never old.'

He smiled then, but already he was beginning to fade. A great wind rose, howling down the corridors, whipping up flimsy white squares of paper and hurling them into the air until she stood in a blizzard of paper. The black wind howled louder, saying, '*Do you think it's only paper I can move? Watch.*' So Liza watched and, as she watched, the black wind tore everything down. The walls of stone that seemed solid enough to last forever, the desks, the filing cabinets, the corridors, all

274

were gone, all destroyed by the bitter wind that blew across the world, and when it stopped blowing she was indeed alone. And beneath her feet neither street nor corridor, but dust, black dust, spreading everywhere. She walked along a lane, head down, a shawl wrapped so tightly round her that only her hands were visible, coarse hands, work-grained. The road led upwards and, as she trudged along it, the sun came up behind her out of the night. She felt its heat on her back, a white sun that produced heat and not warmth, so the black dust gleamed silver at her feet but remained dust. No life anywhere, not even a blade of grass, and still she trudged on alone, alone, up the side of the dark hill. Her shadow stretched out in front of her. The sun crept up the sky, she circled the hill, and her shadow moved round with her, now in front, now behind. But always alone.

Then she saw them, the others, men and women, clambering up the black slope, scratting, like her, for diamonds in the dust. They moved round and round, together and alone, passing each other on their individual circuits like planets. Then, when this had gone on a long time, one of them broke free from his orbit and came towards her. His red, tight, shiny face looked as if it had been skinned. She thought it might crack, so tight and shiny was it, and then it did crack, it burst, and she stepped back, recoiling from him; until she remembered that the sound he made was laughter.

He laughed again and said, 'Three heads, Liza. And one of them a Jerry.' He remembered bones slashed bare, and laughed; he remembered men drowned in mud, and laughed; he remembered promises broken and innocence betrayed, and laughed; and at first Liza was afraid of his laughter. It sounded too much like the black wind that had blown a generation away, and she tried to look away from him, to forget the cracked, shiny face and the laughter that went on and on, and the stump of his arm that he waved in the air. But he wouldn't let her go, he held her shoulder, and made her look into his face, into the moist red cavern of his mouth, the uvula that wobbled as the breath of his laughter swept over it and out across the world, and for a moment she thought he would eat

275

her, like the giant in the fairy story who smelled the blood of Englishmen. But then, just as her fear became intolerable, just as she struggled with the folds of the blanket to free herself, just as she stared into the red cavern of the fire, the quality of his laughter changed. He laughed, and the sun burnt less fiercely on their backs; he laughed, and the sludge quickened; he laughed, and a bare tree, spiky with thorns, put on buds again.

Against a red sky the tree blossomed and burned, and she turned to Frank, to share it with him, to quiet his endless litany of the names of the dead, to tell him it was no longer needed, but he wasn't there. She wandered off in search of him and came to a room where light dissected a face, until the strings and muscles that kept the eyeballs in place were laid bare. She knew she had to close his eyes, and pressed pennies down onto the lids, pennies as black and heavy as night, but his eyes didn't close. He looked at her and said, '*I gave the dead breath, Liza. But you shut them up in a box.*'

'You can't stop here, Missus,' the man with the tin hat said, and led her down into the ground. The earth smelled raw: she didn't want to go down there. If you were going to die, better die on the surface where you could breathe real air, not this damp, earth-smelling muck, full of body sweat and the smell of graves. But there, at the end of the tunnel, was Mrs Dobbin, doughy jowls quivering with fear, though she laughed when she saw Liza, and said, 'I'm glad you've come. I can't make this piece fit.' Liza sat down beside her on the camp-bed. She was doing a Victory jigsaw and the piece she held out to Liza was a young man's face. Tom's face. Liza fitted it into the empty place and immediately all the young men began to march away, shouldering their kit-bags and laughing as they went, dissolving into grey and white dots before they reached the edge of the tray.

I shouldn't be afraid to die, Liza thought. *When so many young men have shown the way.*

The clock on the mantelpiece ticked, but a louder ticking had started inside her. She beat time, not with hands and mind alone, but with every cell of her body. Not a tick really, more like a pulse, it might even be her heartbeat; but no, it was too loud and strong for that. It shook the bones of shoulders and chest as if this pendulum might shatter the case. Pounding and stamping, louder and faster, and then again more slowly as the music ebbed, and she turned away from the circling dancers, from the lamplight and the spinning rope, and looked across the street to where her mother stood in the shadows, holding out her hand.

'Liza!' she called. 'Come on now, Liza. Time for bed.'

It was late, later than she'd ever been before, the clock on the stairs was striking midnight; but she noticed, as she ran towards the shadows, that her mother stood in front of an open door and smiled as she beckoned her in.

16

'I got one of them clear-out firms in the end,' said Mrs Jubb, looking round the living-room. 'Her daughter wanted things sold, but you can't sell stuff like this.' She rested her hand briefly on the sideboard. 'Nobody'll have it. There's not room for it in the new houses.'

'They'll take everything, will they?'

'Oh, yes. Don't give you anything for it, mind.'

The harvest of sixty years' hard labour sized up as junk and shifted in a day.

'What about the box?'

'Oh, Eileen took it back with her on the train. I just hope she values it. It was the death of her mother.'

Stephen sat down abruptly and stared into the empty grate. He'd wanted to see the box again, to confirm his memory of the hooded figure, to try to discern, through the dirt of centuries, what it was that it held in its hands.

'She let too many people see that box. She was always dipping into it and pushing it under the bed. The result was they all thought she had money. I don't know where they thought she got it from. I used to go and get her pension and do her shopping for her and I can tell you there was bugger-all left by the end of the week.'

Through all the horror of Liza's death, the publicity, the police investigation, he'd returned at intervals to the dream, and found to his amazement that the joy he'd experienced on first waking remained. Perhaps it was better not to see the box again, not to search too curiously for an explanation. Whatever had happened would reveal itself more fully in time.

'Would you like a cup of tea?' Stephen said.

'Aye, go on.'

Always in the past when he'd put the kettle on for tea, there'd been a stream of talk and laughter from the next room. Silent now, except for a groan as Mrs Jubb knelt down to empty another drawer. He went back into the living-room.

'It's a worry to know what to do with some of these things,' Mrs Jubb said. 'I wish their Eileen'd been able to stop after the funeral, but, dear me, you only had to look at her legs. I've never seen legs like it. *She*'ll not make old bones. She cried when I saw her off at the station. I says, "Don't worry, love. I'll see to everything." But, my God, I didn't know what I was taking on.'

'Aren't they too good to throw away?'

She was pulling bedclothes out of the sideboard drawers and stuffing them into black polythene dustbin liners.

'Oh, these'll go to the WRV. Seems a shame though, doesn't it? I mean, look at these.' She held up a pair of sheets, the cellophane wrapper still intact.

'I think she'd probably want you to have them.'

'Do you think so?'

'I'm sure she would.'

Rather doubtfully, Mrs Jubb put the sheets to one side. 'She was a great one for putting stuff in drawers and leaving it. My old Gran was just the same. When the time come to lay her out we had a choice of fifteen nighties, and not one of them worn.'

'Anyway, sit down and have this.'

Mrs Jubb looked at the clock. 'Aye, howay, why not?' She sat on the end of the bed and looked round the room. 'Took me hours putting stuff back and now I'm pulling it out again. But the little bastards didn't half make a mess. There was flour on the carpet and all sorts.'

A long silence. Nelson's wing creaked as he stretched.

'He's quiet,' Stephen said.

'He's hardly spoke. He can't get over it, you know, the bed being empty. Nobody'll ever tell me he doesn't understand.'

They sat in silence, the rhythmic swing of Nelson's body from perch to perch the only sound in the room.

'You'll miss her,' she said.

'Yes.'

She nodded, and sipped her tea. 'There's a lot'll miss her. It's surprising how much she meant. I'll be lost, I don't mind admitting it.'

Stephen said nothing, though more aware than ever of the empty bed and the blue-grey ashes in the grate.

'She wanted you to have him, you know.'

Stephen looked up, startled.

'Oh yes. She's lain in that bed many a time and said to me, "He'll look after my bird. I know he will."'

Mrs Jubb looked him straight in the eye, a gaze of such unflinching integrity he knew at once he was being conned.

'They'd only put him down,' she said. 'And there's no mess. It's not like having a dog.'

Sunflower seeds, spat out by Nelson, dotted the bottom of the bed.

'I'll think about it.'

She was wise enough not to press. 'Well,' she said. 'They can knock the whole lot down now, can't they? Nothing stopping them.'

'They'd've done that anyway. She'd've had to move.'

'She'd never've moved. She'd've died in her sleep. She was a determined old woman her. If she'd made her mind up, she'd've done it.'

'Instead of which . . .'

They stared into the grate.

'Some little bugger's shitting himself,' Mrs Jubb said. 'And I think I know who.'

'So why don't you tell the police?'

'I have told them. They were too bloody busy pinning it on my husband. Never done owt like that in his life.'

'I know who did it too. But I can't prove it.'

Mrs Jubb sipped her tea. 'Get him down the station he'd crack quick enough.'

'I don't think so.'

'Don't you? I do. You forget I've watched that lad grow up. He doesn't impress me with his earrings and his tattoos and his

280

this and his that. All right for bullying some old woman, but you get him behind the garages with a couple of good blokes. Be crapping himself in half an hour.'

'I can hardly arrange that.'

'No, but I can.'

She probably could, too. The flats teemed with decent, sentimental, villainous Jubbs, all devoted to crime, dogs, children, old ladies and each other.

'My Joe didn't like being questioned.'

'But isn't that kind of thing best left to the police?'

'Why, what have they ever done? Except poke their noses?'

Stephen gave up. If Zit was in for a spot of homespun justice, serve him right. He wouldn't lift a finger to save him.

'I see they're knocking Jubilee Terrace down.'

'Yes, I know. I come past it on me way to work.' She swung her clenched fist. 'Big ball and chain. Crowd of kids watching. Zit. That lot.'

'Proof.'

'I hope he rots.' On the last word her voice broke. 'I never had a mother, you know. *She* was my mother.'

Mrs Jubb wiped the tears away, leaving two broad bands of dirt on either side of her nose. The dirt gave her face dignity as if she'd daubed it there deliberately, in obedience to an older and purer ritual of grief.

When Stephen left, a few minutes later, he was carrying Nelson's cage. Mrs Jubb went with him to the door.

'You'd best take this pillowcase and put it over him. You won't want him coming out with one of his mouthfuls in the street.'

She looked Stephen up and down and gave a brisk nod, as if he'd passed some test of her devising.

'Well,' she said, stepping back. 'I'll see you around.'

The sunlight was bright on bleached grass as he looked out across the wasteland to the flats. There were two black scars on the ground where the fires had burned on the night Liza died. They reminded him of the other fire that had destroyed her body, and he thought she would have gone into that fire without fear, expecting to meet her loved ones on the other side.

He couldn't share her faith, though walking down her street, holding Nelson's cage, he recalled Skelton's verse.

> Parrot is a fair bird for a ladie.
> God of His goodness him framéd and wrought.
> When parrot is dead he doth not putrify,
> Yea, all things mortal shall turn unto nought
> Save mannés soul which Christ so dear bought,
> That never can die, nor never die shall.
> Make much of parrot, that popajay royál.

He'd been trying to remember that on the evening of her death, but the words had eluded him then. A pity. He would have liked to share it with her.

A crowd of people had gathered to watch the machine that towered over them all. As he walked towards it, he saw the iron ball begin to swing. It crashed into the side of a house, and the wall buckled, leaking plaster from its wounds. The ball stopped, and the remaining force of the impact juddered up the chain.

Most of the crowd were young, excited by the machine's power to destroy, with no memories of the area to make them grieve for these few remaining streets. But he noticed that women, middle-aged or elderly, who walked past on their way to the shops, looked at the machine once and then quickly away.

The machine, ball dangling, had gone into cumbersome reverse.

'Next time,' somebody said.

Stephen took his eyes away from the machine. Only a few yards away, he saw the pink eyes and reddish skin of Whitey and beside him the dark, laughing face of Zit. He watched them intently for a while, until his gaze was drawn away again by the crash of falling brick.

The side of the house was down. You could see the wall-paper in the bedroom with its trellis of roses, streaked here and there with damp. On the landing the paper had come down and hung in strips like silent, lolling tongues.

Stephen felt somebody come up behind him and knew, without looking round, that it was Brian. He turned. Brian flinched, or he might have been shielding his eyes from the sun.

'*They* seem to be enjoying themselves,' Stephen said, nodding towards Whitey and Zit.

'Everybody likes to watch something pulled down. Human nature.'

'Yes, I suppose it is.'

Stephen hadn't heard from Brian since the night he'd seen him beside the bonfire: the night Liza died. Then, he'd been with Zit. The long silence that followed fed Stephen's doubts until they became monstrous. Brian wasn't on the telephone. Stephen didn't feel he could simply turn up on the doorstep, and so he'd wrestled with his doubts alone.

Now he could ask all the questions he wanted. He raised his head to the small, silver sun and realized he no longer cared.

'I'm off to London next week,' Brian said.

'To do what?'

'I know somebody says he can get me a job. Live in. It's not definite like . . .'

'I'm sure you'll find something.'

Or somebody. The ball swung again. At the head of the stairs a pink lavatory was revealed, vulnerable and obscene. Whitey nudged Zit, and said something. They began to laugh.

'I wasn't with them,' Brian said.

'No, I don't suppose you were. But I think you knew.'

Brian looked from side to side before he answered. 'They were drunk, man. I never thought they'd *do* it.'

'You could've gone to the police . . .'

'And said what? They were drunk . . .'

'Or told me.' Stephen waited for an answer. 'But then you'd've had to choose, wouldn't you? And you're not good at that.'

'They're me mates. You don't grass on your mates.'

'No matter what they do?'

283

Brian looked down.

'But you go down London to get away from them. *Very* wise.'

'It's not that. I've been meaning to go a long time.'

'Oh, come off it, Brian. You're crapping yourself. Admit it.'

'No.' He lifted his head and looked directly at Stephen. 'I'm going because there's no jobs.'

Stephen shrugged and turned away. 'Phone me when you get back.'

'Why?'

'Because you might've made up your mind to talk.'

'I'm not coming back.'

He turned away, ignored a shout from Zit and began walking quickly towards the flats. Stephen watched him go, feeling a twinge of pain, but no regret.

He walked back to the car across the wasteland between two rows of houses. Long scars ran through the grass where a vanished street had stood. But all around him, brushing against his chest as he walked through them, grew the tall spires of rose bay willow. No purple flames now: their dry heads rattled in the wind. But from every spire cottony seeds hung. The wind blew, bending the dead flowers, and from one or two of them seeds began to disperse, drifting down across the wasteland, like wisps of white hair.

In the shrouded cage, Nelson stirred and stretched his wings.

'Howay, son,' Stephen said, opening the car door and putting him inside. 'Soon be home.'

He glanced back once only and drove away.